A PERILOUS LAST CONFESSION

―――――◆❈◆―――――

Robert Henson

Copyright © Robert Henson 2019
This book is sold subject to the condition that it shall not, by way of trade or otherwise, be lent, resold, hired out, or otherwise circulated without the publisher's prior consent in any form of binding or cover other than that in which it is published and without a similar condition including this condition being imposed on the subsequent publisher.
The moral right of Robert Henson has been asserted.
ISBN: 9781070975405

This is a work of fiction. Names, characters, businesses, organizations, places, events and incidents either are the product of the author's imagination or are used fictitiously. Any resemblance to actual persons, living or dead, events, or locales is entirely coincidental.

DEDICATION

For Helen, Jan and Megan.

CONTENTS

Introduction	1
1	5
2	7
3	14
4	19
5	22
6	29
7	35
8	37
9	42
10	44
11	47
12	53
13	56
14	60
15	67
16	70
17	72
18	76
19	79
20	82
21	84
22	90
23	94
24	96
25	101
26	104
27	113
28	116
29	117
30	120
31	125
32	128

33	132
34	136
35	138
36	142
37	144
38	148
39	151
40	153
41	156
42	159
43	166
44	168
45	173
46	175
47	179
48	183
49	187
50	191
51	193
52	198
53	202
54	207
55	211
56	217
57	219
58	222
59	228
60	231
61	234
62	237
63	239
64	242
65	245
66	248
67	250
68	257
69	259

70	264
71	267
72	272
73	277
74	279
75	281
76	287
77	289
78	291
79	294
80	298
ABOUT THE AUTHOR	301

Introduction

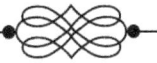

According to Black's Law Dictionary, 'a confession is a statement admitting or acknowledging all facts necessary for the conviction of a crime.' When such an admission is made by anyone knowing their death is imminent, in legal terms, this last confession is referred to as a dying declaration; a rare testimony, protected from the normal vigorous challenges undertaken by opposing Barristers in the High Courts.

Although hearsay evidence is generally inadmissible in a Court of Law, such an admission may be allowed as evidence because it represents the last words of a dying person. The rationale, whether false or otherwise, is that the person making it was unlikely to fabricate such a statement and therefore this hearsay evidence carried a high degree of reliability.

This story is purely fictional and any similarity to any person living or dead is coincidental. It follows the investigation of two police officers, namely Detective Constable John Evans and Detective Sergeant Phil Smith in their pursuit of those responsible for the deaths of two professional criminals and another accomplice. Set in 1964, these two officers belonged to a Northern provincial force, the Leeds City Police. With a strength of only 800 officers, close links existed between them; some healthy, others not so.

It will become abundantly evident of the lack female officers as the story unfolds. In reality, most women were represented within the Service by a 'Police Women's Department,' assigned to uniform duties, predominantly dealing with missing persons and a variety of domestic violence issues. Where criminal offences were identified, those in turn were transferred to their male colleagues for investigation. The emancipation of women into all departments only began to emerge in the late 1960s, several years post our tale. It would take a further twenty-five years before women were significantly represented in all departments and ranks.

Male officers serving in the CID usually remained in their posts for the remainder of their service, only returning to uniform duties either on promotion, or disciplinary matters. Many of the 'older' Detectives drank in the same public houses and Clubs where the local criminals frequented, thus fostering an unwritten code of tolerance and occasional trust. Indeed, this system of 'keeping the villain on their toes' had been actively encouraged. But a new wind of change was blowing down the corridors of all Police Headquarters throughout the land. Discretion was being replaced with transparency and accountability. The mixture between old styles and modern Policing became toxic, with neither side accepting the other.

During this period of imminent change, those 'old school' Detectives, who operated in a twilight zone, vehemently resisted this modernisation. Many judged themselves as the protectors of the public. Occasionally, in order to accomplish this, they sincerely believed criminals should receive the punishment they thoroughly deserved. Rules were frequently bent, or even broken. The 'status quo' consisted of the rich and powerful, supported by the Judiciary. This empowered Police Officers to adhere to a hereditary discretionary code, similar to the Common Law of the land where these rules and customs had been upheld from time immemorial. The word of a Police Officer was sacrosanct, always believed, never doubted and rarely challenged in Court.

This seismic change coincided with the advent of the motorway system in England. Transport links between the urban conurbations dramatically improved the lives of most people; especially criminals. Motor cars became financially more accessible allowing easy access to most parts of the UK.

Criminals were no longer confined to the cities and towns where they originated and operated from. The new roadway system gave them the opportunity of travelling vast distances to areas where they were unknown to commit their preferred criminal activities. Criminals who specialised in 'good class' burglaries, where they broke into premises to steal items to order, were particularly successful.

Their method of committing these crimes was often referred to as their modus operandi (MO). This identified them with the Police; similar to a 'calling card' to the experienced Detective.

Burglars were particularly criminals of habit, rarely changing their methods of entry, always focussing of specific items. Most entered buildings and searched inside to steal small portable items of value. Cash was King but jewellery and small silver antiques were a bonus. It was uncommon they premeditatedly broke into buildings for the purposes of stealing items to order. In such cases, they usually required someone else to sell the property on their behalf.

Such people who supported and financed these burglars were called 'Handlers of stolen goods,' also referred to as 'Fences.' They had usually aligned a buyer for such items with an agreed price paid on delivery before the item was actually stolen.

Police investigations into so-called 'good class house burglaries' became reactionary, often pursuing the criminals after the event. Detection rates and performance fell dramatically, especially outside the London Metropolitan area. This failure of purpose was identified on several fronts; the Police were ill-prepared to meet the changing behaviour of the mobile criminal fraternity and there were too many small ineffective provincial forces. Until 1966, England and Wales was served by 117 separate forces, with criminals moving across their territorial boundaries with impunity. Cross-border cooperation and, in particular, intelligence between Chief Constables was mixed. Compounding this dilemma was the poor recording methods employed by these forces and, other than the Police Gazette published by Scotland Yard, there remained little shared information relating to 'live' investigations.

Following the 'Profumo Affair' in 1963, the Conservative Government, under the newly appointed Prime Minister Sir Alex Douglas Hume, struggled to survive, vulnerable to any further scandal. Within twelve months, a General Election eventually 'swept away' the old establishment rules. A change of public opinion began to gather pace. Long established organisations and reputations gave way to an 'accountability' where the electorate and popular Press expected high standards from all those serving in public office, especially the Police.

Time was now running out for those Detectives who continued to operate in the old ways. Within a decade, many would pay the price, some dismissed from the Service whilst others serving custodial sentences for perjury and/or perverting the course of justice.

DS Phil Smith was one such Detective who trod a very dangerous path in his bid to see a sense of fair play; even if his methods were sometimes unlawful. Yet he was fortunate to have a young colleague, DC John Evans, who was both honourable and trustworthy. He knew the rules and played by them accordingly. Whilst their relationship was enigmatic, with DS Smith being of senior rank, DC Evans normally ruled the day, regularly keeping him in check.

When both officers were confronted by a serious investigation involving the murders of several local criminals, their differing methods were tested to the limit. But one would succeed, where the other floundered. Only through their dogged determination to pursue the truth, and by combining their efforts, did they stand any chance to bring those responsible to justice. Perhaps not justice in the legal sense but nevertheless, justice of a kind.

1

In July 1939, weeks prior to the outbreak of the Second World War, two boys were born on the same day and in the same town, Leeds, where they lived completely different lives. They would never meet, yet twenty-five years later, events would inextricably draw them together.

The first boy was called John Evans, the only child of Emily and Frank, who had chosen to live in one of several newly built housing estates in North Leeds. Along with many of the upper working-middle classes, they migrated from the inner-city areas, synonymous with row after row of red brick Victorian terraced houses. Their new luxurious homes boasted internal bathrooms, well-designed kitchens and even limited central heating. During the War, no destruction was inflicted in those suburbs; they were of no strategic value to the war effort, its residents shielded from the ravages that engulfed most of Europe.

The second boy, Ronnie Ellis was less fortunate. Indeed, he was born unlucky, abandoned by his mother at birth, who was a nineteen-year-old Irish immigrant prostitute. Four weeks premature, he suffered a deformity to his spine and neck, aggravated with malnutrition. Although extremely underweight, he amazed all the medical predictions, surviving the first three months in a Special Care Unit. Unfortunately, this initial ordeal allowed him to face a childhood of sickness, frailty and mental under-development. Like so many young children of this time, his welfare was overlooked by the demands of the War; the increasing numbers of casualties returning from both war campaigns and those caught up in the home front, victims of the German Luftwaffe.

By the time the conflict had finished, Ronnie had been transferred to several orphanages, showing clear signs of mental instability, accompanied by behavioural problems. Medical opinion identified his markedly lack of growth as the cause of his belligerent attitude. This was reinforced through the constant bullying he received from other children, beginning early at infant school and continued throughout his childhood. By the time he was seven he was regularly committing truancy.

2

By contrast, John enjoyed a happy and loving childhood, leaving school at the age of fifteen to work as an apprentice ledger clerk for a large printing company in Leeds. Although he impressed his employers with his enthusiasm to learn, he held no burning ambition to remain. And two years later, whilst waiting for a bus to return home, his career ambitions became crystal clear. He witnessed two uniformed Police Officers travelling in a marked Ford Zephyr saloon car pursuing at high speed two other men riding a motor cycle. The noisy sirens and bells on the police car roof only added to the theatre, alerting everyone to the seriousness of their business. During those fleeting moments, he knew exactly where his ambitions laid.

The following day he wrote to the Leeds City Police Headquarters requesting for information in becoming a Constable. For over three weeks he waited in vain for a reply, until one evening after returning home from work his mother said, 'John, there's a letter for you on the hallway table.' He rushed over and prized open the envelope in full anticipation of them announcing a starting date to join their ranks. But as he read, a bitter sense of disappointment filled his spirit. The final paragraph simply stated, 'apply after completing your National Service.'

Although aware of his impending National Service, where all fit and able men between the ages of 18 and 30 were required for conscription into the Military, he had read in the newspapers certain occupations were exempted from them this. Serving Police Constables were one such exemption.

On his eighteenth birthday, he walked into the Army Recruitment office and volunteered himself for National Service. When asked by the Sergeant why he was doing this, his reply was short, 'So I can join the Police Force as soon as possible.' Within six weeks he had commenced his basic training in Newark Barracks and afterwards, posted to West Germany, assigned to the Royal Signals.

His final assignment took him to Malaya. Fortunately, by 1958 the serious disorder and fighting had diminished. This non-combatant role introduced him to importance of gathering and disseminating intelligence reports from the far-stretched villages, still remotely cut off in the North Jungle. He was far from harm's way and in July 1959, he was de-mobbed and returned home without firing a shot in anger.

Two days later, he caught the bus into town and entered the Leeds City Police Headquarters. At the reception desk, he asked the Constable who was busy writing inside a large ledger for directions to the Recruiting Department. Without looking up he simply pointed at the door opposite him saying, 'Can't you read lad?'

John saw the door sign on the opposite side of the corridor, 'Recruitment.' He strode across and walked through the open door. Standing in the front of a large polished wooden counter he rang the bell attached to the wall and waited. Instantly, a woman appeared smoking a cigarette.

'What can I do for you, young man?'

'I want to join up.'

'Have you already completed the applications forms?'

'No.'

'Here, go in that room and bring them back when you've finished them.' She pointed towards a small office with a single table and chair, handing to him the four-page questionnaire. He walked into the next room, sat down and began reading the forms. But a few moments later she appeared again and handed him a pencil. 'We always use pencils here, that's why we don't make any mistakes.' She gave him a wink and left him alone to read the questions.

Thirty minutes later he emerged holding the forms, returning to the main office. Once again it was empty, so he rang the bell. Her voice bellowed from the back room, 'Have you finished it young man?'

'Yes, shall I leave it with you on the counter?'

'You can, if you want to join us later in the year. But if you want to start now, stay where you are. What do you want?'

'I'd like to join up as soon as I can.'

'Good man. Stay there, I'll get Sergeant Hawkins to see you now.'

John sat down on the long bench and looked at the green painted bare walls. There were no pictures, only a clock hung above the doorway ticking loudly; it was ten-thirty. He could hear the sounds of numerous telephones ringing and other voices coming from within the offices, stretching along the corridor outside.

After thirty minutes of watching the clock, the minute hand pointing vertical, he heard the familiar sound of heavy boots walking across the wooden floor towards him. He knew the wearer of these boots was ex-military and strode with purpose; like all those non-commissioned officers he had met during his military service. The figure of an enormous man filled the doorway. He was aged in his late forties, nearly six feet six inches tall and dressed in a full police uniform. John's assumption was correct; his chest displayed several rows of ribbons, indicating that he had seen a great deal of action during the Second World War. Peering down he said 'Good morning lad, I'm Sergeant Hawkins. So, you want to join up?'

John sprung to his feet 'Yes Sergeant. I do.'

'Come with me and I'll see if you're up to it.'

John followed him back along the corridor until they came to another office named 'Police Personnel.' They entered and sat down. 'I've read your application form and I see you've already done your National Service with the Royal Signals.'

'Yes Sergeant. I was keen to get it over with so I could join the Police as soon as possible.'

'Very commendable. But how old are you?'

'Twenty, Sergeant.'

He looked at the form again 'Oh yes. You're a bit too young for us. We prefer our new recruits to be at least twenty-one.'

John was disappointed. During the two years in the Army he had kept himself physically fit. He was a slim yet muscular young man with dark brown hair with eyes to match. With some assertion he replied, 'Forgive me for saying this, but I wasn't too young to go and serve my Country when they gave me a gun and showed me how to kill. If I was old enough to die, surely I'm old enough to join the Police. I've always wanted to join up, Sergeant.'

'Good point. How tall are you?'

'Five-feet ten inches.'

'It's a little on the short side, lad. But they've recently relaxed the height restriction from six feet. It's up to the discretion of the Police Surgeon, Doctor Slater. Your application will hinge on my recommendation and your successful medical with him. Let me first ask you some official questions. If the answer is 'yes' to any of them, you must disclose this now. Do you understand?'

'Yes Sergeant.'

'Good. Here goes. Do you have any outstanding matters coming before the Courts? Are you in debt? Are you a homosexual? Are there any members of your family who have any previous convictions for dishonesty or connected to the Liquor Licensing trade?'

'No.'

'OK. We'll be doing our checks about you Mr Evans and I can tell you, if they are favourable you will be invited to undergo a medical with Dr Slater. If he finds you fit and healthy and tall enough to perform the role of a Constable, you'll be interviewed by the Chief Constable.'

'Thank you, Sergeant.'

'That's OK. But just before you go; I've got some of my own questions to ask. Can you drink beer and keep a clear head? And can you keep a straight face when the rest of the world is laughing or crying? Don't answer them now. Think about them, because the answer must always be yes. Do you understand me lad?'

'Yes, I do Sergeant.'

The interview was over and within ninety minutes John walked out through the Police Headquarters' back doors, into the streets and took a deep breath of cool fresh air. He was elated; provisionally accepted as a Constable pending his character checks and medical. He felt confident on both counts.

The following week he was summoned to the Town Hall for an appointment with the Police Surgeon, Doctor Slater. The letter mentioned, if his medical was successful, he was to report to Sergeant Hawkins immediately afterwards, where an interview with the Chief Constable would be arranged that morning. Best suit, white shirt and plain tie were mandatory.

Two of the largest civic structures in Leeds were built in the mid

1850s; the Municipal Building housing the Police Headquarters and directly opposite, the Town Hall, where the Magistrates and High Courts convened. The main hall was used for public spectacles and other civil occasions. However, tucked away and hidden from public view on the second floor, laid a large single green painted locked door with no fixed name plate; no indication to passers-by who may be its occupant. This was the office for the Force Police Surgeon, Doctor Slater.

As the Town Hall clock sounded ten o'clock, John climbed the shallow stone staircase to the second floor, following the exact details within the letter, and he knocked nervously on the door. 'Come in' came the reply. He entered a large dimly lit office, the only illumination given by a solitary electric light set in the high ceiling and the old heavy green velvet curtains almost closed, obliterating the daylight outside. The air was thick with tobacco smoke. He turned to his left and saw Doctor Slater. He was nothing like he expected. A morbidly obese man in his sixties, wearing a blue and white striped shirt with dark trousers. The most striking feature of his attire was the thick bright red braces stretching over his large stomach and the matching bow tie beneath his flabby double chin. He rolled forward in his leather chair, placed his newspaper down on the desk and drew deeply from his cigarette. 'What can I do for you, young man?' he asked.

'Sir I'm John Evans, I've come for my medical to join the Police.'

'Come and sit down. You're not out of breath walking up those stairs?'

'No Sir.'

'You must be fit. Come over here and let me look at you. Take your shoes and socks off and hop onto the bed.'

John looked over his shoulder. A large leather-lined bed stretched across the back wall, sat on high legs. For most people, it would have been uncomfortably high to 'hop on.' Nevertheless, he complied and laid on his back with his bare feet protruding over the edge. Doctor Slater waddled over and began to examine each foot carefully, gently twisting them from side to side and checking the soles underneath before placing them back on the bed. 'Sit up and take your shirt off.' John felt the cool metal of his stethoscope and looked upwards as the Doctor listened to his heart rate and breathing. 'OK that's it. Fine pair of lungs, good heart and no flat feet. You're healthy enough, but you need to grow a little. Let me measure your height.'

John swung his legs away from the bed and jumped to the floor. 'Come over here please and stand on the measuring tray.' With his feet together, he stood against the wall in front of the height indicator. Doctor Slater began to adjust the marker, standing proud from the wooden measured pole above John's head. As he lowered the peg into place to record his exact height, he asked 'Let me see you on the balls in your feet young man.' Obeying his instruction, John lifted his weight onto the front of his feet, elevating himself by at least an inch. Doctor Slater nodded with satisfaction, 'Five feet eleven, that'll do.' He gestured John to step away, 'Get dressed and come over to the desk, there's some important paperwork for you to complete.'

With his shirt tucked away inside his trousers and socks inside his shoes, John faced the Doctor. Without looking upwards, he said 'Well done young man. You're fit enough to carry out the role of Constable. Just sign here so I can get my twenty-five guineas. Thank you.'

Within ten minutes, the medical examination was over and John was descending the stairs pondering the doctor's fee; it was the equivalent of nearly a month's salary in his new career. But his thoughts quickly turned to the interview with the Chief Constable. How could he prepare for that? What questions would he ask?

He crossed the road and entered Police Headquarters and walked directly to Sergeant Hawkins's office. He looked up and smiled at John, 'So you're fit enough to fight, eh lad?'

'Yes Sergeant. News travels fast.'

'It does. The Doc has just called me. Now let's get you ready for the Chief. Remember, he's only looking for potential. Don't be telling him you're going to change the bloody world. Tell him it's always been a childhood dream to join the Police. He'll lap that up, the dopy sod.'

Sergeant Hawkins accompanied John to the first floor, overlooking the Town Hall where he had just come from. After knocking loudly on the door, he strode into his office and bellowed, 'Sir. Mr John Evans has successfully completed the criteria to become a Constable. It only remains for your approval.'

Within fifteen minutes, the interview was over. John only recollected the Chief Constable shaking his hand saying, 'Welcome on board young man.'

By noon, he had been examined by the Doctor, interviewed by the Chief Constable and offered the position of Constable in the Leeds City Police.

Sergeant Hawkins took him back downstairs and explained the demographics of City Force. It simply comprised of five Divisions; North, South, East, West and Central. Now all that remained was to be sworn in by a Magistrate back in the Town Hall and attend the Regional Training School for his initial induction course lasting ten weeks. On his return from training he would be appointed to one of the Divisions. Within three hours he had become PC John Evans.

3

On the same day John was sworn in as a Police Constable, Ronnie Ellis was released from Armley Prison. Ronnie had served two years of an original forty-month sentence for several burglaries within the city. He had been released earlier for his good behaviour. Physically, his medical condition had deteriorated, aggravated by the cold damp conditions within his cell and also exasperated by a poor diet. His failing health resulted in him spending many weeks within the hospital wing where the Authorities were enthusiastic in approving his early release, fearful he might perish within their walls. Such deaths in custody attracted the unwelcomed attentions of Her Majesty's Inspectorate of Prisons and the Coroner.

His psychological development throughout his childhood had been impaired by the continual disruption and displacement from one orphanage and school to another. He was regularly taunted and bullied by other boys for his physical deformity and disparagingly lack of normal growth. He was different in so many ways. From an early age, he attracted several offensive nicknames such as 'hunchback' or 'the crippled midget.' The chronic condition within his spine and neck caused him to permanently walk with his head at a forty-five degree angle. In order to facilitate him walking in a straight line, he was forced to turn his head at an awkward angle and move his feet sideways, culminating in a unique crab-like walking gait. Once again this was the subject of hideous and spiteful harassment.

By the age of thirteen his behaviour towards his peers and teachers was one of constant conflict. His school attendance became non-existent. After breakfast, he would leave the Children's Home and spend all his time walking through the city streets and surrounding parks, avoiding contact with anyone who approached. Once he saw an old man sat on a rickety stool, fishing in the Leeds-Liverpool canal. Standing some distance away and hiding behind a tree, he paid close attention to the Angler preparing the bait on the hook before he cast the line. He was curious on two counts; the patience he exercised before landing his catch and the returning of the fish back into the river afterwards.

Several days later he returned, but this time the man had walked along the towpath towards the locks, talking to a barge operator. Whilst he was opening the lock gates, Ronnie broke from his cover and stole the man's rod and all his fishing tackle. Even with his deformity he was able to move swiftly and conceal himself for hours, whilst the Police searched for him. Yet, from that time his life changed for the better. He had an interest and never attended school again. He went fishing instead.

However, this came to an abrupt end when he was eventually arrested for several counts of shoplifting. All committed in Woolworths. He spent his fifteenth birthday inside a Detention Centre, serving a three-month sentence This was his introduction to the cruel and harsh world of penal servitude. But he was a natural survivor. And although his deformity attracted the butt of insults once again, he decided to take the role of a 'Jester,' discovering this approach made his fellow inmates laugh instead of taunting him. His non-confrontational manner gave him some protection. Those who possessed cruel and tough egos tended to fight amongst themselves, ignoring him completely.

On the second month of his sentence he met a sixteen-year-old called Ben White, a prolific opportunist burglar who specialised in entering houses through open windows and doors. But unlike Ronnie, as he progressed through his teens his body had developed and grew larger and was now unable to climb through such narrow spaces. Consequently, he was caught by the Police, wedged between the top sash window and main frame unable to move or escape.

They soon became friends. Ben gave him the nick-name which would be instrumental in defining Ronnie both to the criminal world and the Police for years to come: 'Right-Angled Ronnie.' But he was not offended. This new title gave Ronnie, for the first time in his life, some kudos and identity, which he relished.

During their confinement within their secured dormitory, Ben would talk for hours of how he had committed hundreds of burglaries, mostly private houses but occasionally empty offices. He explained the golden rules for breaking into premises. Silence and stealth; the wearing of soft rubber shoes such as plimsolls and black clothing at night time. Escape; ensure the escape route was quick and easy through an open window or door, preferably different from your point of entry. Speed and recognition; time was everything and identifying the objects as quick as possible was paramount. The most effective method of searching drawers was to scatter them onto of a soft surface. A bedding mattress was best. Selecting only small valuable portable items was essential. Cash was King. Small antiques and jewellery were acceptable, but leave the rest. The secret to a successful career in burglary was knowing when to leave and who you could trust afterwards with the items you had taken the risks to steal.

Ben continued explaining the various methods of entry. Some buildings leant themselves to entering through the windows, others with poorly secured locks, the doors. The recently built 'pre-fabs[1]' highlighted a weakness in their construction; thin walls. Building with easy access to the roofs posed another opportunity; removal of tiles was easy and quickly performed. However, before he grew too large, his preferred method of entry was the cellar grate. Once lifted, access was possible into the heart of the building. It was very rare for the occupants to secure the upstairs cellar door, usually situated in the hallway and leading to the remaining living quarters.

Ben looked at Ronnie, 'With your size, it would be simple to do this.' He explained that as a child he had been successful in squeezing through the narrowest of openings, gaining entry to buildings. He had been taught by his father and uncle, both career criminals, all the tricks of the trade. Unfortunately, they became too bold and complacent and were now serving long prison sentences. With old age approaching and a lifetime of thieving, neither had any material wealth to show for their efforts.

Ben explained to Ronnie how his disability could work to his advantage. After all, now at the age of fifteen, he was only four feet six inches tall, skinny build with severe sloping shoulders.

One evening, whilst the other boys were asleep, Ben gave him his

---

[1] Temporary post-war-built houses

first lesson. Having 'borrowed' a tall wooden stool from the Centre Canteen, he removed the top seat cushion leaving only the frame. Measuring a little over twelve inches wide at the top, he placed it on its side and invited Ronnie to squeeze through the centre, between the four legs.

After several failed attempts, Ben stepped forward and suggested 'Ronnie, point your left arm through the gap first, then lower your shoulder inside. Keep your other arm flat to your side.' He attempted the manoeuvre again. Although he failed to wriggle entirely through, he was able to make sufficient progress for him to pass sufficiently through the gap until it reached his slender hips.

Ben pulled him back out, 'If you were to wear a child's rubber diving suit, coated with washing liquid, you'd have got through. But there are dangers with this. Getting stuck. That's why you should never attempt to enter small confined areas without someone else there, to pull you out, just like I've done with you. Also, you should always wear a rope tied around one of your ankles, especially where the hole has long passageway, like this stool. You can be dragged out backwards. I can tell you that bloody hurts, but at least you're free.'

'How do you know all this Ben?' asked Ronnie.

'My Dad told me, and my Granddad told him. Remember, we're all little people. The trouble was, I didn't take any notice; I went out to break into a house on my own and got bloody stuck. That's why I'm in here with you now.'

Smiling, Ronnie giggled, 'Well, I wouldn't have met you Ben, would I?' They looked at each other and burst into uncontrollable laughter, nearly waking up their fellow inmates. Ronnie had forged a relationship and for the first time in his life, he had a friend.

However, three weeks later, Ben received notification he was going to be placed on Probation and released from the Detention Centre. As he packed his small case, Ronnie asked tearfully, 'Can we meet up when I get out, perhaps we can work together?'

'Sorry Ronnie, I'm going straight. I've got a job at a local Paper Mill. Don't want to end up like my Dad. Take my advice, don't get into crime, otherwise you'll spend most of your life in places like this.'

When the morning arrived, Ronnie waved goodbye to the only friend he had ever known, as he disappeared through the high security gates. Although they would never meet again, Ben had sowed a seed inside his mind. He knew where his ambitions laid. There were no opportunities for a disabled, unskilled teenager with an attitude like his. Ben had been an inspiration, a true friend and someone who had treated him equally without any prejudice.

The following week he was released too, returning once again back into the care of the Local Authority where he was expected to attend several Craft Activity Courses run by the local Technical College. He was taught the rudimentary skills of basket weaving and furniture upholstery in an attempt to introduce him into the workplace. But his underdeveloped physical condition severely restricted his dexterity. Unable to hold objects firmly with his right hand, he became frustrated and confused.

Within weeks, he lost all interest. His attendance became irregular, rapidly falling away to complete absence. Within two months, he became a loner once again, simply wandering the city streets and parks, mixing with many of the homeless and petty thieves. Most of whom supplemented their benefits by completing odd-jobs from the market stall holders.

Ronnie was caught stealing two pies from a butcher's shop next to the Central Bus Station, arrested and brought back before the Juvenile Court again. Unable to legally represent himself coherently, he shrugged his good shoulder towards the Magistrates and pleaded guilty. Although suspecting another period of detention was imminent, he did not expect the six months sentence to the City's Borstal. It was a hard and cruel place, where the bullying continued and all his limited self-esteem beaten out of him.

Indeed, soon after his release, the nightmare continued. He was arrested for stealing food from a market stall and returned to Borstal for a further nine months. As his teenager years grew to a close, Ronnie had been incarcerated for over four years, before finally being sentenced to twenty-four months imprisonment to Armley Jail.

4

It was during this time Ronnie met another fellow inmate called Frederick Cox who would permanently influence his short life. Freddie was a native of Bradford and over thirty years older than him. A portly built man, with balding hair and a pale complexion, his nick-name was 'Freddie the Fence', a professional criminal who specialised in the handling of stolen property, especially precious metals and jewellery. Unlike Ronnie, he had been a lucky criminal. Throughout his long involvement of receiving stolen goods, he had only served a single prison sentence of three years. He was a clever and resourceful operator, always avoiding the attention of criminals who he did not trust. The Police were continuously thwarted in their investigations, unable to connect him with any stolen goods they may have recovered, thereby frustrating their efforts to successfully prosecute him.

His shrewdness also made him a good judge of character, quickly recognising those who attempted to dupe him by offering him low prices for valuables he unlawfully possessed. This approach often brought him into conflict with the criminal underworld and other like-minded dubious dishonest Fencers. Rumours had circulated for years that both serving and retired police officers held an unhealthy friendship with him. This suspicion was reinforced when his house was raided. Any incriminating material and evidence was always absent, leaving little doubt he had been warned. This protection only served to shield him from any imminent prosecutions. Even on those rare occasions when he appeared before the Assizes, he was found 'not guilty', usually through either legal loop-holes in the law, or any mistakes made by the Police during their investigations.

However, at his last Court appearance, he was found guilty of handling stolen goods when several cases of Scotch Whisky were found in his garage. The true irony to this case was that he was innocent, having no knowledge of the property or how it got there. The investigation officer was a local man, born within the slums and deprivation of Leeds. He was a seasoned Detective who had recently taken a post in the local CID office. His name was Detective Sergeant Phil Smith.

This time it was different. After the ruling, Freddie had exclaimed his innocence, 'Sergeant Smith, I've never seen any of this stuff you found in my garage. Please believe me.' Afterwards, when the interview under caution had finished, away from any witnesses, DS Smith whispered into his ear, 'I know you're innocent on this occasion but that's the same reply you've been telling the Police for years. No one believed you then, so no one is going to believe you now.'

'So why do you believe me?'

'Because I put it there. Just think about it Freddie. You got away with it for years because you bribed all the Cops to keep you safe. Well I'm sick of it. You're one bent little bastard that's going down for something you didn't do. And when you come out, I'm going to be watching you very carefully. If you don't go straight, I'll do this all over again. You can't fight the system anymore Freddie, the world is changing. I'm not a bent cop, but I refuse to allow criminals like you to roam freely, selling all the stolen goods you've received from robberies or burglaries alike. If I make life difficult for you, perhaps innocent people can hold on to their valuable possessions a little longer, especially if the thieves have nowhere to fence them to people like you.'

'You bastard.'

'Let's have some respect, Freddie. It's Sergeant Bastard from now on.'

His subsequent trial went as predicted. DS Smith swore on oath of how he had received an anonymous call to the effect that four cases of Scotch Whisky were stacked inside Mr Cox's garage, concealed under a canvas tarpaulin, behind a large chest of drawers. The items were found exactly there and the police photographs showed them in situ, corroborating the anonymous information.

Unknown to Freddie and the Courts, the whisky had been subject to a burglary from a Working Man's Club in the city, several days previously and recovered by DS Smith, concealed in an abandoned stolen van on the outskirts of the city. The whisky was identified by the Club's Steward and returned to their premises promptly. DS Smith knew the guilty burglars would never come forward to incriminate themselves to save Freddie.

Yet Freddie was a realist and knew his fate was sealed. When he was sentenced by the Judge to three years imprisonment, DS Smith escorted him back to the Police Cells to await his short journey to Armley Prison. As they both descended the steps, Freddie asked 'How could you tell all those lies whilst swearing the oath on the Bible?'

With a wink, DS Smith whispered, 'Easy Freddie. I'm an atheist and don't forget that.'

That was in the past. Now, he was sharing a cell with a disabled and dysfunctional eighteen-year-old shoplifter.

However, as the weeks slowly rolled by, their relationship began to blossom. Freddie was very interested in Ronnie's encounter with his previous inmate Ben, especially the story about wriggling through the open wooden stool. He could see a possible opportunity of using Ronnie's unusual skills to enter premises through small openings where he knew there were 'rich pickings' to be made. Likewise, Ronnie had found another friend who ignored his disabilities and treated him a normal person. Once again, his self-esteem began to return.

Unsurprisingly, neither men received any visitors, so they continued the remainder of their sentences together, sharing the same cell and spending countless hours discussing their future plans. By coincidence, their release dates were within ten days of each other, Freddie leaving first, with Ronnie following him the week after. Instead of him aimlessly returning to the Community, Freddie agreed for him to stay with him at his house until he managed to find a place of his own. Ronnie was more than happy with this arrangement. But it came at a price.

Although Freddie had described them as partners, there was no doubt who was the Boss. Ronnie would be sent out to pre-arranged targeted premises to enter and steal valuables on behalf of Freddie, who in turn, would pass them onto the highest bidder on the black market.

5

Probationary Constable John Evans was seconded to the Central Division. This came as a surprise to those more experienced serving officers. Traditionally, only Constables with more than three years of service were allowed to work in the City Centre owing to the hordes of potentially violent drunken people visiting the dozens of public houses and night clubs. This was particularly prevalent on Friday and Saturday evenings.

John was disadvantaged on several fronts; his age, inexperience and lack of physical height. His immediate appointment attracted the butt of many discourteous comments from the older Constables, all of whom were over six feet tall with muscular and overpowering bodies. His first introduction to the shift of thirty-five men was met by one them muttering 'Nay, are we recruiting dwarfs now?'

It was only after the Sergeant nicknamed him 'their dwarf' that John realised perversely it was in fact a term of endearment. His acceptance with his colleagues took an immediate leap forward after attending a serious disturbance in one of the most notorious pubs, the Star and Garter. Without any hesitation and showing no fear, he burst into the melee to arrest a violent drunk. Unfortunately, he failed to see the punch land in his face, throwing him to the floor. Still dazed and half expecting another strike, he heard his colleagues enter and one shout to the others 'Someone's punched the dwarf.' Another officer cried 'The bastards!' Afterwards, all mayhem broke out. Many customers, even those not involved were 'rounded up' and taken away into custody, including the protesting Landlord. John was forever known by his fellow officers as their 'fearless dwarf' and within six months was accepted as part of the team and allowed to make the tea, fully acquiescing to his role as the 'new boy'.

Meanwhile, Personnel Department had assigned him a small bed-sit flat belonging to the officious Landlady Mrs Doris Mathers where strict rules of tenancy were followed. No alcohol, no parties and absolutely no women allowed. His room was on the ground floor of a large stone-built house, set inside a large garden next to the main road in Headingley, North of the city. Fortunately, there were many popular and respectable public houses, a rugby and cricket ground and two cinemas within easy walking distance. He would lodge at Mrs Mathers whilst working his long and irregular shifts but return home to his parents on his days rest or leave. It was the best of two worlds.

Eventually, he was assigned his own beat, close to Leeds University. It was an area predominantly of red brick back-to-back houses with cobbled stone streets, serviced by dozens of small family-owned corner shops. A strong sense of community spirit and identity existed, with strangers usually treated with suspicion and distain. John's predecessor, PC Mills, had worked the area for over ten years, familiar with everyone working and living there including all the active criminals. His local knowledge of all their movements and behaviour allowed him to solve many crimes based on the scantiest of descriptions or the vaguest of detail. His devotion to solving crime on his beat reflected a higher than average successful detection rate. This in turn was rewarded by his recent transfer into the CID. John quickly realised the magnitude and anticipation of the residents in following in the illustrious footsteps of PC Mills.

Nevertheless, within twelve months he made good progress establishing himself with all the tradesmen, licensed premises and clubs, notwithstanding the two major troublesome families called the McDonalds and Wards. When challenged to deal with their truculent behaviour, he was often obliged to call on the assistance of his larger well-built colleagues.

By coincidence, following an escalation of assaults on Police Officers throughout the city, the Chief Constable directed all his Constables to deal with offenders robustly. There was no specific instruction contained within his message, so officer's discretion was expected to be implemented on individual cases. The issue of using 'reasonable force' was subjective and widely interpreted.

Two evenings after this directive was issued, John was summoned to the Swan Inn, the busiest pub in his area. Alone, he entered the large bar room area where all the customers had either fled or hidden behind the long counter stretching the length of the building. Most of the tables and chairs had been disturbed, some damaged. Stood in the centre was a drunken middle-aged man called Sean Ward, holding a knife and shouting obscenities at anyone who dared to look at him. But John's courage was immediately boosted when he saw another Constable walk in. It was the legendary PC Dennis Hay, a once-time professional wrestler and rugby player. A man of few words but quick in action, never smiling, his humour dead pan and dry.

As they both approached Ward, he shouted, 'Don't come near me you bastards, I'm a black belt. I'll kill you both!' Completely unmoved, PC Hay continued towards him and without any hesitation, casually picked up an upturned stool, held it above his shoulder and brought it down forcefully upon the unsuspecting man's head. The impact caused Ward to collapse to the floor in a semi-conscious stupor. PC Hay turned towards John and uttered, 'Never piss about with black belts lad.' Without any further ceremony, he scooped Sean Ward up from the carpet, threw him over his shoulder like a bag of coal saying, 'Get the prisoner van, John.'

The whole of the pub erupted into spontaneous applause. The Landlord asked, 'Will you have a pint officer, while your client is waiting for his taxi?'

'Very hospitable of you, Landlord.'

So, the image of a subdued drunken prisoner strewn across PC Hay's shoulders, whilst drinking a pint of beer, was indelibly etched on John's mind for the rest of his life. He had witnessed a remnant 'old school of coppering,' soon to disappear into folk-law. But this particular incident brought some rewards; never again was John ever questioned by the residents to his status or authority.

Shortly afterwards, John's personal life changed. He met Mary, a young woman working in his local bank. Eventually, after visiting every day for over a week, he plucked up enough courage and asked her out for a drink the following Friday night. Their romance soon blossomed into a serious relationship and within twelve months they were married and had moved into a police house on a large Council Estate in the West side of the city. She was homely and wanted to start a family immediately but John was reluctant, suggesting they should have a few years of enjoying themselves and also time to save for a deposit for their own house.

Against his wishes, she resigned from the bank to become a full-time housewife. But with the cut in their combined earnings, any plans to buy their own house soon evaporated. With John working long hours, she often became lonely and pestered him to change careers. Their finances became strained, culminating in John having to work even more overtime. Mary was deeply unhappy and gradually their marriage began to fracture. This coincided with her parents retiring and moving to Scarborough. Although John initially suggested she should perhaps see them occasionally when he was working extended hours, her visits increased to such an extent she began to spend more time with them than at home.

Ironically, whilst his marriage ran into difficulties, his Police career began to ascend and show promise. As he approached three years service, he knew exactly where his ambitions lay: becoming a Detective. The advice he received from his supervisors was always the same, 'Get some good criminals behind bars first.' He knew all the serious criminals on his patch, their associates and genre of their criminality. He requested for all the reported crimes involving theft and burglary be allocated for his attention. With a high arrest and detection rate, he stood a good chance of being considered for CID. To assist this ambition, John possessed something most of his contemporaries lacked; he was lucky. Very lucky.

On one occasion, he saw a young man knelt beside the front tyre of a small van, attempting to change the wheel with a flat tyre. As he approached him, the man ran away into a nearby park. John instinctively chased after him and eventually cornered him behind the public lavatories.

After he refused to answer the questions regarding his behaviour, John escorted him back to the van and checked inside. Scattered in large bundles, he saw stacks of brand new clothes, mainly gentlemen's suits still attached to their hangers with their price tags. The driver explained, 'I bought them from a bloke in a pub.'

John arrested him on suspicion of theft. Eventually, the thief was charged with ten burglaries from various clothing factories within Leeds over a six-month period. John was commended by the both the Chief Constable and the Judge, bringing him to the attention of several Detective Superintendents. He had made his mark.

But his next arrest and detection swung the balance. Following reports of several burglaries near to the University Campus, two female students had been raped within three days of each other. Both lived alone in separate houses, adapted for student accommodation flats within the same street. The offences had been committed after two o'clock in the morning on a week day, where entry had been gained by breaking the glass to basement windows. A vague description, depicting a white male, 5'10" tall of slim build, wearing a black woollen balaclava with broken crooked yellow teeth, was the only lead. Surprisingly, he had seen fit to wear a condom. Whilst this was fortunate for the victims, it left little or no forensic evidence at the scene.

John had decided to work later that evening after midnight. He quietly walked the streets near to the Campus wearing plain black clothing and keeping close to the buildings in the shadows. As he approached the corner of two converging streets, he heard the muffled sound of breaking glass coming from a basement window on the opposite side of the road. He stopped at the corner of the streets and peered around the wall. He could just make out a dark figure climbing through a small opening into the basement flat. He rushed forward, jumped down the steps and just managed to grab the right leg before it disappeared inside. A man's voice screamed, 'Get off me, you bastard!' but John pulled even harder. Slowly, the man began to emerge, struggling violently until he became free from the window frame.

Suddenly he dropped face down to the paved ground, whereupon John jumped on top and turned him over onto his back. The intruder was wearing a black balaclava, from which two steely-grey eyes peered out and crooked yellow teeth showing through the mouth hole. The intruder attempted to stand, shouting 'You bastard, I'll kill you!' and in the corner of John's eye, something flickered. It was a knife. The intruder sprang to his feet, holding a kitchen knife with an open blade measuring nearly twelve inches long. He stepped forward, 'I'm going to stick this in you.'

Without his truncheon to defend himself, John instantly remembered the advice given to him from his older colleagues, 'Retaliate first.' He lunged towards his left side and punched him square in the face, causing him to collapse to the concrete floor, groaning and holding his mouth. John quickly seized the knife from his grip and threw it over the garden wall, out of harm's way, shouting 'I'm PC Evans and you're locked up. Don't move from where you are, or I shall really hurt you some more. Do you understand me?' But once again, he made an attempt to rush him. John was ready. With a quick jab to his stomach, the prisoner collapsed to the ground in pain, grudgingly accepting there was no escape.

The commotion awoke the young woman in the basement flat. She peered through the broken window screaming, 'What's happening out there?'

John shouted, 'I'm a Police Officer, go to the public telephone box over the road and ring 999 and tell them I've arrested someone trying to break into your flat. Hurry up please.' The door opened to reveal a woman in her early twenties dressed in her pyjamas and bare feet. She looked down at the man curled up in the small yard beneath her broken window, groaning in pain and starred back at John. 'Quickly please. I've just caught him trying to break in. Go and get the Police now.' She nodded and ran passed him, climbed the steps to the pavement and across the street to make the call.

Within four minutes, a large van arrived and two burly Constables came bounding into the yard. One of them smiled, 'Well done. Looks like the dwarf's got our man.' With their usual efficiency, the Constables picked up and carried the prisoner to the police van where he was bundled into the back and handcuffed to a metal rail. John turned to the woman, 'Thanks for that. I'll be back later to tell you all about it and take a statement from you.'

Through her startled eyes, she sighed with relief, 'It's me that should be thanking you.'

John collected the knife from the adjoining garden before joining his colleagues. As he stepped inside the back of the van, he noticed the prisoner was slumped backwards on the wooden bench, now dazed and confused. Under the dim interior light, John reached forward and removed the balaclava from his head. Although he had already suspected this was the rapist, this was confirmed. He matched exactly the description, especially the protruding broken yellow teeth, of which two were now missing.

Six months later, Jake Saunders was convicted and sentenced to twenty years imprisonment for rape, attempted rape and burglary. On the same day he was sentenced, John received an invitation to join the Northern Divisional CID.

Within four years, at the age of twenty-four, he became the youngest Detective Constable in the Force. But this was a mixed blessing; he was posted to the far side of the city in unfamiliar surroundings and colleagues he hardly knew. Once again, he would be the new boy, but this time, no one referred to him as the dwarf.

6

Since his release from Leeds Prison, Ronnie had been learning the skills to his trade too. Burglary. His mentor, Freddie the Fence, had carefully selected the targeted premises, usually homes belonging to wealthy pensioners. Although Ronnie and Freddie lived together in a modest large Victorian terraced house, their living quarters were separate, Ronnie living in the upstairs rooms with Freddie in the ground floor and basement.

Since his last encounter with DS Smith, Freddie had been more cautious about many things. Firstly, he severed all connections with any serving or retired police officers, rented several 'lock-up' garages under a pseudonym name, miles away from the house. He was taking no chances of being connected to any of the stolen property Ronnie was busy stealing, always employing others to collect and store the booty at these various locations. Being doubly cautious, he would arrange for all the items to be continually moved and transferred. Through his network of fellow handlers, he frequently arranged for buyers to be available before such property was in fact stolen. To necessitate all this information, he would hire the services of two people who he could trust. Both of these 'saw a great deal and kept their ears closely to the ground.' The first was a taxi driver called Jim Simms and the second, a prostitute known as the 'Beautiful Brenda.'

Jim Simms had been driving his cab in Leeds for over twenty years and knew every street in the city and just about everything that was happening within them. He had a long-standing business agreement with many of the prostitutes who operated from various hotels and bars in the city centre, recommending punters from outside town who were keen for some 'action.'

Brenda, whose name was Brenda Barker, had 'worked' the bars for over four years. An attractive woman in her mid-twenties, she had turned to prostitution after her husband had deserted her, leaving her with two young children. She received no support from him. She had previously worked in the largest detergent factory in Leeds, known as 'Soapy Joes,' but after six months she was unable to pay the mortgage and meet all her financial obligations. Refusing to sell her only asset, the house, and apply for a Council house, she reluctantly succumbed to the temptation of easy money with short hours. Within a few months she had her regular clients and was always operating from the hotels, never on the streets.

To Freddie, both Jim and Brenda were trustworthy and discreet. Any information relating to their customers, considered to be of value to Freddie, they freely passed on to him. In return, they would receive a reward known as a donation. The value of which would be later determined by the opportunity of what could be stolen from them. For instance, if Freddie was informed a wealthy spinster lived alone in a prestigious suburb, this would attract a good 'donation.' And if Jim offered to take the woman's bags and cases into her house, this would serve an excellent opportunity for him to make a quick visual inspection. If that revealed any security obstacles such as alarms, the types and quantities of door locks, the nature and condition of the ground floor windows and especially cellar grates, this would attract a very generous donation. Cellar grates were of significance. Since his release, Freddie had collected a number of items, including small wooden barrels, car tyres, and assortment of small windows and hatches. They were kept in the back yard, allowing Ronnie to perfect his skills further of squeezing through small openings. They both amusingly referred it to as 'Ronnie's playground.'

Ronnie deployed the advice given to him by Ben White from the Detention Centre several years previously, 'try a rubber diver's suit, coated with washing-up liquid.' Through countless attempts in using this crude apparatus, he eventually mastered the 'art' of wriggling through ridiculously tight apertures.

During the past two years, he had successfully broken into over seventy houses, the majority through the cellar grate. Freddie had advised him about his modus operandi[2] because his method entry was so unusual he must disguise this at all costs. He emphasised to Ronnie that it was like leaving a fingerprint after the crime. The Police would know exactly how many 'jobs' he had committed and who they were looking for in the future by simply comparing the crime scenes. Freddie was aware of the legal term 'evidence of a system.' Most entries were committed by smashing a glass pane. Therefore, to frustrate the Investigators, once Ronnie had committed the burglary, he was to break a window from the outside using brown paper smeared with treacle and replace the cellar grate to its original position. His MO would remain undetected.

To frustrate his chances of arrest, all the burglaries would be committed between 01.45 and 02.30 in the morning, coinciding when the Police were changing their meal breaks or retiring off duty. Even if the noise of the broken glass was heard and discovered during this short time frame, there would be sufficient time to make his escape before their arrival at the scene. A waiting taxi driven by Jim Simms was always parked nearby. He was reliable and never asked stupid questions. His reward was a generous donation.

Once the break-in had been reported, the Police would examine the clumsy smashed window and record it as another common 'opportunist' burglary, probably committed by an amateur criminal. An isolated incident, unconnected to any trend. A 'one off.'

As the burglaries became more frequent, Ronnie was able to save several thousands of pounds from his proceeds, regularly depositing the cash into his local Post Office account. Freddie had advised him not to open a High Street Bank Account; 'Too much attention, especially from the Revenue.'

Whilst his criminal career flourished, Ronnie developed two habits. Chewing copious bars of bubble gum and driving his beloved Mini Cooper car. With only six driving lessons, he achieved the biggest success of his life: passing his driving test. After purchasing it with cash from the local garage, he would spend hours lovingly cleaning and polishing his most precious possession. Unfortunately, the interior did not match the spotless paintwork, with hundreds of empty gum wrappers strewn across the seats and carpets. Occasionally, he would drive Freddie to the shops or into the City

---

[2] Modus Operandi – the method of operation

Centre. On one occasion, Freddie mentioned, 'I don't know how you can find the pedals with all these bubble gum wrappers everywhere.' This became synonymous with Ronnie's previous whereabouts. He would leave a trail of them in the wake of his movements, dropping them unwittingly to the floor. Freddie constantly told him to pick up his litter, pointing out to him the danger of leaving discarded chewing gum wrappers when he was working, 'It's like leaving a paper trail'.

Although his disability meant he could only drive with several cushions stuffed along the left side of the driver's seat, his general driving was not impaired. In fact, the test examiner complemented him on his safe and thorough standard of his driving. Soon, driving became his freedom, offering him independence; something he had never truly experienced before. Visiting the countryside took him away from Freddie, the city and crime. It quickly became his passion. Whenever he had the opportunity, he would drive off with a tank full of petrol and a road map on the dashboard, having no destination planned. Occasionally he would go away for several days.

On one such occasion, having toured the Yorkshire Dales and the Lake District, he returned home to find Freddie in deep contemplation. Later that evening he told Ronnie, 'I've got a special job requiring your expertise.'

Although their relationship was predominately of a business nature, Freddie felt some responsibility towards Ronnie when it came to his physical well-being. He knew his chronic condition had gradually deteriorated, his spine rapidly worsening which left him in constant pain and discomfort. In order to give him some relief, his medication had recently increased but this in turn had brought on side-effects; sudden mood swings of depression and loss of appetite. Freddie recognised Ronnie's days of sneaking and squeezing through cellar grates into buildings were numbered. Before long, his condition would become too chronic and eventually require constant nursing care. Something he would be unable to offer. But for now, he was still the best effective burglar in the country.

This latest 'special job' had come from Jim Simms. It was interesting information regarding the existence of a set of three antique eighteenth century silver snuff boxes belonging to an old retired army officer called Colonel Lewis. He was a widower living alone in a large house called The Laurels, Grove Lane, Roundhay, North of the city. Recently Jim had collected the Colonel in his taxi from the Central Railway Station in Leeds and taken him to his home. During the journey, the Colonel mentioned to him of regularly travelling to France for several weeks at a time, visiting old friends he knew from the War. The house was left empty for most of this time. It was a large Edwardian detached stone building, set inside two acres of garden, completely hidden from the main road.

Upon arrival, Jim had thoughtfully volunteered to carry the old man's luggage inside, whereupon he asked for a drink of water. Whilst the Colonel disappeared into the kitchen, this gave him the opportunity to quickly look through the two ground-floor reception rooms. Inside the living room he noticed a number of small silver antique items including three snuff boxes placed inside a wooden cabinet. This unit stood in the corner facing the fireplace, hidden from the outside by full length heavy velvet curtains draped down each side of a pair of large French Doors. Jim's trained eye quickly assessed that the doors were in a poor state of repair, virtually devoid of paint or recent maintenance. The handles and bolts offered little security.

By the time the Colonel returned with water he had completed his fleeting inspection. He drank a little of the water and returned to his car. Before opening the driver's door, he glanced down the side of the house and noticed a coal cellar grate, set in the driveway about a foot from the wall. It was the original Victorian wrought-iron grate and although heavy, it was only held in position by its own gravity. It was larger than normal and measured approximately two feet square.

Before driving away, Jim had an idea. He returned to the front door and rang the bell. The Colonel appeared again. 'Excuse me Sir, I forgot to offer you my business card. If you require my services to take you to the Railway Station the next time you go away, please don't hesitate in contacting this number and ask for me. I can assure you, I'll offer you a very competitive rate.' All the time he was talking, he looked over old man's shoulder and noticed the internal hallway door held to its frame by a flimsy catch. He assumed it lead directly down into the cellars.

The Colonel looked at his card and smiled, 'Certainly. You've been most helpful.'

On Jim's return to the office, he spoke to Jack the controller, and slid him a £5 note under his newspaper. 'Just let me know when this fare needs a taxi to the Central Railway Station.' He knew that with the Colonel absent for several weeks, this allowed Freddie and Ronnie plenty of time to plan and prepare their entry into the Laurels without fear of being disturbed.

Later, on his way home, he informed Freddie of this valuable information, who promised him £50 when he was certain the Colonel was on the train bound for London.

7

Freddie Cox was a consummate criminal. He meticulously planned all his ventures, always attempting to strike the balance between flamboyance and caution. If he came across some stolen items too risky to sell, he would simply dispose of them in secret. Since his 'set up' by DS Smith and the false conviction that followed, he became a recluse, hardly ever venturing out into the open world. He knew his partnership with Ronnie was on limited time. They had never discussed the future, only their present enterprises. Ronnie was unaware this special job was probably his last with Freddie. Once they could no longer work together, Freddie had decided to retire, sell up and go to live with his sister in Kings Lynn, Norfolk. She was a lonely widow having lost her husband in the war.

In accordance to his high standards of planning and attention to detail, Freddie had acquired plans for the Laurels from the Local Authority Planning Department, purporting to be a small building developer. On behalf of the owner Colonel Lewis, he was applying for outline planning permission to undertake structural alterations and improvements to the roof. Within five days, the house plans arrived showing clearly the layout of the internal walls on three stories, including the cellars.

Throughout the following days, Freddie and Ronnie discussed the planning of the burglary. Once they knew the Colonel was away, Jim would collect Ronnie in his taxi at 1.15 a.m. and drop him close to the Laurels. Jim would remain in the vicinity until his return.

Ronnie would approach the house from the front drive entrance using the bushes and undergrowth as cover and walk directly to the cellar grate. Once he was satisfied the grate was loose and allowed access, he would walk to the front of the house and place his small black bag in the flower bed, close to the French Doors. The bag contained a small hammer, a metal pipe, brown paper and a tin of treacle. Only after the burglary was successfully completed would Ronnie apply the paper, smeared with treacle, to a door window before smashing it with the hammer. Using a metal tube, he would place it over the door handle and force it downwards, breaking the lock. This would cause the door to swing freely open in the night wind. Later, when the Police attended, they would record this as an 'opportunist burglary,' disguising it from the professional burglary it actually represented.

The plans to the house indicated the cellar was subdivided into three separate rooms, converging onto a small area at the bottom of the staircase, before leading upstairs to the main entrance hallway. According to Jim there was no lock, just a small hook and catch. A small shove would dislodge the hook and entry could be gained to the main house. Once Ronnie had made his way into the hallway, the living room laid directly opposite where the cabinet stood containing the silver snuff boxes. Freddie had suggested that once he had seized them, he should quickly search for any other small valuable items in the ground for rooms. But under no circumstances was he to waste time looking for other artefacts not clearly visible. After a maximum of five minutes he must leave the same way. Climb back up through the coal chute and once outside, replace the cellar grate exactly where it had laid and return to the French Doors to break the window and handle.

*

Ronnie would return to Jim, where he would drive him home in a roundabout route just in case they were followed. On arrival, Ronnie would pay him another £50. Job done.

That was the plan.

8

Two weeks after John had been appointed a Detective, he was summoned to attend a briefing on a raid of a Working Man's Club in South Leeds, an area he was unfamiliar with. The Police incursion was due to a number of anonymous reports alleging some profits from the Club's takings had been suspiciously 'skimmed off' by the several members of the Committee. There was little doubt these rumours came from disgruntled club members, who were now no longer part of the scam.

Due to the Club enjoying a Registered Private status, the Police had no legal power of entry, other than in an emergency. It was therefore necessary to obtain a Magistrates Search Warrant to facilitate a raid.

Tonight, the operation was led by a Chief Inspector Green and a contingent of over fifty uniformed officers, accompanied by two Detectives. John was the only Detective at the briefing; the other failing to show. Nevertheless, the raid went ahead. John's only specific role, together with his fellow absent Detective, was to locate and arrest the Chairman Mr Alfred Holmes, before taking him directly to the Police Station. There, Mr Holmes would be interviewed later by the Chief Inspector. Nothing else.

At the stroke of midnight, the uniformed police officers poured through the unlocked front doors to the Club to the amazement of the members inside. Together with two Constables, John remained by the back door in case anyone attempted to escape. Whilst they heard the commotion and shouting inside, suddenly the door flew open under the pressure of a man running towards them. Before

John could react and give chase, he saw him turn left into another doorway and disappear into the rear yard. John immediately gave pursuit, leaving the Constables remaining at the open doorway. As he entered the yard all the lights went out, leaving him in complete darkness. He shouted, 'This is the Police! Stay where you are!'

No sooner as he spoke, someone else tried to rush past him. But this time he was prepared. He lunged forward and grabbed the moving body, throwing himself on top causing both of them to stumble heavily to the ground. A man's voice shouted, 'Get off me, you stupid bastard!'

John tightened his grip further, 'Don't move, or I'll hurt you. You're under arrest.'

Suddenly, he felt a jab in the ribs followed by a thump glancing down the side of his head. John retaliated, punching hard into the struggling man's face. He screamed 'You bastard!' In the darkness, both men rolled over on top of each other across the floor. As they reached the side wall, they crashed together into a stack of empty beer bottles, scattering them in all directions. John managed to break free and was about strike again when one of the Constables approached and shone his torch on both of them. Unable to control his laughter, he giggled, 'Hello Sergeant Smith. I see you have already met DC Evans?'

'Who?'

John stood up, rubbing his face and brushing down his overcoat. 'Yes, I'm DC John Evans. Why the hell didn't you tell me who you were, when I shouted?'

'Cos I was following...' He was interrupted by the sound of a faint noise of a gate opening behind them. Ignoring John, he sprang forward into the corner of the yard and saw a man trying to leave. 'Mr Alfred Holmes. I need to talk to you.'

Mr Holmes was the Club Chairman, a portly built man in his mid-sixties, wearing a dark grey suit carrying a large ledger in his right hand. He asked innocently, 'What do you want?'

John stepped forward, 'Mr Holmes, I'm arresting you on suspicion of false accounting and theft. You're not obliged to say anything...'

DS Smith interrupted him mid-caution, 'Bugger that. You're nicked. Give me that ledger and come with me.'

Both John and DS Smith glared at each other, neither intending to blink first. The Constable took hold of the old man, 'This way Sir, leave them to get on with their differences. I must take you directly to the Police Station.'

Mr Holmes dashed towards the Constables saying, 'Get me away from these two lunatics. I feel safer with you Officer.' John and DS Smith continued with their staring stand-off, both still fuming at each other, neither realising their mistakes nor accepting any blame. Finally, DS Smith broke the silence 'Not a bad right jab you have there. Who are you?'

'I've just told you, I'm DC Evans from North of the city. Who are you?'

'I'm DS Smith, South of the city. Born and bred in this city, but with a punch like that, you can all me Phil.'

'I'm a Leeds lad too. But I must say you fight a bit dirty Sergeant, throwing me to the ground like that. Look at my coat.'

'I'm sorry about that. I'll make it up to you, come with me.'

John followed him back into the main club. All the customers had left, leaving only four officers counting a number of paper forms and bagging several items of evidence inside the Club's office. Without any notice, DS Smith approached his plain police car and said 'Get in DC Evans. There's someone I want you to meet.'

Without any further explanation, John sat inside the car and DS Smith quickly accelerated away towards the city centre. Less than five minutes later, he swung the car in the rear car park of the Duncan Hotel and stopped. Turning to John he said 'Come on, or we'll miss him.'

'Who?' asked John.

'Come on,' he insisted.

They entered the Hotel's service rear door, walked through the empty kitchen that still smelled of recently cooked meals and into the main lobby area. DS Smith strode across the thickly carpeted room into the lounge, where he saw a man standing next to the bar. Without altering his pace, he walked behind the bar and began to pull two half pints of beer. Looking back towards the solitary man he said, 'Hell Jack, it's been a bloody awful night. I want to introduce you to the youngest looking Detective in the city. This is DC Evans and he's given me this,' pointing towards his reddening cheek. 'The little bugger.'

With the beer glasses laid on the polished wooden bar, he placed some money on the till, picked them up and walked back round to where John was stood. 'Well done lad. If you can punch like that, I'll have you on my team any day. But to be honest I've never seen you before.'

'Clearly.'

'How long have you been in the job?'

'Over four years,' John replied defiantly.

'Hell, you must be either good or you're the Chief Constable's love child.'

John refused to answer. He nodded to Jack, 'Please to meet you Sir. Do you really know this man?'

Jack replied 'Unfortunately I do. I invited him for a night cap twelve months ago, but he won't leave me in peace now,' he smiled and continued 'Our Sergeant Phil Smith is an acquired taste. I wouldn't want to get on the wrong side of him. If you didn't know, he's got a bit of a reputation in the town centre.' John stared at Jack, then turned towards DS Phil Smith, unsure of what to say. He had never met any police officer like him.

Still shaking his head in disbelief, Phil gently placed his hand on his shoulder and burst out laughing. It was infectious. John began to weaken, unable to control himself. Very soon they both began to laugh without restraint, leaving Jack looking on perplexed.

Eventually, they both settled down and drank their beer. As Phil wiped the tears from his eyes, he began to talk about his background. Like John, he was born in Leeds and described himself as a Loiner.[3] He was ten years older and brought up in the Old Camp Road, inside the Leylands district, the most economically deprived area of Leeds. He was the eldest of four children who shared a single bedroom with no inside running water or toilets. He spent most of his childhood hungry and watched his alcoholic father regularly assault his mother. All this stopped when he reached fifteen. He had returned home from working in the local woollen mill to find his mother in the scullery, screaming for mercy as his father whipped her again with his leather belt. Phil found the heavy saucepan of boiling water on the open stove and picked it up. Possessed with an instinctive manner to

---

[3] a native of Leeds

protect his mother, he threatened to throw it over him unless he stopped. His father became incensed and ran towards him, but Phil was too quick. Although most of the hot water missed him, he managed to strike the saucepan violently against his father's forehead. The impact caused him to collapse to the floor. Eventually he stood up and rubbed his wound and glared at his son. Expecting the worst, his father muttered, 'That's it. I've had enough of you bloody lot,' before stumbling out of the door and disappearing down the back yard. That was the last time he saw him alive. Twelve months later Phil accompanied his mother to the public mortuary where they identified his dead body laid on the marble slab. According to witnesses, he had fallen into the River Aire[4] in a drunken stupor. These were hard times, especially with the War was in full progress.

However, in the following year he enrolled into the Army as a cadet soldier and eventually joined the Military Police, narrowly missing any conflict. In 1951, he was appointed as a Constable in the Leeds City Police where he spent little time in becoming a Detective in the Southern CID office. He was promoted to Sergeant and remained in the same post.

Unlike John, he was a family man to the core, married to Jane for over ten years with two daughters who had recently started school. John spoke only briefly of his personal circumstances, clearly envious of Phil's life. He seemed to have the best of both worlds.

From their chance meeting in the dark Working Man's Club yard, this encounter forged a bond, linking them closely for many years both within their police careers and beyond. DS Smith's compliment of inviting John to his team soon took on significance in the weeks that followed.

---

[4] River Aire runs through the centre of Leeds

9

Whilst John and Phil Smith were drinking to their new friendship at the Duncan Hotel, several miles away, Ronnie and Freddie looked at the kitchen clock. It was now approaching 1 a.m. on a cold November's night. Jim had contacted Freddie two days previously, having collected the Colonel from his house and driven him to the Central Railway Station. He even accompanied the old man with his luggage onto the platform and saw him leave on the train for Kings Cross. He would be away in France for over three weeks.

Tonight, they were waiting for Jim to park up outside, signalling the start of tonight's work. Ronnie was dressed completely in black with his backpack resting on his knee. Inside, were the tools of his trade, a boy's rubber diving suit, black balaclava, a length of rope, various instruments including screwdrivers, a torch and a metal bar. Stuffed into the side pockets was a plastic container of washing up liquid, brown paper and a small tin of treacle.

'Have you got everything Ronnie?' asked Freddie.

'Yes. I can't see any problems once I'm inside.'

'Just remember, find those silver snuff boxes first and only look for any small items afterwards. You know what I mean. Don't be greedy and stay in there for more than five minutes.'

'Don't worry, I know what I'm doing. If everything goes to plan, I should be back here within the hour. Listen, there's the taxi.'

The sound of the taxi's horn announced the arrival of Jim outside. It was a well-rehearsed routine, having worked together as a team for several years. 'Have you got the fifty for Jim?' asked Freddie.

'Of course.'

'OK. I'll see you later. Be careful.'

As he opened the outside door, Ronnie turned back towards him, 'Don't worry. Just get the kettle on when I get back.'

They both smiled at each other for a moment. Freddie had sent him out into the night on dozens of jobs before but for some inexplicable reason he felt a shudder go down his spine; a premonition that something was not quite right. Why should he have any concerns? They had checked and double checked the planning stages many times. After all, Ronnie was now an experienced burglar. He watched Ronnie leave in the taxi before returning to his seat. This was the worst part of the operation as he looked attentively at the kitchen clock.

Ten minutes later, Ronnie arrived at The Laurels. He was fully conversant with the layout of the building and aware of the large gardens, having driven past it several times and studied the plans from the Local Authority. As he stepped out from the taxi he whispered to Jim, 'I'll be as quick as I can. Give me thirty minutes.' Jim simply nodded and remained silent. He was not a conversationalist; another quality Freddie admired about him.

Ronnie disappeared into the driveway, carrying his back-pack. Since his first meeting with Ben White in the Detention Centre several years previously, he had taken all of his advice and perfected the art of squeezing through impossible openings. All except one important aspect: 'Never go alone.' He had ignored this. Throughout the preceding years he had been lucky, never becoming stuck or discovered.

But tonight, this omission was going to play a significant role in his enterprise.

10

Three weeks after his first meeting with Phil, John was summoned to see Detective Chief Inspector Miller. He had no inclination why the Head of CID (North) wished to speak to him. He knocked on the open office door. DCI Miller waved him inside, 'Now then Evans. As from next Monday, you'll be transferred to CID, South. That's it lad.'

'Is there any reason for this Sir?' he asked.

'No. Just make sure your desk is clear by the weekend.'

*

That was it. No reason. No thanks for the dozens of burglaries and thefts he had detected during the past six months. Now he was history, moving to a part of the city he was completely unfamiliar with. So why?

He made several enquiries with trustworthy colleagues, but it still remained a complete mystery to all. Rather than wait until the following week, John took the initiative and decide to call in at the CID South office and speak to the Detective Inspector. Perhaps he would have some explanation. But on his arrival, he found only one officer present in the office. DS Phil Smith. Showing his delight, he greeted him 'Good to see you John. Heard you were coming next week, so I've fixed you up in a small office off the main corridor. Come and see.'

John followed him out of the office, towards the fire escape to the far side of the building. Opposite to the cleaning cupboard door, Phil stopped and pointed towards a green painted door displaying a hastily written sign; 'Antique Squad.'

'In here John, that's your desk.' He entered a small room measuring only ten feet square with two old metal desks. 'This one's yours,' pointing towards the smaller one under the window.

'What?'

'Right there.'

'Just a minute. I thought I was being transferred to the general CID office?'

'No. You're a specialist Detective now. A member of the Antique Squad.'

'But who else works in here?'

'Me.'

'But I know bugger all about antiques.'

'Me too.'

'Phil, you need to explain. What are you playing at?'

'OK John. Listen, I've been investigating a number of burglaries involving the thefts of antique silverware, mainly in the Southern Division but also within the rest of the city and beyond. There seems to be a pattern with the MOs. All the victims are elderly men or women, living alone in good class dwellings. Although the windows were quietly smashed using the old trick of treacle and brown paper, I'm not convinced they were the points of entry. All the glass that laid inside was never disturbed or trodden on. I believe their MO was deliberately disguised to look like a common opportunist burglary. There's something else not right. All the stolen items were usually expensive antique silverware or jewellery. As you know our regular 'Bertie Burglar' only wants cash or jewellery that can be sold quickly in the pub later. Nothing sophisticated like precious metal antiques. These are different and require an experienced Fence to pass them on.'

'That's all very well. But it still doesn't explain why I'm here.'

'OK. Are you in a good mood?'

'Why?'

'I told the ACC[5] Crime, Mr Jenkins, you had some knowledge in antiques and I needed another officer to help me with all the Inquiries. I hope you don't mind?'

'You did what? Course I bloody mind!'

---

[5] Assistant Chief Constable

'I'm sorry John, but it's a great opportunity to clear up some serious crimes in the City. We've got a free range to go anywhere, choose our own working hours, no bosses to speak of and best of all, plenty of expenses. Mr Jenkins even suggested that if we were successful, we would be looked at favourably in the next promotion interviews.'

'You've just buggered my career up Phil. I was doing alright in the North. Now I been shoved into a Department I know nothing about and working with a Maverick like you.'

'Think of it as a challenge John, not a threat. I chose you because of all Detectives I've seen in recent years, you're the only one I could work with. I trust you.'

'You can go bollocks,' scorned John.

Phil smiled 'I know you really want to come and work with me. Anyway, it's tough shit. You start here on Monday. Let's say nine o'clock, don't be late.'

John knew it was useless resisting any further. Inwardly, he respected Phil and knew he was right. It was an opportunity of investigating unusual and sophisticated burglaries, instead of the mundane crimes committed by 'chancers' who broke into buildings and simply look around for something to steal. These were different. These criminals were professional and knew exactly what they were looking for before they broke in.

John squared up to him, 'Phil, I'll be here as you asked. But never do anything like this to me again. Do you understand?'

'Of course, John. Never again,' he replied unconvincingly.

11

Freddie stared at the kitchen wall clock. It was now four o'clock. He peered outside through the kitchen window into the darkness of the street opposite the house, looking for Jim's taxi returning. Nothing. Suddenly, he saw headlights approach and swing into the small driveway outside. It was the taxi, but he sensed something was not quite right. Jim never parked so close to the front door, always on the street.

Freddie opened the door and immediately noticed he was alone. Before he had chance to open the driver's door, Freddie exclaimed 'Where's Ronnie?'

He shrugged his shoulders, 'Don't know, Freddie.'

'What do you mean? Come inside.'

Standing in the hallway, Jim explained, 'I dropped him off where he told me to park up. He said he would be about half an hour. So, I waited. But when he didn't come back after then I started to get worried. Then, about nearly an hour later, I decided to go and stand in the shadows outside the entrance. Suddenly, I saw the front door open and two men came out carrying something like a carpet. I saw them throw it into the boot and drive towards me. It was a new Jaguar. As it pulled out of the driveway and pass me, I saw the driver. He looked an evil bastard; don't ask me why, I just know. I didn't see the other man sat next to him. It travelled along the Grove and disappeared towards the Ring Road. I managed to get the number; it was JUM 106. I was really worried about him now, so I walked through the main gates to see if I could see anything. There was no sign of him at all. I crept up the drive and walked towards the front of the house. It was then I saw Ronnie's backpack, near to the French doors. Then the lights came on in the hallway, shining through the little window of front door. A few moments later another one came on but this time it was in one of the bedrooms upstairs. The whole bloody place was lit up. Freddie, it wasn't empty after all, like the Colonel had told me. I couldn't stay there any longer, so I went back to the car and waited another thirty minutes. He never turned up, so I came back here. Freddie, I've no idea where he is.'

Freddie walked back into the kitchen and slumped down into his old chair and looked towards Jim again. 'Is there any chance he's got stuck inside the cellar grate?'

'Wouldn't have thought so. He's got through tighter gaps than that.'

'Can we get the backpack from outside the house?'

'Sorry Freddie, but I'm not going back there to try. Believe me, those guys I saw come out of the house looked professionals to me. I've never seen them before, but they looked the military sort. Not exactly big, but carried themselves off like they could handle themselves. I've see those types before, years ago when I was in the army. The one that was driving seemed to have ginger hair and the other seemed to walk with a bit of a limp.'

'OK. We'll have to wait and hope he turns up here. If the Police have locked him up, they'll be here soon enough.'

'Sorry to mention this, but if the Police come here, are you clean? They'll turn this place upside down.'

'Of course, I'm clean. I've even got a TV licence. Meanwhile, can you check the hospitals?'

'Sure. Leave that with me.'

Freddie stepped forward and place a hand on his shoulder, 'Thanks for letting me know Jim, here's your money for tonight.'

'No need for that. Give it to me later when Ronnie comes home.'

'Thanks. Be sure to let me know if you hear anything.'

'Don't worry on that score. You'll be the first to hear.'

Jim closed the door behind him, leaving Freddie alone to gather his thoughts. He had planned this job more thoroughly than any of the others. Ronnie was a resourceful and experienced burglar, never taking any unnecessary chances. Surely, he would have checked to make sure the house was unoccupied? In the past, he had aborted several break-ins where he felt uncomfortable or likely to be compromised. Freddie had never questioned his judgement; that was at the core of their firm relationship. Trust and respect.

Compounding his anxiety was Ronnie's medication. Without the pain killers he would fall into agonising spasms. These had become more frequent in recent months. Three weeks previously he forgot to take them, causing him to lapse into semi-consciousness. Freddie had little choice but to summon an ambulance. Fortunately, at the Hospital he immediately received the necessary treatment, preventing him from falling into a coma. Yet on his discharge, Ronnie had poignantly told him, 'I know I won't make old bones but at least I'm happy doing the only thing I can do well. Screwing houses.'

Quietly, Freddie began to weep, deeply worried about the only true friend he had ever known. Staring at the clock, he rested his head against the high back chair, not realising how exhausted he had become. Soon, he fell asleep, released from all the stress and gradually drifted into peaceful oblivion.

Suddenly and without warning, he was abruptly woken up by a series of loud knocks coming from the kitchen door. He shot a glance at the clock. It was ten-thirty. He sprung from his chair and ran over to the door, fully expecting to see Ronnie but as he flung it open, he saw another man. He was about the same age as Jim, in his middle forties and also wearing a taxi driver's badge. He asked, 'Are you Freddie?'

'Yes. Why?'

'My name is Pete Hayes. I don't think we know each other but I'm a friend of Jim Simms. Have you heard what's happened to him?'

'No. What's happened?'

'He's dead. Knocked over by a hit and run driver just a few hours ago.'

'What?' exclaimed Freddie.

'Yes. About six-thirty this morning. After he parked the taxi outside my house, he walked over the road to buy a newspaper from the corner shop in Shaftesbury Avenue. But when he crossed back over the road, someone drove into him and left without even stopping. The bastard.'

'Why are you telling me this?'

'Jim and I were good friends. In fact, we were partners, sharing the same taxi. He drives during the day, then hands the car over to me to drive at night. He told me a couple of days ago he needed the car for a special job last night. Just before six this morning, he came to my house and dropped the keys off through the letter box like he always does. We live only six doors away from each other. But I was already up and asked him if he wanted a cup of tea. He looked very worried and told me to look out for a disabled guy called Ronnie Ellis who he had lost in The Grove area of Roundhay. And if I heard or saw anything, I was to come to this address immediately and see Freddie. About half an hour after I'd started my day I heard from our Controller that Jim had been knocked down by a car outside his house. When I went around to see what was happening, the Copper told me he had been killed.'

'What's happening now?'

'I don't really know, Freddie. Police are still there now, taking photos and statements. It's all cordoned off. Proper mess.'

'Do we know anything about the car or the driver?'

'No. A mate of mine knows one of the Coppers there. He was told that it appears there were no witnesses, other than a paperboy who saw an old van driving very fast away from the Newsagent's shop. Apart from Jim, nothing else was left at the scene. 'A non-starter' they're calling it.'

Freddie was on the verge of telling Pete about Jim and Ronnie's activities but something held him back. Was this a coincidence? Jim dead and Ronnie missing without trace. He recalled Jim had made it very clear, the men he had seen leaving the Laurels looked professional. But that was in a Jaguar car. This time, it was a van that killed Jim. Could they be connected? Ronnie must have been caught inside the house and forced to tell how he got there. If they had, did they follow him back here? He looked at Pete, 'Bloody hell, that's terrible news. I hope they find the bastard that was driving.'

'Yes, let's hope so. Anyway Freddie, I thought you ought to know. And I hope Ronnie turns up safe and well.'

'Thanks very much for telling me, Pete.'

Freddie disguised his alarm, 'It wouldn't surprise me if Ronnie hasn't gone away for a few days in his car without telling me. He loves to drive in those in those bloody Yorkshire Dales.'

'OK, let's hope so. Bye.'

Pete quietly closed the door behind him, leaving Freddie alone once again. He returned to his chair, sat down and closed his eyes. He began to question himself. What was going to happen next? Suddenly, a chill struck through his entire body. His eyes sprang wide open with alarm bells mentally ringing loudly inside his head. He instinctively realised he too was in danger. If Ronnie had been subjected to any torture, he would tell his captives everything. After all, he was weak and disabled, completely unable to withstand any pain. If he had told them about the arrangements they shared, his position here was severely compromised.

Within a few minutes, he had planned his next move. He ran upstairs and hurriedly packed a suitcase. He would go and visit his sister living in Kings Lynn. She was constantly inviting him to spend some time with her in the tranquil retreats of the Norfolk countryside. Now seemed a good time to disappear from Leeds. With his old brown leather case open on the bed mattress, he unscrewed and lifted two of the bedroom floor boards next to the old wardrobe. He reached inside and seized all the cash he had stashed there for over three years. This was his 'nest egg,' totalling £3,500. More than enough to keep low for a year or two at least. He opened the wardrobe and drawers and grabbed all his clothing and other meagre possessions, before stuffing them untidily inside the case.

He turned off the gas, electric and water meters, locked the doors and walked out through the side kitchen door onto the main road, carrying his case without a backwards glance. Standing in the queue with ten others at the nearby bus stop, mostly of whom were old age pensioners, he pulled up his collar to his rain coat. It began to rain heavily. Apart from the occasional car passing by he saw nothing suspicious. After ten minutes, the bus arrived showing 'City Centre' on the front sign. He looked around to see if anyone else was going to run and catch the bus with him. No one. He jumped on board and sat near the open door, close to the Conductor.

Eventually, the bus pulled into the main terminus, adjacent to the Central Railway Station. It was only two hundred yards away to ticket office. Through the rain and fog he looked in both directions before he crossed the side road. It was clear. But as he stepped off the kerb, he suddenly felt a sharp pain in his lower back. This immediately paralysed him, rendering him into a catatonic stupor unable to move forward or look backwards. It was surreal, he stood in the road momentarily frozen. Curiously, he gently felt someone place their hand under his armpit, preventing him from falling over. Completely incapacitated and unable to move or speak, he was held and dragged forwards across to the far side of the road; his legs and feet dangling awkwardly along the road surface. But before he reached the other side, he lost consciousness. No sound. No images. Nothing.

Sometime later, he began to regain consciousness. He woke up in pain that immediately turned to absolute agony. His left leg pinched, as though it was squeezed tightly in a vice, whilst his right leg felt completely numb. Although laid on his back, he managed to look down his body and saw the full extent of his injuries, before passing out again. He had no comprehension of how long he laid there, but once again a tide of pain swept over his body. Hearing incoherent voices, he felt himself being lifted and gliding through the air. The pain had subsided to some degree and then he heard clearly someone say, 'Careful, let's get him quickly inside the ambulance.'

Freddie opened his eyes slightly. Through his almost closed eyelids, Freddie saw a man in uniform smiling back at him. 'We'll get you to hospital as soon as we can, Sir.' He felt another sharp prick in his arm before collapsing again into a world of complete nothingness. The morphine injection pain killer was now having some effect. He was being carried on a stretcher but the pain in his legs returned, unabated. He looked down again, over his chest and screamed, 'My legs! My legs! What's happened to them? Where am I? What am I doing here?'

He glanced upwards again and saw the inside roof of the ambulance, another man leaning across him. 'Try and hang in there, Sir. Won't be long now before we get you to the Hospital.' Once again, he passed out.

12

Several hours later, Freddie heard another voice, 'Can you hear me?' This was followed by a gentle rub to his shoulder. He surfaced back to consciousness and saw a man dressed in a white coat accompanied by two nurses. 'Where am I? What's happened?'

The Doctor replied, 'Good morning. You're in the Leeds General Infirmary and have undergone an operation on your legs. I'm sorry we couldn't save the right one. Unfortunately, there are other complications. When you were admitted through Casualty Department yesterday, we examined you thoroughly. Sir, you have internal bleeding and although we can keep you on a drip and hydrated, several of your vital organs, especially your kidneys, have been irreparably damaged. It is my dreadful task to inform you there is no hope for improvement and you should prepare yourself for the inevitable.'

'What? Are you telling me I'm going to die?' screamed Freddie.

'We'll keep you as comfortable as we can but I'm afraid there's little else we can do. I'm very sorry.'

'God. What happened? How did I get in here?'

'You were found next to the railway tracks between Leeds and Wakefield.'

'What? How did I get there?'

'I don't know. Are you saying you can't remember how you got there?'

'I just went into Leeds to catch a train to Kings Lynn. I was on my way to Norfolk to see my sister. I've no idea why I was found there.'

The Doctor leaned forward, 'We don't know who you are. You were admitted here with no identification on you.'

'My Name's Freddie Cox. What about my wallet and the suit case I was carrying?'

'I'm sorry but you only came here with the clothes you were wearing.'

'Good God.'

'Now, is there anyone you would like us to contact Mr Cox? The Police want to talk to you as soon as possible. They seem to think you deliberately did this to yourself.'

'Bugger off. Of course I didn't. Someone else did this to me.'

'Just let me know anyway. I don't want the Police talking to you just yet. Let's wait until your medication has kicked in safely. I'm sorry once again to tell you this. Perhaps you might like to think about putting your affairs in order?'

Freddie saw them disappear through the curtains, leaving him to stare at the ceiling and the tubes set into his arms and disappearing beneath the sheets. Although not in pain, he felt cut in two, completely devoid of any feeling below his waist. Resting his head on the starched white pillow, he considered the Doctor's comments, 'put your affairs in order.' Returning his stare back at the ceiling, he tried to retrace his movements. He remembered Ronnie failing to return home, Jim coming to the house, followed by his friend Pete informing him Jim had been knocked down and killed by a 'hit and run' driver.

Suddenly, through the confusion of his pain and the drugs now starting their effects, his mind began to clear. Like a thunder bolt, it jolted his whole broken body. He remembered leaving home quickly to escape any harm falling on himself. Stepping off the bus in the city centre and crossing the road towards the Railway Station, then a sharp stabbing pain in his back, followed vaguely by someone helping him. Afterwards; nothing. How did he get to side of the railway track? What happened to his suitcase? Who were these people and why would they want to kill him?

And now, he had been told he was going to die soon. His recollection of the events as he approached the Railway Station remained unclear, but realised those responsible for Ronnie's disappearance and Jim's death had now succeeded in causing his injuries too. Within the space of a few hours, he had lost two good friends and according to the Doctor's opinion, he would be joining them very soon.

Gathering his thoughts, knowing his mortality was coming to an imminent close, he knew only of one person who could solve this mystery. His nemesis and sworn enemy, DS Phil Smith.

He whispered to himself 'Bugger. What the hell did you find in that house Ronnie?'

13

John's first day in the Antique Squad was uneventful. Phil arrived an hour late and brushed passed him to sit behind his desk. 'Welcome on-board DC Evans.'

'Get stuffed Sergeant Smith,' he retorted.

Ignoring his insubordination, Phil passed a number of files over to him. 'Look at these. Do you remember I spoke about them last week? They're all burglaries committed within the past twelve months both in the city and surrounding areas. All of them record small stolen items of precious metals, normally antiques and where paper smeared with treacle pressed on the glass has been used. When you've looked at those, have a look at these too.' He reached over and handed John a larger file. 'These total twenty-one burglaries in the North of England and the East Midlands during the same period. The MO is very similar. Let me know what you think.'

John examined the undetected crime files, starting with the local reports and finally those from further afield. Phil was right. A clear pattern emerged, linking the similarities of the goods stolen and the questionable points of entry. It took him over three hours to examine the reports before turning to Phil, 'Do we have anyone in the frame for these?'

'No. But I think it's a local Fence whose bank-rolling these jobs.'

'Anyone in mind?'

'The best Fence in town is Freddie Cox. I got him a three year stretch some time ago, but he's gone very quiet in recent years.'

'Perhaps we need to pay him a visit?'

'Good idea. The Collator[6] will have all his details. Get your coat.'

Thirty minutes later they arrived at Freddie's home address. There was no reply to their persistent knocking, and they were unable to see inside through the closed curtains. The only sign of life was the green Mini Cooper car parked in the drive at the side of the house.

Enquiries with neighbours were of little help; all describing the two men residing there as private and secluded, the eldest being in his middle fifty's, whilst the youngest was in his twenties who walked different to other people, sideways like a crab with his head at an angle to his shoulders. Occasionally, he was seen to drive a small green car. Some assumed they were father and son.

'Let's get back to the office John and do some digging on these two, especially the younger one. We'll run a check on the registered keeper of this Mini Cooper. Someone with such an unusual disability should be on our records or someone else's, like the local Doctors Medical Register and Hospitals Out-Patients. Freddie Cox only keeps company with other villains.'

'Shall we go and get a Magistrates Search Warrant?' asked John.

'No. If I want to get in, I'll pick the bloody lock.'

'Not when I'm about,' answered John.

'Of course not. I'm only kidding.'

'No, you aren't, you are a lying sod.'

Both men smiled at each other, each knowing what the truth was as they returned to the office. By mid-afternoon, they had made some progress with the identity of the younger man. He was called Ronnie Ellis, with previous convictions for shoplifting and petty thefts stretching from childhood. John said 'He's just a small-time crook. Not in the same league as your Freddie. And besides, there's nothing recorded against him since he was released from jail over three years ago.'

'You're right. But just because he hasn't come to our notice since his release, only means he hasn't been caught yet. I know those little bastards are up to something.'

'But if he's disabled, how can he commit burglary and supply the goods to Freddie to fence?'

---

[6] Police Officer appointed to record and register information and intelligence relating to criminals – including cross reference with street indexes

Feeling a little despondent, Phil replied 'I don't know. But they're up to something. I just know it. What was the last sighting of Freddie we got from the neighbours?'

John opened his pocket book 'Five days ago, when he emptied some rubbish into the bin outside his back door. Why?'

He was about to answer, when his telephone rang. 'Antique Squad, Sergeant Smith.'

A soft broken voice replied, 'Is that you Sergeant Smith?'

'Yes, who's this?'

'This is Freddie Cox. I need to talk to you urgently.'

'Bloody hell Freddie. I've been looking for you today. Where are you?'

'LGI.'[7]

'What are you doing in there?'

'It seems like I got run over by a train outside Leeds two days ago. Anyway, I want to talk to you urgently.'

'Will they let me talk to you Freddie?'

'Yes. Get over here quickly.'

The telephone went dead. Phil looked at John, 'Bloody hell John. Talk about coincidences. Our Freddie's in the LGI; apparently got hit by a train a couple of days ago. Sounds like he's lucky to be alive. Come on, he wants to talk to us now. I'll check with the Duty Inspector before we go, its George Gregory. His team was working when his happened. He'll give us the 'heads up' of what's been happening.'

Inspector Gregory was sat behind his desk drinking from an enormous mug of tea with his feet placed on the table in front of him. 'What can I do for you never-sweats?'

Phil replied, 'George, I can see you're very busy, but what do you know about a guy called Freddie Cox who got hit by the Leeds to Wakefield train a couple of days ago?'

'Not too sure about that. The BTP[8] are investigating that one. Apparently, the guy had no identification on him. We gave them a hand with escorting the ambulance to the LGI but we had another

---

[7] Leeds General Infirmary
[8] British Transport Police

fatal[9] to deal with ourselves at the same time. A dodgy taxi driver, called Jim Simms, was knocked down and killed by a hit and run driver outside his house. Literally, left him for dead.'

'Any leads?'

'None, other than a burnt-out stolen van dumped half a mile away on some waste ground.'

'Hell, not much to go on there. Do you know if the BTP are treating this case concerning Freddie Cox as suspicious?'

'Not sure, I believe they're marking it down as an attempted suicide. Apparently, it's a popular area for jilted lovers or those seeking Paradise in the next world. But you need to check with them. We only got to know his identity this morning. He had nothing on him to show who he was. Apparently, all his pockets were empty. Lost a leg from the knee down. Must have changed his mind at the last second. Why are you lads interested in him?'

Phil replied, 'He's an old Fence I locked up a few years ago. He's just called me and wants to talk about something. I'll let the BTP know of any developments. Thanks George.'

'You're welcome. It's not every day we got honoured by a visit from the suits.'

'Come on George. I remember you when you wore the best suit in the City.'

He looked out of the window and reflected. 'Yes Phil, those were the days. This is what happens when you get promoted; a big hat, unsocial hours and working with staff who couldn't detect the skin on a rice pudding. You can't turn it down or they'd bust you down to Constable. So enjoy it while you can my friend, this could happen to you.'

Phil smiled. He knew Inspector Gregory very well. He had been one of the best Detectives in the Force until he had an altercation with his Superintendent. Although never seeking advancement through the ranks he was nevertheless promoted into uniform where he would remain for the remainder of his service. It was often referred to as 'punishment by promotion.'

---

[9] Fatal road traffic accident

14

They eventually found Freddie in the Intensive Care Unit where the Duty Doctor gave them strict instructions only to speak to him for five minutes. He informed them of the gravity of his condition and the unlikelihood of him surviving the next twenty-four hours. Although sedated, Freddie opened his eyes and focussed on his two visitors standing next his bed. He was laid on the top of a single white sheet, with two pillows supporting his head. Phil and John were visibly shocked at the sight of his injuries; one leg elevated several inches in the air, the other heavily bandaged below the knee, the stump exaggerating the absence of the lower limb.

Fighting the pain, Freddie spoke softly, 'Well, Mr Smith, I didn't expect to meet you like this, but I need to speak to you in private.'

'Hello Freddie. What on Earth has happened to you?'

'I'll tell you, but with no other witnesses.' He glanced towards John who was stood next to him, completely unaware of the Doctor on the opposite side to his bed.

Phil quietly whispered, 'This is DC John Evans. You can trust him. Probably better than me.'

Freddie looked towards John and uttered, 'What the hell. It's not going to make any difference now.' He paused and tried to lift his head from the pillow. Phil moved forward and pushed it gently beneath his head. 'I'm going to tell you a great deal. Before I do, you must know the Doctors have only given me a few hours to live. Apparently, I have several organs in the brink of packing in. As you know Mr Smith, I've not exactly been a model citizen. In fact, I've been a criminal all my life, never known anything different. Anyway, some years ago, whilst in Leeds Prison for the job you fixed me up for, I met a young man called Ronnie Ellis. He had a disability to his back and shoulder which had stumped his growth since childhood. And when he was released, he came to live with me. He'd been an orphan, bounced from one children's home to another. Ronnie had few social skills or friends in the world but for some reason, we both got on and eventually, he began to work for me. Because of his small stature and disability, he was able to squeeze comfortably though small spaces, especially cellar grates. So, I employed him to break into houses to steal valuable items, mainly small antique silverware.'

Phil and John looked at each other; these were the crimes they had been investigating. Phil gestured to John to start taking notes in pocket notebook. It was imperative his account should be recorded verbatim.

'How many burglaries are we talking about Freddie?' continued Phil.

'Dozens, I'll tell you about them later. Listen, there's something more important I have to tell you about first. About four nights ago, I'm not too sure what day is today, I sent Ronnie out to break into a house called the Laurels, on the Grove, near to Roundhay Park, where an old retired army Colonel lives alone. I had information there were some valuable antique silver snuff boxes in there. It was like any other job. I planned it properly. Ronnie would enter through the cellar grate, find the goods and leave the same way. Once he'd replaced the grate, where it was originally found, he would take from a backpack he had previously hidden some brown paper and treacle and choose a window, closest to where the property was taken. Once the paper was daubed with treacle over the glass, he'd smash it, then leave. At the Laurels, it was different. I advised him not only to break the window, but because they we inside a pair of French Doors, also force the handle down with a metal bar. This would make it look like an amateur job. You know Mr Smith; disguise the MO.'

Phil looked down at him smiling, with perverse admiration, 'Very clever Freddie. And, if it makes you feel any better, it worked. There's been dozens of these types of break-ins all over the North of England. They've never been connected, only for the similarity of the stolen items.'

'They were all ours. There were many other jobs. Not just antiques.'

Once again Phil looked at John in amazement. This could be a serious 'clearance day' for undetected crimes. 'Go on Freddie, we're listening.'

'Well, Ronnie never came home.'

'What was he looking for inside?' asked John.

'Some antique silver snuff boxes. My information was there were three of them in the front living room, in a cabinet overlooking the lawn.'

'Are you sure Ronnie might not have gone somewhere else, instead of returning home?'

'No. He's unable to look after himself and besides, all his medication is at home. If he doesn't take it, he can develop spasms and fits, leading to a coma or worse. And there's something else. He was taken there by a taxi driver called Jim Simms.'

*

Phil shot a glance at John. That was the second time within an hour his name was mentioned.

Freddie continued, 'He was supposed to wait for Ronnie, until he had finished the job, then bring him home. And before you ask, yes, he knew about our jobs too; it was him that gave us this information in the first place. Anyway, he returned later without Ronnie, having waited for over two hours. Jim told me he saw two men leave the house carrying something like rolled carpet. One of them had bright ginger hair and the other walked with a slight limp. They bundled it into the boot of a Jaguar motor car before driving away. Jim said these two men looked as though they could 'handle themselves.' Those were his words. For all I know, Ronnie could have been inside it. Who knows? Oh yes, there was something else, the registration number of the Jag was JUM 106. Jim was absolutely sure about that.'

He laid his head back, wincing with pain. Returning his stare towards Phil, he continued, 'Then someone told me Jim was knocked down and killed about an hour or so after I saw him at my place, near to where he lives. I decided it was time to disappear to my sisters in Norfolk but before I got to the Railway Station, someone nobbled me outside. The next thing I vaguely remembered was being laid across the rail tracks and the sound of a train approaching. I must have been drugged cos I couldn't move. When I saw the train get really close, I used all my strength and managed to roll away, except for my legs. The next thing, I felt nothing until I woke up inside the ambulance. Mr Smith, I believe Ronnie has met the same fate as Jim. Whoever is behind all this have killed two men and wanted me dead as well. I'm telling you this 'cos It seems like I'll never leave this place, until I'm inside my coffin. I want you to try and find out what's happened to Ronnie. I know you can't touch me anymore. And I also know you're a right bastard too. But Sergeant Smith, it'll need a cunning bastard like you to catch these men. I'll give you all the details about the jobs we've done over the past two years. They're all over the North of England, not just Leeds.'

'Bloody hell Freddie. You're telling me you were carried to the tracks?'

'Of course. Why should I want to kill myself?'

'Where's all the stolen property now?' asked Phil?

'All gone and sold. And don't ask me any stupid questions of who or where. I had three and half grand on me when I left home. Like everything else, it's all disappeared.'

'Can you remember anything else about these two men?'

'No. I never saw them.'

John asked, 'Is there anything at your place that would help us clear up these jobs?'

'Yes, there's a small ledger hidden under the floorboards behind an old wardrobe in my front bedroom. I kept records of the addresses and the items taken. Most of your outstanding burglaries are in there Gentlemen. No doubt you'll find that useful.'

'Very efficient. Incidentally, can we have the house keys Freddie?' asked Phil.

'No. Like the money and my identification, all gone missing too. Nothing.'

'Don't worry. I'll sort that out. We'll get the door locks changed. The Chief Constable can pay for those.'

The satire was not wasted. Freddie smiled, 'The only thing I ever got for nothing from you lot and I'm never going to see it.'

The Doctor stepped forward, 'That's enough officers, Mr Cox needs to rest.'

Freddie peered deeply into Phil's eyes. 'Promise me you'll find out who's done this to us. I know you only think of us as low life but we don't deserve this. Promise me you'll find them for me. Promise?'

Without any prompting, Phil replied, 'Don't worry Freddie. I'll get them. I promise you on my life, if I can't get them convicted in the Courts, you'll still get justice.'

Freddie half smiled and closed his eyes. Resting his head against the pillar, he slipped away into a deep sleep. Phil nodded to John, indicating they should leave. But as they made their way towards the door, a continuous high pitch suddenly pierced the air. They spun around and immediately saw the monitor screen behind Freddie's bed displaying the ominous flat line. The Doctor rushed forward and shouted, 'Nurse, over here quickly!' He turned towards Phil and John, 'You two, outside.'

Phil faced John, 'Quick, this looks like a dying declaration, we must write it into our pocket books before we forget any details.'

'I'm impressed Sergeant Smith. I didn't think you kept a pocket book.'

'Only for giving evidence in Court you cheeky bugger. And this could be one of those occasions.' He pointed towards some chairs in the corridor outside. 'Get your book out and get it all written down now.'

'Don't worry Phil, I've already recorded it. What about you?'

'Don't need two books. I'll sign yours, corroborating its accuracy.'

John did not argue; this was serious. The fact that his colleague failed to keep a duty pocket book up to date, required by the rules of evidence, in order to record contemporaneous notes, was yet another example of the Sergeant's 'sloppy old ways.' Fortunately, John remembered virtually every word Freddie had said. He handed his book over to Phil who quickly read the extract, smiled and scribbled his endorsement and signature at the end of the entry.

'Good man. That's exactly what happened,' he said before handing it back to John.

Fifteen minutes later they were joined by the Doctor. He looked flushed and slightly agitated. 'Officers. He's gone. I'm not a Detective like yourselves, but I think something sinister happened here. I assume you will be investigating his death?'

Phil replied 'Yes. So far as I'm aware, he had no next of kin and lived with another man who seems to have mysteriously disappeared too. But that's not for public knowledge Doctor.'

'Don't worry Officer. If I'm asked by anyone, we shall only know him as Freddie Cox, found on the railway line. Nothing else.'

Phil stepped forward towards him, checked his name badge and asked softly 'Dr Banks, did you hear what Mr Cox told us about his criminal activities and the events leading up to his present circumstances?'

'Yes, I did officer. Every word.'

'Then I must inform you that all three of us witnessed his dying declaration. This is legally binding in a Criminal Court of Law and we may require you to give evidence to that effect, if any subsequent trial follows our investigations. We shall require you to make a statement to this effect later. Do you understand Doctor Banks?'

He nodded his head and walked away. Slowly, Phil and John made their way towards the Hospital exit, shocked at Freddie's confession, made only seconds before he died; the allegations of two murders and the attempt of his life. What were they going to do next?

Once outside in the open air, Phil said, 'John, let's go for a drink. We've much to discuss. First thing is, we need to grab that ledger and see what old Freddie's been up to and check out who this Ronnie Ellis and Colonel are. Yes, we're about to stir up a hornets' nest I suspect, so let's keep it ourselves for the time being. Agreed?'

'Why Phil? What don't you want us to report it to the Superintendent?'

Phil had already considered this. He hesitated to take the Inquiry directly to the newly appointed incumbent Detective Superintendent Jones. He had learnt from previous experience that Mr Jones was an extremely ambitious officer and with only fifteen years service. A man who took all the credit for others work and rarely shared his good fortunes with anyone else. There would be no doubt, he and John would be completely overlooked in his bid to advance his career further. To make matters worse; Phil and the Superintendent had a loathing for each other, ever since their last joint investigation when they were both Sergeants. Jones had deliberately neglected to disclose Phil's contributions to the High Court Judge, culminating in only himself receiving a commendation. He was promoted to Detective Inspector the following week.

Returning to John's question, 'Let's just do some digging

ourselves, before we go public. After all, Freddie could be sending us down a rabbit hole. Just trust me on this John for once.'

'OK. But there's one other thing he said I didn't understand. What did he mean 'the job you fixed me up for'? Did you set him up for something he didn't do?'

Phil looked directly at John 'I'm a Detective Sergeant in the Leeds City Police, the finest force in the land. Do you think I would stoop so low as to send an innocent man to Prison?'

'That's not really answering my question, is it?'

'Well that's all you're getting from me John.'

'Listen Phil, I keep telling you, never ask me to do anything illegal or unlawful. I know you might have your misguided reasons and there's no doubt you get results, but I'm not like you. Promise me.'

'OK Buddy.'

15

Later that evening Phil found a local Magistrate and, under oath, obtained a Search Warrant to enter and seize any suspected stolen goods or other items connected with the burglaries mentioned by Freddie, from inside his house. Locating Freddie's ledger was paramount.

As they parked outside Freddie's house, Phil said, 'Listen John. Instead of taking this upstairs to that conniving self-centred Superintendent Jones, first I propose we go and speak to the only senior officer I trust; Detective Chief Inspector Mark Sampson. Do you know him?'

'Not really, but I've heard of him.'

'He's old school. A proper Gentleman. Unfortunately, he's nearing the completion of his service, but he still has that ability of looking at matters with a wider view than most.'

'There's a modern term for this phenomenon. It's was called 'strategic."

'Get stuffed, you clever little shit. Anyway, you'll like him.'

'Why's that Phil?'

'Because he's not like me.'

'I like him already.'

They approached the front door and examined the lock. John considered it was a strange irony; Freddie had been responsible for breaching the security systems of hundreds of homes, yet his own was not fit for purpose. Although the Search Warrant gave them the authority to enter with reasonable force if necessary, Phil took less than two minutes to pick the lock, creating no damage to the door or its frame and saving a substantial amount of public expenditure. They went immediately to the bedroom and found the ledger where he had described. Freddie had been very methodical, chronicling all the addresses of the burglaries and the property stolen spanning a period of over three years. Since his release from Armley Prison, he had orchestrated over eighty burglaries. Furthermore, it included details of the method of entries, most of which were through cellar grates or small windows. All were deliberately disguised later by Ronnie with the smashing of the window panes.

'That should do the trick,' mentioned Phil.

But John appeared pensive. 'Yes, but there lies the dilemma. Even if we can prove Freddie and Ronnie were responsible for committing all these crimes, unless we find Ronnie, we don't have anyone to charge. Do we?'

'No, we don't. But there's something more important here than these burglaries. Just because some people might consider Freddie, Ronnie and this taxi driver Jim Simms to be low-life and even good riddance, they don't deserve to be treated like this. I think we might be looking at some serious offences here. People taking the law into their own hands and killing our very own local criminals. That's not fair, even for me John. Whoever these two guys are, they've really pissed me off and I'm going to get them. I promised Freddie that on his death bed.'

John nodded with approval. He looked down at the last entry in the ledger. 'Phil look, it says 'the Laurels, Grove Lane, Roundhay - Colonel Lewis - 3 x 18th century silver snuff boxes.'

'Now we know for certain he was telling us the truth. It's my belief we are dealing with three very suspicious deaths. Let's have a good look round.'

They searched all the house and seized several minor incriminating items, including balaclavas, a multitude of keys, gloves and lengths of rope, all used as house-breaking implements. Inside one of the bedrooms they saw colourful prints of rally-prepared Mini cars pinned to the walls and the floor strewn with red and white bubble gum wrappers. 'This must be Ronnie's room,' suggested John.

After an hour, they left the house secure and walked into the small rear yard to see the green Mini Cooper again. They tried the handle but it was locked. Peering inside they noticed hundreds of the same red and white gum wrappers scattered on the floor carpet and the front passenger seat. Phil muttered, 'Bloody hell, Ronnie must have worn his jaw out, chewing on all this gum.'

'I've already taken details of it the last time we came. When we get back to the office, I'll run a check through Vehicle Licensing Office to confirm it belonged to Ronnie.'

'Yes, and whilst you're doing that, I'll ring my old friend DCI Sampson. Fortunately, our little Squad comes loosely under his jurisdiction and I know I can trust him to give me some direction on all this before we tell anyone else.'

16

Following Phil's request, DCI Sampson visited their office the following morning. Within an hour he was fully briefed with all the information. After mulling it over three cups of tea, he spoke, 'This is what I suggest you should do. Make some enquiries into how long this Colonel has been living there. It looks like he might be a front to all this. I don't think we should go breaking the front door in at the Laurels at this stage. Incidentally, as anyone reported a break-in there yet?'

'No, Sir' replied John.

'OK. We must assume they will deny any attempted burglary there and besides, we have no specific evidence to support Ronnie's disappearance, other than Freddie' last confession. Unfortunately, there appears to be no obvious observation point to carry out surveillance. So, perhaps we may have to fabricate another ploy to get inside the house and grounds. I think staging some bogus road works outside or telephone wire repairs in the street may be too obvious. It looks like these characters are very security conscious and the only advantage we have at the moment is they have no idea Freddie talked to us before he died.'

'Yes,' agreed Phil

'I'm going to talk to someone I know in the Ministry of Defence about this Colonel Lewis. I'll speak to you later when I've got something for you. Meanwhile, I think we should keep all this under our hats for the time being, until we've got more information.'

'OK. I'm particularly intrigued about these two men seen leaving the Laurels,' replied Phil.

'Yes, they worry me. If they're linked to ex-military, they could be a handful.'

'And I'm going to concentrate on the burglaries,' interrupted John.

DCI Sampson stood to leave, 'It's a very interesting case Gentlemen. This is a classic case of a dying declaration. What Freddie told you was pure hearsay evidence, but as you well know, if it's made when he knows his death is imminent, the Courts may accept this in any subsequent trial. Interesting. Never had one of those before. I assume one of you has made a full pocket notebook entry of what he said?'

'Yes Sir. I did,' replied John, as he looked towards Phil.

'Good. There's a great deal of background investigation and planning to be done. I think someone like Freddie, in his line of business, had many contacts. All criminals I've no doubt. Phil, you have your nose close to the gutter in this city. If anyone can find out more about him, you can. We need to know who they are and quickly.'

'I realise that,' replied Phil.

DCI Sampson added 'Of course, you know we're going to have to inform the BTP about Mr Cox and let the AIB[10] know about the fatal RTA involving this taxi driver Jim Simms, soon. May I suggest I do that at my level.'

Phil agreed, 'Would you mind doing that Boss? Better chance of keeping the lid on it for the time being.'

'Of course. I'll tell them we're following a line of enquiries that may or may not involve these crime incidents. But Phil, it seems we have two suspicious deaths and a disappearance. If your hunch is correct, we could end up charging someone with three murders. This is heavy weight stuff, and completely out of your league. I may have to discuss this with ACC Jenkins. Meanwhile, keep away from the house until I've spoken to him. It's too dangerous on your own. Promise me Phil.'

'Of course, sir. I give you my word.'

He stared at Phil, knowing him too well and continued, 'I mean it Phil. Hold back, there's plenty of other enquiries to be made in the meantime. I must say it all looks promising and worthy of a thorough investigation. Good luck and above all else, be careful.'

---

[10] Accident Investigation Branch

17

Colonel Julian Lewis was a Doctor by profession. Born in 1890, he was the only son to a wealthy textile factory owner in Leeds. As he approached adulthood, he ignored his father's wishes in taking over the lucrative business but instead pursued a career in Medicine. Within six weeks of graduating from Medical School, War was declared with Germany. Like so many of his age, he immediately enlisted into the Army and served as a Junior Doctor in the Field Ambulance Corps. During those terrible four years, he witnessed the full impact of carnage inflicted on an industrial scale by one country on another, frequently referring to this as 'wholesale slaughter.'

Following the Armistice, he decided to remain in the Army. His true passion laid in tropical medicine and only the Military were investing in this type of research. The culmination of the appalling loss of life to tropical diseases, where casualties serving in the overseas campaigns during the Great War vastly outnumbered those borne in actual conflict, was his motive to pursue this ambition. It was widely accepted by eminent medical scientists that most of these diseases and fevers were probably preventable; providing substantial relevant and effective research was readily available and invested.

The proceeding ten years bore witness to this. All serving military and Government Civil Staff serving abroad were immunised against most of the known tropical diseases. The mortality rates dramatically reduced and other countries also shared the benefits of this advanced medical research. Julian Lewis was at the vanguard of this development and eventually promoted to Colonel. Although a high-ranking Army Officer, he always considered himself to be Doctor first before that of a soldier. He collaborated widely with other Countries, especially France and the Unites States, and was universally considered an international leading authority on surviving the tropics. His publication 'Combatting in the real Jungle Enemy' became the blue print for future Jungle conflicts.

However, with the outbreak of the Second World War, he considered retiring and entering a medical research university, consolidating his experiences abroad in Africa and the Indian sub-continent. But following a persistent campaign of both flattery and his call to duty, he felt compelled to remain in service and immediately promoted to Brigadier within the Medical Regiment. He now shared responsibility for the care and development of all British infantry casualties within the European theatres. He remained in post until hostilities ceased in 1945, when he finally retired from the army the following year at the age of fifty-six, only accepting non-executive roles for foreign aid engagements within the African continent.

Shortly after the First World War he married Mary, a biologist with a leading pharmaceutical Company. They had met at a Science Convention in London and shortly after marrying, moved to Leeds and bought the Laurels in Roundhay. Within twelve months she had given birth to the twin boys, George and Charles. Because Julian was absent for most of their childhood both idolised their mother. After attending the local Grammar Schools, they later progressed through University. However, their degrees reflected completely different ambitions. George chose Medicine whilst Charles studied Foreign Affairs. George wanted to follow his father into tropical medicine, whereas Charles preferred to travel the world, fostering ambitions to join the Diplomatic Corp. Yet by the cruellest of ironies their hopes and aspirations were also dashed within months by the outbreak of another War with Germany.

After graduating from Medical School, George, like his father, became a Junior Doctor in the Army. Unfortunately, in June 1944 he was later killed in Normandy several days after D Day; a victim of a booby-trap placed inside a farm house that had recently been captured by the Allies. He and his staff were converting it into a Battlefield Hospital. Along with five other medical orderlies he was instantly killed by a massive explosion. The impact completely destroyed the building. Their bodies were never found.

Mary and Julian Lewis grieved bitterly for their loss, never coming to terms with the prospect of the son's life cut short before it had time to blossom. Then tragically in 1952 Mary Lewis unexpectedly died, leaving Julian alone and distraught. His only comfort during those difficult times was his involvement with the Normandy Landings Association from which many of George's contemporaries were involved. He felt this kept the memory of his beloved son alive. Now, nearly twenty years later he had forged strong friendships with several French families, where he increasingly spent much of his time.

Another distraction was his collection of valuable antique silverware, most of which he acquired through shops and markets. Some were displayed around the house but most stored in a vault, set inside the cellar wall. Several other silver trinkets where scattered through the house, including candle sticks, dishes and three Georgian silver snuff boxes, placed in the living room near to the French Doors.

Now living alone in the Laurels, his only visitor was his other son Charles, who over the years had grown to despise and distrust. He was completely the opposite of his late brother. George had been kind and compassionate, whilst Charles was always self-centred, having little or no regard for others. He had been married twice, with both his ex-wives citing domestic violence against them at their respective divorce hearings.

Charles Lewis had trod a different life path from that of his father and late twin brother. After graduating from University, he accepted a position with the Foreign and Commonwealth Office. This invitation and subsequent appointment had only been made possible by the tireless efforts of his mother. Her family had had the right contacts and it was still the age of 'who you know' that finally counted. Even after all this nepotism, Charles reluctantly took the post. It was only after his father's threat to disown him that he finally accepted a junior position with the Overseas Development Department.

This had been a mitigating disaster, leading to his dismissal from the Foreign Office for inappropriate conduct and behaviour. There was no public explanation for this, nor did Charles ever discuss the matter. The details were forever shrouded in complete mystery. Since then, he was determined never to allow his father to have any authority or influence on his life.

Shortly afterwards, he moved to Gibraltar and established an Export Company, specialising in sales of agricultural machinery to the developing world countries. It later became a facade for the illicit trading of arms. Through the right and influential connections, he soon discovered that the financial rewards of selling guns outstripped agricultural equipment ten-fold.

During the 1950s he was successful in supplying many warring 'hotspots' throughout Africa and Asia with armaments, often to both the opposing sides. Within five years he had secretly accumulated a considerable fortune. Having resided in Gibraltar for several years, his only motive to visit the Laurels was his business connections in Leeds and Birmingham. He would entertain his friends at the house; it was both spacious and accessible. However, Charles's relationship with his father had deteriorated even further over the years. When they were both together in the house they hardly spoke, awkwardly avoiding any contact were possible. Charles's recent interjection was suggesting to his father he should consider moving into a Care Home, leaving the house to him. The Colonel had candidly given his reply 'Charles, get stuffed. Over my dead body.'

18

During the preceding twelve months, Charles had established a strong link with The British Ordnance Company (BOC) on the outskirts of Leeds, which until recent times had been in public ownership belonging to the Ministry of Defence (MOD). However, it had been controversially sold into the Private Sector where it continued to develop and manufacture the latest version of the Challenger Tank for the British Army. Under strict licensing conditions it also exported derivative models to 'friendly' countries, especially in the Middle East. Charles's trading business interests spanned all these nations, even including some countries opposed to them. He possessed those ethics of all Arms Dealers: 'If you can afford to buy it, you can fire it.'

Since the emergence from the ravages and destruction of the Second World War, a new world order began to prevail. The Soviet Union and China were both ideologically and politically opposed to the West, keen to bankroll any opposition to the NATO lead countries. This frequently caused tension and conflict in many of the World's developing regions. The demand for medium and small arms outstripped production. Sourcing and supplying this acute need was shrouded in the utmost of secrecy. Purchasing them at cost and selling for tenfold to highest bidder brought enormous profits. It was illegal and contrary to International Trade agreements. Such enterprises attracted people with no moral fibre. Men like Charles Lewis.

From his office in Gibraltar, with connections throughout the World, he directed his operations. He freely traded with Dictators or those opposed in their arms struggle towards democratically elected

Governments. Providing they paid for the merchandise in US dollars, Charles was prepared to trade with anyone to advance his stature and wealth on the international stage. With his vast accumulated wealth, he was able to tempt and influence those closely connected with the lawful supply of arms.

Recently, he accomplished just that by bribing two Directors of BOC in Leeds with tens of thousands of pounds in exchange for a direct introduction to Ron Earl, the Managing Director of Boddington Armaments, Birmingham. Both of these companies shared the virtual monopoly of producing and exporting arms on behalf of the United Kingdom. Although BOC built significant quantities of heavy armoured machinery and ordinance, their supply of small and medium arms was also consistently high. When military exercises were planned at home or West Germany, the MOD simply requisitioned these companies to supply simultaneously all their ballistic needs and capabilities.

Through his subsequent partnership with Ron Earl, Charles was able to broker deals with both lawful or renegade organisations throughout the world under the auspices of selling and supplying them with BOC and Boddingtons arms. All these transactions were performed through the legitimate to export licence process disguised as Agricultural machinery. Charles was able to syphon enough fully-automatic guns, light to medium field cannons and heavy armaments to supply a small army with all their requirements.

Wherever he travelled, he was always accompanied by his 'minders,' Bill Jones and Joe Mason. Both were born in Yorkshire and had served together as Officers in the Royal Marines. Their friendship was once described by fellow Officers as 'disturbingly close.' Both had separate distinguishing features. Bill was of slight build but incredibly strong for his size with bright curly ginger hair. whilst Joe was much larger with a natural muscular body and walked with a limp, a wound he had received in the Aden campaign three years previously.

Although Joe had recovered from his wounds, his limp caused the Medical Board to recommend him to be medically discharged. He appealed but within three months he was back home in Yorkshire looking for work. The National Coal Board refused to offer him any position within the abundance of Collieries scattered throughout the County.

Shortly afterwards, Bill resigned his Commission and convinced Joe they could earn substantial amounts of money by serving as Mercenaries in several African conflicts. It was during one of their assignments the following year in West Africa they came to the notice of Charles Lewis, who was looking for men to act as his personal security guards. Both had impressed him as being resourceful, loyal and trustworthy. After his enquiries revealed they were martial arts trained, with a reputation of killing their targets quietly, rather than use the lethal force from their weapons, he promptly offered them employment, which they readily accepted. It was permanent, with generous remuneration and relatively safe work.

Their job description was simple; keep Charles's business activities away from any outside interference, at all cost.

19

The Laurels laid less than four miles from the BOC factory. Occasionally, whilst his father was abroad in France, Charles would host small but extravagant dinner parties where the catering was always 'brought in' by a reputable hospitality firm, based in Harrogate, twenty-two miles away. Charles's guests were always the same men. The two Directors for the BOC and Ron Earl. All four men had known each other for several years having accumulated considerable wealth through their collaboration. To safeguard their position further, Ron Earl had fostered a close connection with a hidden branch of the MOD. It was the most clandestine of all Departments within Whitehall, operating through their agents Ron Earl and Chares Lewis.

The economics was simple. The country was still suffering from the financial ruination inflicted by the second World War, with the Treasury close to bankruptcy. Although this illicit trade with so called 'Bandit' organisations amidst unstable countries was morally wrong, the rewards were most lucrative to these men who dared to trade in the shadows. The cruellest of ironies was that it generated a welcomed substantial surplice to the national balance of payments. The whole arrangement between these players and the MOD relied on complete secrecy. Ron and Charles were obsessive if not neurotic with their privacy, avoiding any contact with the public, particular the Press. Any shred of public discovery would certainly jeopardise this arrangement with Whitehall causing the faceless Civil Servants to run for cover, vehemently denying any involvement whatsoever.

Tonight, the syndicate was meeting to discuss their next enterprise and celebrate the success of their last. Charles had arranged for his guests to be collected by Bill and Joe in his new Jaguar from their respective homes and hotels. As always, their role was to protect his guests from any unwarranted attention and remain on standby at the Laurels, ensuring the soiree was held in complete secrecy.

After their meal, they all retired to the drawing room and discussed the supply of five thousand semi-automatic weapons to a freedom fighting alliance connected with the attempted overthrow of an ultra-right Government in South America. Once again, their intelligence suggested the Soviet Union was funding the ruling party. Charles and his Associates were invited to supply arms to the rebels. The UK Government had unofficially described these rebels as 'Freedom fighters' whose objective was to overthrow the tyrannical dictator. They had guaranteed London the installation of democracy through open and free elections. Charles Lewis knew the truth was in fact very different. The fighting rebels were led by just another War Lord, accompanied by his private Militia vying to seize control.

But Charles and Ron were not concerned with such politics, they had already received their first payment from the UK Government, via an international banking account in Switzerland.

One of BOC Directors announced, 'I'll arrange for all necessary paperwork to be collected from here in Leeds. Charles, can your boys pick this up in the next couple of days and take it directly to Ron's factory in Birmingham?'

'Yes, I'll sort that out,' replied Charles. He then turned to Ron Earl, 'When they arrive at your place, will you arrange some transport for the arms? I should think a medium sized lorry should be sufficient.'

'Yes, leave that with me Charles,' replied Ron Earl.

'Thanks. I can send my boys to collect the merchandise as soon as we have the paperwork. They'll transport them from Birmingham then directly to the docks at London where I'll be waiting. I'll arrange for them to be inspected by one of their representatives there and once that's been approved, the second payment will be in our offshore accounts by noon the following day.' Everyone smiled. Charles said, 'Let's drink again to our success and hope that while people are content to kill each other in this world, we can give them the means to fulfil their wishes.'

They raised their glasses in agreement. 'Gentlemen we have all become wealthy men and may it long continue. Our firm alliance exists through trust, secrecy and confidentiality. These are the cornerstones to our success and provided we keep everything tight, we'll continue to make more money in the future. After all, we all know how fickle this business is and the gravy train won't run forever. But if we continue to work close together without involving anyone else, we have a beautiful future ahead of us. Remember Gentlemen, if we didn't supply these weapons, the Soviet Union and Chinese Communists would certainly do. So, I give you, the riches of war!'

They all raised their glasses and nodded in agreement.

20

Shortly after midnight they finally completed their meeting. Charles turned towards Bill as he waved the three men goodnight from the front porch as they were driven away in the Jaguar. 'Does Joe know where to take them?'

'Yes Mr Lewis. He's taking Mr Earl back to the Hotel first and then the other two gentlemen to their homes afterwards.'

'Good. In that case, I'm going to retire for the night. Who's on watch tonight?'

'Joe. I'll wait until he returns before I turn in Sir.'

'Very good. Make sure everything is locked up before you do so.'

Bill nodded as Charles climbed the sweeping staircase to his bedroom at the rear of the house. Bill and Joe's bedrooms were on both sides of the landing at the top of the staircase. This gave them quick access to all parts of the house. As Charles undressed inside his bathroom, he reflected on the nights discussion. Once again, he was delighted with the cooperation the syndicate had made and the opportunities of making vast fortunes in the future.

Whilst Charles Lewis slept soundly in his bed, Joe returned and parked the Jaguar in the garage in the rear yard. He walked through the front door and found Bill sat in the hallway reading a magazine. He looked at his watch, "Not bad Bill. Got all three back and still only 1.30. Do you fancy a night cap? Perhaps there's some of that expensive brandy they were having earlier?'

'No thanks mate. I'm ready for bed. And don't you be helping yourself either. Keep awake. We don't want to mess this cosy little job here. Do we?'

'No, don't worry,' replied Joe.

'Will you take the first shift and wake me up at seven-thirty? I don't think Mr Lewis needs both of us tomorrow, so you can have a lie in till lunchtime.'

'OK. Goodnight Bill.'

As Bill ascended the stairs, Joe walked into the living room and sat on the sofa close to the window. Within five minutes all the lights in the house were out. He stared outside into the winter's night sky, listening to the rustle of the bushes close to the French Doors. He looked back towards the open doorway leading into the hallway, but everything was in darkness. This was the worst part of the job; providing round the clock security to his employer. Thank goodness it was only whilst they were away from Gibraltar.

Although the house was in complete black-out, he was able to hear every sound inside the building. As the wind outside increased, drafts began to enter the old windows causing them to rattle and an occasional creek from the ceiling timbers above. But he recognised all these sounds. After all, he and Bill had visited the Laurels and 'baby sat' Charles for over twelve months.

Suddenly, he heard an unfamiliar sound. The scraping of metal. He stood and walked towards the hallway and heard it again; not a loud noise but it was coming from the cellar. With some reticence, he opened the cellar door and quietly tip-toed down the stone stair case into the black void below. Then he saw a flash of light coming from the room to his right. Someone was in there and coming his way. He crept silently to the lower floor level and heard a footstep approaching. He stooped down and pounced. Lashing out wildly, his fist violently connected with someone.

It was into this world of trained killers and an illegal international arms dealer, a disabled burglar tumbled into.

21

Jim sat, remaining in his taxi, whilst Ronnie collected his backpack from inside the boot. The car was parked over a hundred yards away from the Laurels in a small cul-de-sac, under a large oak tree in the shadows. Jim asked, 'Have you got everything?'

With his mouth busily chewing three sticks of gum, he replied, 'Yes. Same as usual Jim. Give me an hour and then come looking for me. I'm going in through the cellar grate at the right side of the house facing it. If you see the bag outside the lounge window, you know I'm still inside. OK?'

'Sure. Good luck.'

As Ronnie walked awkwardly towards the large house, Jim noticed several gum wrappers on floor and smiled. Typical, always leaving litter in his wake. The lane was lined with large deciduous trees, all bare of their foliage with its dried leaves now rustling loudly beneath his feet. He peered at his watch, 2 a.m.; the presence of police officers on the streets would now be at its minimum, with half of them going off duty whilst the rest were probably keeping warm inside the police stations drinking tea. It was a cold November's night and the wind began to grow stronger and louder. Perfect burglary conditions; any noise he made would be drowned out by nature.

He approached the stone gateposts signed 'the Laurels' and walked through the wide open wrought-iron gates. Stepping cautiously, he moved towards the house using the street lighting as a guide. The gardens were generously adorned with large evergreen shrubs, all affording him with dark cover. He moved from one area of darkness to another. Unknown to Ronnie these were the original laurels, planted by Colonel Lewis and his wife over thirty years previously.

Through the darkness ahead, the house now came vaguely into full view. It was mostly set into the shadows of the larger trees surrounding the grounds. He stepped closer and peered through a side window. There were no signs of life; no vehicles in the front drive or down the side. He smiled and whispered to himself, 'Perfect again. As quiet as the grave.'

This reinforced the information Jim had told him that the Colonel was away abroad. He was alone without fear of being disturbed. He crept towards the front living room window and placed his backpack inside the flower bed, underneath the sill. Remembering the plans Freddie had acquired from the Council, he moved next towards the side of the house where he immediately saw the cellar grate. He stooped down to examine the size; it was just as he had expected, mid-Victorian design, large and heavy. With his jemmy bar, he lifted the edge and placed the bar underneath, allowing him to move it sideways against the wall. It was normal such an undertaking would make a scraping noise but this was unavoidable due to its awkward shape and weight. Thank goodness the wind was howling.

Ronnie adjusted his black rubber diving suit around his shoulder for added flexibility, he tied his black boots tightly to his ankles before finally placing his thick black woollen balaclava over his head. Apart from his face, he was completely black. As he began to manoeuvre the grate entrance sideways he was unaware of an empty bubble gum wrapper, caught between his trouser leg beneath the diving suit, had managed to work free and fall onto the driveway close to the wall. Purposefully, he quickly squeezed through the gap and shone the torch light strapped to his wrist downwards into the black void below.

He crawled down the entrance allowing gravity to do its work. He held his arms tightly against the walls, steadying his weight before falling gently at forty-five degrees onto the pile of coal below. Although his suit and headgear cushioned most of his fall, several chunks of coal were disturbed causing them to roll onto the blacked concrete floor. He was in.

He immediately stood up and shone the torch towards the open wooden door in front of him. He could see beyond the doorway a flight of stone steps leading upstairs into the hallway. Brushing away the coal dust from his rubber suit he stepped forwards, listening attentively for any sounds. The house was empty and he knew exactly where to go and where to find the silver snuff boxes. Smiling again, he produced another stick of bubble gum from underneath his suit; it helped his concentration and steadied his nerves.

But as he was about to unwrap it, he stumbled and suddenly felt a violent punch in his neck. For a split second, he was surprised; it was on his left side, where he was of normal build. It was his right side that had given him a lifetime of pain. He lost consciousness and fell backwards onto the pile of coal.

Seconds later Joe switched the light on. He had blindly struck out with his fist, hitting Ronnie sideways across his neck. He now looked down on the unconscious body of a deformed young man, dressed in a rubber suit, wearing a balaclava and a torch connected to his wrist. He uttered quietly, 'Who the hell are you?' He stooped down and yanked the balaclava away. The intruder was out cold.

Leaving him unattended, Joe rushed back upstairs and burst into Bill's bedroom. He suddenly woke up shouting 'What the …?'

'Come with me now. Quickly,' replied Joe.

Hastily placing his dressing gown over his pyjamas, he followed Joe back down into the cellar. Looking down he exclaimed, 'How did he bloody get there?'

'No idea. I just heard some noises coming from down here, so I crept down and jumped him. Had no time to wake you up.'

'Let's get him sat in a chair and wake him up. He's got some explaining to do.'

Joe went upstairs and returned with an old wooden chair he found in the kitchen. Together, they lifted Ronnie and sat him down, tying his wrists and ankles tightly with some garden clothes line. Once secure, Bill grabbed his hair and pulled back his head and slapped his face, attempting to revive him. Gradually Ronnie began to regain conscious, moaning incoherently before he looked upwards and whispered, 'What happened?'

Bill bent down and looked directly into his flickering eyes 'You've got some explaining to do young man. What are you doing here?'

'I don't know what you mean,' he mumbled.

Without any warning, Joe placed a burning cigarette close to his face, just below the eye. Ronnie immediately felt the heat and screamed, 'I'll tell you. I'll tell you! Please don't hurt me anymore.'

'Who are you and what are you doing here?' he repeated.

'I'm Ronnie and I was told to break in and steal the silver snuff boxes upstairs, belonging to the Colonel. That's all. I promise.'

'Who sent you?'

'Freddie, he's my Boss. I just do as I'm told. Please don't hurt me anymore Sir.'

He looked at his attire and asked, 'How did you get here?'

'Jim the taxi driver.'

'Where's this Jim now?'

'He's supposed to be coming back for me later.'

Ronnie's screams had reached all parts of the house, waking Charles Lewis up from his sleep. He quickly placed his dressing gown around his shoulders and went downstairs towards the voices coming from the cellar. From the hallway he shouted, 'What's happening Bill?'

'One moment Sir.'

Bill appeared at the foot of the cellar stairs and looked upwards, 'We've had an intruder and we're talking to him now.'

'Who is it?'

'Just a disabled kid by the look of it. He was after the silver snuff boxes belonging to your father.'

'Listen Bill, you know what our business is about. Nobody, I mean nobody, must know what we do. I don't want any loose ends that can damage our future prospects. Both of you have made a great deal of money out of me and if you do as I expect; you'll make a great deal more before we can all retire. Deal with this in your own way but make it permanently. No loose ends. No witnesses. No mess. Make it disappear. I don't want to know how Bill. Just do it. Do you understand me?'

'Yes, Mr Lewis. You can leave this with us. Anyone connected with this intrusion will disappear. You have my word on that.'

'Excellent. I'm going back to bed now. Please carry on with your business but not too much noise mind you.'

'Yes Sir.'

Within ten minutes both men had extracted everything from Ronnie; his criminal intentions and those of Freddie and their driver, Jim; where they lived and how they operated. They stripped him of all of his possessions and found a photograph of Freddie. Now they knew what he looked like. It was too easy for these men, they had been trained killers and mercenaries in West Africa where they regularly tortured people to gain information.

Ronnie's life came to a sudden and swift end. After being reassured by his captors of imminent release, he felt relieved his ordeal would come to a close. As Joe offered him a towel to clean his face, Bill quickly stepped forward and pressed his hands against his throat and with all his strength, snapped his neck backwards. Death was instant.

Joe brought an old rug from one of the garages and laid it flat in the hallway. He joined Bill and together they lifted and carried Ronnie's lifeless body upstairs and dropped him into the middle of the rug. Standing at opposite ends they picked it up and took it through the front door and down the porch steps. They continued down the side of the house, passing the upended cellar grate towards the Jaguar parked inside the garage. They lowered Ronnie into the boot of car and threw the corners of the rug over him.

Two minutes later, they drove out of the Laurels into the Grove and disappeared Southwards, taking the main road towards Pontefract. Both men had already made contingency plans for such an event; the permanent concealment of a body. On the outskirts of the town lay one of the largest coal mines in the Country, The Prince of Wales Colliery, overshadowed by its waste heap.

Joe chose this coal mine because his father and grandfather had lived locally and worked their all their adult lives in that pit. Both had died prematurely contracting black lung disease through decades of working at the pit face, continually exposed to coal dust. As a child, Joe often played on these heaps and knew the dangers they posed. Sudden ignition and collapse of the stacks were a constant hazard. The spoil heaps at this colliery were colossal, some rising to over three hundred feet high.

Joe had identified a 'hot heap' after he visited his mother several weeks previously. It had smouldered for many years and was only regulated by the damp weather and the occasional inspection by the National Coal Board (NCB). It was financially prudent to allow this controlled burning to continue, rather than excavate and expose the seat of the fire. Such an operation would cost tens of millions of pounds. Money the Government could ill afford.

In the darkness, on a remote lane skirting the Colliery, the Jaguar came to a halt close to the poorly constructed wire fence. Joe threw Ronnie's lifeless body over his shoulder whilst Bill carried the rug and two gardening spades. The perimeter wire fence presented no obstacle for them, as they trampled down a gap and walked through. They climbed the slope to where the grey acrid smoke was emitting and dropped Ronnie hard to the ground. They immediately began digging away at the embers, taking no time to scoop out a hole measuring a square yard, exposing smouldering fire below. Quickly and without ceremony, they dragged Ronnie and pushed him into his fiery grave, followed by the rug. With their shovels, they returned the coal spoil back into the hole, completely covering him. Within seconds both the body and rug completely vanished without any trace. The fresh air now breathed new life into the fire, incinerating Ronnie's hidden body forever.

There would be no evidence to record Ronnie's violent murder. No one to mourn his passing. His pitiful life continued into his death. He was simply born and died unlucky.

Bill and Joe returned to the Jaguar and set off back to Leeds. With Ronnie out of the way they could concentrated their efforts on Jim, the taxi driver and afterwards Freddie. They knew where they lived and they had to be dealt with immediately.

22

Jim Simms knocked on Pete Hayes' front door. It was normal practice when handing over the taxi keys to have the car cleaned and refuelled ready for service. But this morning was different. When Pete opened the door and saw his partner, he immediately knew something was wrong. 'Come in Jim. What's happened?'

'Listen Pete, I've being doing a job for a special client last night and it's all gone pear-shaped.'

'What do you mean?'

Jim decided to tell him everything. They had been friends and business partners for many years and completely trusted his discretion. After a cup of tea, he stood to leave saying, 'If anything happens to me, go and see this Freddie for me please.'

Pete nodded assuringly, 'I will Jim. But I'm sure everything will be OK.'

Jim left through the front door to buy a newspaper from the corner shop on the opposite side of the road before returning home, several houses down on the same side. Even after speaking to his friend, he was still worried what had happened to Ronnie, fearing he had been arrested by the Police and it was just a matter of time before they called on him too. Worse still, if these two men had harmed Ronnie and were now coming after him, he was in even deeper trouble.

After collecting the newspaper, he came out of the shop and crossed over the road, inhaling deeply on his cigarette. He was completely unaware of the Ford Thames van behind, speeding towards him. Without any warning, the front offside wing hit him at 45 mph, instantly catapulting him twenty feet into the air. He was dead before bouncing violently against the gable end of the terraced house on the opposite side of the road. The force of the impact was catastrophic. His skull smashed into segments like an egg shell and the force ruptured most of his organs. Mercifully, he felt no pain. Yet macabrely, traces of smoke faintly expelled from his open distorted mouth.

Without slowing down, Bill continued driving quickly, glancing in the door view mirror at Jim's body lying at an unnatural position on the pavement. He turned to Joe, 'Better dump this soon. There's too much damage on it.'

Joe pointed ahead, 'There's an old derelict mill down here. We'll park up and torch it to get rid of any evidence. It's also close to the bus stop where we can get back to the Laurels.'

Bill agreed, 'Yes good idea. Now where's this fellow Cox live?'

Forty minutes later they pulled up close to Freddie's house in the Jaguar. As Joe opened the car door, Bill noticed several people standing at the bus stop on the opposite side of the road. One of them included a man in his fifties. He pulled out the photograph he had taken from Ronnie's clothing and compared the image.

'That's him Joe, over there.' Still pointing to the photograph, he whispered to him, 'Go and catch the bus with him but sit far away as possible from him. It looks like he's carrying a suitcase. It's my bet he's got wind of us and he's leaving town in a hurry; probably by train. I'll follow in the Jag. If we get separated, we'll meet up at the Railway Station. That's where he'll heading for.'

'No worries.'

As Bill drove away, Joe sauntered over to the bus stop and stood behind a queue of ten people. He deliberately made no eye contact with Freddie and waited until the familiar green double decker bus arrived displaying on its front screen, 'City Square.' Freddie was the first to board. He sat by the open doorway close to the Conductor, whilst Joe walked passed him towards the front. During the short journey Freddie turned towards the other passengers that had stepped onto the bus with him. But Joe had used a simple method of distraction; he sat next to an elderly woman and engaged in conversation with her. This gave an impression they knew each other and an elderly woman did not match the profile of an archetype killer.

It was noon when the bus came to a halt and stopped in City Square opposite to the Railway Station. Freddie stepped off and walked towards the pavement kerb. Joe saw his opportunity. Immediately breaking off in mid-sentence, he left the old woman and ran towards the exit as the bus was about to set off. He jumped from the platform onto the pavement and approached Freddie who was waiting for an opening in the traffic to cross the road. Joe noticed the Jaguar parked up outside the Station's main entrance some thirty yards away, with Bill standing close by.

As Freddie waited for a gap in the traffic, Joe thrust a needle into his lower back containing a strong sedative causing his legs to give way immediately. Joe dropped the needle and caught Freddie as he tried to touch his lower back, placing his arms around his waist to keep him on his feet. Within seconds Bill joined him, took the suitcase from Freddie's gripped hand and together assisted him towards the waiting Jaguar. With its back door opened wide, they placed him gently inside and although several people had stopped curiously, Bill smiled at them and said, 'Don't worry, it's my Dad, he's having an epileptic fit. Just taking him home to rest.'

They all nodded approvingly. One woman said, 'He's lucky having good boys like you to look after him. I wished my lads would do the same for me. The selfish buggers.' Bill smiled to his friend, thinking 'If she only knew.' Joe propped himself against Freddie and his suitcase in the back seat as they drove away.

Bill drove the Jaguar towards Hunslet, South of the city, following the main Kings Cross rail line linking Leeds to Wakefield. Leading off the main road were dozens of industrial lanes servicing large factories, most of which were now derelict. Although it was in the middle of the day, the whole area was devoid of life; perfect for their purposes. Each of these sites ran parallel to the rail track. Bill turned left into a large disused yard and parked behind an empty warehouse. In front of them laid an open wall, giving direct access to the track line. Fifty yards away stood the entrance to a short tunnel. Both men nodded to each other. Bill suggested, 'This should do.'

Joe immediately opened the rear door. Bill stepped forward. 'Search him and remove anything of identification. And let's have a look in his suitcase too.'

Joe removed his wallet of any documents and money before discarding over a nearby wall. Joe checked the case and found the £3,500 stashed between the folded clothes inside. 'That'll do nicely, Bill. We've got some serious beer money for our efforts.'

Once they had finished, Joe scattered the packed clothing across the dirty yard and threw the empty suitcase over another wall. Joe leant over Freddie and threw him over out his broad shoulders and followed Bill down the small embankment towards the tunnel. They entered the large entrance and looked around. From a distance of twenty feet inside, Joe finally set Freddie down across two shiny track lines. Without speaking, they rested his head against one track, with his legs sprawled over the other. Bill checked him once more, 'He's out cold. Poor sod will never wake up again. When the train hits him, his head and legs will be all that's left of him here. The rest of him will be scattered for miles. Instant death.'

Joe nodded, uttering 'Job done.'

Without looking backwards, they returned to the car leaving Freddie to his fate and drove back to the Laurels. Charles Lewis had left a note for them stating he had caught a taxi to the Railway Station and was returning to his London office. He would meet them at the London Docks, as arranged, in two days time with the 'merchandise.' Their instructions were clear; collect the necessary documents from BOC in Leeds and travel to Boddingtons in Birmingham. There, collect the goods and transport them directly to London. The footnote simply read, 'I trust last night's intrusion has been expedited.'

Bill laughed at the last comment. 'Bloody posh word for what we've been doing for him, eh Joe?'

Before the afternoon's light failed, they searched the gardens and found Ronnie's backpack near to the living room window. They were puzzled to find the brown paper and treacle but burnt everything in the garden incinerator before replacing the cellar grate to its original position.

In accordance with Charles Lewis, all the loose ends were now fully expedited.

23

Charles Lewis looked out from the train carriage window as it sped Southwards through the rolling countryside. He had full confidence in Bill and Joe's ability to make last night's incident disappear without trace. His meeting in London was another important trade deal involving the continued unrest between Israel and its neighbours, especially those of Palestinian heritage. With the Americans and British supporting the Israelis, he saw an opportunity of providing arms to the opposing side. Once again, his contacts with British Intelligence suggested the Soviet Union were in advanced talks with the Palestinians to supply their requirements. It was paramount he spoke with their agents in Beirut within the next few days. He would organise this from his office in London.

Meanwhile back in Leeds, later that afternoon, Joe returned to the Laurels having personally collected the documents from BOC relating to the previous evening meeting. As he parked the Jaguar in the garage, Bill also arrived in a medium size truck, hired from a local commercial vehicle rental company. He entered the house and immediately placed a call to his Boss in London.

Charles replied, 'Lewis Enterprises.'

'We've got the paperwork as you asked Sir.'

'Good. I want you to drive the Jaguar over to Ron Earl's in Birmingham and collect the goods. They'll provide you with everything you need. Leave the car there, load the goods onto it and bring the lorry down here.'

'But I didn't expect to load the wagon?'

'Well you are now. Just get on with it and don't argue.'

Shaking his head with annoyance, Bill simply replied, 'Yes Sir.'

'You know the drill; give him the documents to stamp and bring all the blue copies with you. Don't forget to hold on to your passes, otherwise you won't be allowed inside the Docks. Ron will arrange for your truck to be loaded overnight with the merchandise. First thing tomorrow morning, collect the truck and drive down to the docks here in London. I'll meet up with you there at noon.'

'Got it Sir, tomorrow at noon.'

'That's right. Incidentally, was that other matter dealt with?'

'Yes Sir. Everything is sorted and cleared up. Apparently, it's been a bad week for accidents in Leeds, this week.'

'Too much information. Be careful Bill,' Charles retorted menacingly.

'Sorry Sir. We'll make our way to Birmingham now.'

'Don't be late.'

Bill replaced the receiver and turned to his friend and snapped, 'Come on Joe, we're going to Birmingham, stopping overnight and driving a truck to London, like the last job.'

'What's the matter Bill? Has the bastard upset you again?'

'Yes. When we've finished with him, I might show him some manners.'

'Don't take this personal Bill but he probably doesn't like you, just because you have ginger hair. It's only business and we're making a mint out of him. Let's not kill the Goose, as they say, just yet.'

'Perhaps he doesn't like cripples either?'

'Thanks, Bill, for pointing that out for me. Got that through serving for Queen and Country, you were just born ugly with ginger hair.'

They looked at each other and smiled. For as long as it served their purpose they would obey Charles Lewis for now but their allegiance to him was fickle, always open-ended to better opportunities where the rewards were most lucrative. In their line of business nothing was permanent.

24

John sat his desk looking at the list of suspected burglaries committed by Ronnie and Freddie. They had been professional criminals responsible for dozens of high valued thefts throughout the North of England. Anticipating the list was still incomplete, with some neighbouring forces still in the process of forwarding their crime details, a clear pattern was already emerging. Antique silverware and jewellery had been their target and a broken window smeared with treacle and brown paper, mistakenly believed to be the point of entry had been evident at all of these break-ins. All the buildings, without exception, were serviced by a cellar grate and left in its original position. The total value of all the stolen property to date exceeded £40,000.

It was 9.30 a.m. and Phil had yet to appear when his telephone rang. John reached over and answered, 'DC Evans, Antique Squad.'

'John, this is DCI Sampson. Is Phil there?'

'Not yet Sir.'

'Never mind. Give him a message please. I've been doing some digging on your Colonel Lewis. He appears to be of excellent character with a long and distinguished military record and for a time during the last war he was the Chief Medical Officer for the Armed forces in Normandy. Unfortunately, his son, who was also a Doctor in the Medical Regiment, was killed at that time and that's why I think he spends so much time in France these days. However, he has a surviving son called Charles. Now, he's a different kettle of fish and this is where it gets interesting. Apparently, he was kicked out of the Foreign Office some years ago for certain unknown indiscretions. My

A PERILOUS LAST CONFESSION

contact has no idea what that exactly means but he suspects it was something very shady and embarrassing to the Government. Anyway, it looks like it was all hushed over; probably to safeguard his father's reputation. It seems he lives and works in London and Gibraltar where he runs an export business. I've no further details so you'll need to check with Companies House to see if he's a Director for a registered company, either in the UK or over there. Off the record, my contact has heard he enjoys an international reputation of supplying suspected 'black market arms and ballistics' and regularly returns to this country where he has his contacts.'

'Bloody hell Sir. We're just the Leeds City Police Antique Squad. This sounds a little out of our league.'

'John, that's an understatement. Although the indications are the Foreign Office have no interest in Charles Lewis, I've heard from another source that whilst they're keen to identify his nefarious activities, they would be reluctant to share it with anyone else. They are completely unaware of the suspected burglary at his house, or your involvement through Freddie's dying declaration. However, we have no choice; I'm going to meet with ACC Jenkins this morning and discuss what to do next. It's my intention, you and Phil continue without any interference from London. This could become very political and make things messy. We'll see what Mr Jenkins has to say first.'

'Do you want us to hold back our investigation Sir?'

'No, but as I told Phil yesterday, I don't want you going around to the house until I've spoken to the ACC.'

'OK Sir, got that.'

'Tell Phil. I'll ring him later. Meanwhile, continue with your enquiries into the outstanding burglaries.'

DCI Sampson rang off, leaving John staring at the pages of undetected burglaries spanning over three years. Tucked inside the outstanding paperwork from other forces relating to their respective crimes, he saw a pink folder. It was the vehicle registration enquiry for Jaguar - JUM 106 from the local Licensing Authority. 'Bingo' he whispered. It was registered to Charles Lewis Enterprises Ltd.

He placed a call to Companies House in London and spoke to a Liaison Officer called Katherine. After furnishing her with the details, she returned several minutes later and gave him the company's details. It was a registered limited company showing Charles Lewis as the Director and Ron Earl of Birmingham as the Company Secretary. Although it showed an office in London, close to Vauxhall Bridge, the registered address was listed in Gibraltar. Both had been appointed with the inception of the Company, nearly three years ago.

'Can you tell me the nature of what the business is?' asked John.

'Exporting manufacturing and agricultural machinery. Wait a minute,' she paused. 'It shows Ron Earl holds a permit to export sensitive and restricted machinery to counties within the Commonwealth.'

'What does that mean exactly?'

'Not too sure to be honest. It covers all products that are sensitive to the National Interest. For instance, proto-type machinery that has been developed recently that would be of great value to another country outside the Commonwealth. Like a patent protection scheme. But that's only my opinion.'

'What about weapons or arms?' asked John.

'I suppose so. They would certainly require that type of authorisation from the Government.'

Quickly changing the subject, John asked her if she would enquire into any other businesses interests these men may have. Once again after some delay, 'Yes. Ron Earl is listed as the Managing Director of Boddingtons Armouries, registered in Erdington, Birmingham. He was appointed in 1958, nearly six years ago.'

'Thanks Katherine What about Charles Lewis, does he have any other interests?'

'No. There's no other appointment, only the one registered in Gibraltar.'

'That's great. Thanks very much for your help. As you may appreciate, we're conducting a serious investigation that may involve these men. Can I ask you to keep your eye out on them and let me know here in Leeds whether there is any further activity with their business interests?'

'Yes, I can, but you must submit a formal request via your Chief Constable.'

'Of course. Shall I ask for it to be addressed to yourself?'

'Yes please.'

He recorded all these details before his next call; the Vehicle Licensing Department at Wakefield regarding the green Mini Cooper found at the rear of Freddie Cox's house. The operator simply stated, 'Registered keeper Ronald Ellis, 16 Spring Road, Leeds.' As he replaced the telephone, Phil walked into the office. He looked dreadful. John looked up and asked, 'What happened to you?'

'It's called mixing business with pleasure. Something you're not too familiar with young Evans.'

'What are you talking about? I've been at my desk for over an hour taking important messages from the Boss and making some interesting finds in our investigation, not getting pissed with those from the other side of the street.'[11]

'Excuse me young man. I was on duty all the time, drinking with those who really know what's happening in this city. John, you've got to realise that sometimes you have to get down and dirty to their level, otherwise they won't trust you. Sure, they know I'm a Cop, but they also recognise when I need their help. Freddie and Ronnie came from their side of the street and no matter what your bloody high morals are, sometimes you have to drink with them to get the information you need. Christ John, your arse must squeak when you walk, you're so clean!'

'Thanks for that Sergeant Smith. All I know is you look awful, you stink of beer and frankly, probably are unfit for duty.'

'Bollocks, DC Evans, make me a coffee. And make it strong and black. That's an order!' Following several moments of awkward silence, he sighed, 'Please John, pretty please?'

John shook his head in a gesture of defiance. He respected Phil for his unconventional methods of achieving results, fair-mindedness and generosity but failed to accept his bad, if not illegal, practices. It was an uncomfortable reality; all he could do was to acquiesce and turn a blind eye to him. Yet, with his increasing service and confidence, he resolved never to accompany or witness him in any of these shady practices. He leant over and handed him his chipped mug containing strong coffee. 'Do you want to know what DCI Sampson spoke to me about this morning?'

'Yes, but let me tell you what I found last night.'

---

[11] criminals

'OK. But he's told us to not to go to the Laurels until he's seen ACC Jenkins first. Apparently, Colonel Lewis's son Charles was kicked out of the Foreign Office for some shady dealings years ago. It was all swept under the carpet. Anyway, DCI Sampson is going to recommend we continue our investigation into the burglaries without any intervention from London.'

'Bloody hell. I don't trust that spineless bastard Jenkins. We've got a dying declaration to pursue and no bugger in a suit is going to stop me.'

'You can tell the Chief that yourself. And when he's busted you down to a uniformed PC or even sacked you, what are you going to do then, you pillock?'

'Shut up. What else has happened?'

John related the morning telephone calls and the emergence of Charles Lewis into the investigation and possibly changing the dynamics. He described his business connections with Ron Earl and their Company – Charles Lewis Enterprises Ltd, who were possibly involved with the exporting of arms abroad from their offices in London and Gibraltar. Finally, the Jaguar car JUM 106 was registered to their Company.

Phil stared at John, 'And DCI Sampson is going to tell Jenkins all this when he goes to see him?'

'Yes, I believe so.'

'And what about Freddie's dying declaration?'

'I don't know if he's going to mention that.'

Phil sat back into his chair shaking his head in disbelief, 'I'm not going to give this case up without a fight John.'

'I agree with you Phil, but we're going to have play by the rules for the time being. But as I've just said, DCI Sampson was most insistent we mustn't go to visit the Laurels.'

Phil smiled again, 'It's a too bloody late for that you up-start. But I did find something interesting last night. I mean really interesting.'

John slumped back into his chair. 'Oh God. What have you gone and done now?'

25

Since Phil had been appointed Detective Sergeant in the South Division, he had followed closely to the doctrine of his old mentor, DS Andy Richards; 'The best place to do any coppering is where the criminals drink.' Although he had been long retired and those practices had mainly disappeared, Phil shared drinks and conversation with a multitude of those who operated on the wrong side of the law. He colloquially called them 'his ganifs.' This was an old Yiddish name for criminals.

Within the small enclave close to the Market laid the Leylands, where the community consisted of many ethnic and religious groups, the largest being Jewish and Irish. This was reflected by the countless numbers of small tailor shops, betting offices and public houses. Cross-cultural exchanges flourished except in matters of relationships and especially marriage. However, the whole area had disappeared following the gradual slum clearance after the First World War, with most of the wealthier inhabitants migrating two miles North to a more salubrious area called Chapeltown. This boasted cleaner air and several municipal parks.

For those less unfortunate, they remained close to the city centre and Market area, where the old ways continued. It became a melting pot where crime transcended all religions; this was an integral part of their daily lives. An underworld language existed, mixing both Yiddish and Irish cultures and traditions of which any outsider would fail to comprehend. However, during the early 1920s, the Leeds City Police took the initiative by offering Officers the opportunity of spending some time with selected members of the community in an attempt to understand their secretive language. None had volunteered.

DS Smith was the exception. He spoke the language fluently because he originated from the area. He knew exactly their rules and customs. His old mentor had recognised this, stating 'You speak the lingo lad and this knowledge is power. They will treat you differently provided you don't spoil it. And we need to know as much as we can about these ganifs.'

Phil had taken his advice. Indeed, it became his best protection. He knew everyone in all the ale houses, snooker halls and clubs and more importantly, what they were talking about. Even though he was Copper, he was a native of the Leylands like themselves. And it gained him their resect.

His most frequented 'haunts' were three public houses, all close to the Central Market. The most notorious of all was his favourite, the Market Tavern. Most of the customers were either convicted and active criminals or prostitutes. The remainder were those who operated on the edge such as taxi drivers, rogue traders or those punters simply looking for very cheap merchandise or sex. It had a reputation where you could buy anything at a price.

Into this world of criminality, Phil was comfortable and relatively safe. He never displayed any personal animosity or moral judgement towards the criminals he came into contact with. Many criminals committed crimes because they were poor. He recognised that. He had suffered in his childhood too. But the root of most dishonesty was greed and most people shared that. This unspoken and potentially fractious relationship was generally accepted between him and the criminal fraternity. However, whenever he visited the pubs there was an unwritten contract, 'No one was arrested on the premises on the condition Sergeant Smith was given safe passage to leave.'

Occasionally, Phil saw ganifs who were wanted or unlawfully at large. Because the pubs acted as a type of 'sanctuary,' he simply passed a note over via the Licensee, inviting them to surrender themselves at the Police Station within twenty-four hours. Surprisingly, this unofficial system was largely successful. Most would comply and even seek him out when they presented themselves at the Station front counter.

However, Phil drew the line with violent criminals and suspected sex offenders, especially paedophiles. That was different. If he saw someone suspected of such offences he would simply vanish into the back room and telephone the local Police Station with all the necessary details. His instruction was 'Do not enter, but arrest at a good distance away.' This code of practice generated much respect from the Licensees and their customers.

26

After his last meeting with DCI Sampson, Phil waited until John retired from duty before telephoning his wife to tell her it was going to be another late day. She was used to his long and irregular hours but she never complained. She continually tried to self-assure herself, 'It won't be forever.'

Phil drove his old but trusty Ford Anglia into the city centre. After parking it some distance away, he entered the Market Tavern. Built in 1879, to accommodate the Market Traders and their customers, it was one of the oldest pubs in Leeds, exempt from the permitted hours legislation[12] and allowed to remain open all day. Little had changed to its decor. It was perpetually smoke-ridden with thick yellow nicotine stained walls and ceilings. The floor was rough timber floor boards, heavily soiled by the boots of generations of market workers. It was predominately patronised by men only, with the exception of working women prostitutes. Although universally accepted as an establishment of ill-repute, it boasted the finest beer in the city. The Police were never welcome, nor did they willingly venture inside.

Indeed, there was a Chief Superintendent's directive stating all police visits were prohibited unless answering an emergency. When that occurred, a minimum of three officers and a Supervisor were required to attend. Naturally, it was DS Smith's favourite pub. He preferred to go alone; less confrontational.

---

[12] permitted hours enforced licensed premises to close between 3 p.m. and 5 p.m.

The Landlord was called 'Curly.' He was a small stout man, in his mid-fifties and bald as a billiard ball. Both he and Phil had a mutual respect for each other, both originating from the Leylands. Phil would never unnecessarily disturb his customers. However, occasionally he would allow Phil to use the back kitchen if he needed to talk to someone about police business. All his customers were aware of the arrangement and none overtly objected.

Tonight, he walked through the old battered wooden doors and saw the place was busy and full of customers. As usual, all the loud conversations suddenly stopped. For several seconds, there was just silence. It was always like this. It had become a ritual. Phil would take the initiative by shouting, 'If the Devil could cast his net!'

Someone replied, 'Aye and you be caught in it too.'

Phil laughed, 'Dead bloody right there.' Unlike most police officers, he had a natural ability to connect socially with all levels. Most of them knew of his background and harsh beginnings. Strangely, the criminals had much respect for his audacity and often engaged in conversation with him, playing dominoes or a game of darts. But tonight was different. He ordered half a pint of bitter and turned towards the customers. Some were still fixing their stare towards him, others deliberately looking away nervously. A group of five prostitutes were giggling in the far corner and several men simply walked outside. He drew a breath and shouted, 'Listen in everyone. I need your help.'

'Bugger off,' came a reply.

Ignoring the heckle, he continued, 'You all knew Freddie the Fence. Most of you made a bob or two out of him. Do you know he's dead?'

The customers went silent. 'What happened to him?' someone shouted.

'He was found on the railway tracks just out of town a couple of days ago and I'm treating it as suspicious. If there's anyone in here tonight who has had any recent dealings with him, please speak to me now. Also, for those of you who know right-angled Ronnie, has anyone seen him? He's disappeared about the same time Freddie was killed and I need to find him quickly. He needs to take his medication urgently. You all know who I am. I wouldn't ask you unless it was serious. They both belonged to your side of the street and I need some help to find out exactly what happened to them. I've never come in here before asking for your help and I promise you all, that whatever you say to me will be in the strictest of confidence. Even if its thieving, provided it's not too serious. I'll be in the back kitchen if anyone wants to talk to me.'

He turned and nodded towards Curly who raised his eyebrows and nodded back. Clutching his half pint of beer, Phil stepped into the back kitchen, where he waited for over ten minutes. He had several other pubs to visit and he was playing a very long shot, acutely aware these were all ganif's pubs. No one talked to the Police, especially when it concerned one of their own. He gulped the last remnants of his beer and moved towards the back door, looking towards the bar through the small hatchway trying to attract Curly's attention to alert him that he was leaving. Suddenly the door latch made a muffled sound and opened slowly. Phil moved forwards and pulled it wide open. Stood before him was a woman, probably only in her early twenties yet looked considerable older. Wearing a full length over coat, open at the front to expose her short tight skirt and small top she whispered hesitatingly, 'I might have something of interest for you Mr Smith.'

Reassuringly, he replied, 'Come in love and sit down,' pulling a wooden chair from under the kitchen table. As she approached, he instantly smelt her cheap and overpowering perfume. Her heavily peroxide blonde hair and abundance of make-up failed to disguise her premature ageing, caused by years of soliciting for prostitution amongst the streets and pubs surrounding the market in all weathers. Phil had seen her occasionally in the locality but had never spoken to her.

'What's your name love?'

'I'm Brenda Barker, Mr Smith. You know what I do for a living and so no one's going to believe me, but I don't mind telling you what I do know. Freddie often gave me a few quid for some information about wealthy punters who I did business with. I don't know what he did with it but I was happy to take his money.'

'When did you see him last Brenda?'

'About a week ago; I saw him in here.'

'What did you talk about?'

She hesitated and looked to the floor. Phil leant forwards and spoke softly, 'Don't worry Brenda, I'm only interested in what happened to Freddie. If you were in cahoots with him about some job, I'm not bothered. Just tell me what you were talking about.'

'He told me about a job in Roundhay where an old Colonel lived. He wrote his name for me. It's in my bag here.'

She opened her smudged cream leather handbag and unfolded a piece of paper. She continued 'Here it is; a Colonel Lewis, that's him. According to Freddie it seems this old soldier visited France regularly since the end of the War for some reason.'

'Why was that?' asked Phil as took hold of the note.

'I once told Freddie my Dad was killed in France in 1944, just after D Day. I was a young girl at the time so I didn't remember him. Anyway, Freddie wanted me to go and see this Colonel and tell him that I'd found out from a friend of mine he was involved in the War Graves Commission. Is that what you call them?' she asked.

Phil nodded, 'I think so. Go on Brenda.'

'I've never visited my Dad's grave. I don't know where he's buried but Freddie wanted me to ask the Colonel if he could help me find out where he's been laid to rest. And if he could, would he let me know when he next travelled to France.'

'Why do you think he wanted you to ask him that?'

'I'm not sure, but I suspected he wanted to know when he was out of the country so he could to the job without getting disturbed. Anyway, he offered me £20 and a free trip in a taxi.'

'When did he ask you to do this?'

'Last week, but I've been ill with flu and spent most of the time in bed.'

'So, you didn't go?'

'Oh yes.'

'Tell me what happened Brenda?'

'Well I got dressed up properly, not like this and tried to look respectable. The taxi picked me up at my place and drove me to a posh house in Roundhay. Never been up there before; not for the likes of people like me Mr Smith. I got dropped off outside and walked along the driveway and rang the front door bell. Well I'll be buggered; it was a young man who opened the door, not an old one like I was expecting. I asked him if I could see Colonel Lewis. As you know Mr Smith, I'm used to dealing with rude men but this one took some beating. He asked me why I wanted to see him. So, I explained about trying to trace my father's grave in France. Well he just shouted, 'He's not here. Now sod off and don't come back again.'

'When was this?'

'Yesterday.'

'Then you weren't aware of what had happened to Freddie?'

'No, I called to see him afterwards, but the house was all locked up. I never saw him.'

'Going back to the house. What did this man look like?'

'Not very tall, say five and half feet tall, skinny build in his late thirties. The most unusual thing about him Mr Smith was his hair.'

'His hair?'

'Yes. It was bright ginger and very curly.'

'Who was the taxi driver who took you there?'

'Can't say, Mr Smith.'

'Did he see this man?'

'No. He was parked down the road, out of sight. I know he was upset 'cos his mate Jim had just been killed by a hit and run driver the day before. Very sad. I knew Jim too. He used to do jobs for Freddie and his friend Ronnie. What's happened to Ronnie, Mr Smith? I know he's a bit of a strange man but those two were very close, like father and son.'

'I'm not sure Brenda at this stage. Going back to this ginger-haired man you saw. Would you recognise him again?'

'Definitely Mr Smith, he looked an evil bugger. Someone who could look after himself. You know what I mean?'

'Yes I do.'

'Was there anything else you saw before you left?'

'Not really. Oh, there was a lovely car parked down the side of the house.'

'Can you remember what type of car?'

'Not sure, it wasn't like the ones my punters drive. It was a posh black one, might have been a Jaguar.'

'Thanks, that could be helpful. Now Brenda, can you speak to this taxi driver and ask him if I can meet up with him soon? I really need to find out what Freddie was up to before he was killed.'

'I'll ask him Mr Smith.'

'Thanks Brenda. Here take this and get a drink.' Phil handed her a few pound notes which she quickly placed inside her handbag. As she stood to leave, Phil spoke softly, 'Don't talk to anyone about this Brenda and thanks for your help. Take care love.' She disappeared into the noisy bar and she returned to the corner where he friends were busy chatting to potential customers. He waited for another five minutes but no one entered. He waved to Curly and left through the back door.

As he entered the passageway leading to the rear yard and the street beyond, he saw a figure in the shadows ahead. A man stepped into his view. He was alone and wearing a flat cap. 'Can I help you?' Phil asked.

'Not really Mr Smith, but I might be able to help you. I don't want anyone knowing I've spoken to you about Freddie. I'm not a Grass. Do you understand?'

'Of course. Who are you please?'

'My name is Pete Hayes.' As he spoke, he walked into the light. He was a man in his mid-forties, slightly over six feet tall and very muscular for his age. Speaking with a broad Yorkshire accent, he continued, 'I was a mate of Jim's, the taxi driver who got knocked down and killed a couple of days ago. The Police are treating it as a 'hit and run' but I think it was deliberate. Whoever killed Jim, meant it.'

'Are you the taxi driver who took Brenda to see Colonel Lewis yesterday?'

'Yes.'

'Why did you go?'

'Jim and me go back a long way. We did National Service together and all that. We've been taxi-driving since then and over the years got to know most the bandits in this town. We've both known Freddie for years, he's a proper gent. If I tell you something now, are you going to lock me up?'

'No. Freddie's death is more important.'

'Promise?'

'I can assure you Pete, I won't lock you up if it's about Freddie or Ronnie. I promise. You have my word on that. OK?'

'I wouldn't tell anyone else. But I know you have a reputation of being fair. Although Freddie did say once you were the biggest bastard in town.'

'Yes, I know about that. For the record, a couple of years ago, Freddie overstepped the line and he got caught. But he spoke to me just before he died and made me promise to find out who did this to him and Ronnie.'

Pete paused, 'Right, this is the story. Jim had an arrangement with Freddie. Whenever he picked any fares up from town who obviously had some money, he would pass this information onto him. Freddie was especially interested if they were elderly and lived alone. Better still, if he managed to help with the customers' luggage inside the house and give it a quick casing[13] so he could have a quick look.'

'What was Jim looking for?'

'Freddie was interested in silverware or small valuable antiques. Nothing big or bulky.'

'Anything else?'

'Yes. Whether they were regular travellers and how often they were away. Once inside, he also looked for any security systems and for some odd reason, and I never understood why, the existence of any cellar grates. I think Freddie paid him well for such information.'

'How much?'

'I'm not sure, but he did tell me Freddie once gave him £50.'

'So why did you go to the house yesterday with Brenda?'

'I knew Jim for many years. I also know he was a bit of a villain but he was good to me when I was injured in a car accident and couldn't work. He helped me and the family out until I got back on my feet; literally. He told me he had done this job for Freddie and taken Ronnie to the house just hours before he was killed. I wanted to find out what had happened, so I went to see Freddie. It was midmorning, a few hours after Jim had been killed. When he opened the door, he looked as if he'd just woken up. He told me he had been waiting up all night for Ronnie to return. When I told him Jim had just been run over and killed, he seemed terrified. That was the last time I saw Freddie.'

---

[13] by distracting householder for a drink of water, look inside rooms for valuables

'Did he say anything about leaving?'

'No. But he looked very frightened.'

'Gone on Pete. What next?'

'I started thinking about what happened to Jim, so I returned to Freddie's house yesterday but he wasn't there. I also knew he wanted Brenda to go and visit this old Colonel, so I rang her up and collected her in my taxi. I know it sounds a bit daft, but I thought the Colonel might have seen Ronnie and Freddie. Brenda had no idea of what it was all about but agreed to go with me to the house and speak to the old man about her Dad. I just wanted her to find out whether he was a decent bloke or not.'

'Did you stay in your car when she went to the house?'

'No. I told her I would remain in the taxi but decided to go and have a quick look around whilst she was talking to him. When I saw her go up to the front door, I jumped over the garden wall and crept down the side of the house. I didn't get very far. I stopped behind some tree and saw a black Jag parked in the back yard and a big muscular bloke cleaning the boot out with a bucket and sponge.'

'What did he look like?'

'He was in his thirties, about six feet tall, well built, with short dark hair. When he walked towards the back of the car, I noticed he had a bad limp. Then he looked up in my direction, so I scarpered back to the garden wall and returned to the car before Brenda got back.'

'I don't suppose you got the number of this Jaguar?'

'I did Mr Smith. I remember numbers, first it was trains and bus numbers when I was a kid, nowadays it's expensive cars. The number was JUM 106. Definitely.'

'That's useful. Was there any other thing you can remember?'

'No Mr Smith. Do you know what's happened to Ronnie?'

'Not yet, but I'm working on it.'

'Mr Smith, it's more than a coincidence Jim and Freddie have died within two days of each other, isn't it?'

'I'm working on that too.'

Pete nodded his head. But as he turned away, he spoke softly, 'You know where to find me if you need me. Just find the bastard that's done this.'

Phil made no reply but watched him disappear around the corner leaving him with more evidence than he had hoped for. He pondered whether to report this to DCI Sampson or not. After all, he had given him and John clear instructions to keep away from the house. But now he had discovered some valuable information supporting Freddie Cox's declaration and delaying the investigation further could jeopardise losing even more evidence.

No, he would visit the Laurels now and have a closer look, before it was too late.

27

Phil parked his Ford Anglia some two hundred yards away from the front entrance to the Laurels. Looking at his watch, it was ten thirty and the damp night air shrouded the large grounds in a light mist obscuring the house. He crept through the two stone gate posts, keeping closely to the evergreen bushes growing high on both sides of the driveway. This was perfect terrain for him. Wearing his dark canvas jacket and black woollen hat he was in his element, tip-toeing gently towards the house. The shrubs eventually gave way to lawns as the driveway swept towards the front porch before continuing down the right side towards the rear yard. He thought of Ronnie as he now followed in his footsteps. If he had been discovered; where?

Ronnie was an experienced burglar. He must have felt confident the house was either unoccupied or the old Colonel had long since retired to bed. How could he have been so clumsy as to fall into a trap? Was he caught out here or inside?

Phil approached the front porch. The whole house was covered in darkness with no sign of life anywhere. He moved silently towards the side of the house, straining his eyes to locate the cellar grate. Although his eyes had become used to the blackness, he was unable to see the ground beneath him. With a calculated risk, he took a small hand-held torch out from his jacket pocket and shone the beam along the house wall at ground level, following the large Yorkshire stonework towards the rear of the house. Suddenly he stopped. There it was, placed exactly where it should be; the cellar grate. But there was something not quite right. What was it?

He looked along the whole length of the wall and back to where the grate lay. His experienced inquisitive eye immediately saw the difference. Leaves had accumulated against the wall and ground but the cellar grate was devoid of any foliage. It must have been disturbed recently, otherwise it would have been harder to locate. He bent over and wrapped his fingers around the wet metal slats of the grate and pulled it upwards. With some force exerted he managed to loosen it from the outer frame, allowing it to eventually break free. After sliding it quietly to one side, he shone his torch beam down into the void. After a few moments, he focussed on a single scuff mark scratched into coal dust coated wall, stretching along the shoot before disappearing out of view into the cellar below.

He gently replaced the grate back to its original position and stood backwards. Suddenly he heard a soft rustling noise from under his shoe. He shone his torch downwards and lifted his foot. There, half buried under several leaves was an empty red and white bubble-gum wrapper. The same he and John had found in Ronnie's bedroom and Mini Cooper. 'Bingo' he whispered. Although not substantive real evidence, it was nevertheless compelling circumstantially, placing Ronnie Ellis at the Laurels. He picked it up and placed it into his inside jacket pocket.

Freddie had mentioned to him on his death bed that Ronnie always disguised his MO. With this in mind, he made his way to the front of the house and began to examine the flower beds in front of the two ground floor bay windows. Nothing. They appeared to have remained undisturbed. He crept towards the farthest corner, on the opposite side of the house, to where the cellar grate was fixed and immediately saw a pair of French Doors. Set to the left side was a flower bedding border containing a number of roses. Most had been allowed to roam freely with some flowers still clinging onto life, midst the cold winter's night. Although the bed had been neglected for a long time, he saw several footprints pressed into the soil indicating someone had trodden there recently.

He now faced towards the house and shone his torch inside. Close to the doors, he saw the shape of the cabinet in the near corner come into view. As he lifted his torch he instantly saw the reflection coming from three small silver boxes on top. These were the silver antique snuff boxes Freddie had told him about before he died.

Phil glanced again at his watch; it was now eleven-fifteen. He had spent enough time there and the cold night air was beginning to make him shudder. Returning the same way, he back-tracked out of the gardens and returned to his car. He needed a drink and time to ponder the evenings developments. He would keep quiet about all this for the time being and discus it with John first thing in the morning.

28

'Bloody hell Phil, you were busy last night,' exclaimed John after listening to his previous night's visit to the Market Tavern. 'What are we going to do?'

Phil sat back and studied his question. Eventually, he replied, 'Let's listen to what DCI Sampson has to say before I tell him of our latest information. You realise I've committed all types of criminal and disciplinary offences talking to these people but that's how it used to be. Discretion I call it.'

'I don't think the Chief Constable would call it that.'

'No, he wouldn't, but all that lot have conveniently forgotten the old ways. They're more than happy to revel in the glory of high detection figures, never questioning the unconventional methods some of us have to employ, until the wheel comes off. Then they hang you out to dry. You're on your own. Well, I've got wise to these guys. I don't leave any trail or witnesses to make silly allegations. I get the job done but I need someone like you John to keep me in check.'

'Listen Phil, I'll help you all I can on this but I suspect it's going to become very serious and out of our league. As I keep telling you, don't expect me to do anything illegal in your doggedly pursuit of the truth. Remember we're evidence gatherers not Judge and Jury.'

'OK John, I can't argue with that. Let's see what the Boss has to say.'

29

Charles Lewis was a perfectionist, detesting unpunctuality and late deadlines made by others. Presently, he was waiting in the biting Easterly wind for Bill and Joe outside the old warehouse on the London Docks. He was expecting the large consignment of medium calibre firearms and automatic weapons they had collected from Boddingtons, together with all the necessary permits and documents supplied by BOC. But they were thirty minutes late.

Then he heard the deep noise of a diesel engine approaching before the large rigid-axle lorry came into view. It was heavily laden with its valuable cargo hidden away under the dirty green canvas tarpaulin. As it came to a halt in front of the large open metal warehouse doors, Bill leaned through the driver's window, 'Sorry Boss, we got stuck on the North Circular. There was a serious accident, car upside down. The Police stopped everything.'

Ignoring his excuses, he curtly asked, 'Have you got everything?'

They both jumped down from the cab. Bill replied, 'Yes. It's all in the back. Joe has all the paperwork for you.'

Joe stepped forward and handed over to him an envelope containing the necessary documents from BOC and Boddingtons. Without looking at him, Charles placed them inside his inside coat pocket and watched the approaching fork lift coming from inside the building. Bill walked to the rear and opened the truck's tailgate, whilst Joe was untying the ropes holding the wooden crates to the platform. Bill guided the fork lift driver towards the rear where the operator skilfully maneuvered the extended arms underneath the first wooden crate. As he hoisted the load upwards, another driver in a low-loader approached and pulled up alongside. Eventually, all the crates were individually placed and stacked on the second vehicle.

Charles counted forty-three; that was the agreed consignment. He turned to Bill, 'Drive the lorry back to Boddingtons and then return to the Laurels. Make sure you don't leave any mess. I trust you both dealt with the other matter?'

'Yes Boss, all expedited like you said,' he answered with cynical servitude.

'I don't want anyone sticking their noses into our affairs. Make sure any traces connecting Mr Earl or myself have been eliminated.'

'They have Sir. I won't go into any detail, but I can assure you Mr Lewis, there are no witnesses or anyone else who'll be able to connect the young burglar to us.'

'Are you sure Bill?'

'One hundred percent positive. I don't leave anything to chance; that's why you employ me Sir.'

'I hope so. Once you've sorted out any unfinished business in Leeds, I want you and Pete to join me in Gibraltar. We've other business to look at in Lebanon.'

'Just give me a couple of days Sir. We'll see you back at Gibraltar by early next week.'

'Good man. Provided there's no fallout with this matter, there's a bonus waiting for both of you.'

Charles turned around and followed the heavily laden low-loader into the large warehouse. It was imperative the documents accompanying the crates of arms, now bound for Dubai, was recorded with the Export Dispatch Office on the Dockland Quayside. Unsurprisingly, the original destination had changed since his last meeting at the Laurels several days ago. But with the correct permits and paperwork, these arms could be shipped to any British Protectorate or foreign country who shared membership with the Government Armaments Trade Convention. As he disappeared towards the warm cosy offices belonging to the London Dockland Authorities, Bill and Joe drove their truck away through the Dockyard main gates.

Bill turned to Joe, 'Once we've returned this truck to Boddingtons, we'll drive straight back to Leeds. By the way, the Boss wants us to join him in Gibraltar next week, after we've cleared any mess.'

'But we've nothing to do Bill. We're too professional to leave any clues about.'

'I know. But Mr Lewis wants us to double check. You know what he's like; thinks we're complete fools. Anyway, if he wants us waste more time we'll go back to the Laurels and spend a couple of days putting our feet up and visit some clubs. Remember we've still got that three and half grand to spend we got from the train spotter.'

They both smiled. Joe sneered, 'Mr Lewis has no idea what we've been doing and thankfully, let's hope it remains that way. After all, the Yorkshire Post have reported the deaths of the taxi driver and Mr Cox; the Police are treating them as a hit and run and suicide.'

Bill returned his gaze to his friend and smiled, cynically stating, 'Life expectancy in Leeds appears to be shortening, Joe.'

'Indeed, it is, Bill.'

30

Phil walked back into the office as John finished his conversation with a Detective from a neighbouring Force. The latest total of identified similar burglaries had now increased to sixty-three. All had recorded thefts of silver and gold antiques showing the point of entry through a broken window pane, smeared with treacle and brown paper. John had asked the investigating officers to return to the scenes of these crimes and check as to whether they were serviced by a cellar grate. So far fifty-one had been confirmed.

John was about to inform Phil of these latest developments when the telephone rang again. Phil leant over, 'DS Smith Antique Squad.' He paused, listening to the caller, 'Yes Sir. We'll be there in thirty minutes. Yes, I'll bring all the papers. Bye.'

He turned to John, 'DCI Sampson wants us to meet him in ACC Jenkins' office straight away. Call me a cynical bastard but I think there's something not right here John.'

'You must be joking. We're going to see the ACC in the Ivory Tower?[14] What does it mean, Sergeant Cynical Bastard?' asked John.

'Just a sixth sense. Let's listen to what they have to say first before we tell them anything. I don't want us to go and show our hand first. If I keep quiet, so must you. We'll just listen. Do you promise to do the same John?'

'Yes, but I'm not going to lie Phil or mislead them. I've got my career to consider, don't forget.'

---

[14] Police Headquarters

'Listen, you've no bloody career if you upset this Bastard.'

John smiled, 'Don't worry about me. I'll be the soul of discretion. It's you that fires from the hip. And if you do, I'll step away and leave you to it. Who knows, when they've bounced you back into uniform I might take over as the skipper here.'

'Aye. And they'll call you Sergeant Golden Bollocks. Listen, I'm serious, let's see what they've got to say first. If you like, you can stay here and I'll go on my own.'

'No chance. I want to see how you deal with this. Perhaps you might get your wings clipped?'

Phil smiled back at him, 'We'll see about that. Come on don't let's keep those ESSO's[15] waiting.'

Thirty minutes later they ascended back steps to the first floor of Police Headquarters. John had not entered the building since his interview with the Chief Constable just prior to him being appointed. It was a typical Gothic architectural Victorian Municipal Building set in the shadow of the Town Hall, both now blackened by the decades of heavy industrial and traffic pollution. As they entered, Senior Officers of all ranks passed them in the main hallway and corridors. Most of whom Phil and John had never seen previously. Naturally, as rank and file Officers, all ignored them.

Phil whispered, 'I bet this place is like a Morgue at the weekends. What the hell do they all do here?'

'No idea. Where's the ACC's office?' asked John.

'Not sure. Along here I suspect.' He pointed towards the front of the building. They were the larger offices that commanded better views of the Headrow, the main road running through the centre of Leeds. As they continued silently along the corridor, passing several offices, they finally saw a large oak door with the sign 'ACC - Crime Mr James Jenkins.' Phil turned to John. 'Here goes. Remember, keep quiet.' He knocked confidently on the hard wood and waited for the invitation.

Instantly a loud voice shouted 'Come in.' They entered and saw ACC Jenkins sat behind his impressive large desk staring directly at them. He was in his late fifties, tall and portly built. All his hair was facial. With a balding head, he sported a distinguished handle-bar

---

[15] Officers who enjoyed every Saturdays and Sundays off duty

moustache and thick eyebrows. As a serving police officer at the outbreak of the War, he had been too old to be called up to serve for King and Country. But unlike most, he had a good War, accelerating through the ranks in the absence of any credible opposition. Within six years, he had been promoted from Inspector to Assistant Chief Constable; an impossible fete during peacetime service.

Sat opposite him was DCI Sampson. Although both men were approaching retirement they had never served together, unaware of their characteristic traits. Phil immediately sensed a frosty atmosphere with both men sat with their arms folded and stern-faced. DCI Sampson appeared a little subdued, failing to acknowledge Phil and John with his familiar smile.

'Come and sit down Gentlemen,' ACC Jenkins said curtly, pointing towards the two chairs resting against the wall next to his desk. He continued, 'DCI Sampson has kindly informed me about your investigation surrounding the burglaries connected to this Freddie Cox, who I understand made a dying declaration to you two a few days ago. Can you please tell me what you have discovered so far Sergeant Smith?'

'We're still collating similar burglaries that share the same MOs and similar stolen items. But before I go any further, may I ask sir, why you have asked us to come here today?'

John saw DCI Sampson momentarily close his eyes and slightly shake his head. His body language suggested to Phil not to say too much or argue with the ACC Jenkins. But Phil was oblivious to such signs; as far as he was concerned they were all police officers, irrespective of rank, working together to uphold the law and detect crime, even though some of them were earning far too much money for what they were worth.

The ACC's smile quickly evaporated, replaced with an icy glare. 'Yes, Sergeant Smith. I will tell you. I have examined the criminal records of this Freddie Cox and to be frank, the world is a considerably better place without him. When you spoke to him before he died, had he been given sedatives and drugs to help with the pain?'

'I believe so Sir.'

'I understand he also mentioned an accomplice called Ronnie Ellis who he had sent to break into a house called the Laurels and steal a number of silver items.'

'Yes, that's right Sir.'

'Is this the home address of a retired Colonel Julian Lewis, a highly decorated soldier of the last War?'

'Yes, I believe so Sir.'

'And has the Colonel or anyone else reported a burglary at this address?'

'No Sir, we believe he is out of the country at the moment.'

'I see. Do we know where this Ronnie Ellis is now?'

'No sir.'

'OK. This is what I want you to do. Go and visit this house and make sure Colonel Lewis isn't still there, bearing in mind it seems he spends a great deal of time in France. Look around to see if there are any signs of any entry. If necessary, discreetly speak to the neighbours to see if they saw anything unusual. Once you've done that, report directly to DCI Sampson before you take this investigation any further. Do you understand?'

'I'm not sure sir? What happens if we discover some evidence that may identify an offence has been committed?'

'Let me make this perfectly clear to you Sergeant Smith. The only thing that may appear to have happened is that this Freddie Cox has lead you two down the garden path after he's tried to kill himself. For all we know, his side-kick Ronnie Ellis may be sunning himself abroad, living off the proceeds of all these burglaries he's committed.'

'What?' exclaimed Phil.

'Be quiet Sergeant Smith. My understanding is that preliminary reports from the BTP's Senior Investigating Officer suggest Mr Cox attempted to commit suicide. This Ronnie Ellis appears to have simply disappeared. Perhaps they may have had a big argument between them and this Ellis man ran away with some of the spoils. You know how criminals behave amongst themselves.'

'I don't think so Sir.' Phil bit his lip. What did this man know about criminal behaviour?

'Well, I'm not interested in what you think Sergeant. Did you find anything connected to this break-in when you searched his house?'

'No Sir,' he lied.

He turned towards DCI Sampson. 'I want you to take over this investigation. As I said to you earlier, I don't want this matter becoming unmanageable. Wrap it up soon. Do you understand me Mr Sampson? Sergeant Smith seems to be struggling with my instructions.'

'Yes Sir,' replied DCI Sampson.

'Furthermore, I will advise the BTP to prepare a report to the Coroner that Mr Cox eventually died from his injuries sustained by his attempted suicide bid. The case will no doubt be opened and adjourned until our enquiries are completed. I don't expect them to be protracted Mr Sampson.'

DCI Sampson simply nodded his head without reply. Phil was about to speak when he intervened, 'Sergeant Smith and Constable Evans will do exactly what I instruct them to do. I can assure you of that Sir. I'll take full responsibility for their actions. We'll close the investigation as soon as we can. I'll keep you advised personally with any developments.'

He turned towards Phil and John and gestured with his head to leave immediately. Phil failed to disguise his frustration but with the guiding arm of John under his arm, they both briskly walked out. Two minutes later they were joined by DCI Sampson at the top of the stairway. Phil turned to him saying 'What the bloody hell ...'

'Not here Phil. I've just had my arse hung out on the Town Hall Steps[16] by that bastard. Don't worry my lads, we're not giving this up without a fight. I can smell an enormous stinking rat behind all this. I think it's political. Meet me in my office in thirty minutes.'

With half a smile he turned to John, 'Calm your Sergeant down. That's an order.'

'Thirty minutes' confirmed John.

---

[16] local colloquialism for public humiliation

31

As they arrived at DCI Sampson's office Phil had still failed to quell his anger, despite several attempts from John to calm him down. Phil was the first to step into the office but before he spoke, DCI Sampson said, 'John close the door.' Turning towards Phil he continued, 'Now you listen to me you hot-tempered bugger, if you're going to argue with me I'll kick you out now and you can get on with it yourself without my help. If necessary, I'll transfer you back into uniform. I'm not going to allow you to screw John's career up. For once in your life, shut up and listen. Just take a deep breath whilst I try to fill you in with what's been happening behind the scenes. Now will you be quiet and let me explain?'

Phil simply nodded.

'OK. After we last met, I felt obliged to go and see ACC Jenkins. Especially when you told me all about this Freddie Cox's dying declaration. Unlike you Phil, I must keep to protocol and so will you John if you want to progress further in the Police Service. When I arrived at his office this morning, he virtually dragged me over his desk along with those two other gentlemen apparently from Whitehall. I was given a very uncomfortable interrogation about this Colonel Lewis affair. This was before he had even heard about Mr Cox's demise. When I told him about that, ACC Jenkins simply exploded.'

'Why?' asked Phil.

'Apparently, when I originally made some enquiries with my contact in the Ministry of Defence into Colonel Lewis, it seems like I sent shock waves across the whole of the Department. I've no idea why. As far as I'm concerned, he is a respectable man now living in his retirement both here in Leeds and France. It's my belief that ACC Jenkins has been warned off by the Government Mandarins in Westminster and was ordered to drop the investigation. I have no proof of this but that's what I suspect Phil.'

John asked, 'What's your hunch about this Sir?'

'I think his son Charles is obviously central to all of this. But we need to talk to the Colonel first. Unless we can question him, we have nothing else that connects Ronnie Ellis to his house.'

'Well, that's not exactly true,' replied Phil.

'What are you holding back Phil? Tell me now.'

Phil related all the previous evenings events, leaving DCI Sampson shaking his head in disbelief. 'I told you specifically not to go the Laurels until I authorised this.' Turning to John, 'Did you know about this DC Evans?'

Phil snapped, 'Of course he didn't. He plays by the rules.'

'What do you suggest we do now Sir?' asked John.

'Hell, this is a bag of shit. The choice is clear. We either close the case down as directed by ACC Jenkins or we make some very discreet enquiries later. What we must not do now is to draw any attention to ourselves at this moment.'

'Forgetting Freddie's dying declaration is not negotiable as far as I'm concerned,' stated Phil. 'However, I agree with you; we must allow things to settle down and revisit this investigation in a week or two.'

'I agree,' said DCI Sampson. 'Something is seriously not right here.'

'You're not kidding boss,' replied Phil.

'And there's something else. I didn't tell them about those two characters staying at the Laurels. We need to find out more about them. Their presence in all this is incongruous to the good character of the Colonel. I've decided I'm going to speak to him when he returns from France. After all, ACC Jenkins told me to wrap it up, and so I shall.'

'Won't that compromise your position with him, Sir?' asked John.

'Listen, I'm now in my last year of my police service. What else can they do to me? I just need your assurances you won't interfere with anything for the next few weeks. Are you listening Phil?'

'Yes. But that Jenkins has really pissed me off.'

'I'm sure he has, but don't be so bloody selfish, there's John and myself to consider. Don't go and screw it all up on some Maverick scheme. I want you both to wait until I've had the opportunity of seeing the Colonel. Agreed?'

John replied, 'Yes Sir.'

Phil simply nodded his head, muttering 'Will do.'

32

Bill and Joe returned the lorry to Boddingtons in Birmingham and collected the Jaguar before travelling North on the newly constructed M1. By the time they reached Leeds it was gone midnight. The only place in town serving alcohol was a Jazz Club called the Peel, close to the City Square. They needed more than one drink. Bill decided to park the car overnight in the underground car park, next to the Railway Station, and take a taxi back to the Laurels later.

Approaching the Peel, they crossed the road exactly where they had drugged Freddie Cox several days previously. Bill smiled, 'Hurry up Joe, it's a bit dangerous crossing here. You don't know what might happen to you.'

They both laughed as they entered the club and descended into the basement where the loud music was being played. Once inside the smoked-filled room, they began to drink their beer enthusiastically, hardly catching their breath between the large gulps. Both had taken a keen preference to the local ale, Tetley's bitter. However, in their haste to quench their thirst, they failed to appreciate its strength and the effect it took on their demeanour. In the past, this excessive consumption had made them behave aggressively towards others, occasionally culminating in altercations with the locals.

Tonight, was going to be no different. In their determination to unwind and relax, within an hour they had both drunk eight pints. The frenetic music played by the resident jazz band only served to keep the atmosphere hot and feverish. At one o'clock the Compere called time and the small appreciative audience began to disperse towards the exit. Joe shouted to the barman, 'Two more pints here.'

'I'm sorry Sir, but we're now closing,' sensing potential trouble.

'Bollocks to that. Two more pints. Now!'

The Club owner, Mr Jim Atkinson, was a large muscular man in his fifties who regularly exercised and kept himself remarkable fit for his age. He had seen this type of behaviour hundreds of time before where alcohol had marred the good judgment of some customers. As a retired rugby league player, he was very experienced at dealing with conflict.

He stepped forward and said in a conciliatory tone, 'Gentlemen. We've really enjoyed your company tonight and look forward to you coming back to see us again but we are now closed, so I must ask you to leave.'

Joe thought otherwise and turned around to face him, curtly shouting, 'We want some more bloody beer now.'

'Gentlemen, please leave now.'

Bill moved forward to join his friend but never reached him. Jim Atkinson was ready. Anticipating his move, he brought his fist down on the side of Bill's temple causing him to collapse immediately to the floor. Joe stumbled backwards, looking both surprised and confused. Meanwhile, two other members of staff ran forwards and lifted the semi-conscious Bill back to his feet. He grabbed Joe by the throat and gripped hard shouting, 'Now take your friend out of here now before I put you down with him.'

Through his drunken stupor, Joe quickly steadied himself, realising their time at the Club was at an end. He had never seen his friend Bill dispatched with a single punch before. Now compliance, he nodded and gasped for air, 'Yes Boss. Sorry for any trouble Boss.'

Joe staggered towards the exit steps, whilst Bill was physically lifted to his feet and dragged upstairs by the two men. Once they reached the open doors, they were unceremoniously shoved onto the empty pavement. Miraculously, they remained standing as they drew deep heavy breaths of the cold winter's night air. The sudden shock brought them quickly back to reality. They stared at each other and pulled at their jackets in an effort to straighten them.

Bill rubbed his head again, grunting, 'I'll kill those bastards.'

'Not tonight my friend. Do you remember where the Jag is parked?'

'Yeh, but we'll get a taxi back to the Laurels and pick it up in the morning.'

Joe replied, 'Good idea. We're too pissed to find it anyway. Let's go and find a cab.'

The streets were deserted as they stumbled towards the City Square. The cold rain only added to their misery as they moved from one empty shop doorway to another. But within a few minutes later they arrived in the empty square and saw a line of three taxis parked outside the main Central Post Office Building. All the drivers were talking to each other, sheltering within the large porch, only yards from their vehicles. Joe approached and asked, 'Can one of you take us to Grove Lane, Roundhay?'

'Yes, I'll take you. Jump in,' replied one of the drivers. He stepped out onto the pavement and approached the lead vehicle where he opened one of the back doors. Bill and Joe sat inside as the driver started the engine and pulled away. As they were leaving the Square, Joe asked him, 'Can you tell me where the underground carpark near to the Railway Station is, mate?'

He replied, 'Just over there,' pointing towards the left side of the main entrance to the Queens Hotel opposite. 'Would you like me to show you where it is?'

Bill mumbled 'No, don't bother. We're new to Leeds and forgot where I parked my car earlier. I'll pick it up tomorrow when I'm sober.'

'Very wise Sir. It won't take long to get you to Roundhay. Where about on Grove Lane do you want me to drop you off? If I remember, they're all large houses along there. Which one is it?'

'The Laurels. Do you know it?'

'No, I don't know that one. Never mind, just show me when we drive along Grove Lane.'

They continued on their journey in silence. Bill was still rubbing the side of his head, quietly moaning of his revenge on whoever had inflicted his injury. Eventually the taxi pulled into Grove Lane. The driver asked, 'Whereabouts now Sir?'

'Down here, another hundred yards. Yes, this will do.'

The taxi gently slowed down and came to a halt. The driver said, 'That's thirty shillings Sir.'

Pete gave him £2. 'Keep the change mate.'

Joe leaned over and assisted the injured Bill from the rear seat. Once outside, they walked unsteadily through the stone gate posts towards the house and disappeared into the darkness. The taxi driver smiled as he gently accelerated away. Joe and Bill had been completely unaware of the driver's face, nor his name fixed upon the licence openly displayed on the dashboard. Of all the taxi drivers in Leeds, they had chosen Peter Hayes, the best friend of one of their dead victims.

He returned to City Square and drove directly to the underground car park and saw only three cars parked inside. He was only interested in one. And there it was tucked away behind two concrete pillars in the corner. A black Jaguar registered number JUM 106; the same one he had seen when he had taken Brenda to see the old Colonel.

He had to contact DS Smith immediately, but how could he do that now? It was two a.m. and he would probably be off duty. Then he had an idea.

33

Phil was fast asleep when the telephone rang downstairs in the hallway. His wife, Jane, nudged him in the ribs, 'The phone's ringing. It'll be for you.' Grudgingly, he slid out from beneath the warm cosy blankets, placed his feet on the cold wooden floor and stumbled along the landing, grabbing the handrail as he descended the stairs still half asleep. Eventually he picked up the receiver. A voice asked, 'Is that DS Smith?'

'Yes, who the hell is this?'

'It's PC Brown on the front desk Sergeant. I've got a Mr Hayes here and he says he must speak to you as soon as possible. It's a matter of life or death.'

'What time is it?'

'Just gone four a.m.'

'Put him on.'

Another voice spoke, 'Mr Smith. This is Pete Hayes. We spoke in the Market Tavern the other night.'

'Yes I remember. It better be important Mr Hayes or you're in deep shit!'

'Oh, it is Mr Smith.'

Phil listened to his story as Pete whispered the recent events; collecting the two men from the City Centre and taking them to the Laurels. The description exactly matched those given by Brenda.

'Good man. Let's meet up tomorrow and discuss this further.'

'Mr Smith, I know where their Jaguar is. It's in an underground car park next to the Railway Station and the Queens Hotel.'

'Bloody hell Pete. Are you sure?'

'Oh yes. I've seen it; JUM 106 Mr Smith.'

'Listen Pete, say nothing to the police there and go straight back to the underground car park and wait for me. I know where it is. I'll be there as soon as I can.'

'OK. See you there.'

'Pete. You've done a good job there. Don't take any chances, just wait for me.'

'Will do.'

Thirty minutes later, Phil drove his Ford Anglia into the car park where he saw Pete standing between his taxi and the black Jaguar. After checking the registration number once again, he said 'Pete, I want you to do something for me which isn't exactly legal. You know we're dealing with some really bad bastards who won't stop at anything to avoid prosecution. Are you with me?'

Smiling, he stepped forward 'If it's going to get those buggers behind bars for killing Freddie, Ronnie and Jim; you bet I'm with you Mr Smith.'

'Good. Wait here.' Phil opened the boot to his car and removed a small canvas bag from inside. He took out a pointed implement and a length of stiff wire cable. He said, 'Look the other way Pete, I don't want you to witness this. What you can't see; you can't lie about in a Court of Law.'

Turning his back, Pete spoke softly, 'I do like your style Mr Smith.'

Within twenty seconds, Phil managed to open the driver's door. Stretching out across the front bench seat, he peered underneath the dashboard and began pulling hard at the hidden wiring loom. Quickly he fumbled and connected the necessary wires together. Suddenly the engine instantly burst into life. He lifted his head and shouted to Pete, 'Follow me.'

Five minutes later, Phil drove the Jaguar into a disused railway siding car park roughly the size of a football field. Skirting three sides of the disused site stood rows of brick-built one-storey garages and assorted abandoned lock-ups. The area was originally connected to the main railway terminus close to the City Square half a mile away. Once a hub of industrial activity, it was the secondary railway station, servicing the heavy engineering and wool manufacturers from which much of the City wealth had been built on.

But since the end of the War there had been sudden decline in both these industries. The remnants of the dark satanic mills and foundries bore witness to past times of economic prosperity. Nearly all of the units were empty and disused, with just a few remaining occupied. The whole area was awaiting demolition for the long-awaited modernisation programme where the site would be used as an extension to the main station. But these plans had also floundered. Following the recent Beecham closure programme, funding had been postponed indefinitely. All future investment in the site was now in doubt.

One such unit belonged to a criminal called 'Frankie Knuckles' who was presently serving a lengthy prison sentence for attempted murder. He had used the premises to torture his victim. And Phil had been the investigating officer responsible for all the exhibits produced at Court and after Frankie had been sentenced. Somehow, he forgot to return the keys to Frankie. Phil now had a better use for it.

He turned the steering wheel towards the row of buildings on the far side of the yard and as the Jaguar slowed down, the headlights shone on a pair of green painted wooden doors held together with a chain, draped through two metal handles. The units on both sides were empty and abandoned, all boarded-up and secured with wooden slats. He stepped out from the car and unlocked the padlock holding the chain, opened the doors and drove the Jaguar inside. Carefully, he maneuvered and parked it in the corner before turning the lights off cutting the engine.

For a few seconds, the whole place descended into complete darkness before he stepped away and switched on his torch. Next to the car ran a long wooden bench which housed several gas lamps. He leant forwards and switched them on. But their age and condition had seen better days. The flames struggled to ignite and once illuminated, emitted the dimmest of light; yet sufficient enough for Phil to throw an old oily canvas sheet over the car. He concealed it further by dragging several large crates and cardboard boxes from the other side of the unit and stacking them neatly in front. Now completely covered from view, he turned off the gas lamps and moved outside where he closed the rickety wooden doors together before replacing the lock with a brand-new padlock.

He walked to taxi and sat inside. 'Pete. I want you to take me back to my car. You saw nothing of this. I haven't stolen the Jag. I just want to keep it safe for the time being. When the time is right, I shall have it checked over for fibres or traces of blood by the forensic scientists. No doubt those bastards will report it stolen later today but I can live with that. All you need to do is keep quiet and keep your eyes wide open. No one must know about this. Believe me, I've got my reasons. Do you understand me Pete? It's important you do.'

'Yes, Mr Smith.'

After Phil had collected his car he waved to Pete as he drove away before returning home to his warm bed.

When the alarm clock eventually sounded at Jane's side of the bed, Phil was fast asleep and snoring loudly. Nudging him again in his ribs, she whispered 'It's seven o'clock. Time to get up Phil.'

He shook his head in disbelief. He could have stayed in bed all day. But he knew for the first time since Freddie's last confession there had been a breakthrough. Like so many investigations, 'lady luck' had smiled. He rolled out of bed and showered. Although feeling tired through his nocturnal activities, he muttered under the cascading water, 'I'll have you bastards yet.' He smiled again, 'The old ways were sometimes necessary – after all, it takes a thief to catch a thief.' The location of the Jaguar would remain a secret, known only between himself and a crooked taxi driver.

This was where he felt alive the most. Living on the edge.

34

It was the bright winter's sunlight streaming through the bedroom window on Joe's face that caused him to squint and wake from his drunken slumbers. Rubbing his throbbing head, he vaguely remembered the previous evening's altercation at the Peel Jazz Club. He had lost all recollection of how he and Bill had managed to return home. He rolled over and glanced at the table clock next to his bed. Ten-thirty. He was laid on top of the bed still dressed, wearing his brown suede shoes and feeling very nauseous.

Finally, lifting his aching body from the mattress, he stumbled into the bathroom where he found Bill laid in a hot bath, drinking a cup of black coffee, nursing his bruised forehead.

'You look rough Bill,' stated Joe.

'Have you looked in the mirror yourself this morning?' he answered.

'Can you remember what happened last night?'

'Yes. You became an arsehole like you always do when you've had too much to drink. I only came over to settle you down, when the big geezer thumped me. Bloody typical, I'm trying to calm it all down and get smacked for my troubles.'

Anxious to change the subject, Joe suggested, 'We'd better go into town and get the Jag. It's somewhere in an underground car park near the Railway Station. Can you remember where it is?'

'Yes of course I do, it's next to the Queen's Hotel.'

'How did we get home last night?'

'We got a taxi. Had you forgotten?'

'Yes. I don't remember anything.'

After a light breakfast, Bill telephoned a local private hire and requested a taxi. Within five minutes they were travelling into Leeds, bound for the City Centre. He managed to hide his swollen temple by combing his bright curly ginger hair to one side and wearing a black woollen hat stretched over his ears. Unlike Joe, he knew exactly where the Jaguar had been parked.

After leaving the taxi they walked directly to the underground carpark. They descended the stairwell into the lower level car park and began to search for their car. It was missing. They strode along the length and breadth of all the bays twice before Joe spoke, 'Bloody hell Bill. It's been nicked.'

'Where the hell is it?' demanded Bill. 'Charlie boy is going to go crazy when he finds this out.'

They both looked at each other in silence.

Eventually Joe spoke softly, 'Perhaps we won't tell him.'

'What do you mean, don't tell him you bloody fool?'

'Well, listen to this. Whenever we lock the house up here in Leeds, we always park the Jag in the back garage. Right?'

'Yes. Go on.'

'Well, Mr Lewis will expect us to park it in the garage before we join him in Gibraltar. Right Bill?'

'Yes of course he will.'

'We'll tell him we've done exactly that. Unfortunately, someone will have broken in and stolen it whilst we are in Gibraltar. Now do you get my meaning Bill?'

Bill smiled and nodded. 'I certainly do Joe. You devious bastard.'

'We need to return to the Laurels and prepare the scene for a burglary of our own before we fly out tomorrow morning. Remember, we must have both keys, just in case Charlie boy accuses us of leaving them lying around.'

'Got them here in my pocket. Come on then, let's go for a drink. There's still plenty in the kitty,' replied Bill.

35

DCI Mark Sampson had served all his service in the Leeds City Police, other than the five years spent in the RAF during the War. He was a career Detective now approaching retirement and sought only a quiet mundane professional life. With less than twelve months to serve, he and his wife Helen had planned to retire and live in Dartmouth on the Devonshire coast. They had spent many happy years on holiday there and had already booked a week the following Summer in the Royal Castle Hotel, intending to search the town for a retirement cottage. Helen, a school teacher at the local Infants School, would also retire at the same time.

He had known Phil Smith for many years and had grown fond of his unconventional methods of solving cases. Without wishing to know exactly how he achieved his high detection rates, accompanied by high quality of intelligence he manged to glean, Phil was held in high regard by all his colleagues. In short, he was an enigma. Paradoxically, he was also highly respected throughout the local criminal fraternity, where he had a perverse reputation of 'the only cop in town you could trust.' No one messed with Detective Sergeant Smith.

Since his first meeting with Phil and the impressive young prodigy DC John Evans, he knew the suspicious deaths of Freddie the Fence, Jim the taxi driver and the disappearance of Ronnie Ellis, were more than just coincidental. His sixth sense screamed 'foul-play.' This was further confirmed after the initial enquiry regarding Colonel Lewis he had made with his old pal, who had once worked with in Special Branch before being recruited into the Ministry of Defence.

Somehow this simple and benign enquiry had caused utter consternation. And without any warning he had been summoned to see ACC Jenkins where for two hours he had been subjected to intensive questioning by him and the two strangers dressed in pin-striped suits. Clearly, they were all concealing the true motive for their reticence. Why should these enquiries in Leeds, involving three local criminals, have such serious implications connected with Whitehall?

Each time he had asked them what all the fuss was about, ACC Jenkins simply said, 'Answer the damn questions Chief Inspector.' Such short measures from his Boss only served to infuriate him more. After all, he was a hard-seasoned Detective possessing a sixth sense of recognising bullshit. And now he could smell it in buckets at close quarters.

His resolve stiffened. Seizing the opportunity, he asked the men in suits, 'I'm not suggesting for one minute Colonel Lewis is a suspect in this investigation. I'm only trying to build up a profile of the man. After all, he may well have been the intended victim of a burglary.'

Smiling through an expressionless face, one of the suits replied, 'Chief Inspector Sampson, apparently, there has not been any recorded burglary at this address. So I do not want you to approach Colonel Lewis and talk to him about this matter.'

'The hell I can. I'm a serving Police Officer and the Judges Rules[17] clearly state I can interview anyone in the land, other than her Majesty the Queen herself, if I believe they may have any material information about any suspected criminal investigation.'

'Careful Chief Inspector,' interrupted ACC Jenkins.

'I'm sorry Sir, but they're asking me do something unlawful. You must defend me on this, surely?'

Before he had the chance to reply, the other man in the suit stood and walked towards the window. ACC Jenkins looked attentively at him, clearly subservient to his status. He turned around and softly spoke, 'Chief Inspector Sampson. Of course, you're right. We would never suggest you do anything likely to compromise your legal position. I'm sure you realise there are certain aspects of your inquiry that have enormous hidden implications on a political scale. As you

---

[17] set of guidelines for police to question witnesses and suspects of crime

know, we have a newly elected Government. The Prime Minister Harold Wilson has vowed that a number of old outdated principles inside certain Departments would be swept away and a new dawn of transparency was to prevail. I'm unable to tell you exactly what that really means; only to say that the new Government cannot afford to have a scandal like his predecessor Macmillan had. It would cause tremendous political and economic hardships; perhaps even a run on the pound. So, let's get things into perspective here Chief Inspector, your investigation could jeopardise the financial stability of the Country. However, I can assure you, Colonel Lewis enjoys the full confidence of the Government and is considered a valuable servant to the Nation. If you need to speak to him, so be it. I also appreciate you have a duty to investigate the serious reports of these suspicious deaths; but I would ask you to seriously consider there are other important matters at stake regarding our National Security. Your criminals appear to have stepped into a far more sinister and dangerous world. I'm sorry Mr Sampson, but that's all I'm prepared to say.'

DCI Sampson sat back and reflected on his comments. He had never before in all his service heard so much patronising drivel. His nostrils were now blocked up with all this bullshit. They were deliberately keeping him in the dark, not wishing to share any possible vital information that could be used in his investigation. So far as he was concerned, three men had been murdered by unknown forces, perhaps even with Whitehall's sanction. This was akin to George Orwell, not the democracy he stood for. Having listened, he kept his counsel and remained quiet. Inwardly, he was now even more determined to find out who was responsible.

From that moment, he simply nodded his head and complied. 'I understand Sir.' He decided not to disclose any further details. They would be unaware of the evidence Phil and John had discovered and especially the details of the two men mentioned in Freddie's dying declaration.

For a few moments, there was an awkward silence before the two Westminster men nodded to each other. One of them said 'Thank you, Assistant Chief Constable for your time. I'll leave this matter in your capable hands. We must return to London now.' Hastily, they collected their briefcases and overcoats from the adjoining table and left quietly, leaving DCI Sampson to face the wrath of Mr Jenkins.

Once they had disappeared some distance away along the corridor, ACC Jenkins turned his seat towards DCI Jenkins. 'Listen to me. When Smith and Evans arrive here in twenty minutes, you will do exactly what I say. Otherwise, I promise I'll find you a broom cupboard somewhere where you will serve the remainder of your career. Do you understand me Chief Inspector?'

DCI Sampson thought carefully of just what had been said in past fifteen minutes. His mind returned to his early police days, being cross-examined at the Assizes[18] by the Defence Council. He was attempting to explain why he had followed an unlawful order, given by one of his senior officers. The Judge poignantly reminded him, 'As a Constable, your allegiance is not to your Superiors, but to the law of the land.'

He knew that to be true. And for that reason, since that day, he purposely displayed a photograph of his wife and children on his desk, so as to remind him when he was forced to make difficult decisions, the law of the land and his unconditional love for his family were his only true allegiances.

But for the time being he would acquiesce and pretend to cooperate with his demands. That way, he might discover what they were all hiding.

'Yes Sir, I'll do as you ask. And so will those two as well,' he lied.

---

[18] Forerunner to the introduction of the Crown Courts

36

Following their disastrous meeting with ACC Jenkins, Phil, John and DCI Sampson agreed to delay their investigations for a couple of weeks. Now sat alone in his office, DCI Sampson pondered how he could attempt to contact the Colonel. Without having a face-to-face talk with him the investigation was going nowhere. The dichotomy between the Colonel's excellent reputation and the violence inflicted on the two men presently lying in the City Morgue was beyond his comprehension.

After browsing through the notes taken from his meetings with Phil and John, several hours later he formulated a plan. When Phil had been approached by the prostitute Brenda, she had mentioned her father being killed in France during the War. As she was never going to return to the Laurels, he would use this story for himself but invent another fictitious solder in the Medical Corps killed at the same time, perhaps a relative of his. He would write to the Colonel and seek his advice for any further information. Since John held the house keys to Freddie Cox's house, he would use that as his address.

Later, he composed the letter.

Dear Colonel Lewis

Please forgive this intrusion, but I was given your name and address by a friend of mine who is an active member of the British Legion and he suggested you may be able to help me.

In August 1944 my uncle, George Sampson, was killed in action near to

Caen, Normandy. He was a leading orderly with the Medical Corps attending to both Allied and German injured soldiers in a field hospital when they came under an artillery attack. It is my understanding you were the Commanding Officer for the British Medical Services during this time. Although he was buried in a nearby Military Cemetery, my mother wanted to know what was known about her younger brother in those days before she lost him.

I appreciate this is a highly improbable request but I wondered if you could perhaps see yourself assisting us in our endeavour. If you are unable to furnish any further information, would you be able to recommend any other person? I await your reply with anticipation.

Yours sincerely

Mark Sampson

With some decorum, he decided to sign the letter with his own name and wait for his reply in the forthcoming weeks. Until then, he would keep a low profile and hope for developments in the near future. And to his amazement he did not have to wait long.

37

The following week, John arrived early for work. Since their last meeting with DCI Sampson, Phil had become quiet and withdrawn, appearing pre-occupied with other unconnected thefts of antiques discovered inside the homes of active burglars within the Leeds area. Although he had occasionally asked for Phil's opinion of their last meeting with ACC Jenkins, he remained aloof, shrugging his shoulders muttering 'Those idiots we call Chief Constables seem have lost all connection with hard working coppers like us. They're all sycophantic bastards with no balls.' John sensed he was still fuming below the surface, preferring to keep his own counsel.

Alone in the office, he began to look through a series of documents when the telephone rang. He answered 'Evans, Antique Squad.'

A familiar voice replied, 'John, it's DCI Sampson. Is Phil there?'

'No Sir.'

'Good. It's you I want to speak to anyway.'

'I'm sorry, I don't understand.'

'Listen John, I don't want to really go behind Phil's back with this, but I know how he reacts. You have a level head and so what I'm about to tell you, it's between us. Do you understand?'

'I think so Sir.'

'Let me put it another way. John, you will not discuss this with anyone else without my permission. That's an order. Does that make it clearer John?'

Feeling a little uncomfortable, he replied, 'Yes Sir. Crystal clear.'

'OK. After our meeting with ACC Jenkins, like you and Phil, I was annoyed. I mean really annoyed. I was pretty much hauled over the coals by him and two men you missed. I had no idea who or where they were from, other than from inside some nameless Department in Whitehall. At first, they warned me off from any contact with Colonel Lewis, even accusing me of withholding information from them. I must confess that's not entirely untrue but they did really piss me off. ACC Jenkins had told them about Freddie's dying declaration but they dismissed it without any comment. The bottom line is this; I was ordered to make sure this investigation disappeared. Well John, bollocks to all of them. I didn't join this service to serve those who follow perverse political instructions. I serve the law of the land. So, this is what I've done.'

He told John about the plan he had formulated to speak to the Colonel, hoping his deceptive letter about his fictional Uncle would allow him the opportunity of perhaps establishing who else had access to the Laurels other than the Colonel himself. John sat dumbfounded. This cunning old Detective was nearly as unconventional as Phil. He continued, 'I gave the Colonel Freddie's address as my own.'

'Really Sir?' asked John

'Yes. Now, I want you to go with the keys to Freddie's house and check the mail. If it's there, bring it straight to my office. If it's not, I want you to keep trying a couple of times a week until it's delivered. It's important I try to make some contact with him.'

'Can't I just come and see you this morning and give you the key? Then you can visit anytime you want Sir.'

'Not really John. I don't want the key leaving your office, otherwise Phil will get suspicious and spoil everything. Anyway, I've got too many important things to do and I want you to go on my behalf. Now will you please go this morning for me?'

'Will do Sir. I'll go now. But why can't you tell Phil about all this?'

'I admire your loyalty. However, I want to do this my way and prevent him going off in one of his wild idea ventures. You know, as much as I admire Phil, he can be his own worst enemy.'

'Ok Sir. But I'm not very happy about this.'

'I know you're not. And I'll tell him when the time is right.'

'Alright,' John replied reluctantly.

'Thanks John. Remember, not a word to Phil.'

Without any reply, John placed the telephone down, feeling uneasy. What should he do? DCI Sampson was right in one respect: Phil was a 'hot head' and often failed to see the bigger picture. But their working relationship had always been based on trust and openness. Contemplating DCI Sampson's request, he felt like a Judas, betraying his good friend and going behind his back. Reluctantly, he decided to visit Freddie's house where hopefully there would be a letter and this dilemma would quietly disappear.

John collected the house key from inside the office safe and was about to leave when the door opened and Phil entered. He asked, 'Going out?'

Feeling awkward, he replied, 'Yes, just a little job in the Northern Division. What are you doing today Phil?'

'Got some information about some silver candlesticks being hocked at the Cash for Goods Shop[19] in town. They might be subject of a burglary in Halifax. Do you want come with me?'

'No thanks but I'll meet you here later for lunch perhaps.'

'OK.'

John slid the keys inside his pocked and left. That was the first time he had lied to Phil and promised himself it was the last. He drove directly to Freddie's house and unlocked the front door. He stooped down and picked up the pile of correspondence and immediately saw a plain hand-written envelope addressed to Mr Mark Sampson, posted locally in Leeds two days previously. He dropped the remainder of the mail onto the floor, locked the house and made his way to DCI Sampson's office.

Thirty minutes later he knocked and entered, 'I have the letter Sir.'

'Good. Let's have a look at it.' He quickly opened the envelope and started reading the letter, before handing back to John. It was short in detail, simply apologising for not being able to personally recollect his uncle, George Sampson, but would make some enquiries at the War Graves Commission next time he visited Normandy. However, in the final paragraph he wrote 'please contact me on this telephone number 675273 or call at the Laurels, Grove Lane, Roundhay if you require and further assistance.'

---

[19] presented for sale at the pawnbrokers

'Great,' exclaimed DCI Sampson. 'I'll contact him later today and try to arrange a meeting at his place. Perhaps we might be able to make some progress on this investigation after all John.'

'To be honest Sir, I'm not happy about leaving Phil out of all this. If he finds out what I've done this morning, he'll never trust me again and to be honest, I wouldn't blame him.'

'After I've spoke to the Colonel, I'll tell him then John, I promise.'

38

Yet Phil had not been idle. His motive for keeping John unaware of his investigations was simple. He was deploying old styles of policing practices now universally shunned, even by his rank and file colleagues. The less John knew, the more he was protected. It had been over a week since he had secreted the Jaguar inside Frankie Knuckle's empty lock-up and each day since then he had checked with Force Control to see if it had been reported stolen. Nothing. This was an expensive luxury car, so failing to report its theft merely confirmed to him the seriousness of the investigation; it was not just a botched burglary.

Although he admired his older colleague DCI Sampson, he believed the attraction of his impending pension had marred his reputation of 'getting results.' Conversely, Phil's belly was full of determination. Determined to vigorously pursue this inquiry no matter where it took him or who it offended. He would continue in his own way until he eventually uncovered sufficient evidence that no one could ignore; not even Whitehall. Working alone brought no constraints.

Shortly after midnight, the eve before John visited Freddie Cox's house on behalf of DCI Sampson, Phil entered the grounds to the Laurels. He had several contingency plans, all depending on what he discovered. As he quietly approached the front of the house he stopped and listened for several minutes. It was a cool still dark night with no moon. Eventually his eyes became accustomed and, together with his previous visit, gave him a good idea of the general layout of both the house, back yard and surrounding gardens.

Once he was satisfied all was clear, he made his way into the rear court yard where the large garage stood. The solid wooden doors were slightly ajar. He shone his small torch onto the lock and found it to be broken. The metal was still shiny, suggesting recent damage. He stepped inside the garage and found it empty apart from a long bench set on the back wall. Resting on top were several empty buckets and an assortment of cleaning sponges. He switched off his torch and pondered in the darkness. Why should the garage appeared to have been broken into, where the Jaguar was usually parked? Strange?

He slipped back out through the doors and began walking along the rear of the house, checking the windows and doors as he progressed until he reached the opposite side. After examining all sides to the house, he found no further signs of interference or damage. Once again, he stopped and considered the insecure garage. He was confused.

Then it suddenly dawned on him. The Jaguar belonged to Charles Lewis, the Colonel's son. If these two men were working for him and had been using it without his full knowledge, this could prove embarrassing to explain to Charles Lewis why it had been stolen; especially from a car park in the centre of Leeds. Therefore, if they planned a burglary here, no one would be the wiser. He whispered to himself, 'Nice one Ginger.'

But Phil also had a devious mind. 'Two can play that game.' If they had arranged a bogus burglary to the garage, he would set another one for the house.

Returning to the back garden, he approached the French Doors. Standing exactly where Ronnie intended to deceive his entry, Phil took a deep intake of breath, picked up a nearby brick-end and broke one of the window panes. Wearing his gloves, he reached inside and yanked the wrought-iron handle violently until the door sprang open, causing the remaining shards of glass to fall on the thick carpet beneath and allowing the night air to enter the room, fluttering the curtains in all directions. Turning around, he threw the brick into the bushes and walked briskly back to the road, checking to see if any traffic or anyone was exercising their dog along Grove Lane. Nothing. It was all clear.

He returned to his car and drove towards home. A little over a mile away, he stopped at a public telephone box and rang 999. Once connected to the Police Control Room, he placed his handkerchief over the receiver and said, 'I've just walked my dog along Grove Lane here in Roundhay and I've just heard the sound of breaking glass coming from the old house. I think it's called the Laurels. It has two large stone gate posts outside.'

The operator replied, 'Thank you Sir. Can you give me your name and address?'

'Come now, I think they're still in there.'

Phil immediately hung up. He would now retire to bed and hope his uniform colleagues would attend and discover the burglary. They would ensure the house and garage were secured and a crime for suspected burglary would be submitted. With some negotiation and story-telling, the investigation would be allocated to him. This would allow him the opportunity of speaking directly with the Colonel and inspect the house thoroughly. Filled with a sense of self-adulation and smugness he retired to bed, smiled and rested his head on his bed pillow thinking, 'The old ways still hold; now I'll get some results.'

39

Late the following morning, Phil walked into his office. John was absent, having left a message on his desk, 'Interviewing a suspect for burglary in the West Division and returning after lunchtime.' *Perfect,* Phil thought, as he placed a call to the North Divisional CID, asking for Detective Inspector James. A few moments later he said, 'Good morning Boss. This is DS Phil Smith. How are you?'

'I'm fine Phil. What can I do for you?'

'I've heard you might have a burglary recorded from last night in Grove Lane?'

'Yes, it came in early this morning. Someone called it in, but we've been unable to trace them. It's a pity. We might have a good witness, but they hung up. Probably some lily-livered Liberal living in the same street. Why the interest?'

'I've got some information that may link it to some other ones I'm dealing with. Would you mind if you pass the investigation over to me?'

'Only if you record it as 'detected' in our area.'

'Of course, Boss. No problem.'

DI James continued, 'The uniform lads found both the house and garage broken into. They made some enquiries with the neighbours, but they didn't see or hear anything. Apparently, it's a retired Colonel who lives there but spends most of the winter in France. We've left a message inside the house for him to ring Force Control with the crime number when he returns. I'll let them know you're now dealing with it. Do you want me to send the papers through the internal mail?'

'Don't bother, I'll come and collect them this morning. I've got another job in town, I'll drive up and pick them up myself.'

'It's all yours Phil. I expect I'll read about what's happened with this later Phil. You're a man of many secrets. Good luck.'

Phil smiled as he replaced the receiver. He had never been accused of as being a Liberal. So far so good.

40

After taking the letter to DCI Sampson, John returned to the office to find Phil reading various reports. As he looked up, the telephone rang. 'Antique Squad, DS Smith.'

To John's utter amazement he heard Phil reply, 'Yes Colonel Lewis, I'm the investigating officer looking into the break-in at your house. I've been waiting for you to contact me so I can speak to you about it in more detail. May I come over this afternoon to see you Sir? Thank you, I'll be there within the hour.'

He replaced the telephone and looked directly towards John. 'Come on, we're going to talk to the Colonel at the Laurels. Apparently, his house and garage were screwed[20] last night. Now we have the opportunity of getting in there and finding out who else is operating out of there.'

John sat opened-mouthed, unable to speak. How the hell had he managed this? He felt completely out of his depth. DCI Sampson had fabricated a ploy to speak to the Colonel through a fictional dead uncle and now he was looking at Phil who clearly had orchestrated another ploy. But how had he managed to beat the DCI? Now he was on his way to speak to him. Nervously, John asked, 'How did you arrange this Phil?'

'Do you want to know John? I mean really want to know?'

'Hell, yes I do. I'm working with you and DCI Sampson on this case and frankly you've both lost me in your Wild West tactics. Just tell me what you've done before we leave this office.'

---

[20] break-in; subject to burglary

'Do I have your word you won't tell anyone?'

'Phil, you're a bloody good cop and your ways are not necessarily mine, but if you promise me you haven't behaved dishonestly, then of course I won't tell anyone. Now tell me what's happened.'

'Before I answer that question, let me confirm something with you. Under the Larceny Act, if you steal any property, must there be an element of permanently depriving the owner of it. True?'

'Yes, that's right. Why?'

'Well I moved the Jaguar a couple of weeks ago from the City Centre to a safe place, whilst our friends 'Ginger' and 'Limpy' were too drunk to drive. They never reported it stolen. Last night, I staged an amateur burglary at the Laurels and it has been allocated to me for investigation. That's it John. Still on board?'

'Just a minute. Before we go anywhere, I'm going to ring DCI Sampson.'

'Bugger off. He's too squeaky clean these days. Can't blame him; his retirement and fat pension is just around the corner.'

'I wouldn't be so sure about that Phil. I think you may have underestimated him. I'm in the middle of you two and frankly, you're both the bloody same; obstinate and definitely old school. Before I ring him, I've got something to tell you.' With some hesitation, he relayed the account of DCI Sampson's deception, paying particular attention of being ordered to keep quiet and not discussing it under any circumstances with Phil.

After finishing, he looked at Phil, 'If you want me to transfer back to Division I will do. I can't serve two masters. You and DCI Sampson better get this sorted out between you, because it makes life impossible for me.'

'John you're staying right here because I trust you and I think you might make a good Detective one day. But I'm disappointed about one thing.'

'What's that?'

'If a colleague ever tells you not discuss anything, you keep that secret to your dying breath; what the hell are you telling me about it now? Can't you keep a secret these days young man?'

'I thought you'd go mad because I went behind your back?'

'Hell, no John. Frankly, I must congratulate the Chief Inspector for such imagination. I'm impressed.'

'So, what are you going to do? Will you speak to DCI Sampson so we can pool our resources? You know he has a great respect for you but he's afraid you'll upset the apple cart with your manner.'

'Bugger off. There's nothing wrong with my manner, you cheeky sod.'

He smiled and John smiled back. 'Let me ring him now Phil and let's get this sorted out now. After all, we've got enough enemies out there, both in and out of the job.'

'Go on then but I'm going downstairs to the canteen. It's a bit odd John, you might only be the Constable, but you're now the negotiator between your Boss and mine. Get it sorted. I'll trust your judgement. Come downstairs when you've finished and we'll go and see the Colonel.'

After Phil had left the room, John sighed, took a deep breath and picked up the telephone. His conversation with DCI Sampson was surprisingly shorter and more pleasant than he had expected. He simply stated, 'When you are sworn to secrecy, you take it to the grave, but under the circumstances, I see you had little choice.'

'That's exactly what Phil said.'

DCI Sampson laughed. 'Go and see the Colonel and both come over here afterwards.'

Thirty minutes later they arrived at the Laurels. This was Phil's third visit; but on this occasion, he was on lawful police business. It appeared different during the daytime. The grounds seemed larger and the house more imposing, with the large central porch supported by two circular columns. They climbed the shallow stone steps and rang the doorbell.

41

Seventeen hundred miles South of the Laurels, laid Charles Lewis's office and apartment in Gibraltar. Separated only by three hundred yards, both overlooked the wide bay and quayside between the airstrip and the mainland of Spain. Although within less than two miles from mainland Europe, General Franco repeatedly placed strict movements between the two frontiers, thus restricting access by road or rail to the rest of the Continent. Occasionally he relented and for a short period movement between the two territories relaxed. Unfortunately, every Christmas, relations between London and Madrid dramatically cooled. The season of good will evaporated. The frontier was effectively closed, with access to the 'Rock' only by air or sea.

Charles had returned five days before Bill and Joe to the warmth of the Mediterranean climate, a welcomed change from the cold damp weather in England. Recently he became heavily involved in secret talks with Agents acting on behalf of factions to the Rhodesian Government. Her Majesty's Government in London had agreed in principle to full independence, provided free and fair elections were held representing a multi-racial balance. However, the ruling white party was strongly opposed to these conditions and vehemently blocked any such power-sharing.

In recent months, a rumour began to circulate within Rhodesia and its neighbour South Africa, of the intention of the Prime Minister Ian Smith to declare a state of 'Unilateral Declaration of Independence'(UDI). Such action would cause severe political, social and economic consequences. The major fear of the incumbent Rhodesian Government was their security and readiness to protect the white population from both external and internal conflict. To accommodate their ambitions, they desperately required an increase of their military capability immediately; such an undertaking was vital before any attempt of threatening UDI was implemented.

Arms Dealers such as Charles Lewis stood to make a considerable fortune. And his talks with these Agents were now in an advanced state. The final arrangements of three large consignments of medium and heavy weapons, dispatched from the UK to Cape Town, South Africa, had been completed. Charles had given Bill and Joe three days leave to spend in Morocco before returning to the UK for Christmas where they were to facilitate the movement of the merchandise. Charles had learnt from years of experience such operations were now entering a delicate stage. Any signs of unusual behaviour from the Agents, customers or the Banks would throw the whole deal into jeopardy. Arms dealing was the most secretive of all trades, its enemy being public attention. The last thing Charles wanted now was any unnecessary outside interference.

As he pondered and looked out of his office window, the telephone rang. 'Charles Lewis.'

An unwelcomed but familiar voice answered, 'Charles, it's your father. I've just returned home from France and found a note from the Police to say the house and garage have been broken into.'

'Has anything been taken?'

'Nothing I can see from the house, but your car has gone.'

'What?'

'Charles, the garage has been broken into as well and your Jaguar car is missing.'

'Bugger.'

'Don't worry Charles, the Police are coming around this afternoon so you'd better give me the details of it.'

Charles instantly recoiled at the thought of the Police trampling and snooping about the Laurels asking stupid questions. He did not want any involvement of the Authorities, especially now. He decided to cut his losses. 'Thanks for letting me know father but the Jaguar wasn't parked in the garage, it's being used by a friend of mine until I return home. And if you've had nothing stolen from the house, tell the Police not to bother coming. After all you know what they're like, they just want to know all our business.'

'I can't stop them from coming around Charles, but I'll tell them there's nothing missing. It was probably kids anyway. Don't worry I'll sort it out.'

'OK. But will you ring me back after they've gone?'

'Yes Charles. Incidentally, will you be home for Christmas this year?'

'Unlikely father, I've got some serious business commitments here at the moment.'

'I wish I knew what you did son that's so important you can't see me. You're the only family I have.'

'I'll see what I can do father. I promise.'

Charles replaced the telephone and looked out towards the bustling dockyard and grey naval ships beyond. He had a strong suspicious nature and acute sense of self-preservation. He perpetually feared being scrutinised and overseen by others, often over-reacting to the slightest movement of change from the norm. In all the years since building his multimillion-pound business there had never been any trouble at home. Yet within weeks of a bodged burglary and the forcible abduction and disappearance of the culprit, the Police were now visiting the Laurels. He could smell a rat.

He urgently needed to speak to Bill and Joe and establish what exactly happened in the days following the break-in. He would send them back to Leeds to clean this mess up. But until their return from Morocco, frustratingly, there was nothing he could do.

42

Phil rang the front door bell and stepped backwards. John decided not to say a word, allowing his partner to ask all the questions. They waited patiently in the front porch until they saw movement inside through the opaque stained-glass window panes set either side of the large oak door. As the wide door slowly opened, they saw Colonel Lewis for the first time. He was now in his mid-seventies, of slight build with white balding hair and a light brown moustache. A Harris tweed jacket with brown leather patches over the elbows hung loosely from his shoulders, covering his baggy grey trousers and blue shirt. The cravat tied around his neck portrayed the stereotypical nature of a retired military officer.

Phil stepped forward, 'Good afternoon Sir. Are you Colonel Lewis?'

'Yes. You must be the police officers investigating the break-in.'

'Yes Sir. May we come in?'

'Of course, but I don't think you'll be able to do much.'

Looking slightly puzzled, Phil and John followed him through the large mosaic tiled hallway into the living room where he invited them to sit down. 'May I offer you some tea?'

'No thank you Sir. You've just mentioned that we'll not be able to do much. How is that?'

'When I returned home from France late last night, I went straight to bed. Unfortunately, it wasn't until this morning that I noticed the note your colleagues left. The French doors had been broken and one of the window panes smashed.'

Although the doors had been pushed closed by the Colonel, small shards of broken glass remained scattered across the fading carpet. He walked over towards them, followed by Phil and John. 'I haven't cleared the mess up as you can see but I've checked everywhere and nothing has been taken.'

John looked at the scene again and saw the fruits of Phil's labours; it looked like a genuine attempted burglary. He looked around at the rest of the room and immediately saw the three small silver boxes set on top of an ornamental cabinet close by. The Colonel noticed John's attention saying, 'Yes they are part of my larger collection of antique snuff boxes and other silverware. I keep most of it in the wall-safe downstairs in the cellar. I've checked it all and it's not been interfered with. As I've said, there doesn't appear to be anything missing.'

Phil asked, 'Colonel, have you checked the garages in the back-court yard or other out buildings you have in the garden?'

'Yes, I did. I found the garage doors had been damaged and my son's car missing. But I've contacted him this morning and he's told me it wasn't in there anyway. Apparently one of his friends is using it until he comes home. So, as I've just said, we've been really lucky. Nothing has been stolen.'

John peered closely at Phil as he continued asking, 'Does your son live here with you too Sir?'

'Not really, he lives mainly in Gibraltar where he runs his business and before you ask what he does, I can't honestly tell you, I've no idea.'

'What type of car does he own Sir?'

'It's a Jaguar I believe. A black one. I don't think he's had it long, but he never keeps his cars long. As I've just said officer, he comes and goes all the time. With me away in France and Charles in Gibraltar most of the time the house is empty. I hardly see him.'

'What's your son's full name Sir?'

'Is this necessary officer?'

Casually, Phil replied, 'No of course not. It's an occupational hazard; I'm always asking too many questions Sir. My wife tells me off all the time. But we'll still have to record this as an attempted burglary. So, for the report we have to mention and detail all the residents who live here, whether permanent or temporary. I fully appreciate your concern; in fact, I agree with you, there's little we can do here. But if there are similar complaints of burglaries within the neighbourhood, we can start building up a larger picture. It's my experience that when the culprit is eventually arrested and charged, the more offences we have, the longer the prison sentence it attracts.'

'Yes, I can see that.'

Phil continued, his pocket note book open and pen poised. John inwardly smiled 'a rare sight.' He asked, 'Now Sir, your son's full details please.'

'Charles Edward Lewis. He was born 2nd March 1919 in London but lived here as a child with his brother George before he was killed in the War. As I've said officer, I have no idea what he does, other than he lives and works mostly in Gibraltar and obviously travels extensively around the world.'

'How do you know that Colonel?'

'I've seen all the tags and stickers on his suitcases when his boys bring them into the house.'

'Are these 'boys' in his employment?'

'I suppose so. I don't know anything about them at all; rough lot to me.'

'Is one of these men using his Jaguar whilst he's away in Gibraltar?'

'He didn't say. I shouldn't think so; they usually go back to Gibraltar with Charles.'

John realised Phil was asking too many searching questions about his son. He interrupted, 'Sergeant, I don't think we need to bother the Colonel about his son anymore, we've got all we need.'

Phil turned around towards John, momentarily showing his annoyance at being stopped but immediately realised his mistake. 'Yes, you're right. There you see, asking too many questions again. But before we go Sir, can we have a quick look around, we might find something, you never know?'

'Yes, help yourself.'

'May we look inside the cellar first?'

'Yes, but I've been down there to check the safe. Everything is where it should be.'

'We'll have a look anyway Sir, we have local criminals that

sometimes target cellar grates and their openings to gain access inside the house.'

'I understand. I'll leave you to look around. Let me know when you've finished, I'll be in the study writing some overdue letters.'

Phil and John followed him though into the hallway. He stopped halfway along and opened the internal door leading to the cellar down a flight of stone steps. The Colonel switched on the light, 'I'll leave it with you. You know where I am if you need me.' He walked along the hallway and disappeared into another room at the rear of the house. Phil and John descended the stairs into the cellar. When they reached the bottom John asked, 'Did you notice those antique silver snuff boxes upstairs?'

'Yes, I did.'

'Are you looking for anything specific Phil?'

'Not really. Let's have a good look at the pile of coal beneath the shoot.'

They both stooped down and started lifting various lumps of coal from the edge of the pile. Suddenly, Phil froze and muttered, 'Bloody marvellous,' as he picked up a red and white wrapper containing bubble gum. 'This is the sort Ronnie ate. Remember when we found these inside his Mini Cooper?'

'Yes, we've got them back in the office safe.'

Phil placed a hand gently on John's shoulder. 'There's something else I forgot to tell you.'

'Bloody hell Phil! What?'

'When I came back here last time, I found one of these outside, close to the cellar grate.'

'Really?'

'Yes. I examined the cellar grate and it had been moved in recent times. Nearby, I found another empty wrapper just like this one.' Reaching into his jacket inside pocket, he pulled out his wallet and took it out from inside, placing it next to the one they had just found.

John scrutinised them both replying, 'They are the same, Phil.'

'Yes. Although it's not conclusive, so far as I'm concerned, these wrappers place Ronnie outside, next to the cellar grate and down here. It's my belief John something happened to him right here where we're standing.'

'I think you're right Phil. But what are we going to do now?'

'Once we've finished here, we're going to see DCI Sampson. John my boy, you're going to witness a couple of 'old school' cops working in the shadows. If you don't want anything to do with this, you'd better tell me now. Otherwise, you're on board and we're going to sort these murdering bastards out.'

'What are you talking about?'

'Someone's protecting this Charles Lewis and I'm going to find out why. I'm very interested in getting to know who these two gorillas he employs are. They fit the description Freddie told us. So why does he need them?

'Listen Phil, I'll help you all the way, but please don't ask me to commit any criminal offences. OK?'

'Alright, but you're getting to sound like a bloody broken record now. What about possible breaches of the Discipline Code?'

'Maybe. Perhaps.'

'Good boy. We'll start with some enquiries into the Colonel's son, Charles Lewis. I'm satisfied the old man is completely unaware of all this, but I need to ask him a few more questions before he leaves for France again.'

'OK, but be careful you don't get too intense. And by the way, don't call me boy.'

'Shut up, you dopy sod. It means I like you. Otherwise it would be DC Evans.'

John placed the bubble gum inside his pocket; he would bag and label it later back at the office as evidence - found at the scene of a possible murder. They climbed the steps and returned to the hallway. The Colonel was still inside the study. 'John, go and talk to him and advise the old man on some crime prevention methods; locks and outside lights etc. You know what I mean. Keep him occupied, I'm going to have a look around upstairs.'

'Bloody hell, Phil.'

Without any warning Phil pushed John into the study where the Colonel looked up and said, 'Have you finished officer?'

'Yes. Before we go, can I talk to you about your security measures? The locks appear completely inadequate and not really fit for purpose to be honest.' Phil waited for a few moments until he was satisfied John had the Colonel's complete attention. He quickly ran silently upstairs and began to enter the bedrooms. The first was clearly being used by Colonel Lewis; his suitcase was still half full of his clothes and the bed remained unmade.

The second room looked more promising. Hung inside the large open wardrobe were several suits. He slipped his hand inside of a dinner jacket pocket and found a small business card. He lifted it out and read 'Ronald Earl, Director, Boddingtons Armouries Ltd, Birmingham.' Placing it inside his own pocket, he continued checking the various jackets. He found nothing else of significance. The third and fourth bedrooms each contained a single bed. Again, he quickly searched the wardrobes, but they were both empty. But as he was leaving the final room, he saw a pillow case, thrown into a waste bin. He bent down and noticed small traces of blood on it. As he picked it up he saw underneath a pink sheet of paper. He examined it closely. It was an invoice from a major local garage. Appleyard's Ltd of Leeds. It was for £20 of petrol on account, during the past three weeks for Jaguar motor car JUM 106. At the bottom of the paper in handwriting it read 'received £20 with thanks from Mr Joe Mason.' Again, he pushed it inside his pocket, dropping the blood-stained pillow case back into the waste bin.

Phil knew he was out of time. He descended the stairs two at a time and casually entered the study as the Colonel said to John, 'Thank you for that officer, but as I've said before, I shall invite a joiner in to repair the doors and install a sturdier lock. It's a good idea for additional lighting outside, especially around the garage area.' John looked at Phil with much relief, 'We'll be on our way now Sir, but if there's anything you find afterwards, please don't hesitate to contact me on this number.' He wrote the office telephone number on a police letter headed business card and handed it over.

Phil stepped forward, 'Thank you Sir for your time. We might contact you later if our investigations link this incident with others of a similar style.' He nodded to John and walked towards the hallway and front door. The Colonel followed them to the front door and shook hands before they left. Phil gave him a wave as he placed the police car into gear and drove slowly away. He turned to John. 'Let's go and see the Boss. You're going to learn some of the old ways, John my boy.'

Twenty minutes later they parked in the station car park. As Phil switched the engine off, he said, 'This is going to be interesting. Are you sure you want to be part of what we're going to be planning?'

'Yes, but nothing criminal. Remember?'

'Oh shut up!'

43

As John and Phil entered DCI Sampson's office in Leeds, a telephone rang in Charles Lewis Enterprise's Office, Gibraltar. 'Is that you Charles?'

'Yes father. Have the Police been?'

Yes, you were right about one thing, they wanted to know a great deal about you.'

'What did you tell them?'

'Not much really. I naturally told them who you were and that you worked abroad. But let's be honest Charles, I've no idea what you do or where you go anyway. Other than you seem to live mostly in Gibraltar and travel the world extensively on business, I know nothing else about your activities. Apparently, they wanted both our details because they'll be recording it as an attempted burglary.'

'Did they have a look around?'

'They appeared to be interested in the cellar, I've no idea why but that's where they went first.'

'Where you with them?'

'No Charles, I left them down there, I had some letters to write. Why?'

'Nothing really. But did they go anywhere else?'

'I don't think so. One of them gave me some crime prevention advice. The other, I'm not sure. He was somewhere about, but I don't know exactly where. They're the police; it's natural for them to check the house and garage for any other signs of damage. Why are you so concerned Charles?'

'There's no reason, father. It's just that I've travelled throughout the world and frankly, I've learnt to distrust them.'

'These officers appeared to be very professional and concerned about our security. They promised to contact me if any similar incidents come to their attention.'

Charles bit his lip. He knew his father always had a blind allegiance to the British Authorities, never questioning their actions. After all, he was an honourable man. Several years ago, it had been rumoured in some quarters that he was to be nominated for a knighthood for his medical services to the Armed Forces. His unblemished character and widely respected name was recognised as a 'tour de force' by many. But his son's dismissal from the Foreign Office had scuppered any likelihood of such a decoration. By contrast, Charles was shunned by the establishment, operating in the murky underworld of illicit International Arms dealing; trading with despots, murderers and renegades where honour and integrity were non-existent.

In a split second, he made a decision, 'Father, I've changed my mind, I will come home to see you in the next few days. I'll probably be bringing Bill and Joe with me. Is that all right?'

The Colonel sighed, 'To be honest Charles, I don't know why you employ those men. They look and behave like thugs, especially the ginger haired one. Can't they stay in a local hotel?'

'OK, I'll sort that out.'

'Good. Look forward to seeing son.'

Charles replaced the telephone and returned to his reports. Where the hell were Bill and Joe?

44

As Phil and John entered his office, DCI Sampson pointed towards the two chairs in his office, 'Sit down.' He continued, 'Right Phil, it's time for us stop fooling about behind each other's back, otherwise we're going to make an utter mess of this investigation. No more secrets from now on. Agreed?'

Phil nodded his head, 'Agreed.'

'Good. Now will you tell us what you've been up to and then I'll fill you in from my side? It seems our John probably knows what we've both been doing.'

'I do. And I must say it's not exactly comfortable for me to watch you two operate out of some self-styled policing and to hell with all the rules, no matter how honourable you both consider your motives to be.'

Phil turned to DCI Sampson, 'What's he talking about?'

'I know exactly what he's talking about Phil. What's more, he's right. John represents tomorrow's 'policing' and frankly it's going to be far more difficult for him in the future to prove his criminal investigations than for the likes of us. As our old Prime Minister Harold MacMillan once said, 'We've never had it so good.' But these days are quickly coming to an end. I can visualise in the near future we will have to be more accountable to the public, certainly presenting evidence in the Courts and especially the Politicians.'

'So how are we going to deal with this matter?' asked Phil.

'Let's see what we've got and take it from there. I'm still going to see the Colonel now I've got an invitation to his house, but we must be careful. Tell me everything you've been up to Phil. And I mean everything. Leave nothing out, our careers may depend on this.'

Whilst DCI Sampson and Phil discussed their actions, John was busy writing all the details down. After twenty minutes, Phil turned to him and asked, 'What are you doing?'

He stopped writing and explained, 'I'm recording a visual log of what we know. It's the latest method of collating all the information and intelligence into a flow chart that can quickly be understood. Apparently, it stimulates the inquiring mind. It's called psychology. I learnt it on my last CID refresher course, Phil. You should try and make an effort in attending some of these in the future. They're very useful. You never know, you might learn something.'

'Bollocks. It's all twoddle. Written by so-called academic armchair investigators.'

DCI Sampson interrupted. 'Shut up Phil, you're just too long in the tooth for any changes. Show me what you've done, John.' He stood and drew on the large black board facing DCI Sampson and Phil, copying his notes.

Victims

Ronnie Ellis - House burglar
Disappeared from the Laurels
Freddie Cox- Fence
Murdered
Jim Simms- Taxi Driver, drove Ellis to the Laurels
Killed – fatal hit and run RTA three hours later

Exhibits

Freddie Cox's dying declaration
Jaguar JUM 106
Bubble gum wrappers found in **Ellis's car and Laurels**
Note with Colonel Lewis's details written by **Freddie Cox**

Witnesses

Brenda Barker – prostitute, sent by Cox to scout the Laurels, saw 'Ginger'
Pete Hayes- taxi driver, saw man with limp at rear of the Laurels
Dr Banks ICU Leeds General Infirmary – witnessed Cox's dying declaration

Suspects

Charles Lewis – resides occasionally at Laurels, main residence in Gibraltar, possible Vauxhall Bridge, London. Co-Director of **Charles Lewis Enterprises Ltd** along with

given to **Brenda Barker**	**Ronald Earl** – Director
Business Card – **Ronald Earl**	Boddingtons Armouries
Boddington Armouries	**Male 1 - ginger haired**
Birmingham	**Male 2 - with limp**
Invoice Appleyards Leeds fuel for Jaguar JUM 106 named **Joe Mason**	Both these men possibly ex-military and one may be called **Joe Mason**

After he finished, both men stared at the chart in silence. DCI Sampson nodded, 'Well done John, that's good. Even these dinosaurs agree with me. Don't we Phil?' He made no comment other than an expressionless reluctant grunt.

John continued, 'This chart allows us to see what we've got but more importantly, what we need to do. It is my belief that Charles Lewis is central to all of this investigation and what he does for a living may determine the reluctance of why ACC Jenkins is so anxious to sweep this inquiry under the carpet. It may be something very political and sensitive; we don't know at this stage. But I think we should delve some more and find out what this gentleman is up to. After all, these two thugs working for him are running amuck all over our city and killing our own home-grown criminals.'

Phil asked, 'What do you suggest we do now Boss?'

'I've still got some of my budget left in the Divisional purse. I'll write that off as overtime. Your overtime. First you, John. Have you got a passport?'

'No Sir.'

'Go to the Post Office and collect the forms. Bring them to me for signature and I'll let you have some money from the 'expenses jar.' Apply for five days leave, I'll sign that off too. Then go to the Manchester Passport Office tomorrow with the forms and get one. From there, I want you to go to the Airport and fly out to Gibraltar. It's important we check out Charles Lewis; where he lives and works and try to establish the true nature of what his Company represents. You'll be travelling as a tourist, visiting some relative of friends over there. Make up a story for yourself and stick to it. I know it's a bit old school but we don't want to cause any unnecessary attention. Do we?'

'Absolutely not. I'll go over there and find out all I can Sir.'

'Yes. If you can connect Charles Lewis with these two characters we know only as 'ginger and 'lame boy' then that would be very useful. Call in at the TSU[21] and collect one of their covert cameras. Apparently they have one that resembles a tie pin. I'll sort the paperwork out for that too.'

'Yes Sir.'

'And one other thing John, leave your Police warrant card here at home. Don't want to take any unnecessary chances, just in case you get your pockets dipped.'

'I'll leave it in my desk.'

'Good man. Now, I'm sorry it's the week before Christmas but that's good for your cover. Many people travel to Gibraltar this time of the year. Remember, at night time it'll be crawling with Servicemen all getting pissed; so, keep out of trouble. No unnecessary risks, John.'

'I understand Sir.'

'Incidentally, I hope your wife will be OK about all this?'

John stopped momentarily to think about that. No, Mary was going to be furious. He had promised to go with her and visit her parents in Scarborough next week before embarking on their Christmas shopping. He was in trouble; again. Lying, he replied, 'I think she'll understand Sir.'

Turning to Phil, he continued, 'I think you should go to Birmingham and make some inquiries into this Boddington Armouries firm and in particular one of its Directors, Ronald Earl. As you know, he's also a joint Director of Charles Lewis Enterprises too. Also, can you visit Appleyards, here in Leeds, and see what you can find out about this Joe Mason? What exactly is the account he has with the Jaguar car.'

'No problems. What are you going to do Boss?'

'For the time being, the Jag can stay where it is. In a few days, I'm going to arrange for it to be thoroughly examined by someone in SOCO I can trust. It seems very likely that Ronnie and Freddie were transported in it. That reminds me Phil, I need the keys.'

Shaking his head, 'Don't have any. Hot-wired the little beauty.'

'How the hell did you do that?' exclaimed John.

---

[21] Technical Support Office – suppliers of Home Office approval covert equipment.

'Listen. That's what I do John. I listen to good hard working ganifs who steal good quality cars. After I've nicked them, I make them show me the tricks of their trade. Once you know how to get into the car and locate the wires under the dashboard, it's simple. You just yank those that are connected to the ignition switch and cross-wire any two of them. Once the engine fires up, you get the two you need and twist them together. That's how I did it. I don't suppose they teach you that at these refresher courses you go on, do they?'

This admission left John speechless.

DCI Sampson was unfazed. 'OK. What about the keys to the lockup? I can arrange for it be examined there when the time is right. Afterwards, I'll arrange for it to be trailered from there under the tarpaulin during the hours of darkness to the main police garage.'

'Fair enough,' replied Phil as he slid one of the two keys across the desk.

'When I go and see the Colonel, I'm going to try and place some listening devices inside the house. I know where we can locate some of the latest equipment from another friend of mine who used to work in the Security Services.'

Phil nodded his head in appreciation. 'I'm impressed Boss. I thought you were losing your nerve now your retirement looms closer.'

'Bugger off.'

Once again, John rolled his eyes and asked, 'When shall we meet up again Sir?'

'This time next week; here in my office, unless there are any urgent developments.'

'Bloody hell Boss, that's the day before Christmas Eve,' replied Phil.

'I know, so don't get too pissed. It's the best time to go sniffing around people's movements; when they are off their guard, celebrating. Meanwhile, let's keep a low profile. John, you're taking a few days holiday before Christmas and Phil, please be discreet in Birmingham.'

'Of course, Boss. Discretion is my middle name from now on.'

Neither DCI Sampson or John made any comment.

45

John was right. After returning home that evening and informing Mary he was going to be away for several days, she screamed in utter astonishment, 'But I've been looking forward to seeing Mum and Dad for months! You know how much it means to me. Your sodding job always comes first. It's just not fair John!'

He attempted to console her by explaining how important it was for him to go away and it would only be for three of four days and there would still be time to go and see her parents for Christmas. But she vehemently dismissed all his excuses, 'No John. It won't do. I spend most of my life waiting for you to come home, never knowing when that is. It wasn't like this when we first met; you were in uniform then and working regular hours. I knew when you were coming home and we had a life together. I'm warning you John, if you don't do something about this and spend more time with me, there will be consequences.'

She stormed out of the room and went upstairs and slammed the bedroom door. He stared down at the solitary dinner plate setting on the table realising the seriousness of the situation. He wanted to tell her he still loved her and that this case was unusual. He wanted desperately to suggest she found a job for a while to help with the finances and they were perhaps too young to start a family. If she returned to work it might also give her a stronger sense of purpose in life and her days would be less lonely. But he knew this was too sensitive a subject to broach. His fractured marriage was now in imminent danger of falling apart completely.

Like so many professional Detectives, he was torn between the horns of a dilemma; his marriage and career. Presently, he chose the latter for which he later came to regret.

46

John slept in the spare bedroom. Mary refused to speak to him whilst he packed a small suitcase and as he opened the front door to leave, she remained resolute; failing to say goodbye. He drove to the office via the TSU office, set in an old Government prefab building on the outskirts of the city. He signed for and collected the miniature camera together with several roles of special film.

As he entered his office, Phil and DCI Sampson were studying several past burglaries they suspected Ronnie had committed. DCI Sampson said, 'John, sign these forms. One is for your leave, the other is for £50 for your expenses. Remember to get receipts when you can. Have you packed enough clothes for several days?'

'Yes Sir.'

'Good. You must take the train to Manchester and collect your Passport. It's all ready for you. Afterwards take a taxi to the Airport. Here are your tickets. Your flight is at four thirty. I've left the return flight open; just in case you have to come home early or later. OK?'

'Yes Sir. Thank you.'

'Off you go. Phil will drive you to the Station. Good luck and John, be careful.'

Within thirty minutes John had caught the trans-Pennine train to Manchester where he later collected the Passport and before three o'clock, he was waiting in the lounge for the small schedule plane for Gibraltar.

Finally, after a bumpy flight, he landed on the runway that stretched across the flat sandy causeway connecting the island to mainland Spain. By seven thirty he had booked into the Rock Hotel Gibraltar. His small room overlooked across the busy naval dockyard towards the Spanish mainland. The Mediterranean Fleet was in harbour. John checked his notes and, according to Companies House, he was less than two hundred yards away from Charles Lewis Enterprises Ltd registered address.

He sat on the bed and began to examine his 'state of the art' small lapel automatic camera. In accordance with the boxed instructions, he discreetly fixed it behind his jacket lapel, poking the lens through the button hole, giving the impression is was a small blood donor badge. With its wide-angled lens camouflaged as a badge and specially designed to take over 200 images, it was triggered by thin wire connected to a small button pierced through the fabric, running down to the inside of the jacket sleeve. By placing a hand in his pocket, he could easily take photographs quietly and covertly. He finally hung his jacket inside the wardrobe and went to sleep exhausted.

The following morning, he woke up to brilliant sunshine and swung the windows wide open. He breathed in deeply the warm Gibraltan air and smelled the slight breeze coming from the nearby sea. What a change from the dark December weather back in the UK.

After eating a full breakfast, he walked along the cobbled High Street towards the Governor's Residence passing dozens of small shops and bars, until he finally saw what he had been looking for. Fixed to a stone wall, next to a dark wooden door between a liquor store and jewellers shop was a list of business names engraved on a brass plaque. Alongside these, corresponded press-buttoned door bells. Holding a street index map he had acquired from the hotel, he pretended to be in search of somewhere else. As he examined the page, he cast his eyes sideways and quickly scanned the names. Second from the bottom, in the smallest of print he saw 'Charles Lewis Enterprises Ltd.'

He reached inside his jacket pocket and took several frames before continuing along the street. After a few yards he hesitated; what to do next? He turned around and saw a small bar on the opposite side of the road. He looked at his watch; 10.15 a.m. The street was already bustling with local shoppers and Navy servicemen in their blue uniforms, many of whom were engaged in their Christmas shopping. This poignantly reminded him of his broken promise to Mary. After the previous night, he expected she would visit her parents whilst he was away, leaving him unsure of what sort of Christmas he was going to be returning to.

He crossed over and looked inside; no customers. This allowed no cover, so he strolled further along until he found a newsagent shop selling English papers. He bought the Telegraph and returned to the bar. This time he saw several shoppers enter, so he decided to follow them inside. To his surprise it was in fact a hotel. He went to the counter, ordered a coffee and sat in the empty window seat facing the door on the opposite side of the road, pretending to read his paper.

After two hours and several cups of coffee no one had entered or left the building. He was about to return to his hotel for lunch, when he saw two men approach the dark wooden door and stand outside. One of them pressed a bell. Although he was unable to see accurately which bell, one of them had bright ginger curly hair and the other walked with a distinct limp to his right leg. Both wore similar casual clothing of grey trousers and short brown leather jackets. John instinctively knew them to be Charles Lewis's men. They matched the descriptions given by Brenda and Pete when they had visited the Laurels a few weeks earlier. He quickly walked to the hotel front entrance and stopped outside, some thirty feet away from them. John looked in the opposite direction, sunk his hand inside the jacket pocket and pressed the shutter button several times.

John paused, turned and looked into a shop window. He was able to see them clearly through the reflection in the bright sunlight. Eventually the door opened. He tried to turn around but they quickly disappeared inside without a trace. Who had let them in? Was it Charles Lewis?

He returned to the bar and ordered a plate of sandwiches and another cup of coffee. Now, he was prepared to wait all day until they came out. But as he took the first bite, the door opposite opened again, revealing the same two men. As they stepped outside, another man suddenly appeared, dressed in a smart business suit carrying a leather attaché case. He looked very different. *This must be Charles Lewis*, thought John. Leaving his food, he walked quickly outside and followed them down the busy shopping lane. The smartly dressed man seemed to be in deep conversation with the others, waving his arms slightly and pointing towards their chests. As John drew closer, he noticed the smartly dressed man became agitated and upset, spurning them for something. The ginger haired man waved his hand in a gesture of apology but this was instantly dismissed.

Cautious not to approach too close and taking nothing for granted, John moved from one side of the street to the other, careful not to attract their attention. After following them slowly for five minutes they eventually came to a crossroads; the two men peeled off to the left leaving Charles Lewis continuing ahead. John decided to follow Charles Lewis. Eventually, after a further two hundred yards he saw him enter a luxury block of apartments called 'Nelson House.'

John waited nearby for twenty minutes before approaching the block. The front lobby was empty with the polished wooden door wide open. With some hesitance, he entered half expecting to be challenged by one of the residents. Once again on the rear wall was a list of names, apartment numbers, names and their corresponding door bell. There were twenty in all but none with the name Lewis or any similar name. He double-checked again, nothing. Then something caught his eye. 'R. Earl.' That seemed familiar. He took two photographs of the list of names.

He walked back outside trying to remember the name. Suddenly he muttered, 'Of course. Ronald Earl, co-Director in Charles Lewis Enterprises Ltd.' Although he had been unable to take any quality pictures of the three men, he had established where Charles Lewis lived and worked. All he needed to do now was to find out what the nature of his business was and the identities of the two thugs he hired. He decided to return to the Rock Hotel and telephone DCI Sampson of the developments and ask for further instructions.

47

Earlier that day, Charles Lewis was perusing his teleprinter machine. As he read the messages, typing incessantly from an Agent operating in Central America, the outside doorbell rang. Leaving his office, he descended the stairs and opened the outside door. Without any civility, he said, 'Come in.' His two lieutenants, Bill and Joe, entered and followed him upstairs. Once inside the office he turned and sarcastically said, 'I'm glad to see you two. Hope you had a pleasant break.'

'Yes Sir, very enjoyable,' replied Joe

'Good, cos I've got some unfinished business for you.'

'What's that?' asked Bill.

'Apparently there's been a break-in at the Laurels. When my father returned a few days after you left, he found a note from the Police to say to the garage and the house had been broken into.'

Bill and Joe quickly glanced at each other in shock. They expected the garage but not the house. Bill asked, 'Have they stolen anything from inside the house?'

'Not according to my father.'

'How did the Police find this out? Asked Joe.

'Good question. Apparently, some anonymous caller heard the sound of breaking glass.'

Bill said, 'What, from the road? Impossible; it's too far away. I don't like this Mr Lewis. Something's not right.'

'I agree. Did you make sure the place was clean, like I asked you before you left?'

Bill replied, 'Of course Sir. There was nothing that could connect your business with the intruder. Believe me Sir, he disappeared without any trace.'

'Did you secure the house and garage properly before you left?'

'Yes Sir, Joe and me double checked. It was all in order. What about the Jag?'

'It's missing. I've told my father it's not been stolen; a friend of mine is using it instead.'

'Do you want us to find out where it is Sir?'

'Not at this stage, but I don't like the Police snooping about like this. I want you both to return to Leeds and make sure nothing has been overlooked. I don't know exactly what you did but make sure there are no lose ends. Do you understand me?'

They both nodded and instinctively said, 'Sir.'

'Take tonight's six o'clock flight back to Manchester and go directly to the Laurels. Tell my father I will be returning next week on Christmas Eve. When you've made sure nothing has been left to chance, I want you to check into the Royal Hotel in Leeds and wait for my instructions.'

'Can you let us have some cash Boss until we get back to the UK?'

'Yes. Walk with me back to Nelson House I'll let you have a couple of hundred pounds until I see you in a few days. As soon as you've got it, I want you both to leave; I'm meeting Ron Earl there at lunch.' Turning directly towards Bill, he continued, 'And make absolutely sure everything is watertight back in Leeds.'

'Will do Boss.'

They all moved towards the door and left the building together. As they continued along the busy street and approached a crossroads, Bill suddenly stopped. 'Boss don't look around, but I think we're being followed. Just carry on, we'll turn off here and if it's you he's interested in, we'll double track back and cover you. Just prod me in the chest as though you're giving me a proper bollocking.'

Charles knew exactly how to react. Without flinching, he poked his fingers into his chest and spoke loudly, 'I'm bloody well fed up with you two. If you don't improve your ways, you can go and find somewhere else to work. Do you understand?'

Bill raised his arms up in the air but Charles pushed them away, ignoring him and continued ahead. Bill and Joe walked the other way and out of sight.

Charles carried on, knowing if anyone was following him, Bill and Joe would deal with them in a manner as not to compromise his personal safety or privacy. Yet Charles's natural cynical disposition wondered if it was Bill's intention to purposefully make him feel threatened and make them become indispensable. But for the time being he would comply with his instructions.

Once he arrived at Nelson House, he resisted looking around for any one following him, entered and walked through the lobby. Instead of immediately taking the lift to his flat on the third floor, he approached the lobby counter and suddenly crouched down behind it and waited. Several minutes passed before he heard someone enter the hallway and stop in front of the apartments list. Carefully, he raised his head sufficiently enough to see a young man standing in front of the sign, examining the list. Lowering his head back down, he waited for about thirty seconds before he heard the intruder leave.

Slowly Charles stood upright and saw him walk across the street in the direction he had come from. Bill was right. He was being followed. But who the hell was he? Bill and Joe's still had some work to do before they returned to the UK.

Once the young man had disappeared from sight, he summoned the lift and ascended to the third floor and walked along the corridor to Apartment 36. This was rented to Charles Lewis Enterprises Ltd and jointly shared between himself and Ron Earl. As he entered, to his surprise, Ron was standing in the middle of the lounge welcoming his partner, 'Hello Charles. Good to see you again. How are things?'

Ignoring the implications of his previous stalker, he smiled, 'I'm very well Ron. What time did your flight arrive this morning?'

'Actually, it was on time. Ten thirty.'

'Let me pour you a drink before we talk properly,' suggested Charles.

'Good idea. Just a tonic water please.'

Ron explained their latest shipment of arms for the Rhodesian Government would be arriving in Cape Town the following day. Some aspects of the business plan had changed relating to their transport and storage but this was quite normal, indicative of their clandestine activities. Improved security was often maintained by continually changing their arrangements.

'We'll go to the office and sort it out later.'

As they both settled into their comfortable seats, Ron sighed with some relief, 'I was up really early this morning Charles. Would you mind if I have forty winks before we go to the office?'

'Of course not, Ron. Put your feet up, there's no rush.

As Ron drank the last of his tonic, he rested his head against the back of the chair and slipped quietly into a light sleep. Charles was far from feeling sleepy, his mind was elsewhere. Was the stranger a Police Officer? Why should his Jaguar be stolen now? Did Bill and Joe do something catastrophically stupid that has attracted this unwanted attention?

He decided once Ron awoke, he would tell him of the burglary at the Laurels but nothing else. He now needed Ron to speak to his contacts in Whitehall urgently. Obviously the first warning to abandon the investigation against himself had been ignored. A more robust approach was now the order of the day.

48

John returned to the Rock Hotel and went immediately to his room. He looked outside the window towards the dwindling sunlight falling over the harbour, completely unaware of the two men stood outside the main entrance. He placed the call to DCI Sampson. 'Hello Sir, I think I have now made the connection between our two suspects with Charles Lewis. I've managed to photograph them all together walking through the town centre. I've also located his office and an apartment belonging to Ron Earl.'

'Excellent John. What have you done with the camera and film?'

'It's with me now.'

'OK. Listen, just to play it safe, I want you to take it immediately and put it in the Hotel's safe. Now.'

'Will do. What else do you want me to do Sir?'

'If you can find out exactly what Charles Lewis Enterprises are up to that would be marvellous. Also, try to establish the identities of these two thugs. But be careful, they're dangerous men. Don't forget, we can always have them arrested there at a later date. So far as I'm concerned, they're still on British soil.'

'I fully understand.'

'I want you fly back home tomorrow. If you can't uncover any further information, don't worry. After all, everything will be closing down for Christmas.'

'OK. I'll ring you back this time tomorrow when I arrive back in Manchester.'

'Very good John. Don't forget, take the camera now to the Hotel safe. And talking of safe, you make sure you look after yourself too. Bye.'

John replaced the receiver and unpicked the camera away from his jacket, removed it from his lapel and placed it along with the spare unused rolls of film inside a plain brown envelope. He went downstairs and approached the small reception desk where the duty Manager greeted him, 'Good afternoon Sir, how may I be of assistance?'

'I shall be booking out tomorrow. Until then, would you place this inside your safe along with my passport, until I collect it?'

'Of course, Sir.'

John handed over to him the small package and passport, turned around and left through the main entrance. He decided to visit one of the nearby jewellery shops and buy a watch for Mary for Christmas. She had intimated on several occasions her old one had been erratic, sometimes losing an hour within the week. He knew it would not nullify the unhappiness she held for the commitment he held for his career, but it might temper her attitude a little. Perhaps this would allow him some time to start making amends and improve their relationship.

As he stepped outside, the late afternoon had now faded to early evening. The December air was still warm and inviting. People were walking in all directions, some finishing their last-minute shopping while others were looking for a place to relax and enjoy a drink. John was in search of both. He found a jewellers near to the Governor's Residence. He purchased a watch for Mary and although it was considerably cheaper than in the UK, the price still represented a month's salary. The shopkeeper gift-wrapped it neatly inside Christmas paper. John smiled and placed it safely inside his jacket pocket.

Now he needed a drink. Tomorrow morning would be spent attempting to establish the true nature of Charles Lewis Enterprises and finding out more about the two other men before he flew home. But tonight, he was going to indulge in some site-seeing and relaxation.

He noticed a bar advertising Danish larger where live music was being played. He stepped inside and descended into a dimly lit cellar. He coughed as he inhaled the thick tobacco smoke belching out from the large room. It was full of customers, mostly men listening to the smooth hypnotic sound of two live saxophones. Although not his favourite genre of music, he ordered a large glass of larger and began to soak up the ambience, soon forgetting his domestic problems. He found a bench seat in the corner nearest the entrance and watched several couples dancing on the wooden floor in front of the band.

After two drinks, he decided to return to the hotel. But as he rose to his feet, he felt someone touch his shoulder. Instinctively, he turned around and for a split second looked into the cold green eyes of a smiling man with bright ginger curly hair. Before he managed to gather his senses, he felt a sharp pain in his left thigh. He involuntarily touched it but immediately lost all bodily feeling. Although dazed and confused, he was aware of slumping downwards towards the floor. He attempted to speak but no words came from his mouth. He was completely locked inside his body.

As he collapsed, two arms supported him under his armpits. He was now being lifted back onto his feet, unable to speak, with his eyes wide open seeing the people watching him as the band continued to play. But he could hear nothing. He looked curiously to the man by his side who appeared to smile again. Then his whole world went blank as he slipped into a bottomless black void.

Bill and Joe were holding John tightly upright, supporting his body weight. They dragged him towards the entrance and virtually carried him up the steep stairs towards the entrance door. Joe smiled at two sailors entering. One of them smiled, 'Christ, he's started on the booze early.'

Bill replied, 'You're right mate, we keep telling him to slow down, but he never takes any notice. Not a proper drinker like us.'

The sailors grinned and disappeared inside. Bill whispered, 'Come on Joe, let's get this sorted out. We'll take him down to the docks and make it look like a robbery. We need to empty his pockets first.' They dragged him down the side of the club into another back street devoid of any overhead street lighting. Only the glow from the nearby apartment windows shone over them as they started to strip John's jacket and shoes. Bill searched the pockets and found the small package wrapped in Christmas paper. He threw it to the ground and stamped on it firmly. John was unable to hear the crunch of his month's salary present for Mary. Joe removed the brown leather wallet and started quickly picking through the papers, counting the modest amount of money inside. Apart from making it appear he was a victim of robbery, it was vital they knew who he really was.

But after searching him several times they were surprised to find no identification. His wallet only contained £35. No driving licence or any other details. He turned to Bill, 'There's not even a bloody library ticket in here. Who the hell is he?'

'We can check at his hotel,' Bill replied.

'Yes, we can. Do we know anyone working there?'

'We'll go to the back door and speak to one of the Spanish cleaners. Five pounds will go a long way back on the mainland.'

Joe shook his head in agreement, 'Let's get rid of him first. You take his other arm and we'll drag him down to the bay, then tip him over the edge. With a bit of luck the current will sweep him over to Spain, then no one will be the wiser.'

Although John was completely incapacitated, he sensed he was being dragged along the ground, his shoeless feet painfully feeling every cobble stone. His agony allowed him to gather some degree of focus. He could hear voices next to him. His basic sense self-preservation told him his life was in threat. These were dangerous men intending to place him in harm's way. He started to struggle and attempted to shout but the pressure on their grasp simply tightened. With all the strength he could muster he shouted, 'Help!' as he felt himself collapsing to the ground. Once again, he was back in the black void.

49

Bill was an expert in surveillance, both in the pursuit of targets but also being acutely aware of those who may be watching him. He had first noticed John observing them through the shop window reflection after they had left the office. It was an amateurish technique, adopted by those unfamiliar with this field of covertness and when he followed them along the street, this simply confirmed his suspicions.

Tipping Charles off about the 'tail' allowed Bill and Joe to peel off in another direction, double track and follow John with relative ease. They had followed him to Nelson House and return later to the Rock Hotel. The failing late afternoon sunlight gave them good cover as they waited in the shadows outside the hotel for him to reappear.

Two hours later they saw John leave the Hotel through the main entrance. At a distance of over fifty yards, they followed him to the jewellers shop and then into the club where the loud music was coming from. Bill smiled; how fortunate to snare his target under the distraction of his favourite music. Using the same hypodermic needle used on Freddie Cox, he injected a highly toxic hallucinate drug into John's thigh, causing immediate paralysis.

It was all so predictable. They knew exactly what effect it would have on him. As with Freddie, they lifted him to his feet and supported his body to prevent him falling down. They carried him outside, removed his Harris tweed jacket and shoes in a nearby courtyard and searched him for identification.

Unfortunately, Bill's plan began to unravel from that moment. As they dragged him across the course cobble stones towards the harbour, somehow John had miraculously regained enough consciousness to shout 'Help.' This cry had caught the attention of three sailors returning to their ship who stepped forward and asked Bill and Joe what was happening. To Bill's amazement, Joe suddenly let go of John and ran away, leaving Bill to face the inquisitive Matelots.

The sailors immediately realised John was in some distress and rushed forwards. Bill thumped the nearest in the face and pushed John towards the others, causing him to collapse to the ground. Like Joe, Bill turned around and ran away in the same direction, still holding on to John's jacket.

The first Sailor stumbled backwards whilst the other two lunged forwards in an attempt to catch John before he collapsed. Unfortunately they were too slow. John hit the ground hard. His head fell awkwardly on the road surface causing a deep cut to his forehead. For a moment, the sailors gave a token chase before deciding instead to return and deal with John's urgent needs.

Meanwhile, Bill eventually caught Joe on the Main Street close to the Rock Hotel. He shouted, 'Wait a minute Joe, I've got something for you.'

He turned around, 'What's that?'

Bill ran towards him and sunk his fist into his stomach causing him to bend double in pain. Before Joe could gasp for air Bill pulled his head upwards by the hair and whispered in his ear, 'Never do that again to me, or you're a dead man. Do you understand me, you cowardly crippled bastard?'

Replying through his clenched teeth, 'I'm sorry Bill. I just panicked. I don't know what came over me.'

'Now wait here, I'm going to find out who this guy really is. It's all too suspicious for someone who doesn't live here not to have any identification.'

Still clutching his stomach, Joe replied, 'I'm sorry Bill. I promise you it won't happen again.'

'You're bloody right there.'

Bill disappeared down the side of the Hotel towards the kitchens. There he found the back-door wide open and the smell of cooked food coming from within. Without any hesitation, he entered and saw dishes of prepared meals, ready for the guests. Standing in the far corner was a middle-aged man washing dozens of saucepans in a large ceramic sink. Soap suds spread across the draining board, down his dirty apron and up his hairy arms. He looked towards Bill and stopped cleaning. In a heavily Spanish accent he asked, 'What you want?'

Bill approached him holding five new £1 notes, spread out like a fan. Without any conversation, the cleaner was mesmerised with the cash flashing in front of his face. Bill nodded and gestured for him to follow towards the back door. Once outside, Bill placed the pound notes into his wet hand and asked, 'I want you to go and ask the Receptionist to come here and see me. That's all. Tell him I have some money for him.'

Although he looked confused and bewildered, he quickly stuffed the money into his grubby trousers, 'Wait here Sir. I'll see what I can do'.

He disappeared but within a minute he returned with another man dressed in a grey suit who also spoke English with in a Spanish accent. 'What can I do for you Sir?'

'Would you mind if we speak in private?'

He looked at Bill nervously, 'Why?'

Bill took £50 from his pocket, ten £5 notes and in a similar manner fanned them out for maximum effect. 'I just want to ask a few questions, that's all.'

The receptionist starred at the money; he would have to work twelve hours a day for a month to earn that amount of money. 'What do you want to know?'

Bill pushed John's jacket into his hands. 'Do you recognise this? It belongs to one of your guests.'

He looked closely and replied 'Yes, he went out about two hours ago.'

'Good. I want to you to go and check his Passport and let me know who he is. Everything.'

'I could be dismissed for doing that.'

'I'm fully aware of that. That's why I'm offering you fifty pounds. Tell me who he is and don't ask any questions. Will you do that for me? No one else will ever know. I promise.'

He stared at the money again and licked his dry lips. This money would allow him to visit his family on the mainland and buy his three sons the best presents they ever had for Christmas. He convinced himself this was an opportunity to earn some money with the minimum of risk. This was a chance he could not ignore. Yet he was being tempted to break the Hotel's cardinal code of honour: confidentiality. But honour did not pay the bills. He took a deep breath and without any further prompting he spoke softly, 'Wait here.' He turned around and left the kitchen.

In less than five minutes, he returned. 'According to his Passport in our safe, his name is John Evans.'

'What other details?' asked Bill.

'He lives in Leeds in the County of the West Riding of Yorkshire.'

'Anything else?'

'Yes. He's a Police Officer.'

Bill's suspicions were now confirmed. The unknown woman coming to the house asking to see the old Colonel, the disappearance of the Jaguar from the underground carpark, the attempted break-in and the visit by the Police, all served to heighten his suspicion. They had been placed under surveillance and probably suspected for the murders. He slipped the money into the Spaniard's jacket pocket and left the kitchen to re-join Joe outside. He found him still rubbing his stomach. 'Come with me. I think we have to re-assess our position with the Boss.'

'What's happened Bill?'

'We're in deep shit. The Cops are on to us. We've just put one in hospital. If you hadn't have run away, we could have dumped him in the dock and given us more time to get out of here. I don't like it Joe. We must go and see his lordship; he's got powerful friends. And he's going to need them now. But let's go for a drink first.'

As Bill and Joe entered another bar, John was being admitted into the British Military Hospital some three hundred yards away from where he had fallen. He was initially placed in the Intensive Care Unit where he remained semi-conscious for several hours. Eventually, just before noon the following day he finally opened his eyes and saw the uniforms of the Civil Police standing at the edge of his hospital bed. Temporarily confused and with the worst headache of his life, he breathed a sigh of relief. Now he was safe. But what had happened and where was he?

50

'He's a bloody Copper,' exclaimed Bill to Charles Lewis.

'What!'

'I can't say I'm that surprised. Think about it, Boss; the strange woman calling at the Laurels asking for your father, the break-in and the Coppers stamping all over the house, especially down in the cellar.'

'And the Jaguar,' added Charles.

'And the Jag,' Bill confirmed.

'Are you sure he's a Police Officer?'

'Yes, there was absolutely no identification on him when we searched his clothing, so I checked at the Rock Hotel and his name is John Evans from Leeds. That was according to his Passport.'

'How the hell did you find that out Bill?'

'I crossed a couple of Spaniard's palms with some cash. Money always talks.'

'OK. Where is he now?'

'He's in the British Military Hospital. I couldn't find out anymore.'

'Is he going to survive?'

'Yes of course. He's got some strong shit going through his veins and probably a big lump on his head. But he's a young man; he'll survive. What do you want us to do next?'

'Nothing. Return to Leeds as we've discussed but go straight to the Hotel and wait for my instructions. I'll be coming home on Christmas Eve. Now Bill, I know it's Christmas in a couple of days but I can't stand you and Joe down, there may be a few things I want you to do. Don't worry, I'll be giving you a large bonus for your troubles but you must both keep a low profile. Do you understand?'

'Yes Boss.'

'Meanwhile, I'm going to make a telephone call to try and make this problem disappear.'

'You must have friends in high places?' enquired Bill.

'That's an understatement. Just make sure you're ready in Leeds when I call for you Bill. Christmas is cancelled this year.'

'Bugger,' whispered Joe.

51

DCI Sampson was busy chairing a meeting with his three Inspectors, discussing the Christmas duties and operational cover over the following week. Tomorrow was Christmas Eve. With no active serious investigations in his Division, he anticipated a skeleton cover. Yet his mind was elsewhere. John should be arriving in Manchester later in the afternoon and Phil had returned from Birmingham with no material evidence. As the meeting drew to a close, his telephone rang. He picked up the receiver and immediately heard the dulcet threatening voice of ACC Jenkins. 'Sampson, I want to see you in my office now!'

The phone went dead leaving him speechless. His colleagues looked on before the eldest Inspector asked, 'Is everything alright Mark?'

'Yes. ACC Jenkins wants to see me now apparently.'

'Don't worry, he wants to wish you a happy Christmas and offer you a drink.'

'Let's hope so,' he replied unconvincingly.

Thirty minutes later he nervously knocked on his door. 'Come in,' the voice bellowed from within. He entered but before he reached the desk, ACC Jenkins launched into a rage, shouting, 'Where the hell have you sent DC Evans?'

Half expecting the question, he replied, 'He's taken some leave Sir. Why?'

'Don't you bullshit me. He's recovering with a serious head wound in a Military Hospital in bloody Gibraltar. What's he doing there Sampson?'

'I don't know Sir. Why should this involve me?

ACC Jenkins paused before replying. 'I've been told he was observing Charles Lewis. Is this true?'

'No Sir. Frankly I've no idea what you're talking about.'

'Sampson, think very carefully before you answer my next question. Did you send Evans over there to look at Charles Lewis?'

DCI Sampson paused to consider his next move. This was a career-defining moment. He stepped closer towards him replying, 'Mr Jenkins, it is my genuine belief that Charles Lewis and two of his associates are strongly suspected for the murder of Mr Cox and the disappearance of Ronnie Ellis.'

'Didn't I give you specific instructions not to pursue him in your investigations?'

'Yes, you did. But you have also obstructed in me in the execution of my duties without fully explaining why.'

'How dare you speak to me like that ...'

'I haven't finished yet Mr Jenkins. Unless you explain to me to my satisfaction why you want to pull the plug on this investigation, I have no alternative but to take this matter to the Chief Constable himself.'

'I think you have said enough. I am relieving you immediately of your command and you will take garden leave[22] with immediate effect until further notice. You may return to your office to collect your belongings but on the way, you can go and see Mrs Evans and perhaps explain to her why her husband won't be coming home for Christmas. That's all. You're dismissed.'

'Before I go, can I ask you how you got to know about DC Evans circumstances before I did?'

'No, you can't. Your failure to obey my instructions has now caused me to make formal arrangements for DC Evans to be seen by the Governor General's Office. I shall have to deny this officer was engaged with any investigations over there and was just visiting Gibraltar as a private citizen. So far as I'm concerned, he can make his own arrangements to return to the UK. And when he does, I'll insist he submits a full report as to the circumstances. Sampson, this

---

[22] unofficial paid leave – suspended from duty

is a bloody mess and you will likely face disciplinary charges. Now get out of my office.'

'And a happy Christmas to you too,' he replied sarcastically.

As he walked towards the door ACC Jenkins shouted, 'Get back here Sampson!' Ignoring his last outburst, DCI Sampson continued towards the doorway, stopped and glanced backwards before slamming the heavy door shut in its frame. The sound caused the whole corridor to reverberate. He muttered defiantly to himself, 'Bollocks to you, I'm not finished with this yet.'

He returned to his office, collected his briefcase and all the papers relating to the Freddie Cox investigation and telephoned Phil. He said, 'Can't talk, meet me in the Regent pub in thirty minutes. It's urgent.'

'What's happened?' asked Phil.

'Apparently John's in a hospital in Gibraltar. No more talk.'

'Understood.'

The Regent was a popular meeting place for the Police. Unlike those Phil frequented, it was patronised by law abiding and good-mannered customers and boasted no less than seven lounges and snugs, ideal for private conversation. The two Detectives sat alone in one of them drinking their half pints of beer. Phil asked, 'What's happened to John?'

'I don't know. ACC Jenkins told me this morning before suspending me from duty.'

'He's done what?'

'Someone's tipped him off. He told me it was the Gibraltan Authorities had warned him but I don't believe that.'

'Me neither,' answered Phil.

'He knows I sent John over there to look at Charles Lewis. Something has happened, and poor John is now in a Military Hospital. I think he wants me out of the Service before I can make his life anymore awkward.'

'Listen Boss, I'm going out to Gibraltar today to get John. He could be in more danger over there than back here at home.'

'Yes, I know that Phil, but has ACC Jenkins been in touch with you yet?'

'No, but I bet the bastard's going to now.'

'I agree, you'd better make yourself scarce for the time being. Take some unexpected leave now and go and find John. I've still got some authority to grant you some additional expenses before they retire me permanently.'

'What are you going to do now?'

'Exactly what I've been told to do. I want you to take the papers for the case, I've got them all here for you. Jenkins wouldn't tell me how he got to find out about John. If he told me the Gibraltarian Authorities had informed him, then I would have taken that as face value. But I think there are other players behind the scenes who are pulling the strings. I told him I was going to see the Chief Constable but frankly, I don't trust him either.'

'You're right there. They all piss in the same pot. As far as I'm concerned, he could be following the same orders too and Jenkins is simply the messenger.'

'Eloquently put Sergeant Smith. But let's be serious. It's important you go out there, rescue John and bring him home first. If you can, try and find out whether the Authorities over there contacted our Mr Jenkins. If they did, all well and good. But it's my belief someone else may have found out about John and told those suits from Whitehall I saw in Jenkin's office the other week.'

'I'll try my best, but John is my priority.'

'Of course, I feel dreadful for sending him out there Phil, he's not as street wise as you and I.'

Phil placed a hand on his shoulder, 'Don't be stupid Mark. I'll go and sort this mess out and be back here with John as soon as I can.'

'Thanks Phil. There's one other important thing. When you and John are eventually questioned by Jenkins, you must tell him you were acting under my instructions. If you do that, you'll be able to blame me and perhaps discreetly carry on this investigation behind his back.'

'Do you want me to ring you at home?' asked Phil.

'No. The bastards may have my phone tapped, try my sister Margaret, she lives just two doors away from me. Ring her on this number when you've seen John. It doesn't matter what time it is, she won't mind. Jenkins has buggered up all our Christmases.'

'He's certainly done that. Fortunately, I've got a very sympathetic wife, unlike John. Mary's going to take this bad. I think she's away visiting her parents in Scarborough.'

'Don't worry about her, I'll go and see her and explain what's happened.'

'Good luck on that.'

After their meeting, DCI Sampson drove to John's house; unsure whether Mary was still away visiting her parents. But as he parked outside, by coincidence he saw her returning from the local shops, walking down the front garden path towards the front door. As she opened it, he approached her and asked, 'Hello, excuse me, but are you Mary?'

'Yes. Who are you?'

'My name is DCI Sampson and I need to talk to you about your John.'

Twenty minutes later, he left her tearful and bewildered. Because he was unsure about John injuries, he deliberately kept the purpose of his visit to Gibraltar vague, describing his condition as 'not serious.' Worse, he was unable to re-assure her John would be home for Christmas.

Whilst her love for her absent husband had diminished in recent times, she felt an overwhelming sense of duty to go and visit him, especially now he was in hospital. But DCI Sampson had told her his repatriation was already in progress. His colleague DS Smith was going out on the next available plane to make the arrangements. He had promised her to let her know of his condition, once John had been seen. Mary stared at their wedding photograph on the wall and burst into tears. 'What's happened to us John?' Suddenly, something unexplainable snapped inside her body. Wiping her face, she picked up the telephone and rang her parents in Scarborough.

Within ten minutes she packed her suitcase and rang for a taxi to take her to the Railway Station. Whilst waiting, she wrote a short note, 'Dear John I hope you have recovered but I have no idea where you are or what you are doing. If you want to speak to me, I'm spending Christmas with Mum and Dad.'

52

The plane touched down at Gibraltar on the runway between the Craggy Island and the Spanish mainland. As Phil stepped down onto the airstrip tarmac, he welcomed the warm gentle Mediterranean air brush his face. For a moment, he closed his eyes; the last time he was abroad during the winter, was fifteen years ago in Aden during his National Service. There, he was dodging bullets; hopefully this visit would be less hazardless.

Like John, he booked into the Rock Hotel and immediately walked directly to the Military Hospital. It was close to nine o'clock but after some persuasive pleading with the Night Matron, he managed to find him in a private room next to the main staircase. As he approached the bed, John opened his eyes and spoke softly, 'Am I glad to see you Phil, you ugly bastard.'

'Less of the ugly and remember Constable Evans, it's Sergeant Bastard to you.' They both smiled. Phil leant over the bed and gave his friend a welcomed embrace. 'Before you tell me what happened, how are you? What are your injuries?'

'I'm OK. I've got this large lump on my head with a few stitches and that ginger bastard injected some substance into me like he must have done with Freddie Cox. I've asked for a blood sample so we can compare it with Freddie's at the Morgue, but they've just ignored me.'

'Never mind about that. Have they given you a time when you can be discharged?'

'No, but I think they're only keeping me here under observations.

I really want to go home to see Mary.'

'The Boss was going to see her and tell her what's happened to you.'

'She's not going to be too well pleased to hear I'm here in Gibraltar.'

The door opened and the duty Doctor entered. 'Good evening Mr Evans. How are you feeling now?'

'I'm fine Doctor. I want to discharge myself and fly back the UK tomorrow.'

'I have no objections with that but you must continue with your medication and see your own Doctor back in the UK after Christmas.'

'Thank you. I'll go and see my Doctor later.'

With some assistance from Phil, he slowly dressed and limped out from the Hospital, walking purposefully back to the Rock Hotel. His head was still pounding and his breathing laboured. As they entered and approached the reception desk, the Spaniard behind the desk was astonished and relieved to see him again. Since accepting his bribe, he feared John's circumstances had been due to him betraying his identity to the ginger haired Englishman last night. This was true but with a sense of remorse, he said, 'Hello Mr Evans, we were all worried what happened to you after the Police came last night to tell us you were in hospital. May I ask you what happened?'

'Just had a disagreement with someone in a club that's all.'

'So long as you're alright now Sir. Thank God. Unfortunately, I'm afraid your room has been closed like most of them in the hotel for Christmas, but we still have your suitcase in the office and other belongings in the safe.'

'Don't worry about that, he can sleep in my room,' said Phil.

John asked, 'May I have my passport and the small package I left in your safe the other day please?'

'Of course, Sir.'

'What's in the package?' asked Phil.

'My little camera with, hopefully, plenty of incriminating photographs.'

Phil swung around to face John, 'You managed to take some snaps of those bastards?'

'I did, but we must make sure they don't fall into bad hands before the film is developed.'

'You crafty bugger. Well done.'

The Spaniard collected the keys from the shelf beneath the counter, but before leaving for the office where the safe was kept, he said 'Excuse me Sir. If you require some photographs to be developed, I have a cousin who owns a Chemist Shop just over the road from here. They will develop them tomorrow morning while you wait, for at a very competitive rate.'

John considered his suggestion, 'What time does the shop open?'

'It's opens at eight. I'll ring tonight to let them know you've a film to be developed urgently.'

Phil said, 'Our plane leaves at eleven, so that gives us plenty of time.'

John nodded and turned back towards the Spaniard, 'OK. If you can arrange that now, that would very helpful. Thank you.' He collected his passport and camera whilst Phil picked up his small suitcase. Together, they climbed the shallow stairs to the first floor and retired to the bedroom. Once inside, John collapsed onto the bed fully clothed and fell into a deep sleep, leaving Phil on the sofa wanting desperately to ask his friend exactly what had happened to him.

With John snoring loudly on his bed, he placed a telephone call to Margaret, DCI Sampson's sister. After apologising for the lateness of the hour, within five minutes a voice answered, 'Phil, is everything alright?'

'Yes. I've got John here with me in the Hotel, sleeping on my bed; can't you hear him? I haven't had the chance to speak to him properly yet. It seems he was drugged like Freddie Cox before being abducted. He's got a nasty cut to his head, otherwise he'll be fine. Incidentally, he's taken some photographs which we're getting developed in the morning before we fly back.'

'Good, make sure no one sees them but you two. Now listen Phil, apparently Jenkins has been looking for you and suspects you're over there. When you come back, he'll want to see you both immediately; you must tell him you were obeying my orders like I told you. If you don't, he'll suspend you both too and then we'll never be in any position to get to the bottom of this. At least with you both still serving, we have a chance. Do you understand Phil? It's really important?'

'Yes Mark. Don't worry I'll tell him it's all your fault. You're right, with John and myself still on the inside, we have a better chance of sorting all this mess out. Perhaps we can also get you back to work before you retire.'

'Perhaps. By the way, my friend at SOCO has examined the Jag in your secret den and took some finger prints and fibres samples of clothing from inside. All we need is a copy of prints from those two characters and seize Freddie Cox's clothes from the Coroner's Officer and have them both compared.'

'Don't worry, I'll try and deal with that too. Is it possible you can meet us at Manchester tomorrow? The plane arrives about four-thirty.'

'Yes, no problem. I'll see you then.'

Phil replaced the telephone and laid back on the small sofa thinking how the investigation was progressing. Not well. He began to plan a new approach. The interference from ACC Jenkins and the suspension of his old friend DCI Mark Sampson only confirmed his determination to root out those responsible for John's dilemma. He was going to play by his rules from now on, using the Christmas spirit of goodwill to maximise his evil yet well-meaning intentions.

53

John was first to wake up. It was Christmas Eve and although he continued to suffer from a severe headache, his energy levels had slowly returned aided by a cool shower and change of clothing. Sitting on the edge of his bed, he picked up the telephone and placed a call to Mary, unsure of her reception. But after several minutes there was no answer. He now suspected she had gone to see her parents. He replaced the receiver and walked over to the window. Looking outside, the dawn was breaking, revealing Royal Navy ships neatly moored in the harbour below. He began to reflect on the state of his marriage. The present he had bought had been lost and with no funds to replace it, this was not going to be the happiest of Christmases, especially on his own.

Phil eventually stirred from his less comfortable slumbers and within thirty minutes they were enjoying their breakfast in the Hotel restaurant. John relayed all the events that had occurred two days previously. Afterwards, Phil told him what had happened to DCI Sampson. John exclaimed, 'It's bloody dreadful what's happened to Mark Sampson; he's an honourable, conscientious hard-working copper, like us. Why should he be treated like this at the end of his career?'

'Probably to save the careers of others,' replied Phil.

'We must do something to change that.'

'Don't worry my friend, I've already made plans.'

'Hell Phil, this sounds bloody ominous.'

'Not really. When we arrive back in the UK, we have to convince

Jenkins we were ordered by DCI Sampson to come over here. If we can show we had no choice but to do as we were told, we've a chance of staying where we are in the Antique Squad.'

'Yes, I understand that. But it's still not right all the same. We'll have to pretend to be fall into line.'

'Something like that. But as you know, that doesn't come natural to my habits either,' complained Phil.

'You'll have to work on your subservience, Sergeant Smith.'

'Get stuffed Constable Evans. Listen, it's nearly eight o'clock, let's go pack our things and take the film over to the road to get it developed. That still gives us plenty of time to catch the plane to whatever future we have with the Leeds City Police.'

Twenty minutes later they entered the Pharmacist. The shop had remained unchanged for decades. It was darkly lit with wooden panels everywhere, shelves displaying countless apothecary jars and cupboards stretching from the rickety floor to old oak beamed uneven ceiling above. A middle-aged couple stood behind the counter.

John produced the small role of film to the Spaniard. 'Did your cousin phone you last night about an urgent film we would like to develop before we return home?' To his surprise, the woman approached and spoke, 'Oh yes, my cousin phoned last night about this. I'll go and develop it now. How many copies of prints do you require?'

'Two please,' replied John.

Turning to her husband, 'Julio, I'm going into the back to develop this film. Please look after the shop.'

As she held her hand out to collect the camera, Phil stepped forward, 'I'm sorry for asking, but these photographs may prove to be legally important in an English Court of Law. I must insist that one of us is present whilst you develop them. Of course, we'll pay you extra for any inconvenience.' She looked surprised but simply nodded her head in agreement, glancing at her husband for his approval. He shrugged his shoulders in a nonchalant manner. Phil turned to John, 'You must go with her as you took the photographs to keep the continuity of the evidence trail.'

'Hell Phil, I'm impressed. You're keeping to the rules of evidence for a change.'

'Don't get too carried away. Once we're out of here and back on my own turf, all hell's going to be break out.'

Under the red light, two copies of thirty-eight black and white prints were developed. After processing them, she placed two sets of copies into envelopes and handed them to John, before returning to the shop. Phil paid for them with his recently acquired expenses, courtesy of the Chief Constable and looked immediately at the images. Nodding his head with approval, he said, 'Nice one John.'

He was especially interested in the appearances of the three men and the flat belonging to Ron Earl in Nelson House.

'I'll take one copy and you the other.'

'Good idea,' agreed John.

'Come on, let's get down to the airport.'

'You can hardly call it an airport,' sighed John 'The terminal is a small building at the side of a runway that starts and ends in the sea.'

'You're right my friend, but it's going to be the next step before we get home.'

'Yes, I tried to contact Mary this morning. She's not at home, probably gone to Scarborough. So, I've no idea what's waiting for me at home.'

'I'm sure everything will be alright when you walk through the front door,' Phil said unreassuringly.

'We'll see.'

They strode down the hill towards the airport carrying their suitcases. There was increased activity today, with the vast majority of aircraft belonging to the RAF. Only recently had Gibraltar been opened to regular scheduled civil aviation, with only two flights to the UK; one to Heathrow, the other Manchester. Their flight was the last available plane before the whole base closed down for the Christmas holidays.

As they approached the small tiny wooden terminal, a remnant of the last World War, Phil suddenly pulled John's arm and nodded. 'Look at the man getting out of that car. Isn't that Charles Lewis?'

'Let's have another look at the photographs,' suggested John.

'Yes, it's definitely him,' exclaimed Phil. 'He's never seen us has he?'

'I don't think so, only his thugs.'

'Are they here with him?'

'I can't see them,' replied John.

'Right, this is what we're going to. You catch the plane with Lewis but try to keep out of his view. I'm staying here. When you get to Manchester, Mark Sampson will meet you there; he'll be expecting us both. Tell him the whole of Gibraltar has closed down for the holidays. This gives me the chance of finding out a little more about Charles Lewis and the company he keeps. I don't want any arguments from you. I'll remain here until the day after Boxing Day, when I'll try and get a flight back.'

'Where are you going to stay?' asked John.

'The Hotel will bound to have an empty room even over Christmas. Don't worry about that, just go and leave this with me. I'm going to find out more about these bastards before they hurt us anymore. It's personal now, John. You go back home and spend some time with Mary.'

'What about your Jane and the girls?'

'Obviously, I wish I was home with my girls, but they've become used to it. Anyway, I've promised them all a holiday in the sun at Easter. Apparently, there's a new destination, according to Jane; it's called Majorca. It's warm for most of the year and not too far from where we're standing right now.'

'OK. But promise me Phil, please don't do anything too stupid, will you?'

'Just give me that fancy camera before you go.'

John reached into his pocket and handed it over. 'Take these two roles of film as well. It's all automatic. Please, make sure you don't lose it, or I'll be back in uniform before the new year.'

'Bugger off and leave me in peace.'

They both smiled at each other. John shook Phil's hand and walked towards the wooden building, turning around to wave at his friend before disappearing through the front door. Phil collected his case and walked back across the road and headed directly back to the Rock Hotel, hoping there was room for him on Christmas Eve. The Biblical irony was not lost on him.

As he arrived back, the last guest was checking out. The Spanish receptionist appeared puzzled, 'Is there anything wrong Sir? We are about to close for the week until the new year.'

'Not really. I just need somewhere to stay over for the next few days. I've got some urgent business that can't wait.'

The Spaniard knew John Evans was a Police Officer. He had read this on his Passport and so assumed this man must be too. He could still feel the bundle of pound notes bulging in his jacket pocket and the imminent threat of being discovered as a disloyal servant to the Rock Hotel. A feeling of guilt and regret now grew in his stomach. He was spending Christmas with his family on the mainland. What could he do for this unfortunate Police Officer?

Then he remembered the spare room in the basement, served by an exterior door and used in cases of emergency when members of staff were locked out at night time. 'Mr Smith, I can let you have the small room downstairs until we re-open again. It's very basic with only a bed, toilet and wash basin. But it's clean and there's a small cooker. If you go to the shop on the corner, you'll be able to buy enough food to last you a couple of days. After then, some of the local cafes will be open and there's always the Military Base near the Harbour where they have their own shop. The NAFFI, I think they call it.'

'Thanks very much. I'll take it,' he replied.

Five minutes later, Phil was sat on the edge of his single bed. He was going to have a busy Christmas and he knew exactly what to do and where to start. Get some food and visit Nelson House.

54

The return flight was uneventful. Before boarding, John checked to see if Charles Lewis was travelling alone and not accompanied by his 'minders.' Sitting eight rows behind him in the opposite aisle, John remained out of his vision, hidden by a newspaper. He was taking no chances, never averting his gaze away.

Finally, the plane landed at Manchester in the darkly lit and damp afternoon, he remained in his seat until Charles Lewis had stepped off the plane and began walking towards the large terminal. Entering the lounge, John held back to see if Charles Lewis was collecting his suitcase from the arrivals carousel. No, he walked straight through the exit, past the 'nothing to declare' desk, carrying only his brief case. John followed through the same doors and immediately saw DCI Sampson waiting behind the barrier. 'Merry Christmas John and welcome home.'

'Merry Christmas Sir.'

'You can call me Mark until I get re-instated. We've got lots to talk about on our way back to Yorkshire.'

'Did you see Charles Lewis? He was on the same flight?'

'No. Remember I've no idea what he looks like.'

'I'll show you an image of him when we get in the car. I've got some good photos of him and his thugs.'

'Marvellous. Wait a minute. Where the hell's Phil?'

'He's decided to stay, after seeing Charles Lewis board the plane.'

'Hell, I know what that means.'

'There's something else I've got to tell you on the way back. But before we talk, I must ring Mary to tell her I'll be home soon.'

'Sure, there's some phones over there near the exit.'

For over two minutes the home telephone rang out without reply. He tried again. No answer. He stepped out from the small kiosk and asked 'Sir, have you seen her?'

'Yes, I saw her yesterday after my meeting with ACC Jenkins. She had just returned home from shopping. Obviously, she was upset to hear what had happened to you but unfortunately, I didn't know exactly what had happened to you. Jenkins told me he had been notified by the Gibraltan Authorities about you but when I pressed him further, he threw me out of his office. I'm now suspended until further notice. I sent Phil out to bring you back.'

'Yes, Phil told me that. I'm really sorry to hear that. Can I ask you how Mary reacted when you told me I was in Gibraltar?'

'John my boy, I can't lie to you. She couldn't understand why you were over there and hadn't contacted her. Naturally, I tried to convince her you were very busy investigating a major crime and sometimes communication was impossible. That was all I could say. I bet she's gone to see her parents until you return home. I'm sure she'll be happy to see you.'

'Those bastards stole my wallet and Mary's present, including the house keys. It's going to be a crap and lonely Christmas.'

On their return journey to Yorkshire both men had the opportunity of telling each other in detail what had happened since their last meeting. DCI Sampson was insistent, 'John, when we get back, take a few days off and return to work as normal. I can promise you, Jenkins will be seeing you immediately. It's imperative you tell him I ordered you to go to Gibraltar. That way, with a bit of luck and some acting on your part, you will remain in post and hopefully, safeguard your promising career. I've told Phil exactly the same. With both of you still working as Detectives, something may happen. We just need get lucky.'

John described in detail his movements following the three men and the connection with Ron Earl's apartment in Nelson House, where Charles Lewis was staying. He was less informative about Phil's motives for remaining there, attempting to appease his concerns, 'I think he was just going to tie a few loose ends up. That's all.'

'Let's hope John, for both our sakes, he doesn't do anything stupid or we're in deeper trouble than we are already now.'

At exactly 6 p.m., the car came to a halt outside John's house. It was in complete darkness. 'Hell, she's not in and I don't have a key.'

'I'll get you inside your house without any damage, that's no problem John, but do you really want to stay in there on Christmas Eve alone? You're very welcome to come and stop with us.'

'No thanks Sir. I'll be OK. Just show me how you can break into my house.'

'Come with me.'

They both stepped out of the car. DCI Samson lifted the boot lid and took out his blue coloured tool box. Reaching forward and fumbling in the dimly lit compartment, he produced a large brace and drill complete with a medium sized bit, a two-foot long curved steel rod and a lump of putty. 'Bring the torch, John.'

As they walked towards the house along the footpath, he turned to John, 'Which of these windows has the best wooden frames?'

'The bay at the front.'

'Good. Have you got any step-ladders or something for me to stand on?'

'Just a minute.'

A few moments later, John re-appeared with a wooden stool he found in the garden shed. Without any hesitation, DCI Sampson stood on top and began to twist the brace and bit in a clockwise motion. The drill quickly penetrated the wood and exited inside fractionally below the handle. He withdrew the bit and inserted the metal rod, easing it gently upwards until the handle flicked away from its holding. Pulling the rod towards him, he bent it further, allowing its curve to become more exaggerated. Once again, he inserted the rod until it reached the latch on the sill. With some delicacy, he manipulated it sufficiently to loosen its grip, causing it to spring upwards and release the window. He stepped away from the stool, 'I think you can manage the rest John. Just remember to fill the hole with some of this putty. When it sets, give it a lick of paint.'

'Where did you learn that from Sir?'

Tapping the side of his nose, he said, 'Old school son, old school. I'm going home now; ring me if you need anything. Otherwise get into work the day after Boing Day if you can. Happy Christmas John.'

Once inside, John switched on the lights and found the note Mary had left. He was right. She had gone to see her parents in Scarborough but they had no telephone. He would have to drive in their old Morris 1000. But not tonight. He was exhausted and desperately needed to sleep.

55

As John fell into a deep sleep, back in Gibraltar Phil was busy taking advantage of the chaotic Christmas Eve celebrations. Although the hotels were closed, the bars were enjoying a brisk upsurge in the sale of alcohol, with the majority of customers being sailors in uniform on shore leave. Clearly, all had ignored the orders to behave themselves and not to bring the 'Senior Service' into disrepute as their singing and loud incoherent voices becoming louder with every drink. The Military Police were overwhelmed, often turning a 'blind eye' to verbal disturbances, dealing only with those engaged in violence or serious disorder.

Phil had studied the photographs of Nelson House and made his way through the Main Street where most of celebrations were in full swing. He stooped down to pick up an empty beer bottle, held it loosely between his fingers and continued with a slight stagger. To an unsuspecting eye, he was like all the revellers, enjoying his night out.

Within ten minutes, he entered the front foyer to Nelson House where he glanced at the board displaying the flats and their occupiers, he quickly recognised Flat 36 – R. Earl. It was just as John had mentioned, on the third floor. He pressed the button to summon the lift. His heart rate began to increase as he stepped inside the wooden panelled compartment and ascended. The doors opened automatically to reveal a plush carpeted corridor with six apartments, three on both sides. Number 36 was at the far end, on the left. He stopped for a moment to listen for any sounds. It was all silent. The whole building was as quiet as the grave. He approached the door displaying '36 R-Earl' and he pressed the doorbell. If someone answered he had a story ready. Holding his empty bottle of beer, he pretended to be foolishly drunk. But no one came.

He knelt down and recognised the key to be a standard three lever mortice lock. Reaching into his coat pocket he produced his prized possession; a set of skeleton keys for a variety of lock manufacturers. He had confiscated these several years previously from a recidivist house burglar. Once convicted and sentenced to prison, the Court had issued an order for their destruction of these keys, handing them over to Phil for him to carry this out. Several days later, he signed the necessary paper work, endorsing the property had been destroyed in the Leeds Municipal Incinerator; 'Would never be used in crime again.' Since then, Phil had used them occasionally where legal channels to enter premises were denied.

It took less than two minutes before he heard the lock tumblers quietly click. Checking behind him, he turned the door handle and stepped inside, quietly closing it behind him.

He waited a few minutes for his eyes to become accustomed to the dark before approaching each of the windows in turn and closing the thick curtains. He switched on his small torch and returned to the entrance door and turned the main lights on. The décor was both expensive and luxurious, with soft cream leather sofas resting on an enormous Persian carpet. Original oil paintings adorned all the walls. The living room was open plan, with large windows facing towards the harbour on two sides and another door leading along a short passageway to a small kitchen and two large bedrooms. At the far end laid the bathroom and a walk-in wardrobe.

Phil soon located the personal hand-written telephone book tucked inside the small table drawer. He photographed the pages and noticed a loose piece of paper with some scribbling on. Carefully, he straightened it and saw written 'Bill and Joe - 27 Jubilee Gardens.'

'Bingo,' he whispered to himself. Could that be here in Gibraltar? He snapped a photograph, before placing it back inside the book. He continued with his search, ensuring nothing was disturbed, leaving no signs of disturbance as he moved swiftly between rooms. Eventually, he found a brown leather briefcase inside a cupboard of the master bedroom. It was closed with both the metal catches containing three-number combination locks. He memorised all six numbers before attempting to release them. Turning the catches outwards, to his amazement, both sprung open, releasing the metal case flaps.

Obviously, Charles Lewis was not anticipating any one snooping around in here.

He peered inside and noticed four folders of loose papers. He delicately lifted out all the files together, resting them on the carpet before him, spreading them out in a line. He centred his attention on the first file; it contained invoices for large quantities of side arms and automatic rifles with the relevant ammunition from Boddington Arms Manufactures, Birmingham. The second and third files revealed dozens of permits and export licences to most Countries within the Commonwealth. The fourth and final was the most interesting. These papers referred to a large transaction of medium armaments manufactured by the British Ordinance Company (BOC) in Leeds, the agent being Charles Lewis, underwritten by the Ministry of Defence. The destination simply stated, 'South Africa Export.' Attached to the main file were the records of meetings between Charles Lewis, Ron Earl and other directors of BOC. Phil was about to skip to the next page when he noticed the date of the meeting. It was the evening before Ronnie Ellis committed the burglary at the Laurels and Freddie Cox met with his fate on the railway line. He photographed all the papers and returned them into the briefcase.

Behind one of the paintings he located a Burg Watcher wall safe, far too difficult for him to tamper with. However, he had successfully connected Charles Lewis with the Government and the possible explanation as to why ACC Jenkins had been instructed by Whitehall to 'play down' any investigation, serious or otherwise, that could implicate him in any way. He returned to all the areas of his search, double-checking to ensure everything had been returned to its exact original position. He quickly glanced across the living room before switching the lights off. Everything was where it should be.

In the darkness, he drew back the curtains and slowly opened the outside door, peering along the communal corridor. Waiting for a moment, he walked out and approached the lift. Then he heard the quiet whirling noise of the winding gear operating within the elevator shaft. Someone was coming up. Taking no chances, he sprinted towards the stairway and ran down the stairs two at a time, until he reached the reception area. It was empty and within seconds he stood outside in the cool night air. His next visit was 27 Jubilee Gardens.

As he returned towards the Main Street, he saw two members of the Military Police in their distinctive red caps. He dropped the empty bottle of beer over a low wall and approached them. 'Excuse me Gentlemen. I'm looking for Jubilee Gardens. Can you tell me where this address is please?'

The Corporal replied, 'Yes Sir. If you walk down this side of the road, you'll eventually come to an old stone archway, it's part of the old fortifications, turn right and make your way towards the Docks. Jubilee Gardens is the row of old houses on the right.'

'Thanks very much. I hope you have a quiet night.'

He smiled through the corner of his mouth, 'Now you're taking the piss Sir.'

'Sorry, but thanks anyway.'

Phil left them to continue their unenvious checks of the bars. He remembered, as a uniform Constable, working on Christmas and New Year's Eves; by far the worst tours of duty in the calendar year. Everyone smelled of alcohol and mainly fell into two groups. Those who loved you and wanted to kiss and buy you a drink, or the others who held a pathological hatred and wanted to rip your throat out. It was absolutely impossible attempting to rationalise with people who were under the influence of drink.

Following their directions, it took Phil only ten minutes to find himself standing outside the front door of 27 Jubilee Gardens, a middle-terraced house facing the Dockyard and dimly lit from the small street light nearby. All the houses including this one, were in darkness with no sign of life. He stooped down to look through the letter box. Nothing but darkness from within. He examined the lock and found it to be something he had never seen before. Probably of an old crude Spanish type and as old as the house dating back to the mid-nineteenth century. The key would be large and very heavy. In fact, too heavy to carry back to the UK. He pondered. What would he do with a key that size? Keep it somewhere safe and handy. He looked along the front of the houses and saw several enormous terracotta urns the size of beer barrels, containing differing sized oleander shrubs. He walked to the nearest and fondled about in the weeds covering the soil. With a warm sense of smugness and joy he immediately felt a metal object and removed it from the foliage. A large iron key.

He approached the front door again and offered the key to the loosely fitting, well-worn key hole. And with the slightest of turns he opened the rickety old door on its enormous hinges. He looked behind him in all directions before stepping inside. There was no one in sight. Using his torch, he shone it into the room. Unlike Nelson House, this was an austere and poorly furnished house with few comforts. There were no curtains to close here, only dilapidated wooden blinds hanging precariously from their brackets. This gave him no choice but to use his torch as he searched the small house. His first move was to locate and open the rear door leading into a back courtyard. It was surrounded by an embankment of shrubs that adjoined to other yards beyond. This was his instant escape route if disturbed.

His prime objective was to attempt to establish the identities of the two men. He looked around and instantly noticed several items of significant value. The first was a photograph, propped up against an old clock on the fireplace; two soldiers in Royal Marine uniforms holding their automatic weapons in the air and smiling broadly into the camera. Written below; 'Captain Bill Jones & Lieutenant Joe Mason Aden 1961.' He instantly recognised them as the same on his photographs and remembered his tours of duty out there in that hot and foreboding country. But that was several years before this was taken. Sat on a low table were two small wine glasses with traces of dregs at the bottom. He could clearly see under his torch beam several good quality fingerprints on both.

He seized the photograph and emptied the dirty glasses on the floor before placing them inside a plastic envelope. Hopefully, the fingerprints would yield an exact match with those in the Jaguar. As he continued his search, he saw the stairs leading to the bedrooms. This was a dilemma; ascending these would leave him vulnerable; temporarily preventing his escape. He decided to take the risk. He bolted upstairs and shone his torch into the darkest of areas of the two bedrooms discovering only dirty clothing on the floor and unmade beds.

Quickly, he turned around and went downstairs and turned left into the kitchen. Surprisingly, this was clean and tidy. He swung his torch across the empty worktops and inside the open cupboards before turning his attention to the floor. Unlike the rest of the tidy room, he saw a large waste bin, brimming with fresh potato peelings and stale bread. The smell suggested the food was perhaps only two to three days old. They had obviously left at short notice.

As he began to rummage through the mess, disturbing several

empty bottles of beer and discarded food holders and old newspapers, he noticed an empty whisky bottle. He picked it out and suddenly saw something familiar. Two crumpled red and white bubble gum wrapping papers, tucked down the side of the waste bin. He whispered, 'Hell Ronnie, I'm finding these everywhere I go.' Once again, he took several images of the wrappers in situ before also placing them inside another envelope.

He stopped to look at his watch. He had been inside for over fifteen minutes. Too long. Switching off his torch, he closed and locked the back door and made his way towards the front. Slowly, he opened it and checked for any movement outside. Nothing. Only the noise coming from the dozens of bars in the town centre several hundred yards away. He double checked for any sign of his intrusion before closing the door shut and locking it. Finally, he walked passed the terracotta urn and tossed the old key back into the shallow undergrowth.

Phil breathed a sigh of relief as he walked back the Rock Hotel. Half an hour later, as he laid on his bed inside the servant's room, he reflected on his circumstances. Although it had been a fruitful night of discovery, he was a long way from home and his family on Christmas Eve. The next few days would mark the worst Christmas in his life, alone and hiding from his Assistant Chief Constable. 'Interesting times,' he mused, but promising to himself he would never be absent from Jane and his girls again this time of the year for the rest of his life.

56

The dawn of Christmas Day brought mixed blessings for the Police Officers. Towards noon, the telephone rang next to John's pillow, rescuing him from a disturbed and restless sleep. He picked up the receiver, 'Hello John, this is Mary. When did you get back?'

Drowsily he replied, 'Late last night. Are you still at your Mum and Dad's?'

'Yes. Will you come over here? I didn't know when you were coming home and I've been really worried about you John.'

'Yes of course. I need to find the car keys. I'll be there later this afternoon.' As she replaced the receiver, his spirits rose. Perhaps he could try to make amends and save their marriage. She sounded concerned and the last few days had been fraught with stress and danger. He was lucky to be alive and after all, it was Christmas. He showered and dressed. Eventually he found the spare front door key and then embarked on the two-hour journey to Scarborough in the temperamental Morris 1000.

*

Meanwhile, Phil was resting on his bed in the Servant's room beneath the Rock Hotel waiting for the next available flight back to Manchester. Fortunately, he managed to speak to Jane and his girls from a public telephone box Although they were disappointed in not seeing him, their spirits rose too when he promised he would take them on holiday abroad in the next summer holiday.

DCI Mark Sampson was less fortunate. His wife Helen had developed another migraine followed by bouts of dizziness and nausea. She had become extremely anxious about her husband's career, worrying if he would ever return to work. How would that effect his pension? Would they be able to retire to Devon as they had always planned after all? By nature, he had been a private husband never discussing his work at home. Whenever she asked him about his work, he always replied, 'Helen, I leave all my problems there. I don't want to bring them home.'

She had respected this. But this time it was different; if his pension was lost or even reduced, this affected her too.

57

If DCI Sampson was having a miserable Christmas Day, ACC James Jenkins's was even worse. The Chief Constable, William Steele, rang him while he was playing with his grandchildren. 'Jim, I've just had the Police Liaison Executive at the Home Office on the phone screaming at me to the effect that an officer from his force had been interfering with the movements of a highly respected agent belonging to the Ministry of Defence, namely Charles Lewis. He reminded me this was the second instruction from the Ministry relating to this matter and of the potential major political fallout for the Government and in particular, yours. Under no circumstances was this investigation to progress any further, otherwise I would be advised by the Home Secretary to dispense with your services.'

'What? It's Christmas day for God's sake.'

'Never mind about that Jim, I thought we had all this under control. What the hell's happening?'

'DC Evans went to Gibraltar without my knowledge and DS Smith has disappeared on leave. I made it crystal clear to all of them I wanted this investigation winding down. I gave DCI Sampson specific instructions to ensure these orders were carried out to the letter. He gave me his word this would be done. After we both found out about DC Evans landing up in hospital in Gibraltar, you decided to suspend DCI Sampson and quarantine DS Smith from all further investigations. In fact, you recommended they be returned to Divisional uniform duties. However, I suggested that wasn't necessary as it would attract the intervention of the 'Federation'[23] and you agreed with that for the time being.'

'Yes, I know that, but London are furious. They have threatened me with a 'D' notice on any statements I give in response to this affair becoming public, citing bloody National Security. This Charles Lewis appears to wield enormous political influence and we could become casualties if we don't take full control immediately. I want DC Evans and DS Smith reigned in. Now.'

'OK. But I've no idea where DS Smith is, he's not at work nor at home. He's taken some leave and disappeared.'

'Have you checked to see if he's at home?'

'Yes. I spoke to his wife. She doesn't even know where he is.'

'That's unusual. Surely, he must have told her, it's Christmas for Christ sake?'

'He's old school. Even if he had done, she wouldn't tell us.'

'What about DC Evans?'

'As far as I know he's still in Gibraltar. I'll contact the hospital to see how long he's going to be there, but I'm going to struggle today. Most of the international lines will be down.'

'Bugger. When they surface, get them in your office and officially take him off the case before transferring them back to Divisional CID. And make sure they're kept busy. DCI Sampson can stay where he is; we'll pension him off as soon as we can.'

'It's a pity. DCI Sampson has had an exemplary service record and is well respected by most of our officers.'

'I don't care, Jim. He's history and I'm the Chief Constable. Get these two other officers found and trim their feathers. So far as Sampson is concerned, I don't want him ever to return to duty. Get rid of him. That's an order!'

'Yes, Chief Constable.'

The line went dead but he still held the receiver tightly in his hand. Slowly, he replaced it and looked into the mirror on the wall, starring at the furrows in his forehead and well-defined bags under his eyes. With over thirty-two years service, he and his wife Marjorie had been planning to retire to Portugal the following year. But the stress of the

---

[23] Police Federation – similar to a trade union for rank and file officers from Constable to Chief Inspector

'Lewis' affair had brought him sleepless nights and a sharp rise in his blood pressure. He returned to the living room, ignoring his grandchildren and sank into the deep cushioned sofa, contemplating his future. He had little respect for William Steele, the newly appointed Chief Constable transferred on promotion from Manchester. As an outsider, he had no knowledge of the force or even the city boundaries, spending more time playing golf with the civil dignitaries than at his desk. He was keen to delegate most of his responsibilities to his Deputy and three Assistant Chief Constables, including himself.

He weighed up his options. Acquiesce with William Steele and his political cronies or stand by his officers, risking an earlier than expected retirement. His Christmas was now in ruins and today he faced the biggest decision of his career. Play the game or take the honourable path irrespective of the consequences. Eventually, following two large brandies and two hours of reflection, he finally came to a decision. Nodding his head, he whispered to himself, 'That's it. I know what I must do.'

Within those few moments, the rest of his life irretrievably changed.

58

ACC Jenkins attempted to contact the Military Hospital in Gibraltar but there were no available operators working on the main international switchboard. Replacing the telephone, he resigned to accept tracing Phil and John was going to be impossible. However, at least he knew where DCI Sampson was and decided to make a telephone call.

'Is that DCI Sampson?' he asked.

'Yes. Who's this?'

'Mr Sampson, this is ACC Jenkins. I appreciate it's Christmas day but I need to speak with you now. It's a matter of great urgency. May I come and see you now?'

'But I'm suspended. Don't you remember?'

'Yes of course I do, but it's very important and I think it's in both our interests if we meet up this afternoon.'

'My wife is in bed sick. If you come here, you'd better reconsider my position before I let you through my door.'

'If you agree to see me, then perhaps after we've spoken, I will be a position to rescind your suspension.'

'Very well. But don't ask me to do anything that will compromise my reputation.'

'Of course not. I'll be there in half an hour.'

As the old Grandfather clock set in the hallway corner struck three o'clock, the front bell rang loudly. DCI Sampson opened the 1930s fan styled stained-glass door and reluctantly invited the Assistant Chief Constable inside. Without any welcome, he curtly said, 'I won't wish you a happy Christmas and, frankly, I think you've got a bloody cheek coming here to see me today of all days.'

'Yes, Mr Sampson I understand your annoyance, but you must give me a hearing.'

'Come in here and sit down,' pointing towards the living room.

'Are you alone?' he asked.

'No, as I told you, my wife is unwell and in bed. She is too upset to hear what you have to say and you're probably the last person in the world she would want to see.'

Both men sat down facing each other. There was an uncomfortable calmness before ACC Jenkins began, 'What I'm about to tell you is in the strictest of confidence. No one, I mean no one, should be privy to what I'm about to tell you. Before I go any further, do I have your guarantee and assurance on this?'

'Yes. Go on.'

'When DS Smith and DC Evans first brought this affair involving our local criminals Ronnie Ellis and Freddie Cox to your attention, you had no idea what a Pandora's Box you were opening. After you made the inquiry with one of your old contacts in Westminster about Colonel Julian Lewis, a number of alarm bells rang in the darkest corners of several Government buildings. It wasn't the Colonel they were concerned about, but his son Charles.'

'Why?'

'Have you any idea what he does?'

'Not really, but I suspect he's involved with the sales of arms because of his connection with BOC here in Leeds and his business partner, Ron Earl, a Director for Boddingtons Guns in Birmingham.'

'Yes, you're right. Before I say any more, I don't have any proof of this but I also believe he supplies arms to rogue states and organisations with the knowledge of the Ministry of Defence.'

'So why are you telling me this Mr Jenkins?'

'I've been under a great deal of pressure from the Chief Constable to pull the plug on any investigations concerning Charles Lewis.'

'Why do you think that?'

'There's one thing I've come to recognise since I was appointed Assistant Chief Constable. Treachery. Charles Lewis appears to enjoy the favour and protection of many influential people, inside and out of Government. As you know, the scandal of the Profumo Affair effectively brought the previous Government down and was unable to hold onto power even with the appointment of Sir Alex Douglas Hume following Macmillan. The recent General Election has heralded in a new Labour administration with Harold Wilson. It is the considered opinion of Whitehall that this Government is being scrutinised by the Press and one more embarrassing disclosure could sweep them away too, triggering a Constitutional crisis. Public confidence in the rule of law could flounder.'

'What are you suggesting?'

'Mr Sampson, I know I've been a thorough bastard to you and your staff, attempting to interfere with the investigation surrounding the suspicious deaths of Freddie Cox, the taxi-driver Jim Simms and the disappearance of Ronald Ellis. For that, I apologise unreservedly. If you had not spoken to your contact in the Ministry of Defence regarding Charles Lewis, perhaps your investigations would not have been thwarted from the beginning. Conversely, I've little doubt some influence would have eventually been used to impede our efforts, once Lewis had been formally interviewed. What I'm about to tell you is in the strictest of confidence. I must have your assurance on this before I continue.'

'Mr Jenkins, you and I have served with the Force for a considerably long time. Although our paths have never crossed, I can promise you I will remain silent on anything you tell me, providing it's not contrary to the law, or places my staff in jeopardy. I'm not prepared to sacrifice their careers to protect yours or mine.'

'Excellent. Now will you allow me to continue and may I call you Mark?'

'Not for the moment Mr Jenkins. Let me hear what you have to say first.'

'OK. Having spoken with the Chief Constable Mr Steele, I'm satisfied that Charles Lewis is working on behalf of the Government. Perhaps not directly, but certainly as an Agent. His line of business is...'

'Arms Dealer,' interrupted DCI Sampson.

'Yes, that's right. But I suspect he's involved with the supply of arms to the opposing side the Government openly deals with.'

'How do you mean?'

'It's all about our National Wealth. If the country exports more than imports, the wealth of the country increases. When it comes to Government Departments, the Treasury is by far the most important of all, even more than our Justice Department. Charles Lewis appears to be involved with the sales of this invisible and clandestine arms market. The way the Country's balance of payments and finance are concerned at the moment, the UK makes enormous profits by supplying both the Governments and their opposing parties.'

'Aren't there International laws forbidding this trade?'

'Yes. That's why it's political dynamite. The deaths of some of our local criminals are, I'm afraid to say, too insignificant to expose.'

'Bloody hell. We're caught in the middle, aren't we?'

'Exactly.'

'So where does that leave me?'

'Until my recent conversation with the Chief, out in the cold. But I've now had time to reflect on what he said to me.'

'And what is that?'

'I'm not going to dance to his tune any more. He might have sold his soul out to the Politicians, but I'm going to make a stand. But I need your help Mr Sampson.'

'If you are serious about that, first we need to formulate some sort of a strategy to expose Charles Lewis and his cronies without making it too obvious we had any hand in it.'

'Thank you. You're right. We need to work together and sort these bastards out now. Things may get a little messy. Like Charles Lewis, if we are to succeed, we'll have to work in the shadows. So, can we trust and depend on DS Smith and DC Evans?'

'Well, there lies the rub. DS Smith is like me, 'old school' but John Evans is the epitome of the modern police officer. Trustworthy yes, but he will not undertake any duties he considers bad practice at best, or unlawful at worse. However, to his credit he's very discreet and provided we keep him out of any 'unconventional' policing activities, I'm confident he would be a valuable member of the team.'

'Do you trust me enough to tell me where these two are now?'

'DC Evans is back home on leave over the Christmas period. I collected him from the Airport yesterday. He managed to collect some very useful information about Lewis.'

'Where is DS Smith?'

'I'd rather not say at this stage.'

'He's out there in Gibraltar. Isn't he?'

'I'd rather not say.'

'I understand your reluctance after our last two meetings. When he returns, will you please contact me so we can have a meaningful conference? We all need to place our cards on the table. I'm relying on you Mr Sampson to prepare the ground; I don't want any more conflict between us from now on.'

'How can I contact you Mr Jenkins whilst I'm suspended?'

'You're not. I've re-instated you from this moment. Will you please return to your office the day after tomorrow? I'll contact you then and discuss where we need to progress on this.'

'Yes Sir. Thank you.'

'Once again please accept my apologies. Please don't take this the wrong way but I'm also taking a risk with my career coming here today and discussing it with you. For all I know, you could be taping our conversation from the moment I walked in.'

'It's Christmas Mr Jenkins, the time of good will and peace to all men.'

'Exactly,' he replied.

Both men starred at each other, neither blinking nor stirring from their seats. Eventually ACC Jenkins broke the silence, 'We're both old school. I'm sure we'll get to the bottom of this.'

'Listen Mr Jenkins, although I want to trust you; remember, there's a great deal at stake here. You tried to ride rough-shod over us without any explanation. Let me talk to the other two and we'll meet up later.'

'You're right. I deserve to be treated with suspicion but unless we come together on this, you and I are starring into the abyss called early retirement with a reduced pension. That's why we need to be clever and start thinking like these bastards. It's my understanding, DS Smith is a master at this. If he hadn't have become a police officer he would have made a hell of a good thief, probably living in the lap of luxury. We desperately need him, he's going to be a king-pin in our operations.'

'Yes, he would make a formidable adversary.'

ACC Jenkins stood and made his way towards the hallway where he saw Helen Sampson leaning on the doorway. 'Good afternoon Mrs Sampson. I'm sorry to intrude on this of all days. Please forgive me.'

'Mr Jenkins, is my husband a dishonest man?'

'No, far from it. He's an honourable man who is going to help me investigate those who have designs in harming our careers and reputations. So far as I'm concerned, you should be proud of him, as I am. After all, he one of my most trustworthy Detective Chief Inspectors.'

'Is he still suspended?'

'No. He still works for the Leeds City Police until his retirement. Then Mrs Sampson, he's all yours.'

She smiled as he walked outside into the front porch before turning around, facing them both. 'I'll take my leave and wish you both a happy Christmas.' They stood and watched as he drove away. Helen asked softly, 'Does he really mean that Mark?'

Looking slightly perplexed into her eyes he answered, 'No, does he hell. He's one dangerous self-centred little bastard.'

She asked meekly, 'What are you going to do now?'

'It's very clear now my darling. I'll play to his game for the time being until I've built enough damning evidence against him and the Chief.'

'How will you do that Mark?'

'We've already retrieved a great deal of evidence so far. But he's just supplied me with the best we have yet.'

'How's that?'

'Silly sod, he underestimated me. I recorded all the conversation. I used that tape recorder you bought for me last year in the sales. It's over there behind the magazine stand. Don't say anything before I go in there and switch it off. Don't want anyone to listen to what we get up to in our own house, do we?'

Helen smiled at her husband 'No we don't. Anyway Mark, I heard everything he said too.'

59

For Charles Lewis, Christmas Day was both peaceful and frenetic. He spent the morning with his father reminiscing through his childhood and his brother George, especially their holidays in Devon with Mother. For a few hours it appeared a normal loving relationship between a middle-aged son with his elderly father. However, shortly after their Christmas dinner, whilst sitting in the living room where a large coal fire roared in front of them, Colonel Lewis changed the topic of the conversation. 'So, what is it you do exactly, Charles?'

'I export goods all over the world father.'

'But what sort of goods?'

'Anything and everything,' he answered curtly.

'Can't you tell me anymore?'

'No father. Please don't ask any more questions.'

Now they sat in silence, avoiding each other's stare, neither wishing to continue talking. Suddenly the telephone rang in the hallway rang. Charles jumped out from his chair, 'That'll be for me,' and briskly walked out of the room, closing the heavy wooden door behind.

The Colonel looked into the flames and whispered, 'Charles, what are you up to? Why can't we spend more time together without these arguments?' Although it was twenty years since his other son, George, had been killed in France, he still missed him so much. Unlike Charles, he was polite, generous and possessed wonderful social skills; always thinking of others before himself. It was so cruel how he had been taken away from him at such a young age. His wife Mary had never recovered from their loss, grieving until her untimely death some years later.

Since then, for the past twelve years, his only family was Charles. They had become estranged from each other for most of that time. Yet he hoped this Christmas might thaw their frosty feelings towards each other and perhaps bring forward a more promising future. He had tried his best but Charles remained distant and aloof.

Outside in the hallway, Charles picked up the receiver, 'Hello, who is this?'

'Boss, it's Bill. We're booked into the Royal Hotel in town. What are your instructions?'

'I've spoken with my contact. He has assured me the investigation has been curtailed but I don't want to take any chances My source has told me the officer in charge is a Detective Chief Inspector Sampson who is now approaching his retirement. It would appear he is reluctant to follow the instructions given to him by his superior officers, so I think we should arrange for him to collect his pension earlier than expected. Do you understand exactly what I mean?'

'Yes.'

'The other person in the hospital we know about, has apparently returned home and spending an uncomfortable Christmas with his wife. He's only a Constable, so I think we can assume he'll do as he's told and won't interfere with our plans again. It's just his boss we need to look at.'

'Leave that with me Sir. Do we have an address for this Sampson?'

'Yes, he lives in a small village just outside the city, with his wife Helen. Have you got a pen?''

'Yes, go ahead.'

Charles read from a piece of paper he had scribbled on from an earlier conversation with his contact. After he had given Bill the details he said, 'Tomorrow is Boxing Day. There are many drunken drivers on the road then. Personally, I wouldn't drive tomorrow, because of that.'

'Got that Sir.'

Charles replaced the receiver and whispered, 'That should tie up any loose ends.' He returned to the living room and found his father asleep in his chair directly in front of the fire. He stood motionless over him, wondering how he would be like at this age; no children or loved ones to share his later years. He knew George had been his favourite son. His death had caused a long dark shadow stretching over his early adulthood and the entire family. His refusal to consider a career in Medicine only exasperated their relationship

Suddenly, he shrugged the emotion from his mind and concentrated on his only passions; power and wealth. He had successfully accomplished both without the benefit of his father's influence. Unlike him, Charles had abandoned any sense of honour or morality. Such integrity was an obstacle to his future ambitions. The selling and supplying of arms required a certain unique penchant. Charles Lewis had no conscience and slept soundly every night despite the devastation his actions caused to humanity throughout the world.

60

DCI Sampson also slept well that evening following the visit from the Assistant Chief Constable. He was relieved on two counts; being re-instated and having the proof of high political involvement into their investigation. Helen also shared her husband's improved circumstances. Now their retirement plans were back on track, she could continue with her plans in seeking for a small cottage in Devon. So far as she was concerned, Mark's retirement could not arrive soon enough.

As they were finishing their lunch, the telephone rang. 'Who on earth can this be Mark?' asked Helen.

Without reply, he picked up the receiver, 'Sampson.'

An unfamiliar voice said, 'Mr Sampson, this is the Police Headquarters Control Room. I have a message from DC Evans for you to meet him outside the main Central Market gates.'

'What does he want?'

'I'm sorry Sir he didn't say. He rang two minutes ago and told us to contact you at home as soon as possible. Sir, he sounded very anxious. That's all I can tell you.'

'Very well. Leave that with me.'

'Thank you, Sir. Do you want me to log the call?'

'No. Not for the moment.'

He replaced the receiver and shouted to Helen in the kitchen. 'I've got to shoot out love. It's that young Evans. For some reason he chose to pass a message to me through the Control Room. I don't really understand why he didn't contact me here. Apparently, he wants to see me now as a matter of urgency. There's something not quite right Helen but it shouldn't take me long. I'm meeting him outside the Market.'

'Alright, but please take care and don't be long. I've made your favourite trifle and we've been invited next-door for drinks later.'

He ignored her last comment. Meeting John would be more interesting than listening to their neighbours chatting incessantly about the most mundane of topics imaginable; gardening. They had both retired from teaching several years ago and failed to explore the wider world for new horizons and challenges, even though they enjoyed the best of health. By contrast, he and Helen were determined to take the opposite route.

As he walked out into the porch he turned and said, 'I'll be as quick as I can.'

For some unexplainable reason, Helen said, 'Be careful,' as she watched him drive his new Ford Cortina out from the drive, towards Leeds. Although she had seen him go to work thousands of times before, with a slight shudder passing down her back, she seemed to have a negative premonition today. Was he heading towards harm's way?

Thirty-five minutes later he pulled into the entrance to the main market gates. As he expected on a Boxing day, everywhere was deserted. No people, no traffic and certainly no John. He remained stationary for a further ten minutes looking casually in all directions. But apart from the occasional car passing, he saw no movement.

Suddenly from nowhere, a woman approached him from behind the car. She was in her twenties but looked considerably older with shoulder length peroxide blonde hair, wearing a distinctive faux leopard full length coat with a red collar. She shuffled forwards in her white stiletto heel shoes and tapped on the window. 'Are you Mr Sampson?'

He wound the driver's window down and replied, 'Yes. Who are you?'

Ignoring his question, she continued, 'If you're waiting for John, he's round here. Follow me.'

'Where are you going to?'

'Just around the corner. He can't come himself; you'll see why if you follow me.'

With some trepidation, he stepped outside the car onto the empty pavement and looked in all directions. There were signs of any life, just the unusual silence of a city on a Bank Holiday.

Then it happened. Without any warning, he saw in a split second in the periphery of his left eye, a figure slam into his side causing him to lose his balance and fall heavily to the hard, damp pavement. He tried to scream but was prevented by someone's hand, roughly gagging him with leather gloves over his mouth. In the corner of his eye he saw another man run towards him and faintly heard the woman's stiletto heels run away.

Unfortunately, Mark Sampson was a man in his late fifties and not in the peak of physical condition; no match for the strength used against him by the two younger men. He managed to glance sideways at one of his attackers and saw the distinctive colour of ginger hair, before a hood was placed over his head and his world sank into complete darkness. He lost consciousness as he was placed back inside his car, slumped against the steering wheel. He had been drugged and completely unaware of the circumstances. With the hood removed, it gave the impression he was fast asleep.

He neither heard nor felt the other vehicle collide into the back of his new car. The impact was so catastrophic it catapulted him through the front windscreen onto the road surface, some twenty-five feet away. His broken body remained unattended in the empty road, until the arrival of a passing motorist ten minutes later. Fortunately, the driver was a Doctor travelling to the nearby Leeds General Infirmary starting his shift within the Accident and Emergency Department. His day began prematurely, attempting to save the life of Mark Sampson.

The driver in the other car was already dead, sprawled across the front seats with a large section of his scalp missing.

61

Bill and Joe had been busy. Charles Lewis had cancelled their Christmas and his instructions were unambiguous; make it look like an accident. To facilitate their plan, they left the Royal Hotel near City Square and stole a car from the same underground car park where the Jaguar had been taken. It was a Hillman automatic. They had also discovered, only fifty yards away, a dishevelled homeless man laid on a pile of newspapers, huddled within a multitude of filthy blankets, stretched out inside an empty shop doorway.

*

Joe approached the man and offered him a bottle of whisky, 'Happy Christmas mate. Drink this fine malt, it'll keep the cold out.'

Joyfully and astonished, he accepted his kind gift, 'God bless you Gov.'

He immediately gulped the amber liquid and quickly fell into a stupor. With his body already full of cheap sherry, the drug laced alcohol soon accelerated his drunken condition. Within five minutes he slumped back onto his blankets and fell into an alcoholic-induced coma.

Joe was joined by Bill, driving the stolen Hillman. Within two minutes, the unconscious itinerant was bundled into the front passenger seat, with Joe in the rear. The man had now defecated himself, leaving the interior stinking beyond imagination. With the car windows lowered, both men held their breath in fear of vomiting, as they travelled the short journey to the Central Market. They parked the car inside a small alleyway down the side of the main entrance, concealed from the front gates. Bill approached a public telephone box and made the call to DCI Sampson's home address.

They had deliberately chosen this location. It offered a good degree of privacy with the whole market closed over the festivities. Although the main entrance area was completely empty, set within several hundred yards were several pubs, open and enjoying a thriving trade. These in turn, attracted a number of the local prostitutes plying their trade outside, in a hope to replenish their spent Christmas earnings. One such regular was called Lillie Bell. She stood alone in cold draughty side entrance to the adjoining Victorian built Corn Exchange. Dressed in her familiar long fake leopard skin coat, she was known locally as Fag-Ash Lil. This was her 'stand'[24] where she regularly leant against the old weathered doors, chain-smoking her woodbine cigarettes.

Bill approached her, 'Hello love, do you want to earn some money and keep your knickers on?'

'How do you know I've got any on, you cheeky bugger?' she quickly retorted.

'You're right I don't. But if you want to make twenty quid for just speaking to a driver in a car outside the Market gates in a few minutes time, you'd better decide now. How about it?'

'OK. What do you want me to do?' she asked as she stubbed her cigarette butt against the black smoked sandstone wall.

'Follow me and keep quiet.'

'Just a minute Mister. Money first before my services.' She rubbed her nicotine fingers together and reached out for her payment. He placed four £5 notes into her grubby hand, snatching it quickly before he had any chance to change his mind. Bill pointed towards Joe who stood on the opposite side of the road.

'He'll tell you what to do.' As she crossed the deserted road, Bill returned to the car where the itinerant man was still unconscious and sat in the front passenger seat. As Lillie approached Joe, Bill started the car engine and pointed the car towards the Market Main gates and waited.

After twenty minutes a car stopped in view and Joe nodded to her to approach the driver. He told her exactly what to say and impressed on her the importance of persuading him to leave his car. The

---

[24] prostitutes were very possessive of their place for soliciting.

moment Bill saw the driver stand outside, Joe rushed him from behind and threw him to the ground. Bill dashed over the road and joined his partner. They completely over-powered, sedated and hooded their victim. Lillie ran away, not looking backwards until she was completely out of sight. Gasping for air, she lit another cigarette, dragging deeply on the stub. 'That was easy money,' she whispered, smiled and continued on her journey home.

Meanwhile, they propped Mark Sampson against the steering wheel and returned to the stolen car, parked a hundred yards away. Wearing his gloves, Bill slid the filthy unfortunate man into the driver's seat and pointed the Hillman towards the Ford Cortina. Again, holding his breath, he leant through the open door and wedged the man's old boot between the accelerator and the brake pedals. This caused the engine to rev uncontrollably. Finally, he poured the contents of another whisky bottle over his clothing before he carefully, amidst the din, knocked the automatic gear stick into drive mode with a pole. Immediately the engine lurched forward and car quickly picked up speed. As if attracted by an enormous magnet, the car accelerated away in a straight line, never deviating from its path until colliding directly into the rear of the Cortina at a speed of over forty miles per hour. With neither driver wearing seat belts, the impact was immediate and devastating.

Bill and Joe noticed DCI Sampson being thrown forwards through the windscreen and landing on the road surface ahead. They looked momentary at each other before nodding and casually walking away. Bill uttered, 'The Detective Chief Inspector will no longer be investigating us anymore, even if he survives that.'

'I agree. Bloody streets are full of drunken drivers.'

'Yes. Let's go back to the Hotel and resume our interrupted Christmas.'

'Good idea partner.'

62

As ACC Jenkins replaced the telephone in his living room, he began to feel twinges of regret and remorse. He had just been informed by the Force Control Room that DCI Sampson had been seriously injured, involved in a road traffic accident outside the Central Market gates. Initial indications suggested he had been sat inside his stationary car when another vehicle collided into him. The second vehicle had been stolen from a city centre car park and the driver was a homeless itinerant, called George Bagley who had been pronounced dead at the scene.

He immediately placed a call to the Chief Constable, William Steele, at his home address. 'Have you heard about Sampson?' he asked.

'Yes, just now.'

'It's bloody dreadful. The man may die. You told me to let the MOD have his details, so they could conduct a surveillance operation on him. What the hell's happened? You just wanted to speed up his retirement and close the case. For God's sake, there was no suggestion that anything like this was going to happen.'

'Calm down Jim. I'm just as disgusted as you. But it's out of our hands now. We can't go against National Security and all that.'

'Do you really believe all that bollocks?'

'I know that I'm the Chief Constable, and I'm responsible for supporting the Government of the day, whoever that might be. Yes, our roles do become political but that goes with the job. Get real Jim, you knew that when you became ACPO[25] status all those years ago. Stop being so bloody naive.'

'So, what happens now?'

'Simple. Sampson will no doubt be pensioned off now, Smith and Evans can be dealt with how you feel fit. Promote them if necessary, just get them off the investigation regarding our local men. Call me when you've fixed that. Goodbye Jim.'

The telephone went dead. ACC Jenkins stared again into the mirror and pondered. He would let things settle down first before going to see DCI Sampson but first, he must find out where DS Smith was. Although Mark Sampson refused to tell him of his whereabouts, he failed to deny he was in Gibraltar. If that was true, he would be unable to deal with him until his return. Meanwhile, he would concentrate his efforts on the young DC Evans and pay him a home visit tomorrow; perhaps reward him for his loyalty and tenacity. If he was going to be awkward, threaten to return him to operational uniform duties. Paradoxically, he now felt some empathy towards Sampson, Smith and Evans. Used and betrayed. After all, they were only protecting their own careers and reputations like himself. How was this all going to end?

---

[25] Association of Chief Police Officers – includes Assistant, Deputy and Chief Constables

63

John returned home the following day from Scarborough with Mary. His recent estrangement and potentially serious injuries had dramatically re-ignited her feeling towards him. Although predominately through pity, she had decided to give their marriage another try. John had promised he would reduce his hours at work and once this case had been solved, apply for another post in CID at the local police station to where they lived. They would spend more time together planning for the future. She wanted more commitment from him and above all else, children. He was still reticent but agreed to allow nature to take its course.

Later that evening, after settling down to watch the television, the telephone rang. A woman's voice asked, 'John, have you heard what's happened to my husband?'

'No. I'm sorry, who is this?'

'This is Helen Sampson, Mark's wife.'

'What's happened Mrs Sampson?'

'He's been involved in a road accident in Leeds yesterday afternoon, waiting to meet you.'

'I don't understand, I've been away over Christmas with my wife in Scarborough. What's happened?'

'He left home about midday after getting a phone call from someone telling him you wanted to see him in town. Then I got another call from Police Headquarters about an hour later to say he was in the Leeds General Infirmary with a suspected broken neck. I rushed down there to see him. When I got there, they were waiting for the Surgeon to arrive, remember it was Boxing Day, but I managed to speak to Mark before he went into theatre. He told me not to talk to anyone apart from you and Sergeant Smith.'

'Of course. But is he alright now?'

'Yes. He had the operation to remove the pressure from his neck. He's heavily sedated but comfortable. He's strapped up from the head to his waist and looking very sorry for himself. He'll survive, that's the main thing. He also wanted you to have the tape recording of his conversation with ACC Jenkins here the other day.'

'What do you mean Mrs Sampson?'

'Yes, ACC Jenkins came to see him on Christmas Day to tell him he was re-instating him and would help him find out who's responsible for some killings. I don't know anymore because Mark never discusses work with me. That's how he prefers it. I don't know what Mr Jenkins meant but I did over-hear most of what he said. Anyway, the recording is here in front of me and I must give it only to you. Oh, there's something else Mark said, 'Don't trust that bastard Jenkins!' Yes, that was it, word perfect.'

'Do you know what happened?'

'Not really. I hoped you could find out for me. Mark hasn't a clue.'

'OK, leave that with me, but will he be alright?'

'The Doctors are hopeful he will recover sufficiently enough to walk again. But he'll probably have a pronounced limp with one leg slightly shorter than the other. I'm afraid his policing days are definitely over.'

'I'm really sorry to hear about this. When can I go and see him?'

'Oh yes, that's another thing. He doesn't want you to visit him in hospital. He believes he's being kept under watch and anyone visiting him other than me are being scrutinised. It's all very confusing to me, John. Can you wait until he gets home?'

'Of course. When can I come over to collect the recording tape?'

'Will tomorrow morning be alright?'

'Yes, that's fine. I will come see you on my way to work. Thanks for letting me know, Helen. I'm really sorry to hear what's happened to Mark. I promise you, those who were responsible for this will be brought to justice.'

'Thank you. Please take care of yourself.'

John replaced the telephone and looked at Mary. She knew something was wrong by his pale ashen complexion on his face. He spoke quietly, 'Mary, I never tell you about the things I'm involved with at work, but I must on this occasion. My friend Mark Sampson has been badly injured and I believe those responsible were the same that wished me harm in Gibraltar. Sit down, I'm going to tell what's been happening and why I need you to be patient with me until this case has come to some conclusion. I know I've promised you I will reduce my hours, but I must get to the bottom of this first. Do you understand?'

'Yes, I think so John. But what's all this about?'

John sat down next to her, held her hand and began to relay all the circumstances surrounding their investigations, beginning with the suspicious deaths of Freddie Cox and Jim Simms, together with the disappearance of Ronnie Ellis. After forty minutes, he sat back in his seat. 'So, Mary, that's why I had to go to Gibraltar. And this has caused DCI Sampson to be injured so seriously, he'll never return to work. Someone has decided to permanently take him out of the investigation.'

'What are you going to now?'

'Wait for Phil to return. He's going to go bloody ballistic when he finds this out. To be honest Mary, I think you should return to your parents in Scarborough until this is all over. It could get very unpleasant and at least I'll know where you are. In any case, it looks like I'm going to be working all hours.'

'I'll go back for a couple of weeks, but I'm not happy about leaving you here alone. Will Phil be alright?'

'Oh yes. I feel sorry for those bastards who hurt Mark Sampson. DS Smith will unleash all hell with his 'old school' coppering skills on them now. Even I'm going to run for cover when I first tell him what's happened.'

64

John left his house shortly after 8 a.m. and drove directly to see Helen Sampson. As she opened the front door, dressed in her neat dressing gown, he could see had been crying. 'Come in please. I'll get you the tape.' He stood in the hallway whilst she entered the living room only to reappear with the small audio tape recorder. She continued, 'The tape is inside. I think it's not been unwound but Mark suggested you should make a copy as soon as you can and give it to Phil.'

'Thank you, Mrs Sampson, I'll do that. Please give my regards to Mark and tell him I will keep him informed of any developments. I won't go and see him in hospital but wait until he returns home.'

'Thank you. I don't understand what all this is about John. All I know is that Mark has worked hard and devoted all his working life to the Police. If this is how he ends his career, I don't know how he will take it. Please find out who's responsible.'

'I will Mrs Sampson. When Sergeant Smith returns, we'll be sorting things out. I can assure you of that.'

'Just be careful.'

He took hold of the tape recorder and placed it inside his brief case along with the photographs he had taken in Gibraltar and drove directly to the office. He wondered how he would make another copy of the tape and where to keep all this evidence securely. For the time being he would wrap it all inside a plain bag and place it inside the Connected Property Stores, with his name and a fictitious investigation title. His mind drifted towards what sort of a reception he would experience, once he arrived at the Police Station. And who would be waiting for him?

He did not have to wait long. As he parked outside his office, he saw a familiar figure standing close to the outside entrance to the Police Station. It was Phil. He approached and opened John's car door, 'Don't get out, let's go for a short ride. We need to get out of here for the time being. It wouldn't surprise me if our office is bugged!'

John exclaimed, 'Bloody hell.'

'We need to talk.'

Phil sat inside as John drove away. 'Have you heard what's happened to DCI Sampson?'

'Yes, about twenty minutes ago.'

'I've just come from his house where I saw his wife Helen. There's more you should know.'

'I thought so.'

John drove to the nearby Library where he relayed all the events surrounding the visit from ACC Jenkins, the tape recording of their conversation and the telephone call that lured him into town, where he was subsequently injured. Afterwards, Phil spoke in detail of the developments he had uncovered whilst in Gibraltar. Inside the Library they located a small office set aside for reading and plugged the tape machine in the mains. With the volume on low, John played the tape. Once it had finished, he turned to Phil, 'What are we going to do now Phil? With DCI Sampson out of the picture and our ACC Jenkins and probably the Chief himself, who obviously we can't trust, who are we going to confide in now?'

'No one my friend. It's now down to you and me. If that bastard Jenkins is up to his neck in corruption and deceit, you can bet that up-start of a Chief Constable we have, is also currying favour with Whitehall. I need to think about our next move, John.'

'But we can't deal with this; it's far too big and involved. After all Phil, we're just a couple of hairy-arsed coppers with absolutely no clout.'

'Don't underestimate us. We are a good team and I'm not going to lie down whilst they get away with murder.'

John murmured, *Illegitimi non carbourundum.*'

'What?'

'It's Latin for don't let the bastards grind you down.'

Phil smiled and nodded. Suddenly he thumped the top of the table, 'Bollocks. As my old Boss once said to a clever thief, 'If I can't get you in a Court of law, well I'll just bloody get you.' Let's think about this John. I can't think of anyone we can take this to; can you?'

'No.'

'OK. This is what I propose. We'll return to the office and convince ACC Jenkins we have stopped all our investigations into this matter because we were taking our instructions from DCI Sampson. We shall resume our duties with the crimes allocated to our office and for all intents and purposes, drop all our attentions with this case completely. Let them think we are no longer interested. After a period of time, say two to three weeks after the dust has settled, we'll start to look at Charles Lewis more closely. I can tell you John, I'm a very patient man and will gladly wait for my opportunity. I'll be operating in the shadows from now on, so perhaps I'll keep you out of the loop with some things. Do you fully understand what I'm saying?'

'Yes Phil, I do. But will you tell me when you start your shady activities?'

'Perhaps.' Phil smiled again and gently slapped him on the shoulder. 'Let's get back to the office and face the music. Just remember, I'm sure our conversations may be compromised, so we'll use it to our advantage.'

'Who do you think has rigged the office?'

Phil smiled and shook his head. 'You're so naive sometimes, John. Those bloody Rubber Heelers.[26] That's who. They'd hang their own Grandmother, the bastards. Anyway, let's start moaning about how we were acting on the orders from Mark Sampson. That's our only chance. Meanwhile, we must keep all our evidence in a safe place. Definitely not the Station.'

'What about the Connected Property Stores?' asked John.

'No, you daft sod. First place they'd look for.' He paused 'Hang on a minute. They have locked cabinets here in the Library for those using valuable research books. I'll go and get a couple of keys.'

John nodded his head, 'Yes, it'll be safe here alright. Now let's go and see if we've still got a job.'

---

[26] Police officers belonging to the Professional Standards Dept.

65

Within an hour of their return, ACC Jenkins walked unannounced into their office. Instinctively both men stood to attention. Phil said, 'Good morning Sir.'

'Sit down Gentlemen.' He pointed directly at Phil and shouted, 'Where the hell have you been Sergeant Smith over Christmas?'

'On leave Sir. I gave the leave request forms to DCI Sampson and he approved it.'

'Yes. But where exactly have you been?'

'To be honest Sir, I needed to get away from the job all together. I went up into the Yorkshire Dales on my own for a couple days, walked on the hills and stayed in a couple of small bed and breakfasts on the way. I'd had enough after DCI Sampson had sent DC Evans to Gibraltar on a wild goose-chase about this Charles Lewis case. And when I heard he'd got robbed by some drunks for his troubles, I just had enough. It's a bloody mess and we want to just get on with our job catching crooks stealing antiques.'

'So, what have you uncovered about Charles Lewis? I must know!'

'I'm sorry Sir but we don't know much about him and frankly I'm not bothered either. I can't imagine he's involved with the secret and shady world of antique theft. I don't know why Mr Sampson had such an interest in him.'

'Are you telling me you both were only acting under his orders?'

'Of course, Sir. I understand he's been injured. Can you tell us how he is?'

'Unfortunately, DCI Sampson will not be returning to work.

Never. His injuries are too serious for him to make a complete recovery before he retires. It appears whilst he was sitting in his stationary car in town, a stolen Hillman hit him from behind. The other driver was an itinerant who must have stolen the car a few minutes earlier from an underground car park near City Square, before he collided into Mr Sampson's car.'

Phil shot a glance at John as ACC Jenkins continued, 'He was killed, so we'll never know why he did it.' He turned to John and continued, 'How are you feeling now Evans?'

'Much better, thank you Sir.'

'Good. Until I appoint a new DCI, you'll continue to work on the outstanding crimes that I've no doubt have been accumulating in the pending tray. You will under no circumstances pursue this inquiry or any others that refer to Charles Lewis. I will personally take responsibility for all the investigations into the deaths of Freddie Cox and the taxi driver, Jim Simms. Do you understand?' He looked at John and asked, 'What enquiries did you make over there?'

'None to be honest Sir. I was told to go and see where Charles Lewis was operating and what he was up to. But I got robbed before I manged to do anything. I never found out anything about him.'

'So, it was a complete waste of time Evans?'

'Yes Sir. I had all my money stolen and wallet taken. Fortunately, I'd kept my passport at the hotel. Otherwise, I would have been in a real mess.'

Phil stepped forward, 'To be frank Sir, I don't want to be disrespectful, but I told DCI Sampson all this before he sent DC Evans over there, but for some unknown reason he chose to ignore me.'

'Well Gentleman, you are officially off the case. Permanently.'

'Thank you, Sir,' Phil lied convincingly.

Without any notice, ACC Jenkins turned and walked out the office, leaving them speechless but satisfied. Their ruse appeared to have worked. Phil winked at John and scribbled a note and passed it over. John glanced down and saw 'look at the top of the office clock.' He looked up and noticed a small object resting on the wooden clock case. It was about the size of his thumb nail, black in colour without any visible markings. Phil broke the silence, 'Thank Christ we're off that bloody case. Perhaps we can get on with our normal work now.

What do you say John?'

'Absolutely. Won't let myself be hood-winked into doing anything stupid like that again Sarge. After all, we're supposed be running an Antique Squad, solving the burglaries and theft of fine art, not some crap about a bloke called Charles Lewis.'

Phil smiled and nodded approvingly. 'Right, let's see what's been building up in the bloody tray.'

66

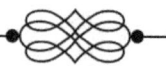

Charles Lewis answered the telephone at the Laurels. A familiar voice said, 'Charles, I now have assurances from the Chief Constable that you will not be hindered by any unnecessary visitors and the officer in charge has been relieved of his command. In fact, he's been retired early.'

'Excellent. I shall be returning to Gibraltar tomorrow where we can continue with our enterprises. Thank you for letting me know Ron.'

'My pleasure,' he replied, before replacing the receiver.

Ron Earl carried enormous influence within Whitehall, especially the MOD. The unexpected break-in by an insignificant local burglar at the home of a major Agent, working on behalf of the UK Government, had sent shock waves through the establishment. Inter-departmental cooperation between Ministries was often fraught with distrust and ambivalence. However, on this occasion the Chief Civil Servants running the Foreign Office, MOD and the Home Office had been closely allied to one single goal: the safeguarding and protection from public scrutiny of the lucrative arms trade to disreputable third parties throughout the world.

Following a hastily convened meeting, all these Departmental Heads agreed to close ranks in their efforts to quash any investigations that threatened to expose the exportation of these arms. However, it was unanimously agreed to monitor the movements of two police officers working for the provincial Leeds City Police force, for the foreseeable future. If, at any time, they continued to pursue this investigation, the matter would become the responsibility of the MI5, where they would deal with matters accordingly.

Ron was the link between Charles Lewis and the vast profits the Treasury and their small company enjoyed Since the newly elected Labour Government had come into power, there had been several runs on the pound. Indeed, the Bank of England was on the brink of devaluing sterling. Therefore, no one was going to upset the 'status quo.'

67

As the office clock sounded 4 p.m., Phil looked up and said, 'John, that's enough for today. Can you give me a lift home, my car's in the garage for repairs?'

'Yes, of course.'

'Come on then. Let's go.'

As John drove away from the Police Station car park, Phil searched the interior of the car until he was satisfied there were no listening devices present. He nodded with some relief, 'Hell that was a long day, but I think Jenkins bought it. John, you were a convincing liar this morning. Proud of you my boy.'

'What are we going to do?'

'Been thinking about that all day. First, while we're in the office, we must keep up this pretence for the time being until they're satisfied that we've stopped fishing about. Meanwhile, I've got a few things up my sleeve. I'm not going to tell you exactly what they are just in case the bloody wheel comes off. I don't want your precious career on my conscience. I'll only tell you after I've worked my magic on some of these bastards. They've no idea what I've got in mind for them.'

'Phil, am I wasting my time in telling you to be careful?'

'Bloody right. Don't waste your breath. I'll see you in the office tomorrow morning. You'll need to be bright and breezy for both of us. I shan't be getting any sleep.' He pointed towards the next bus stop. 'This will do nicely. See you tomorrow.' And before John had time to apply the hand brake, Phil was out of the car, clutching his leather brief case and running towards the approaching double decker bus signed 'City Centre.'

He jumped on board the open platform and paid his fare for the central bus station. Ten minutes later, he left the busy terminus and walked up the slight hill towards the Leeds General Infirmary. As he entered through the main entrance, he enquired into the whereabouts of Mark Sampson. The Receptionist looked down the register list and finally said, 'Ward 36, Brotherton Wing.'

Climbing two flights of stairs he saw the sign for Ward 36 to the left. As he approached the doors, he noticed a man sat on a wooden chair, reading a paper-back book. He looked official in his grey suit and completely out of place in the clinical surroundings. Phil instinctively became suspicious.

But he had anticipated this. He turned around and walked away in the opposite direction. Set to one side he found what he was looking for, a door with the notice 'male staff toilets only.' Without hesitation, he walked straight inside and closed the door behind. Next to a sink were two cubicle toilets, both with their doors wide open. He chose the left one and locked it behind him. Quickly, he removed his outer coat, opened his brief case and produced a white medical knee length coat with buttons running down its front, together with a genuine medical stethoscope. He stuffed his coat inside the bag, buttoned his coat and hung the scope around his neck and returned to the sink. He peered into the mirror and smiled as he placed a name plate on his breast pocket; 'Dr Barry Jones – Neurology Dept.'

He left the toilets and made his way to the nearby Ward 36, striding purposely passed the seated Guard, towards the Nurse sat behind the Ward reception counter. Phil asked, 'Excuse me Nurse, I'm looking for a patient of yours, Mark Sampson.'

She glanced at his badge and immediately replied, 'Yes Doctor, he's over there in the corner, bed nine. I've been told he's not see anyone without the Consultant's permission.'

'Of course, I fully understand. I won't be long, but can you give me some privacy? I'm here to ask him some questions about his wife. She's a patient of mine with quite a vulnerable disposition. I'm concerned about her welfare too, so I need to talk to Mr Sampson about his aftercare after he leaves from here.'

'Certainly Doctor, I'll close the curtains around the bed and give Mr Sampson his pain killers now. If I'm not here when you've finished, I'll be doing my rounds with the meds. Should be back in thirty minutes.'

'Oh, don't worry Nurse. I'll only be a few minutes.'

'Please come this way.'

Phil followed her towards the corner bed where he immediately saw the patient. Mark Sampson looked dreadful. Apart from the face, his head was completely hidden by bandages with his neck in traction, supported by straps and several weights. He was asleep. The Nurse spoke softly, 'Hello Mr Sampson, there's a Dr Jones who would like to speak to you.' He slowly opened his eyes and focused them on Phil, immediately reacting with astonishment. But before he could say anything, Phil interrupted, 'Thanks Nurse. If you can leave us alone now, that would be helpful.' She stepped backwards and pulled the side curtains together leaving then both staring into each other's eyes.

'What the hell are you doing here, Phil?'

'I need to talk to you about why you are in here.'

'You know they've got someone outside monitoring my visitors. I don't want you getting sucked into this mess any further. It's obvious we're dealing with some powerful faceless people. I assume you know I got a visit from ACC Jenkins the day before I received all this?'

'Yes, I do.'

'Have you got the tape recording between Jenkins and myself?'

'Yes. Safe and sound together with plenty of other incriminating evidence.'

'And the people that did this to me?'

Phil interrupted, 'We both know those two arseholes working for Charles Lewis did this. Well, I've found out who they are when I was in Gibraltar. You got set up Mark. And I'm going to sort them out. ACC Jenkins is up to his neck in this affair and along with the Chief probably.'

'You're right Phil, but what can we do?'

'As it stands at the moment, we have sufficient evidence to arrest a number of people, including Lewis and his cronies, but I believe they will be protected by the same forces that put you in here in the first place.'

'So, what next?'

Phil leant forward and whispered, 'If we can't get them in a Court of Law ....' he paused momentarily.

DCI Sampson quietly replied, 'Well, we'll just get them.'

'Exactly,' replied Phil.

'Tell me what happened when you were parked outside the Market Main gates?'

'Well it all started when I received a phone call on Boxing Day at home.' He recited the events leading up the collision, vaguely describing the woman who approached him.

Phil asked, 'What did she look like?'

'I think you'll know her. She looked like a hard-working Tom operating out of the Market area. In her twenties, perhaps older, peroxide blonde hair'

'That would fit most of them Mark. Do you remember what she was wearing?'

'Of course. It was a cheap imitation full-length leopard skin coat with a colourful collar I recall.'

'This collar. Could it have been red?'

'Yes, that's right. Definitely red.'

'I know who wears a coat like that, Fag-ash Lil. I'll go and see what she has to say.'

'OK Phil. Leave me now and don't get caught. Make sure you keep young John out of your old-school activities.'

'Don't worry. He won't be involved. Just get better and I'll come and see you when you're out of here.'

With a smile and a measured wink, Mark Sampson nodded and turned his head away. Phil pulled back the curtains and returned to the reception desk to find another nurse administering several trays of patient's medicines. Casually he remarked, 'Thank you.' But she only half acknowledged him, too pre-occupied with the medication she was counting. He walked past the 'suit,' also too busy reading his book. And without a glance backwards, he descended the stairs to the next floor where he located another staff toilet. He entered, quickly swapping his coats and walked downstairs, returning to the main reception area. Mingling with dozens of visitors who were hurriedly dashing in all directions, he slipped out of the Hospital and made his way towards the Market Tavern, in search of Lillie Jones, alias Fag-Ash Lil.

The clock behind the bar sounded seven o'clock as Phil walked through the front door. Similar to an old Western film, the door sprang back on itself, crashing into the other. This signalled the arrival of all those that entered. Curley, the Landlord, cast him a half-smile. Phil approached the bar where he asked, 'Usual Mr Smith?'

'Yes please, Curley.' As he waited for his half pint to be pulled, Phil scanned the pub for Lil. There she was, sat amongst the other prostitutes with her back to him, wearing her distinctive coat with the red collar. Curley passed him the beer. As he paid, Phil asked, 'Can I use your kitchen for a minute?'

'Sure,' he replied.

Phil approached Lil, tapped her gently on the shoulder and whispered into her ear, 'I need to speak with you now, in the kitchen.'

She swung round in an attempt to argue, but she could see the determination on his face. Shrugging her shoulders, she stood and followed him through the side door into the kitchen. Suddenly she swung round and demanded, 'What's this all about?'

'Listen Lil, you're not in any trouble, but I need your help. A couple days ago, on Boxing Day, you saw a man parked in a car outside the Market Main gates, where you gave him a message. Right?'

'What about it?'

'That man was an off-duty Senior Police Officer who was seriously injured minutes after you spoke to him.'

'I don't know anything about that!'

'I know you don't. All I want is to talk to you about the men who asked you to do this.'

'I don't know who they were.'

'Tell me Lil what they looked like.'

'A pair of strange looking bastards. One had ginger hair and the other walked with a limp.'

'Yes, I know who they are Lil. But where did you see them?'

'I was working outside the Corn Exchange where I always stand, on the off chance I could find a punter. It was a quiet as the grave. Then this ginger haired bloke came up to me and asked if I wanted to earn some easy money. He just told me to go and speak to the bloke parked outside the gates and pass a message to him about a friend of his.'

'Can you remember exactly what he asked you to say?'

'No, just that if this bloke was looking for his friend, he was to follow me.'

'Where to?' Asked Phil

'Down the side of the Market, where I'd spoken to this ginger haired man. I assumed he was the friend he was looking for.'

'After you spoke to the man in the car, what happened next?'

'I gave this bloke the message but as he got out of his car, he was rushed by another man I'd never seen before. I knew something was wrong, so I decided to run away and leave them to it. I didn't want to get involved.'

'Is that all Lil?'

'Yes. I did what I got paid to do and I didn't want any trouble. But when I was walking down the other side of the Market, out of sight, I heard a loud noise. It sounded like a car accident. I carried on walking and decided to catch the next bus home from City Square. I remember having to wait for ages, cos the buses weren't running often, it being Boxing Day. Anyway, whilst I was in the bus shelter, I saw the same men walk almost past me on the other side of the road and go into the Royal Hotel. Then my bus came, and I've never seen them again.'

'And are you sure they were the same men Lil?'

'Yes.'

'And you're sure they went into the Royal?'

'Definitely. I still go in there for the odd drink, that's all. When I was younger, I used to work out from the lounge before some bastard complained. Since then, I've been out on the streets.'

'That's great Lil. Thanks very much for your help. Here take this as a token of my appreciation.'

'I'm no grass, Mr Smith.'

'No, you're not. Let's call this a business transaction.'

She smiled and took the £5 note and walked back into the bar. Phil attracted Curley's attention, 'Thanks Curley. Oh, can I leave my bag here, I'll pick it up later?'

'Sure.'

'Good man, I'll see you soon.'

He left by the back door and walked directly to the Royal Hotel. It had been two days since the attempt on DCI Sampson's life and Phil knew it was unlikely the two men were still guests. Yet, there was an old saying ringing in his head he frequently heard throughout his investigative career as he whispered to himself, 'You never know your luck in a big city!'

He entered the public bar and ordered a small beer. Surprisingly, there were at least thirty people inside, sat in small groups at various tables scattered throughout the long room. Most of them were men working away from home on business, enjoying the opportunity of drinking during the week on their firm's expenses. Phil found a quiet corner where he had a good view of all these guests and the main entrance to the hotel lobby. Hoping for the best but expecting only disappointment, he picked up a newspaper lying on the table next to him and began to examine the crossword.

After several drinks and nearly two hours later, he looked at his watch. It was 9 p.m. Suddenly, he heard a loud man's voice shouting, 'Come on, give us another drink!' He looked up and saw them. The first man he saw was stood at the bar, swaying slightly from one side to the other. He demanded from the bar keeper, 'Are you bloody deaf? I want some more beer. Now!'

The barman shook his head, 'Sorry Sir, I can't serve you anymore alcohol. The Manager has told me you've had enough again.' Phil's mouth dropped slightly when he saw the second man come into view. He had bright ginger hair and also appeared the worse for drink. Phil whispered to himself, 'I've got you little bastards. Now it's my turn to play dirty.'

68

Charles Lewis replaced the telephone, enraged to find Bill and Joe were not in their hotel room. He had previously left instructions for both of them to contact him immediately at the Laurels. It was imperative he spoke to them before his flight to Gibraltar the following morning informing them they were to accompany him.

His father had retired early to bed, stating he was feeling unwell. In truth, the Colonel had disguised his utter contempt and disapproval towards Charles' guest, Ron Earl. From their very first meeting he found him conceited, arrogant, boastful and completely devoid of any compassion towards anyone other than himself. He especially despised Ron Earl's advocacy of eugenics and the survival of the strongest, with war providing the perfect antidote for the over-populated regions in the world. He was the owner a company who manufactured weapons on an industrial scale, thus providing the means to cull the world's unwanted growing population. The Colonel was aghast to discover his son shared his views too. He shuddered to comprehend that his only surviving son completely disregarded basic moral standards and behaviour he had sworn to uphold. In short, he was thoroughly ashamed of him.

Charles returned to the living room where Ron Earl had settled in a leather sofa, drinking a glass of his vintage brandy. Ignoring his displeasure in failing to speak to Bill and Joe, he smiled at Ron saying, 'I bought that bottle in Gibraltar from an old sailor. I think it was booty from the last war.'

'Yes Charles, lovely and smooth. Now changing the subject completely, I've spoken to my contact in Whitehall and they have assured me the plug has been pulled on the investigation into the burglary here. However, they did have some concerns about your two boys and suggested you should put some distance between them and yourself. To coin their phrase, they have become a 'liability' and could threaten your position as our agent in the future. I'll put it bluntly Charles, get rid of them!'

'I agree, leave that with me. I intend to return to Gibraltar with them tomorrow. There, I'll make the necessary arrangements and pay them off. Besides they both live there, so there's no reason why they should turn up again here.'

'Good man. I also have assurances that the Chief Constable here in Leeds has 'pensioned off' the investigating officer and his small team taken off the case. Apparently, they've posted a watch at the hospital where this officer is recovering from a road traffic accident. This will last for the next couple of days, just to make sure he's kept in complete isolation from any of his colleagues. The moment he's discharged from there, he'll no longer be a serving Police Officer.'

'Hopefully that will be the end of the matter.'

'Yes. I can't see any of subordinate ranks wanting to pick up the gauntlet now.'

Charles nodded in agreement, took a sip of his brandy and said, 'Ron, I've decided when I return to Gibraltar, I shall conduct all our future business from there. This stupid incident here at the Laurels potentially jeopardised all our future arrangements. I cannot allow that to happen again. Thank goodness Ron you have such influence in Whitehall, otherwise I could be facing the full riggers of a criminal investigation. In any case, my father doesn't need all this aggravation on his door-step at his time of life.'

"Very wise Charles. Collect you boys tomorrow and disappear back to Gibraltar. In a few days, we should have heard from our agents in Cape Town about the Rhodesian consignment. Perhaps you should fly out to Cape Town and check on our investment. Incidentally, you might want to recruit someone else whilst you're out there. I can give you a contact I know who works in the South African Police.'

'Thanks Ron, but let me get rid of these two first.'

69

Phil walked to the telephone kiosk set in the far corner within the Hotel's reception where he placed a call to the Market Tavern. Upon hearing the dulcet tones of Curley's Yorkshire accent, he asked, 'Curley, this is Phil Smith. Is Pete Hayes, the taxi driver, there?'

'Hang on, let me have a look.'

By the noise coming through the receiver, Curley was having a very busy night. Phil could hear the din with a mixture of shouting and bad language. Suddenly, he heard Curley abruptly shout loudly, 'Is Pete Hayes here?'

A voice replied, 'Who the bloody hell wants to know?'

'Telephone call for you.'

After a few moments of shuffling and groaning, 'Who is this?'

'Pete, this is Sergeant Smith. You promised me you'd help me find his killers. Well I need your help urgently. Now.

'Yes, Mr Smith. Where are you?'

'Come straight away to the Royal Hotel and meet me outside in the car park. I think I might have found the bastards who killed Jim.'

'On my way.'

'There's something else that's important. Ask Curley to give you my briefcase. It's behind the counter. Don't forget.'

'No problems Mr Smith.'

Five minutes later, Pete drove his Austin Cambridge taxi into the Hotel car park, where he saw Phil standing near to the back door. He stepped out of the car and said, 'Sergeant Smith, where are they?'

'Just a moment Pete. We must play this right. I'm going in there to try and convince them to come with me to a club on the outskirts of town where there's plenty of women and booze. I want you to stay here for the time being. But when I come outside with them, I don't want you losing your temper. We'll overpower them here and take them to my lock-up where you helped me last time with their Jag. You remember?'

'I do. You're a naughty boy, you are Mr Smith.'

'Yes I am. And I'm going to get a lot naughtier before tonight's over. Are you with me Pete?'

'Hell yes. Breaking the law with a Copper doesn't get much better than that. After all Mr Smith, you're only seeking proper justice for my dead friend. You bet I'm with you.'

'OK. You must do exactly what I ask of you Pete. Do you understand?'

'Sure. I'll be waiting here.'

'Incidentally, did you bring my briefcase?'

'Yes it's here.'

'Good, I'll need it later.'

Phil returned inside and walked directly into the bar. To his amazement, both men had managed to convince the Management they would behave themselves and were presently quietly talking and drinking their beer at a nearby table. Knowing they had never seen him, Phil approached and asked, 'Excuse me Gents, forgive me for asking but are you looking for any action tonight?'

Bill replied, 'What sort of action have you in mind?'

'You know, some girls and gambling. A bit of cannabis and dancing if you want.'

'Why are you telling us?'

'I work on the taxis here in Leeds and I know everything what's happening in this town. For a small fee, I'll introduce you both to a night of pleasure you'll never forget. It's entirely up to you. If not, I'm sorry to have troubled you.'

'How much is your fee?' Joe asked.

'Twenty quid and I'll take you there. That's all. If you're not happy, I'll give you your money back. After all, I'm not going to mess with you two. Am I?'

They both looked at each other. Bill nodded, 'Why not, there's nothing going on here. Lead the way.'

Phil smiled and placed his hand out for payment. Bill shook his head, 'I want to see where you're taking us first. You could be anybody, leading us down the garden path.'

'I wouldn't do that. If you'd like to follow me, my friend's outside in his taxi to take us there. It's not too far.'

Phil stood and gestured for them to follow him. Leaving their drinks, Bill and Joe rose to their feet, excited at the prospect of a night of sinful pleasure. They fell in behind Phil as he made his way towards the back door. To Phil's delight, they appeared even more unsteady than he had anticipated as they swaggered in a drunken manner towards the back door. He noticed the taller of the two had a severe limp, exaggerated by his stupor. However, the smaller man with the ginger hair appeared more alert and aware of his surroundings. As they stepped down the two shallow steps, Phil pointed towards the waiting taxi, in the far corner of the car park.

Phil said, 'This is my friend, we'll take you there now.'

Bill replied, 'Where are we going?'

But as the neared the car, Phil slowed down and allowed them to walk in front of them. Pete opened the driver's door and said, 'Good evening Gentleman.' It was at that moment Phil struck Bill on the side of his head with his police issue truncheon he had concealed under his coat sleeve. This caused him to collapse immediately to the ground. Before Joe had any time to react, Pete jumped out from his car and struck him squarely on his jaw. Like his friend, he collapsed to the ground unconscious.

'Quick Pete, get them into the back seat, we must get out of here before anyone sees us.'

They lifted each man and pushed them into the back of the taxi, Bill falling awkwardly against the central door pallor, whilst Joe slumped forward into the floor well, spreading his arms down the back of the front seats. Within seconds, the doors were closed and Pete was driving out of the car park, with Phil keeping a keen eye on their hostages.

The short journey to the lock up took only four minutes. Pete looked intently at Phil. Although a man who feared no one, this was far removed from his comfort zone. He was stressed, unlike his accomplice Phil who seemed to revel in the uncertainty and danger. Phil asked him, 'Are you alright?'

'Not really Mr Smith. What's going to happen when these two characters wake up?'

'Don't worry. I've got it all sorted. Remember, we're avenging the deaths of your friends. We're on a mission.'

'Yes. But they weren't your friends.'

'No Pete, they weren't, but I'm not having these bastards getting away with justice even if it's not the proper judicial rules.'

For Phil, his motives were clear. Mark Sampson and John had suffered badly through the cruelty of these two men. Now it was his turn and the illegality of his actions was not going to obscure his sense of justice. He and John had collected sufficient evidence through their investigations to charge these men with three counts of murder and the attempt on Mark Sampson's life. But they had been obstructed by ACC Jenkins and the Chief Constable, probably under the direct instructions from the Home Office. If justice was to be denied in the Criminal Courts, then Phil was going to invoke the ancient 'common law' rule that preceded all statute law.[27] From time immemorial, communities had judged the actions of others by applying the simplest of tests; 'would a person of reasonable sound mind believe an offence had been committed and were these two men guilty of those deeds beyond all reasonable doubt?'

Inwardly, he knew this philosophy was completely fallible. It was simple cold-blooded revenge. Yet conversely, if he ignored the opportunity that now presented itself, he would regret failing to challenge these men's misdemeanours for the rest of his life. Provided Pete was not present when he interrogated them, his conscience was clear. His moral compass pointed towards the perverse path of true righteousness. The true pathway according to DS Phil Smith.

As the taxi's headlights swept across the dark deserted yard, it eventually focussed in the old doors fixed to the crumbling brickwork. 'Give me a moment to open the door,' asked Phil.

'Quick as you can Mr Smith. I'm not very happy about this.'

'Don't worry Pete, when I've got them inside, I want you to leave.

---

[27] written law produced by Parliament

I can manage without you and besides it'll be better if you don't see any more. You understand?'

'Yes, thank you.'

Once the door was open, they carried Bill and Joe inside and tied them to two old metal chairs set to one side, next to the parked Jaguar. The temperature inside the garage was cold and damp. This now began to have an effect on their stupor. With their breathing becoming deeper, they started to shiver uncontrollably, accompanied by inaudible mutterings.

Phil turned to Pete, 'Off you go. Thanks for helping out. I'm going to talk to these two and get the truth from them. Perhaps I can find out exactly what happened to your friend Jim. I just want your promise, you'll keep this to yourself, this is between both of us. OK?'

'Oh yes, Mr Smith. You can depend on me not saying anything. What you are doing is both right and wrong. I'm not cut out for this. Just let me know when it's all over. You know where to find me.'

He followed Pete to the door, where they shook hands. As Phil closed it behind him he turned towards the men and whispered, 'Now my little beauties, you're going to tell me everything you know.'

70

Phil turned towards the two men tied securely to the old metal chairs, their arms and legs bound tightly with rope and sticking tape across their mouths. He waited several minutes until both had their eyes wide open. He asked menacingly, 'Can you both hear me?'

Joe was the first to nod, whilst Bill looked deliberately down at the ground. Phil kicked his chair to attract his attention and repeated, 'Can you hear me, you piece of shit?' With some reluctance, Bill acknowledged him before averting his gaze downwards again. 'Good. I'll start with you,' pointing to Joe. 'First of all, who are you, Joe or Bill?'

Both men stared at each other in complete bewilderment. How could he know their names? Phil continued, 'Look at these photos. Any idea where I might have got them from?' From his pocket, he produced the old black and white photographs taken from their small house in Gibraltar. Continuing he said, 'I know all about you and the dirty work you do for Charles Lewis. I know you murdered the young disabled burglar who broke into the Laurels, then the taxi driver who took him there. You then abducted the older man who planned all this in broad day light before drugging him and placing him on the rail tracks in South Leeds, not too far from here. Well I can tell you this; he didn't die at the scene. He died two days later in hospital but not before he had time to tell me all about it. Then, you tried to kill my friend in Gibraltar and also my boss a couple of days ago, here in Leeds. Oh, I nearly forgot, you also killed that poor wretched tramp you stuffed into the car before it rammed it into the other car.'

He approached Joe and ripped the tape from his mouth. 'Who are you?'

'I'm Joe.'

Bill began to struggle against his ropes, rocking sideways in an attempt to unbalance the chair. Phil slapped him hard against his right cheek and tore the tape from his face too. Immediately, he shouted to his friend, 'Shut your mouth! Don't say anything. If he's a Cop, he can't do anything to us.'

Phil stooped over him and casually said, 'You know you're right about me being a Cop. But I'm old school and I don't give two bollocks what happens to you both. Let me explain before you leave here, you're either going to tell me exactly what you've been doing, or I'm going to hurt you so badly, you will never cause any trouble to anyone else for the rest of your life.'

'You're just bluffing Cop!' shouted Bill.

Phil walked over to an old bench stretching alongside the garage wall and picked up an old hammer. Holding it in one hand he said, 'I want to make it perfectly clear to the both of you. You overstepped the line when you tried to kill my friends. It's now personal. Very personal indeed. Like you two I've served in the Army in Africa and Aden, seen terrible things inflicted on hostages tied up like a Christmas turkey. Just like you are now. I don't give a shit about the rules. You two have been on a killing spree in this City and I'm going to stop it right here and now. Your precious Charles Lewis can't save you now, nor can all those powerful people who support him. You're on your own. You will talk to me or so help me God or I'll bloody knee-cap the both of you.'

He stepped forward and stood over Joe's legs. He lifted the hammer and looked at his knees. Suddenly Joe screamed, 'Don't! I'll tell you what you want.'

For a split second, Phil looked away from Bill and failed to see he had wriggled his arms free from behind the chair. In that instant, he fiercely lunged at Phil. With his legs still attached to the chair legs, he still managed to push Phil violently against the metal bench, knocking his head against the top corner. Phil had been caught completely off-guard.

It took several valuable seconds for him to regain his composure but by then it was too late. Bill had produced a flick-knife from nowhere and cut free the ropes free from his legs. As Phil attempted to stand, Bill punched him in the face causing him to hit the bench again. Now with Phil slumped over the edge, Bill took a deep breath and turned towards Joe. Without any warning, he plunged the knife into his Joe's chest. He did not scream nor feel any pain, just astonishment. His wide opened eyes watched him escape towards the door and vanish into the darkness outside. Why should his partner, who they had shared so much over many years, do this to him? Why?

Phil eventually staggered to his feet and looked at Joe. He was still sobbing as he looked straight into Phil's eyes, whispering, 'Why Bill, why?' But Phil had no time to check his welfare, Bill was loose outside in the disused Railway yard, along with the other rats and vermin that infested everywhere.

71

After he let Phil out from his car to catch the bus, John returned home. Mary had already left. She grudgingly agreed to stay with her parents in Scarborough for a couple of weeks whilst he continued with his investigation. Without her disapproval, he felt slightly emancipated as he settled into the sofa with the fish and chips recently bought at the corner shop. Especially eating them directly out of the paper would be something she would never allow him to do.

Afterwards, he began to reflect on the day's events. Clearly, Phil was planning something tonight. But what? He suspected it would be clandestine yet felt a shared responsibility for the investigation. This uneasiness began to manifest itself into real concern. Now he was anxious. Phil was exposing himself to further danger and operating alone. He had to help him but where would he start?

Firstly, he telephoned his home and spoke to one of his daughters; she simply told him he was still at work. Knowing he never discussed his job at home, John thanked her and replaced the receiver, whispering, 'Where are you Phil?' Suddenly, out of the blue he remembered one of his haunts; the Market Tavern. He had never visited the place. It had a dreadful reputation for being 'anti-police' with most of its clientele consisting of active criminals and prostitutes. He was also aware of the Chief Superintendent's directive, clearly instructing the terms of Police Officers visiting the premises. Even entering off-duty was a serious breach of the Disciplinary Code. This brought a smile to his face. Recently this had been mentioned to Phil by another senior officer who had dismissed his comments, saying, 'Sod off, I prefer to drink with people who I know what they do, even if they're all thieves and vagabonds.'

Nevertheless, he would start his quest to find him there.

He parked his Morris 1000 directly outside the rickety doors to the Market Tavern. As he entered, the atmosphere immediately transformed from a rowdy and boisterous gathering to a quiet deep sense of suspicion and hostility. Ignoring the severe stares and muttered obscene remarks levelled against him, he approached the bar and spoke to Curley. Unaware of his name, John asked, 'Excuse me, I'm looking for Sergeant Phil Smith. Has he been in here tonight?'

'Who wants to know?' Curley enquired.

'My name is Detective Constable Evans.' He produced his Warrant Card to confirm this and continued, 'It's a matter of real urgency I speak to him as soon as possible. Has he been here tonight?'

'Can't say I've seen him officer,' he replied.

John knew he was lying but felt vulnerable in persisting. 'I know Sergeant Smith is the only Copper you trust, but he's also a close friend of mine. Please, I'm begging you. Can you tell me where he is? I honestly believe he may be in great danger. I'll go and sit in my car outside and wait for an answer. But please don't make it too long.'

Although it only took twelve strides to leave through the sprung-held wooden doors, John feared he was about to have something thrown in his direction at every step. With some relief, he reached outside and immediately sat inside his car. Five minutes later there was a faint tap on the front passenger's door window. He stared up and saw towering over the car roof a man about 45 years old, over six feet tall and well built. He stooped down, opened the door and asked, 'Who are you?'

John faced him. 'I'm a copper, like Phil Smith and he's my partner at work. You've got to believe me, he might be in danger. Can you tell me where he is?'

'If I tell you, he might be in greater danger. So why should I trust you?'

'OK. Phil and I are investigating the murders of Freddie Cox and the taxi driver, Jim Simms. I can't tell you anything else other than we've been hindered in our investigations. If you know him as well as I do, you'll also know he's not a conventional copper. He often bends the rules. In fact, sometimes he bloody ignores them altogether. It's my belief he may be in danger so I need to find him quickly. Will you please help me?'

Pete the taxi driver smiled; this officer obviously knew him well. He spoke softly, 'I'll show you where I last saw him. If you're not levelling with me, I'll hurt you. I mean it.'

'Don't worry, I am levelling with you. I am his friend. Take me there now, please.'

Pete walked around his car and sat inside and uttered, 'Wellington Street.'

Within five minutes, John drove into the old railway sidings car park. It was covered in darkness with no signs of life. The Morris 1000 headlights shone on the old doors. One of them was slightly ajar.

Pete said, 'Pull up here. Stay in the car, I'll go and check with him first.'

John saw him approach the open door and enter. Suddenly he ran back out shouting, 'Quick, come here!' John jumped out of the car and entered into the dimly lit building. He instantly saw a man lying on the ground next to a black Jaguar car. Stooping over him, he saw the man had suffered a deep wound to his chest. He was gurgling and attempting to speak through his blood-filled throat. John asked, 'What's happened?' Attempting to focus his eyes on John, he lifted his head slightly and muttered, 'Bill's stabbed me, smacked the copper and pissed off. I know I'm done for, so I need to put things right.'

'I'll go and get an ambulance.'

'No need. I've seen enough violence in the world to know what's happened to me. Bill stuck the blade in deep and I've no feeling in my legs. I know what's going to happen.'

'Do you recognise me?' asked John.

'No. Should I?'

'Don't you remember? Along with your friend, you drugged me in Gibraltar a few days ago leaving me for dead.'

'Christ! It's you; the copper. I know I'm dying so all I can do is say I'm sorry. We were paid to get rid of you.'

'What's your name?'

'My name is Joe Mason.'

'Do you know where my friend is Joe?'

'After Bill stabbed me, he ran out through the door. Your mate ran out after him. He can't have got too far cos Bill had a lot to drink and your mate hit him hard over the head before he brought us here.'

Pete interrupted. 'He's right. Mr Smith gave the other bloke a good punch.'

John exclaimed 'What? Why didn't you stay here with him?'

'He told me to go. He was going to question them about what they had been up to.'

John turned to Pete, 'Stay here with him whist I go and find Phil. He may be in trouble.'

'No, you stay, I'll go,' replied Pete before running out through the garage doors shouting, 'Mr Smith, where are you?'

The dying man continued, 'Me and Bill, his full name is Bill Jones, work for Mr Lewis.'

'Is that Charles Lewis who lives at the Laurels, here in Leeds?'

'Yes, that's right. Well me and Bill have done some horrible things for that Mr Lewis. Just over a month ago, a young bloke broke into the house. We caught him in the cellar. It seems he was trying to steal some silver snuff boxes. Anyway, Mr Lewis told us to get rid of him and leave no trace. Bill decided to kill him. After he'd done it, we dumped his body in the back of the Jag and drove it to somewhere near Pontefract. We carried his body to a burning slag heap where we put it into the smouldering fire, before covering him with more burning coal. I don't suppose there would have been much left of him after a couple of hours.'

John asked impatiently, 'What about Freddie Cox?'

Turning his head slowly he replied, 'Who's he?'

'Freddie was the man this young burglar was working for. He was the fence. What did you do to him?'

'Oh yes, that was awful. Bill again decided to kill him too. We waited until we saw him in town near to the Railway Station. Bill went up to him and drugged him with a needle, like we did to you. Then we virtually carried him to the car and drove him unconscious to the main railway line between Leeds and Wakefield where we dumped him on the tracks. As far as I know that was the end of him.'

John paused and said, 'But it wasn't Joe. You now know that. His name was Freddie Cox and he survived for two days, in time to tell me about the plans for stealing those silver snuff boxes from the Laurels. So, you see we were on to you from the very start. Now I want to know about the other man, the taxi driver who was killed before Freddie?'

'I didn't want to do that. Honest to God. Bill made up his mind to make sure he would never talk. After he drove him down, we took the van to some waste ground nearby and set it on fire. That's the God's honest truth.'

'His name was Jim, a married man with three children and he was a good friend of the man that's just come here with me tonight. Your mate killed him outside his house. That's what you bloody did!'

'I swear on my mother's life, I didn't want anything to do with that. Bill was driving the stolen van when he knocked this guy down.' Joe lifted his head further but began to choke violently, blood belching from his mouth. An enormous convulsion caused his back to arch, his eyes filled with mortal trepidation. Finally, he slumped back onto the ground. He tried to speak but John could only read his lips, 'Sorry.'

John stared at the dead man for several moments, realising he had witnessed yet another dying declaration. According to the rules of evidence, he should record everything as soon as possible, but his friend was out in the darkness with a serial killer. That was more important. He must go and find him, but where could he be?

72

Pete ran from the garage door into an empty yard and suddenly stopped. With no lighting other than the distant street lamps some two hundred yards away, he listened for any unusual noise. Nothing. Then he saw a moving green light, followed by the unmistakable sound on an approaching steam locomotive railway engine. As his eyes adapted to the darkness, he carefully walked towards the six feet high wire fence separating the yard from the railway track beyond. He shouted, 'Mr Smith, where are you?' But he heard only the loud hissing sound of emerging train releasing its steam-pressure valves. He was completely unaware of the dark figure crouching next to him within the leafless buddleia bush. Once again, he shouted, 'Mr Smith!'

But Pete never saw the attack coming. Armed with a half-brick, Bill struck him from behind across the side of his head. Fortunately, in Bill's impatience to strike the mortal blow, he missed his intendended target, the base of his skull and the brick glanced along the side of his jaw. However, the impact sufficiently stunned Pete enough for him to collapse onto the cinder laden ground, rendering him semi-unconscious. Bill stooped over him and kicked his motionless body into the ditch running along the car park perimeter. With no time to complete his 'kill', he continued towards the fence searching for any gaps to allow him to escape onto the track.

The train was close now, its front lights illuminating the shiny tracks and the wired boundary fence. Then, out from the gloomy night air he saw the gap. The fence had been breached over a broken concrete post and trampled down to waist height. Like a cornered wild animal, Bill sprang forwards. His adrenalin coursed wildly through his veins as he ran full speed, jumping over the opening into freedom and escape.

But with the limited light from the passing steam locomotive, he misjudged his landing. Although clearing the fence, he fell heavily on the course gravel stones that supported the rail sleepers and track. The noise from the engine was now deafening as he stood to his feet. But the awkward landing had sprained his ankle. As he bent down to rub away the shooting pain, like Pete, he never saw his attacker either. Phil mustered all his strength as he smacked him hard between the shoulder blades with a piece of timber.

However, Bill's tough physique managed to absorb most of the strike. Instead of falling again, he swaggered to one side and managed to stumble away in the same direction of the passing train. Phil attempted to give chase, but the recent injury inflicted on him by Bill was now taking its toll. Unable to keep up with him, Bill was in fact experiencing a 'second wind,' his strides becoming longer and his pace increasing.

Phil was struggling; unable to endure the pain, as he gasped for breath. His lungs felt as though they were exploding in agony. He was utterly out of shape and much older than Bill. With only fifty yards covered, he knew there was no chance of catching him. In desperate resignation he stopped, bent over in pain and gasped for air. He was unable to continue. With straight arms supporting his exhausted body on his bent knees, he looked up and saw Bill reach the front of the train and disappear from his view. The train continued relentlessly towards the approaching Station.

Phil could only walk slowly ahead, his mind racing; everything had gone to shit. What was going to happen now? The other suspect was dead, murdered by his associate. Several witnesses saw him leave the Royal Hotel with Bill and Joe and he was still no closer to capturing those responsible for all the deaths and hurt they had inflicted. And Charles Lewis was free to continue in his shadowy world of selling death on an industrial scale. No doubt Bill would return to Gibraltar with Charles Lewis and he had lost his only opportunity of discovering the truth and administering some kind of retribution. It was the lowest point of his life. His mind was racing as he stared at the train approaching the Station. His career was in ruins, his liberty in doubt. He had failed his friends and above all else, chose his career instead of his beautiful family.

The train continued unabated towards the Railway Station, its bright rear red lights throwing a warm glow across the parallel shiny track lines. Phil was about to return to the garage when something caught his eye. It glistened through the reflection of the disappearing train rear lights; a small silver coloured metal object lying in the middle of the track. Suddenly, he noticed other objects of varying sizes and shapes scattered about the track, again glistening in the fading red lights. He walked forward towards the silver metal, crouched down and picked it up. It was a knife; a flick-knife. Instantly, he realised this was the weapon Bill had used against Joe. He looked again down at his feet and realised in horror through the dim light, the scattered pieces covering the tracks were the smashed and severed mortal remains of Bill. He must have tried to dash in front of the train, but lost his footing and stumbled.

Without waiting to inspect the scene any longer, he walked back to the gap in the fence some two hundred yards away and made his way towards the garage. As he strode over the perimeter ditch, he heard another noise. A groan, accompanied by a cry, 'Help me.'

Phil shouted, 'Who's there?'

'Help' repeated the voice. He looked down and saw the outline of another body lying awkwardly against the wire fence, legs twisted with a hand aimlessly waving in the air. 'Mr Smith, help me.'

'Christ. Is that you Pete?' exclaimed Phil

'Yes, I'm hurt.'

Phil bent down and saw his head was bleeding slightly from the crown. 'What happened Pete, and why are you here?'

'Never mind that, did you get that bastard?'

'No, but the Kings Cross to Leeds train did.'

'Is he ...?'

'Oh, very much so. They'll need several bags to put him in.'

Pete smiled, 'Result then, Mr Smith?'

'Yes, but why are you here?'

'Do you have a friend called John?'

'Yes, why?'

'Well, he's here. He told me you were in danger. I wasn't too sure about him at first to be honest, but he convinced me you were in need of some help. He was right Mr Smith, wasn't he? Anyway, he's back in the garage with the other bloke.'

Phil helped him to his feet and together they walked back towards the garage.

'What are we going to do now?' asked Pete.

'You're going home first Pete, but I think I may have a plan. Can I borrow your taxi?'

'Of course. You'll probably need my badge too.'

Slowly, they made their way back to the garage to find John standing outside. He asked Phil, 'What's happened?'

'That bastard Bill tried to hurt our friend Pete.'

John nodded in concern, 'Yes, and he's murdered his mate inside the garage. Did he get away?'

'Not exactly John. He ran into a train. What's left of him is scattered over the tracks near to the Station.'

'What?'

'Let the BTP boys deal with that in the morning. After all, they were keen to put Freddie's death down to suicide, let's see what they've got to say about this one.'

'Well Phil, even by your standards, this has been a 'bugger' of a night. So far, you've found our two suspects and they've wound up dead.'

'I know, you're right John. But I'll still sleep soundly in my bed; they both finally got what they deserved. So far as I'm concerned it's justice my boy!'

'Bloody right there, Mr Smith,' agreed Pete.

'So what do you suggest we do now Mr Smith?' asked John sarcastically.

'I have a plan Mr Evans.'

'Oh Christ. Does it involve me?'

'Only a little bit.'

'I was afraid of that. Remember, don't ask me to do anything that's illegal. You know the rules.'

Pete asked, 'What's he on about Mr Smith?'

'Pete, meet the face of tomorrow's cop. Squeaky clean. Always speaks the truth, hardly ever swears, never lies, doesn't drink much or smoke tobacco and definitely wouldn't be seen dead in the

Market Tavern.'

'Don't trust them,' retorted Pete.

'Bugger off you two,' protested John. 'Anyway, this cop has something that might be of use to you Mr Smith. It's a Yale key attached to a fob belonging to the Royal Hotel - Room 137. You might need this.'

'Where did you get this from?'

'On Joe in there. Found it in one of his pockets.'

'That's useful,' replied Phil.

John continued, 'Incidentally, Joe told me a number of things before he died; what they did to Ronnie Ellis after he broke into the Laurels, the killing of Freddie Cox and how Bill deliberately ran over your mate Jim. They were acting in accordance with instructions from Charles Lewis.'

'Hell, another dying declaration?' said Phil.

'Yes, but who's going to believe it, especially coming from me?'

'Exactly John. That's why we're going to dispense some more Justice tonight. Before we take Pete home, let's stop by the Royal Hotel first. I want to have a look inside room 137. Perhaps there might be something of interest in there.

73

Whilst John and Pete remained in the car, Phil entered the Royal Hotel and walked through the back door into the lobby. He continued directly to the lift and ascended to the first floor. Tucked away at the back of the hotel, facing down on the refuse bins, he soon found Room 137. He tried the key and the door opened freely. A double bedroom with two single beds neatly made was the only orderly manner of the room. Clothing was scattered across all the furniture and carpets and a smell of body odour, stale alcohol and spent cigarettes permeated throughout. Phil remembered the similarity between here and the small house belonging to them in Gibraltar.

Wearing thin cotton gloves, he searched the drawers and suitcases placed above wardrobes; nothing of interest. Then he turned his attention to the walk-in bathroom and found, placed behind a wicker basket, a black leather holdall concealed under several bath towels. He unzipped the flap and peered inside. There it was; exactly what he was looking for. A small box containing a hyperaemic needle with ten ampoules of clear liquids. There were three empty spaces where previous glass vials had laid. The remaining ones were clearly marked 'Caution – Neuromuscular Blocking Drug.' He suspected the missing three had been used on Freddie Cox. Mark Sampson and John, rendering them incapable of protecting themselves.

Phil seized the box, left the room and made his way passed the reception towards the public telephone boxes next to the lounge. There, he made a local telephone call. A few moments later he spoke. 'Good evening Sir. Is that Mr Charles Lewis?'

'Yes, who is this?'

'Sir, I'm very sorry to disturb you at this time. My name is Jason Green, I'm the General Manager of the Royal Hotel in Leeds. We appear to have a problem with one of our guests called Bill Jones who has unfortunately been taken ill. He suddenly collapsed outside his room early tonight and his friend Mr Joe Mason has gone with him to the Leeds General Infirmary. Mr Mason requested me to contact you as a matter of urgency, as he left with his friend in the ambulance. He wondered if you would be able to meet him at the hospital as soon as possible. I can arrange for one of our contracted taxis to come and collect you and take you there now. Will that be in order Sir?'

'This is very inconvenient.'

'I apologise, but I'm just passing the message on to you.'

'Very well. How long will your driver be?'

'I have your address as the Laurels, Grove Lane, Roundhay. Is that correct?'

'Yes.'

'He'll be there in less than ten minutes. His name is Peter.'

Without any civility Charles Lewis hung up. Phil smiled and replaced the telephone whispering, 'Got you. You little jumped-up bastard.'

Phil returned John's car and asked Pete, 'Where's your taxi? I need it now.'

'Parked up down by the side of the Market Tavern.'

'Good. Let's go John and pick it up.'

As John drove away, he asked, 'What are you up Phil?'

'We're dropping Pete off first and I want you to return to the lock-up garage and wait for me there. I won't be long. Then you'll see what's going to happen. You must trust me on this John.'

'Hell. this is going to be a long night,' John said with resignation.

74

Charles Lewis replaced the telephone receiver and returned to the living room. His friend Ron Earl was stood in front of the open burning fire, gazing at the flickering flames. 'Sorry about that Ron, it appears one of my boys has collapsed and been rushed to hospital. The other one is with him now. That was the Hotel where they are staying. Apparently, Joe wants to see me urgently. If it had been the other fellow, Bill, I'd ignore this. But Joe's different; he wouldn't normally bother me. It must be important. Ron, I'm really sorry about this. We'll have to curtail our pleasant evening until we meet up next week in Gibraltar, unless you stay the night. You know you're most welcome to stop. Hell, we've got plenty of rooms.'

'Kind of you to offer Charles, but I'll make my way back to Birmingham tonight. There's a Board meeting tomorrow anyway and I must be there. No, you go and sort this matter out at the hospital. Perhaps this might be your excuse for dumping them when you return to Gibraltar? They're getting too toxic to hold on to Charles. Anyway, good luck and thank very much for the delicious meal and fantastic vintage brandy.'

'Thanks Ron. The Hotel is sending a taxi for me to take me to the Hospital.'

Ron Earl made his way along the hallway towards the front door, he stopped and said, 'Good luck,' before disappearing into the winter's chilly night air. Charles found his overcoat in the cloakroom and stood inside the hallway, anticipating the impending arrival of the taxi. He decided not to disturb his father; that would take too much explanation.

A few moments later, the doorbell rang. He opened the door and was surprised to see Ron again. 'Charles, I've just had a thought. I'm going through to Leeds; I can easily drop you off at the Hospital. Cancel the taxi and come with me.'

'Ok. If you don't mind, Ron. Just give me a moment please.'

He walked over to the telephone and looked for the Royal Hotel number he had previously written down, when he attempted to contact Bill and Joe. He dialled the number and immediately spoke to the Receptionist. 'I wish to speak with your General Manager, Mr Green.'

There were several moments of silence, followed by, 'I'm sorry Sir, who did you wish to speak to?'

'Your General Manager, Mr Green,' Charles replied impatiently.

Again, there was silence. 'I'm very sorry Sir. But our General Manager is not working tonight. I can put you through to the Duty Manager, Mr Higgins.'

'Do you have a Manager working for the Royal Hotel called Mr Green?'

'No Sir.'

'Have you arranged for a taxi to collect me at my house, here in Roundhay now?'

'No Sir.'

'Are you sure?'

'Certainly. We haven't sent a taxi to anywhere tonight and I've been working since six o'clock this evening. Perhaps you got the wrong message Sir?'

Charles replaced the telephone without answering and whispered to himself, 'No, I think I got the right message.'

Ron Earl stepped forward and asked, 'What was that about Charles?'

'I'm not sure Ron. In a few minutes time a taxi is going to arrive here and supposedly take me to the Leeds General Infirmary. I've just spoken to the Receptionist at the Royal, and guess what? They have no Manager called Mr Green nor have they sent a cab.'

'It's a set-up Charles. What are you going to do?

75

Once John had parked his Morris 1000 outside the Market Tavern, Phil took the keys for the taxi from Pete together with the Leeds City Hackney Carriage Badge that hung loosely from a silver chain around his neck. Turning to his two friends he said, 'Pete, I'm afraid you'll be doing no business tonight. John and I will drop the car off at your place in the morning. We'll tell you everything that's happened then. Are you sure you don't want us to take you home now instead?'

'Hell no, Mr Smith, the wife will want to know what's happening. I'll have a few drinks here and get a lift home later.' Pointing towards the row of cars parked alongside the pub, he continued, 'The car's over there. Good luck Mr Smith and be sure to look after yourself.'

'I will Pete. Thanks.'

Pete stepped out of the car and walked towards the Market Tavern. Phil turned to John, 'Drive back to the garage, I'm going to collect Charles Lewis and bring him there. We'll see what he has to say.'

'How are you going to manage that?'

'He's had a message from the Manager of the Royal to say one of his boys had collapsed suddenly and been rushed to hospital. The Hotel was sending a taxi to collect and take him there.'

'What are you going to do with him when he knows he's not being taken there?'

'I have a plan, which I do not feel I want to discuss with you right now.'

'You've got something unpleasant in mind, haven't you?'

'John, what you don't know, you can't testify against me.'

'Oh bugger. You really are going to harm him.'

'Of course not. I promise. Just be ready for me. I'll be there in about thirty minutes but give me forty-five, just in case.'

John nodded, Phil opened the door and walked briskly over to the taxi. John saw him turn the roof light on and drive away towards Roundhay. He looked at his watch; it was nearly half past eleven. It had already been a long day and there was no sign of when it was going to end. With a sigh, he drove back to the railway sidings and pulled up outside the garage doors. He switched off the car's headlights and peered through the windscreen; it was in complete darkness. Opening the door window, he could only hear the intermittent noise of distant locomotives coming from the main city Railway Station half a mile away. The thought of it being as quiet as the grave caused him to shudder. Inside the garage laid the dead body of Joe Mason and not too far away, laid the shattered remains of his friend. He shuddered again as the cold winter's temperature began to plummet below zero.

Meanwhile, three miles away, Phil drove the taxi into the driveway of the Laurels and parked outside the front porch way. He sounded the horn twice and waited. No one came appeared. He pressed the car horn again and looked towards the front door. Slowly, it began to open. A figure emerged and signalled to Phil. A voice summoned him, 'Driver, sorry about this, but can you help me please with my case?'

Without reply, Phil stepped out of the car and walked cautiously towards the door. Charles was standing in the shadows of the porch way, silhouetted only by the hallway lights inside. As Phil climbed the shallow stone steps, he failed to see the Browning revolver in his right hand. With only six feet between them, Charles moved forwards. Phil saw the firearm and stopped. 'Get your hands in the air and get inside now before I shoot you where you are.'

He knew it was useless attempting to deny the motive for his visit but realised his own chance of survival was stalling for time. Time enough for John to grow suspicious and come to help him again.

Holding his arms aloft, he walked into the hallway where he saw another man who he had never seen before. He was about fifty years of age with grey bushy hair, medium height, slightly overweight, wearing a smart pin-striped suit. Charles pressed the barrel of the

Browning hard into Phil's back. 'In there,' he snapped, as he pushed him along the hallway towards the door leading to the cellar. Phil instinctively knew if he went through the door, his chances of coming out there alive would be little. He turned to face Charles and defiantly said, 'You know I'm a Police Officer. Although they have just abolished hanging for murder, the Courts will send you to prison for the rest of your life.' He turned towards Ron Earl, 'And the same goes for you too. Your smart clothes and powerful connections won't save your skin either.'

'You have no idea who I am?'

Phil guessed, but he was now desperate, fighting for his life. Taking a deep breath, he replied, 'I believe you are Ron Earl.'

'And how would you know that?'

'I know you are a Director of Boddingtons from Birmingham and both of you are Directors for Charles Lewis Enterprises Ltd with offices in Vauxhall, London and Gibraltar. In fact, I've been to your office in Gibraltar and found some very useful information.'

Charles Lewis shouted, 'What do you mean you've been to our offices in Gibraltar? You don't know where it is?'

'Well that's where you're wrong. I've even been inside your apartment; Flat 36, Nelson House, as I recall.'

Suddenly, Ron Earl's phlegmatic tone evaporated. 'How the hell does he know all this?'

Phil now sensed a shift of fortunes and pressed ahead. 'Mr Earl, do you really think the Police have ignored Charles' activities in last few months? He has employed two 'heavies' called Bill Jones and Joe Mason to do all his dirty work, starting with the abduction and murders of a young disabled burglar called Ronnie Ellis who had the misfortune to pick the wrong house to break-in and his accomplice Freddie Cox who was trying to escape and disappear indefinitely to his sisters. To make matters worse, they even killed the taxi driver who brought the young man here.'

Charles snapped, 'And where's your damned evidence?'

'Freddie Cox didn't die on the railway tracks where Bill and Joe left him to his fate after drugging him. He lived for another two days. Long enough for him to tell me everything about the burglary here and the disappearance of Ronnie, his burglar. This is called a dying declaration and it was said in front of other witnesses. We have your

Jaguar in which the bodies of these two were carried. You are no doubt aware from you father that we visited here recently and down there in the cellar found chewing gum wrappers use by Ronnie, identical to the ones I retrieved from Bill and Joe's place in Gibraltar. Do you really want me go on?'

Charles turned to Ron and screamed, 'I thought you had arranged for all this to be dealt with by your contacts in London?'

Phil replied, 'Yes, we were advised not pursue our investigations. And to be honest, most Officers would have complied with the instructions given by their Assistant Chief Constable. But Gentlemen, I'm not your average compliant cop. I have no idea what you two are up to. I suspect you're both up to your lousy necks involved with the illegal sales and supply of arms to anyone in the world who is prepared to pay for them. Frankly, I don't give a shit about your business. But when you start murdering people on my patch, whoever they are, and threaten the lives of my colleagues, then I won't stand idly by and let you get away with this. Now you can do what you want to me. But I can tell you now, Bill and Joe are in custody and we have recovered samples of drugs together with the hypodermic needle from their room at the Royal. Those will be compared with the forensic toxicologist tests, carried out on Freddie Cox's remains. Oh and incidentally, did you really think I would come here on my own? Charles Lewis, the game's up.'

Ron stepped to one side and walked towards the front door. 'Charles, I'm having nothing else to do with this. I would suggest you seek out the services of a good Barrister. This is a complete and utter mess, brought on by your over-reaction and overzealous ham-fisted team. Our partnership is over.'

As he neared the door, Charles screamed again, 'Where are you going? You can't leave like this!'

'I'm sorry Charles, it's over.'

He was about to fire the revolver when a sudden movement caught the corner of his eye. He swung round and in complete panic fired the gun once. For a split-second, Phil and Ron stared at each other, wondering if the other had been the intended target. Realising both had not been shot, they looked over Charles' shoulder towards the bottom of the staircase. Simultaneously, they took a sudden intake of breath and glared in absolute disbelief at the figure thrown backwards against the wooden stairs as it began to tumble down towards the hallway rug. It was the fatally wounded Colonel Julian Lewis. The only sound was the load resonation of the gun fire, echoing against the wooden panelled walls.

Charles dropped the gun and rushed forwards screaming, 'Father! What have I done?' He bent over and cradled the Colonel's head, failing to notice the gaping hole in his chest. Phil was stunned and remained anchored to the ground, unable to move or comprehend what he had witnessed. Ron Earl had no such condition. He instantly ran out through the front door and within seconds, jumped into his car and quickly drove away down the driveway.

Phil bent down and carefully picked up the revolver and placed it in his jacket pocket. He looked over to Charles and saw he was still holding his father's head firmly to his chest. Truly remorseful for what he had done. Without distracting his attention, Phil walked over to the telephone and picked up the receiver. Even the Chief Constable could not disguise what had happened. Charles Lewis had shot his father at close range and no amount of influence from Whitehall could protect him now from lawful justice.

As he was about to ring 999 for the Police, he saw in his peripheral view the figure of Charles running towards him. Unfortunately, Phil's reactions were too slow. For the second time that night, he was hurt. Charles slammed violently into his back, throwing him immediately to the floor and across the large rug. All his stamina and strength had gone. Although the impact would normally have been sufficient for Phil to quickly recover from, this second assault on his bruised body was too overwhelming.

The force caused him to slide across the polished wooden floor, colliding into an old hat stand, knocking it over and spilling out the various walking canes and umbrellas housed in its cage. They rolled haphazardly in all directions. Although confused and slightly disorientated, Phil managed to regain some composure as he saw Charles approach him. His rage was palpable, shouting, 'You made me kill my father, you bastard!'

But in his hurry to reach Phil, he failed to notice the walking sticks scattered beneath his feet, his heel rolled over the round cane causing him to momentary loose his balance. Phil grasped the moment and lunged forwards with all his available strength, rugby tackling him from the waist and landing heavily on top. Charles screamed again, 'Get off me you bastard!' He darted his head from one side to the other, trying to locate his fallen revolver, unaware it was inside Phil's coat pocket.

They rolled over across the wooden floor until Charles hit head against the deep skirting board. The impact jarred him sufficiently enough to loosen his grip. Phil fumbled about inside his other pocket and found the small box containing the hyperaemic needle. He quickly pulled away from the casing together with a vial. Snapping the glass into the holder, he squeezed the plunger until the clear liquid inside spurted upwards through the needle. Quickly, he stuck the needle into Charles's neck and pressed firmly with all his strength.

Charles subdued struggles ceased immediately, rendering him completely incapacitated. His body went limp before rolling over onto his back, unconscious. Phil placed him in the recovery position and walked outside into the cold fresh air. After several minutes, he approached the taxi and opened the rear door and returned inside the house. The Colonel laid awkwardly at the base of the staircase, blood spreading onto the floor. He quickly examined him and discovered the gunshot wound had penetrated his rib cage above the heart and exited through his back between his shoulders. His injuries were catastrophic. Death would have been instant. With care and respect for the old man, Phil placed him gently where he had fallen and walked over to Charles. He starred down at him with some pity. He was asleep now but when he awoke, his life would never be the same. How would he ever come to terms with killing his father?'

He grabbed Charles by the shoulders and dragged him along the hallway through the porch and down the shallow stone steps before finally placing him across the back seat. He returned inside the house. There was a vital item he needed to locate before he could ensure his plans would succeed. Fortunately, it took only three minutes to find. Inside the hallway occasional table drawer, he found the ignition keys to the Jaguar. Swiftly he placed them inside his jacket pocket and left the house through the front door. Leaving it slightly ajar, he drove the taxi out from the Laurels hoping John would still be there inside his garage.

76

John looked at his watch; it was nearly an hour since he saw Phil drive away. He was worried about what might have happened to him. If he drove to the Laurels he might not be there and Phil would discover him missing at this end. Nevertheless, it was now too long for him to have collected Charles Lewis and return.

Finally, he made the decision. He would go and search for Phil. He drove away from the old railway yard and travelled North towards Roundhay.

As he pulled in the Grove close to the Laurels, he walked quietly up the driveway until the house came into view. He was surprised to see several lights were still illuminated inside but more worryingly, no taxi. Where the hell was he? He continued approaching the house, all was silent with no signs of life. He paused and wondered what to do next. Cautiously, he climbed the shallow steps and placed his ear to the front door. Silence.

Slowly and without any pressure, the door began to move inwards. He stepped back, anticipating an attack but the door continued opening slowly on its own axis. With some trepidation, he pushed gently against it until it was completely open. John stared inside and froze. He could see the figure of a man lying at the base of the staircase. He rushed inside and immediately recognised it to be the late Colonel Lewis. He instantly knew he had been shot. He had seen injuries like this during his time in National Service. He shouted loudly, 'Hello? Is there anyone here? This is the Police!'

Amidst the silence he uttered, 'What's happened and where the hell is Phil and Charles Lewis?' This was a game changer. A respectable old man had been shot dead in his own house. He had no choice. He walked over to the telephone and made the call. Within seconds he spoke to the operator, 'Get me the Police, I want to report a murder.'

77

Within ten minutes, the first police car pulled up outside the front door where John stood. The driver climbed out from the plain Ford Zephyr and starred menacingly at him. It was ACC Jenkins. Without any time to compose himself, he asked, 'What have you found DC Evans?'

'Good evening Sir. Sergeant Smith contacted me earlier this evening to say he'd come across some vital information linking Charles Lewis and the men he employs with the possible murders of three people.'

At that moment two further plain police cars entered the driveway, whereupon four Detectives entered the house and expressed their surprise at seeing the Assistant Chief Constable already in attendance. ACC Jenkins turned to the senior Detective, 'Inspector Jones, please take over here. DC Evans found the body but I need to speak to him first.' He turned to John and nodded towards the living room, uttering, 'In there, DC Evans.'

John followed him into the room where he continued, 'What information?'

'I don't know Sir. He just told me he was coming here to confront him with this and see what he had to say about the matter. But when I got here about fifteen minutes ago, I found the old Colonel over there. I checked to see him, but he's dead, shot through the chest at close range, I suspect. DS Smith and Charles Lewis were not here Sir.'

'Didn't I give you and Sergeant Smith clear instructions to distance yourself from Charles Lewis?'

'Yes Sir.' John realised he must keep his conversation with him to a minimum until he saw Phil; it was now obvious he had run into trouble once he arrived at the Laurels. Whether he had forced Charles Lewis as a captive away or vice-versa, his best course of action would to remain vague, especially now ACC Jenkins was asking him awkward and embarrassing questions.

'So why are you here?' he screamed.

'Because DS Smith told me to meet him here. I was just following his instructions Sir.'

ACC Jenkin's complexion became flushed and blotchy. Clearly the stress of two junior officers ignoring his orders was too much to bear. He was about to verbally explode when the telephone rang on the coffee table next to him. Without waiting for the tirade of abuse, John stooped down and snapped up the receiver. It was Phil. As he began to speak, ACC Jenkins deliberately placed his ear next to John so he would be privy to their conversation.

As Phil was explaining his version of events, ACC Jenkins's eyes began to protrude grotesquely, his breathing heavier and his mouth opening wider. What he was hearing alarmed him, especially the mention of Ron Earl. He had heard that name before and knew he was connected to the Whitehall. He now feared the whole pack of cards would collapse, exposing the full corruptive practices exercised by several Government Ministries, their Agencies and himself. The concealment of the Colonel's violent death was now impossible and there was little doubt the Chief Constable would be looking for a scapegoat and he would be the sacrificial kid.

Could his career be saved? Perhaps these two officers could shield him from such an impending disaster. Perhaps the offer of promotion?

78

Whilst the Police were in attendance at the Laurels, Phil entered the garage to find John absent. Shaking his head in bewilderment, he returned to the taxi and checked Charles. He was still in a deep sleep. Phil knew exactly what he must do. Although he had planned this moment for Charles whilst he was in Gibraltar, the discovery of his taxi ruse and the subsequent shooting of his father were completely unforeseen. However, he would stick to the original plan.

Reaching into his coat pocket he produced four items. The Browning revolver, Bill's flick-knife, the ignition keys to the Jaguar and a pair of police-issue handcuffs. He walked over to the car and pulled away the tarpaulin, sat inside and started the engine. It started on the first twist of the key and the engine immediately burst into life, its six cylinders announcing its potential power. He reversed it carefully outside into the yard, parking directly in front of the garage doors, alongside the taxi.

Wearing his gloves, he wiped the steering wheel and the chrome plated handbrake and turned his attention to the revolver and flick-knife. With the Jaguar driver's door opened next to the taxi's rear door, Phil began to shuffle and lift Charles out from one into the other. Eventually he placed and sat Charles into the Jaguar's driving seat. He was slumped backwards with the steering wheel resting on his stomach. He reached over him and pressed both the revolver and the flick-knife separately into his clammy right palm before dropping them onto the car floor carpet below. Then he wrapped his arms firmly around the steering wheel and locked them tightly with the handcuffs between the spokes to his wrists.

'Job done,' he whispered. Taking one look around the garage, ensuring everything was exactly where it should be, he walked out and half closed the doors behind him. He drove the taxi away and within two minutes parked it in a side road near to City Square. Within walking distance lay a row of red public telephone boxes. From there, he telephoned the Police.

Once he was connected to the Force Control Room, he asked to speak to the duty Chief Inspector. Seconds later a voice announced, 'Hello. This is the Chief Inspector. What can I do for you?'

'Sir, this DS Smith from the Antique Squad. Can you send a unit to the Laurels, Grove Lane Roundhay? Colonel Julian Lewis has been murdered. And another to the disused Railway Sidings on Wellington Street, Unit 14. There you will find his son Charles Lewis. I saw him shoot his father earlier tonight and also stab one of his employees Joe Mason. He also tried to kill me as well. He took me there by force after he killed his father. But I managed to overpower him and handcuff him to his Jaguar car. Please hurry.'

'OK Sergeant Smith, I've got all that, but where are you now?'

'Calling from a phone box in City Square, just around from the Railway Sidings.'

'Units are on the way now. You must return to Wellington Street and liaise with the officers in attendance.'

'Yes Sir.'

'Incidentally, we already know about the Laurels; your colleague DC Evans discovered the Colonel half an hour ago.'

'Got that.'

'Good work Sergeant, but I suspect you'll have a 'shed full' of explaining to do when the Chief finds out about this. Colonel Lewis was a respected and fine upstanding member of the Community. No doubt this will attract a great deal of press attention, nationally.'

'Yes Sir.'

He replaced the receiver and made another call. Fortunately, it was John who answered. 'Thank God it's you.'

'Sergeant Smith. Are you alright?'

'Of course, I'm alright. Why did you leave the...?'

Completely out of sync, John cut across his intended question saying, 'I was worried about you. I thought you'd be here. What happened? Did you have some trouble with Charles Lewis?'

Phil sensed something was not quite right. John was very distant and deliberately stopped him from asking any further questions. Whether it was telepathy or otherwise, he realised that perhaps someone else was listening to their conversation. So, he continued cautiously, 'Charles Lewis shot his father; I was there, and so was Ron Earl. Charles forced me here at gun point. It's a lockup garage in some Railway sidings off Wellington Road. I managed to get the better of him and handcuffed him to his Jaguar. Yes, the Jag that was reported stolen But that's not all, there's another man here. He's been killed too. I think he was one of the men that worked for him; don't know where the other guy is, probably ran off somewhere. Anyway, I escaped and sounded the alarm. There are units on their way, might even be there now, so I'd better get back.'

'I'm sorry for not getting here sooner like you asked but I didn't expect you would be in any danger.'

Suddenly, without any warning another voice spoke, 'Sergeant Smith, this ACC Jenkins. I want to see you now, along with DC Evans. Where are you?'

'I'm in City Square but I'll be returning soon to the old Railway Sidings on Wellington Street where I left Charles Lewis with one of his dead servants. Other units should be there now.'

Clearing his throat, ACC Jenkins spoke curtly, 'I want to see you both in my office in one hour. Don't be late.'

'No Sir.'

Phil stepped out from the telephone box and smiled. He walked back along Wellington Street towards the Railway Sidings to join his colleagues. And for the first time in his career, he was actually looking forward to his meeting with the Assistant Chief Constable.

79

John and Phil assisted the Detectives at their respective crime scenes. Following protocol, neither were allowed access to the immediate crime scene area. That belonged to the Scenes of Crime Officers. Their role was simply to examine, preserve and gather evidence for impending forensic science analysis.

The scene outside the garage became chaotic. The Detectives had found Charles Lewis. This coincided with him regaining consciousness. And once he realised his predicament, he immediately protested his innocence, unable to give any explanation as to why he was sat inside his own Jaguar with two murder weapons lying underneath the driver's seat. He was cautioned and arrested on suspicion of murder and screamed, 'This is a set up!' When he was finally released from the handcuffs and free of the steering wheel, he accompanied the Detectives inside the garage, where he stared with astonishment at the body of Joe, slumped dead in the metal chair. Again, he shouted, 'I don't know anything about this!'

He was taken away and driven to the Central Police Station.

Using one of the Detectives personal radios, Phil placed a message to John, still in attendance at the Laurels. He simply asked, 'When will you come free from there?'

'About an hour, Sergeant.'

'Good. I'll meet you outside Headquarters before our appointment. Understood?'

'Yes.'

The Town Hall clock struck five o'clock. It was still freezing cold and a light shower of snow now drifted between the smoked-blackened Town Hall and Municipal Building. John and Phil met at the side door where junior ranks entered. Phil spoke softly, 'You must allow me to do all the talking John. In fact, I would prefer you not to say anything. Remember, someone might be listening to every word we say. In my briefcase I have brought all the items of evidence we had collected, including the tape recorder machine. I can't wait to hear what this spineless bastard has to say.'

John smiled, 'I know you're up to something. So, I'm not going to spoil your moment of fun. As long as you know, you carry my career with you in your hands. Please don't waste it!'

'Shut up, you wimp. I know I've got a habit of shooting from the hip but on this occasion, trust me.'

'Bugger,' replied John, unconvinced.

They climbed the flight of stairs to the first floor. Everywhere was deserted as they continued along the corridor, walking towards the only office where any light was coming from. As they reached the open doorway they saw ACC Jenkins staring out of the window towards the Town Hall's black satanic walls on the opposite side of the road. He was deep in thought, unaware of their presence. Phil broke the silence, 'You wanted to see us Mr Jenkins?'

He looked up and nodded, 'Yes, of course. Please come in.'

'What's happening with Charles Lewis, Sergeant?'

'He's being interviewed as we speak, but I've no doubt he'll be charged with the murders of his father and his employee, Joe Mason.' John glanced towards him, knowing that he had not murdered Joe. In fact, Joe had confessed to him with his dying breath, that it was Bill. But Phil already knew this. Ignoring John's attention, he continued, 'We may have further evidence that will link him to the murders of Freddie Cox, Ronnie Ellis and Jim Simms.'

'I see. Well under the circumstances, it's been a successful night and I look forward to reading the report.'

'Thank you, Sir. Incidentally, the remains of Charles Lewis's other employee, Bill Jones, have just been found on the rail tracks near to the Station; just a couple of hundred yards away from the garage.'

John continued with his gaze, his mouth slightly opening in disbelief. What else is Phil going to say that he was unaware of? ACC Jenkin's eyes grew larger. Tonight's events were spiralling completely out of control. However, in a calm tone he said, 'Very well. That will be all for now. Thank you for coming.'

John stood to leave but Phil remained seated. ACC Jenkins said, 'Was there anything else Sergeant?'

'Yes, there is. But it might be better if we can talk alone.' Both men looked towards John. Phil stood and placed an arm on his shoulder, 'Stand outside John. I don't want any witnesses. Please.'

'I'll stay. This is too important for me to miss,' replied John.

'No DC Evans. Leave; that's an order.' Phil smiled and gave him a wink, whispering, 'Please John.' With some reluctance, he left the office and closed the door firmly behind him. He walked along the corridor but as he reached the stairwell, he stopped and quietly he crept back to the door, placing his inquisitive ear on the wooden door panel.

John did miss the opening salvo launched by ACC Jenkins but clearly heard him shout, 'How dare you come into my office and talk to me like that!'

There was a moment of silence followed by Phil raising his voice. 'Listen to me. You are a conniving, spineless little bastard who obstructed us from the first day in our investigation into the suspicious deaths and disappearance of the criminals we were interested in. Although they might have been habitual criminals with little moral standards, they didn't deserve their fate. Not by Charles Lewis, his henchmen or even yourself.'

ACC Jenkins stood and began walking around his large desk screaming, 'Get out of here now! You can consider yourself dismissed from this Force, forthwith.' But as he approached Phil, he was completely taken by surprise when John flung the door opened and burst in. Without any reservation, he pointed his finger and asserted, 'You are a disgrace to the rank you serve. I shall not stand idly by to see you destroy this officer's career because you have been influenced by people in high places. We may be just simple Detectives of junior ranks, but we have the courage of our convictions. We may also serve you and the Chief Constable, but we serve the rule of law first. You have broken all the rules of command by failing to support us in the execution of our duties and placing your career before the lives of others.'

He stared at John, speechless. Phil walked over to the bookcase next to his desk and plugged in the tape recorder. Phil turned and said, 'Listen to this, you piece of shit. It's the conversation you had with DCI Sampson at his house, the day before he was nearly killed.'

ACC Jenkins remained still, unable to move as he heard his voice through the speakers of the recording machine. No one spoke until it had finished. Finally, he returned to his seat and slumped down. Sheepishly, he asked, 'What now?'

'I haven't finished yet. I can promise you sooner or later Charles Lewis will implicate Ron Earl in this affair. Remember he was a witness, like me, when he shot his father whilst attempting to abduct me. He'll start squealing like a pig to the Home Office, who in turn will want to hang someone's arse out in public. That'll be yours and probably the Chief Constables too. Ron Earl is too much a valuable asset to the prosperity of this country and will avoid any prosecution, free to return to his murderous trade of death. In fact, I would place my pension on him attracting a knighthood in the near future, for 'services to the country'.'

'You seemed to be well informed,' said ACC Jenkins.

'Yes I am. I read the newspapers and keep my ears and nose close to the ground. Unlike you, I've worked with criminals all my career and there's one thing most have in common: greed, ego and a ruthless protection to save their own skin. Just like you Mr Jenkins and Charles Lewis.'

'So, what now Sergeant?' he spoke softly in a subdued tone.

Turning towards John, he asked, 'Please leave me alone with him now. We have things to discuss which I would feel happier if you weren't here. Please.' John nodded in agreement and left the office again. This time he continued down the stairwell and waited close to the outside door. Meanwhile, Phil faced ACC Jenkins and whispered, 'This is what you're going to do.'

80

Six months passed. Charles Lewis appeared before the York Assizes and was convicted with one count of murder and another for manslaughter. He was sentenced to life imprisonment. He pleaded guilty to the involuntary manslaughter of his father, but not guilty to the murder of Joe Mason, vehemently denying causing his death. He accused Phil of 'setting him up' having no knowledge of the existence of the garage belong to Frankie Knuckles or ever driving the Jaguar where he was found sat in.

As expected, Ron Earl was not subpoenaed but agreed to attend in camera. Called as a Prosecution Witness, he was given 'Judicial Immunity.' He testified against Charles Lewis and refused to answer any questions regarding their business activities, citing 'National Security' as a defence. He denied any knowledge of the existence of Bill Jones and Joe Mason.

All the evidence collected by Phil, John and DCI Sampson was presented to the Director of Public Prosecutions. They accepted the evidence of Freddie Cox's dying declaration and concluded that the three men involved with burglary at the Laurels had been unlawfully killed by Jones and Mason.

The day following the trial, Phil and John were busy sifting through the latest crime reports when a knock came from their office door. 'Come in' shouted Phil. With neither of them looking up to see who their visitor was, a voice said, 'Don't you normally stand up when a Senior Officer enters the room?' They were astonished to see DCI Sampson standing in front of them, leaning on his thick walking stick.

Phil replied, 'But I thought you were retiring?'

'No. For some reason, the last thing ACC Jenkins did before he resigned was to allow me to return to work and complete my service.'

John said, 'He must have had his reasons Sir, most just get pensioned off before they have that chance.'

Looking at Phil, he replied, 'I know. I must have friends in high places, don't you think Phil?'

Smiling, he replied, 'You must have.'

'Anyway, talking of such people, I have the pleasure to tell you DC Evans, you are to see the newly appointed Chief Constable tomorrow. One of his first duties is to promote you to Sergeant following the successful outcome of the Freddie Cox Inquiry. Congratulations my boy.'

'Thank you, Sir. But we never detected the crimes against him, Ronnie Ellis or Jim Simms, did we? The DPP wouldn't accept Joe Mason's dying declaration. Their deaths still remain 'on file'[28] and no one will be held to account for them.'

'You're right John. Apart from your promotion, there are no real winners in all this. Unfortunately, those two thugs avoided a criminal trial. There was no justice for them after all.'

Phil intervened, 'Not so sure about that Boss. They got the justice they deserved. Perhaps not through our legal justice but justice of sorts nevertheless.

'You may be right Phil. Anyway, changing the subject, Helen has invited you both round for dinner tomorrow night. See you then.' He turned and shuffled out with his walking stick and disappeared along the corridor.

John looked at his friend, 'Phil, what exactly did you talk to Jenkins about that morning?'

'I allowed him the opportunity of making amends, before he resigned. That's all.'

'What did he get out of it Phil?'

'A cheap electric recording machine containing a poor-quality tape of his conversation with Mark. And his good reputation. That's all.'

'That's another thing. I thought we placed the tape recorder inside

---

[28] an inquiry that is perpetually left open and undetected

the locker at the Library?'

'No John, I kept it inside my briefcase all the time. It was at that moment, when I decided to implement my plan. It was all going to happen that day. I couldn't tell you John because you're not old school. Sorry.'

'You devious bastard.'

'DC Evans. Do I still have to keep reminding you? My name is Sergeant Bastard.'

ABOUT THE AUTHOR

Robert Henson served for thirty years in the Police Service and Home Office. Upon retirement, he graduated with a Master's Degree in Education and became a free-lance training consultant working closely with several Government Agencies teaching the Criminal law and Investigation Procedures.

He now lives in the country, spending his retirement in tranquility with his wife and two terriers.

CPSIA information can be obtained
at www.ICGtesting.com
Printed in the USA
LVHW081718140819
627625LV00029B/692/P